The Secret Heir

C.J. Toca

Saddle Ridge Publications, LLC—Madison, WI
ISBN: 979-8-9868996-0-2
eBook ISBN: 979-8-9868996-1-9
Library of Congress Control Number: 2022916375
Title: *The Secret Heir*
Author: C.J. Toca
Digital distribution | 2022
Paperback | 2022

Visit www.cjtoca.com

To my brother who gave me the confidence to publish this novel.

Chapter 1
March 4, Blueberry Lake, New Jersey, USA

Stefania stood looking down the barrel of a pistol held in the shaking hand of an unshaven twenty-something psychopath wearing a stained white sleeveless t-shirt and black track pants. In the background the squawk of the television blared old re-runs of some American sit-com in the dimly lit room. His tribal neck tattoos framed his chin. Below his dilated brown eyes two inked teardrops adorned his whiskered cheek.

"Wanda, go in the back and get me some of those zip ties out of my pack," he ordered. "You two, keep your hands where I can see 'em."

A waify toothpick of a woman, looking slightly older than her probably thirty years, got up from a beaten old blue sofa, her braless pierced nipples poking out from a tight white tank top which hung below her pant-less waist. A brief glimpse of black hipsters visible, covering a portion of a tattoo of a snake which started at her ankle and wound its way up her calf, to her thigh and beyond.

"Sure Duce," she replied. Wanda disappeared through a doorframe into the back of the ramshackle bungalow.

"I think we're going to have some fun with these two," he said.

I want to get into position to kick that pistol out of his hand, Stefania thought, as she shimmied toward him. *I need to get a foot or so closer.*

As far as Stefania knew, Thomas stood behind her, all six feet of him, hands in the air, in his blue down jacket and black wool hat covering his blond hair.

"Just my luck," commented Thomas in his English accent from behind. "I'm going to die in a rundown old hovel at the hand of some philistine named Duce in a place with the dubious moniker of Blueberry Lake, New Jersey."

"Shut up blue eyes!" Duce yelled.

"I'll be just another victim of America's gun violence," snapped Thomas. "My God, does everyone in this bloody country run about armed?"

"I said shut up you fuzzy foreigner!" Duce shouted again, seeming to come slightly unhinged. He took a few steps toward Stefania. "Now you, with the dark hair, green eyes, and yoga pants, I've got some plans for you. I think what we got here's a Latina."

And I have some plans for you. A few steps closer please. I've been in this situation before jackass.

Sweat seeped out of every pore in Stefania's five and a half foot frame, beading on her forehead and under her nose.

Duce's eyes narrowed, and he gave Stefania the once over from head to foot.

"Yeh, I got some excellent ideas," he said, followed with a cackle. "Wanda, where the hell are you with those ties?" He yelled as he took two steps closer to Stefania. He looked back over his left shoulder toward the door frame behind him, "Wanda?" he shouted.

Stefania leapt into the air her right foot hitting his right hand knocking the pistol out, skipping across the stained hardwood floor. Duce collapsed, his head hitting the old floor planks, taking a bounce and settling into a growing puddle of blood. Like road kill he lay there motionless, a crimson drip seeped out of the back of his skull onto the floor.

"Oh Madonna!" exclaimed Stefania.

She looked up. In the shadow of the doorframe where Wanda had disappeared stood a figure wearing a black sweater, black knit cap and holding a smoking pistol equipped with a silencer.

"You!" Stefania exclaimed.

Four Days Earlier
March 1, Leblon, Brazil

Stefania walked into the living room of Uncle Mateus' white *casa grande* in Leblon. The wood beamed ceiling, white marble floor, and broad open floor to ceiling windows looking out on the Atlantic Ocean, sun gleaming off the waves on the one side, and pool terrace on the other side, made this one of Stefania's favorite places to visit. Her white sundress rippled in the slight ocean breeze. Uncle Mateus sat on a brown leather sofa, thin, and handsome, Mateus looked the part of a successful physician, with olive skin and slicked back gray hair. Cousin Hércules in his blue uniform as a captain in the Brazilian Navy rose from a high backed white upholstered chair. Stefania hugged and kissed Hércules on the cheek, and bent over and kissed Mateus on the head.

"Welcome my dear niece, please sit," said Mateus.

Stefania sat down in a matching high backed chair across from Hércules.

"Uncle Mateus, dear Cousin, I am so honored to be invited to see you. But your invitation was quite mysterious," said Stefania.

"I understand that Hércules wants to discuss some private matters with you. I'll be in my office should you need me," Mateus declared, as he stood up and left the room.

"Some delicacy, hmm, Hércules, now I'm interested."

Hércules sat back down, but leaned forward, toward Stefania slightly.

"Stefania, do you recall the Air Sao Paulo Flight 221 crash off the coast of Brazil a week ago?" asked Hércules.

"Yes, it was worldwide news. It was a flight from Sao Paulo to London as I recall, why?"

"My navy ship was involved in the salvage operations. It was quite terrible I must say. We recovered scores of corpses, personal belongings and the like. We had to catalogue and store all possessions and items recovered."

"That must have been an awful experience Hércules."

"Indeed, it was, but there was one particular passenger recovered which resulted in an interesting discovery."

"Okay, I'm not sure where this is going, but what is this all about?"

"As you know I am deeply devoted to the church, I'm a deacon and therefore also a chaplain in the Navy and I've been made a knight of Malta by the pope."

"Yes, okay, what—"

"One of the passengers on Flight 221 was an assistant to the papal nuncio to Brazil. His body was recovered as well an aluminum attaché case which apparently belonged to him. The attaché case bore the seal of the Holy See, and it contained a rather sophisticated lock. When I recognized this could be of some importance to the church one of my sailors pried open the case. I did not list the attaché case in the catalogue of items recovered. When the Brazilian Navy informed the papal nuncio, he denied knowledge of his assistant or that he was on the flight. Likewise, the Vatican pled ignorance. They eschewed knowledge of the briefcase as well."

"How did you know he was the papal nuncio's assistant, maybe he was just some errant priest?"

"In the briefcase we found his identification papers including a Vatican passport, and a UK passport under the same name. There was no question as to his identity. He was not Brazilian. He was from the UK, which makes one wonder why an English priest was the assistant to the papal nuncio to Brazil. The papal nuncio in Brazil said he wasn't assigned there. We've found no evidence that he's ever lived in Brazil, at least under that name."

"Yes, that's curious, but I'm even more curious as to what you found in his attaché case."

"Other than his identification papers, and flight information for the flight from Brazil to London, and then from London on March fourth to Newark, New Jersey, the only other items in the attaché case were a thumb drive sealed in a watertight plastic tube, and a set of keys. Apparently he must have opened the case after he got on the plane and placed his flight and identification papers back in the case."

"Well, what's on the thumb drive?"

"That's why I called you. We were quite surprised the thumb drive wasn't contaminated with sea water. The tube it was in kept it dry. The thumb drive, well it's encrypted. I recalled that English fellow you are friends with has close connections with the Vatican. I figured you might wish to run this by him to see what he can make of it. If this priest was involved in something confidential for the Vatican, I didn't want to blow his cover."

"Was there anything found in his clothing?" asked Stefania.

"No," replied Hércules. "Given the violence of the crash, and the wave action on the bodies following, our assumption is that anything he had on his person, such as a wallet or cell phone, was ejected or lost in the sea. Many of the bodies recovered had little on them in terms of wallets, phones or identifications. We were lucky because his body was still buckled in his seat, we were able to cross-reference his seat number, and apparently he was sitting over the wings. The bodies of the passengers over the wings were the least damaged in the crash."

"Interesting. Do you have the thumb drive?"

Hércules took out a manila envelope and handed it to Stefania.

"Here, this envelope contains the identification papers, flight information, and the thumb drive. The corpse was never claimed. It was cremated and interred in a potter's field here in Brazil."

Stefania took the envelope from Hércules and placed it in her ever-present over-size black leather shoulder bag.

This gives me an excuse to contact Thomas.

March 3, Kensington, London, UK

Sitting at the table at a fashionable Italian restaurant in Kensington, Stefania waited for Thomas. She hoped he'd offer his assistance over lunch. They'd texted back and forth, but she hadn't seen him in over a year and missed the intimacy of their adventure two years ago in connection with her last journalism project, which went sideways.

I never really fell out of love with him. I've kept him at arm's length, I don't want to get hurt.

Wearing a low cut red sweater, and a black pleated skirt with black leggings, her jet black tresses pulled back in a ponytail, she thought she looked sexy, but not overly so. Her green eyes focused on the door to the restaurant waiting with anticipation for Thomas to enter. Thomas had picked the restaurant, and Stefania didn't really mind making the trip from Rome to London. The London trip related to an assignment, she told Rodolfo, her editor at the *Italian Monthly Journal*, so the *Journal* paid her expenses.

The glass door opened and Thomas appeared, looking no different than their last meeting two years ago. Smartly dressed in a gray wool blazer with a black sweater underneath and, black gabardine trousers, Thomas looked about for Stefania. The door attendant pointed toward the back of the restaurant. Stefania sat in the last table, her back to the wall under a framed painting of the Roman skyline from the Spanish Steps. Thomas's piercing blue eyes looked at her, and he swept his strawberry blond hair across his forehead with his right hand. His six foot athletic frame waltzed over toward Stefania, serpentining around the other tables.

The thirty-foot walk took a few minutes. Someone at every table seemed to know Thomas and greeted him.

She heard "Thomas," "Radcliffe," and "duke," muffled through the soft banter of the restaurant.

Stefania stood as he finally approached, and the two exchanged a hug and a brief kiss on the cheek.

"I'm so happy to see you," said Thomas in his ever so wonderful English accent, "You should always seek me out when you are in the UK for a project. You look wonderful; you're so incredibly gorgeous."

I normally would be put off by such a direct comment, but given my history with Thomas, I'm flattered.

"Thank you Thomas, it's nice to see you as well. You never change; you always look the same."

The two were interrupted by the waiter, and they put their drink orders in. Stefania ordered a glass of valpolicella, and Thomas ordered a gin and tonic.

"Thanks, I think, dearest. So what brings you to London?" asked Thomas.

"I'm working on another project which might interest you."

"Oh, how so?" he inquired.

"Well, it involves the Vatican," responded Stefania, taking a sip of her red wine.

Thomas laughed.

"The last project of yours involving the Vatican almost got us both killed, but as I recall made you a great deal of money, and I lost my phone in the bargain," Thomas replied, laughing again. "In all seriousness, I owe you a million times over for what you did."

"Yes, I remember, and I thank *you* again for all of your help, despite it being for naught," she replied.

"You know I'm just joking. We both had fun, it was a wonderful adventure. So spill the beans, what's your new project?"

"As you recall my cousin Hércules is an officer with the Brazilian Navy."

"Oh yes, although I think he's one of your few relatives I've never met."

"Yes, well in connection with the salvage operation of the Air Sao Paulo Flight 221, he uncovered some information from an English priest who was on the flight."

"Crikey," responded Thomas with modest alarm. "I think there were maybe one-hundred or so passengers from the UK who were on that flight. The wife of one of my Sandhurst classmates died in that crash. Terrible business. Anyway, so who was this English priest?"

"His Vatican passport indicated his name was Charles Smith, as did his UK passport, no middle initial, but when the Brazilian Navy notified the Vatican, it denied knowing anything about him. No one claimed the body, and with that name he was virtually impossible to trace. It is like this man never existed. I went to his address in Whitechapel, but no-one was there."

"Do you have the passports?"

"Yes, here they are." Stefania took the passports out of her ever-present black shoulder bag and slid them across the table to Thomas.

Thomas paged through the Vatican passport.

"Hmm. This is a diplomatic passport from the Holy See. There are very few of these issued. Was there anything else found on his person?"

"Yes, as a matter of fact there was. I was kind of going to ask for your assistance."

"You know dearest I'll always assist you and am forever indebted to you for the secret you've agreed to keep, much to your prejudice I'm sure. Well, let's have it then."

"It's a thumb drive, encrypted." Stefania handed it to Thomas. "The Brazilian Navy couldn't get anything out of it. The priest had it in a locked briefcase when discovered, together with a booking for a flight from London to Newark, New Jersey, for tomorrow."

"Hmm. I'll wager whatever it is on this thumb drive has something to do with his scheduled trip to the States tomorrow," theorized Thomas tapping the table with the USB.

"I agree," said Stefania, nodding.

"And query why was he coming to London first," Thomas added.

Thomas took out his phone, and appeared to scroll through his contact list.

"What are you doing?" asked Stefania.

"You remember my colleague Harry Foster?" Thomas asked.

"Oh, yes, the Australian investigator guy," responded Stefania.

"Yes, that's him," Thomas answered as he held his phone to his ear.

"Harry, yes it's Thomas. Where are you now? Do you have time to nip by Frederici's. I've got a little assignment for you. Consider yourself on the clock. Smashing, see you in ten."

"What'd he say?" asked Stefania.

"Harry should be here in ten minutes. He lives close by. Unless you object, I'll see if Harry can access the information on the thumb drive."

The waiter served Stefania's wine and Thomas' cocktail.

"Great, we can put our food orders in while we wait. I'm famished," said Stefania.

Ten or so minutes later Harry Foster walked in. He appeared as Stefania had remembered him, a beefy, bald sixty or so year old gruff Australian. Wearing a plaid shirt and gray vest with blue jeans, Harry walked over and sat down.

"Good afternoon Harry. You remember Stefania?"

"Yes, nice to see you again," Harry replied.

"Well, what do you have for me mate?" asked Harry in his characteristic Australian accent.

"Seems like Stefania has come by an encrypted thumb drive. Any chance you can decrypt it?" asked Thomas.

"I thought you said this was a small job?" Harry said with a chuckle. "I can certainly try. My contacts can do almost anything with computers, hard-drives, cyber."

Thomas' eyes cut to Stefania.

"Here it is," said Stefania, producing a glassine envelope from her black shoulder bag containing the thumb drive and handing it to Harry.

"Anything else?" asked Harry.

"Of course," responded Thomas. "Here's a UK passport for a Charles Smith with an address in Whitechapel. See what you can find out about this chap. He also may, or may not be, a Catholic priest. He died last week on Air Sao Paulo Flight 221."

"Mate, the last blokes you had me investigate with Vatican connections all got killed, and you and Stefania nearly. Why do you insist on living dangerously?"

"I'm not sure this is dangerous yet. Can you move fast on the thumb drive Harry?" asked Thomas. "We may need an answer by tomorrow."

"I'll do my best," said Harry. "I'll call you on your mobile as soon as I know anything. I'd best be off."

Harry got up and hurried off.

"I'll text or call you as soon as I hear back from Harry," said Thomas.

"Thank you so much," Stefania said with a smile, her green eyes making contact with Thomas' piercing blue ones.

"As I said, I owe you a million times over dearest," Thomas replied, returning the smile.

While the meeting served a business purpose, Stefania secretly wanted to see Thomas. She wanted to talk to him, hear his voice in person, see his eyes, his expressions, feel his embrace, hold his hand, and run her hand through his hair. The luncheon lasted all afternoon, and the one glass of wine turned into four or five. Stefania took in Thomas' every facial expression, the intonation in his voice, his hand movements. She had not gotten over Thomas, and she knew it. Had he gotten over her though? Stefania desperately wanted to know the answer to that question.

March 4, Kensington, London, UK

Stefania lay awake in her hotel bed wearing only a gray tank top staring at the ceiling thinking of her time with Thomas the day before. Delighted but at the same time melancholy, she missed their time together, but didn't realize just how much. The sun had just risen, and early morning light started to filter through the drawn curtains into the room.

The silence of the hotel room was broken by her ring tone. At 0700, it was early, but Stefania knew she should have been up already. Reaching over to the nightstand she looked at her mobile.

"It's Thomas," she whispered to herself, still in a groggy state.

Grabbing for the phone, she missed and knocked it to the floor.

"Oh Madonna," she yelped, extending her arm for the phone, she loped out of bed onto the carpeted floor, her naked legs tangled up in the bed sheets. Finally she secured the phone and accepted the call.

"Yes, Thomas," she said.

"Good morning Stefania, how are you?" he said in Italian.

"Very good, and you," she responded, also in Italian.

"Listen, I've heard from Harry. The thumb drive contained only one piece of information."

"Well, what was it?" she asked.

"It is a longitude and latitude for a location and a time and date, that being today," he responded.

"Well where is it?" she asked.

"The longitude and latitude information corresponds to a place called Buttermilk Falls, New Jersey, in the States. The time, half-past seven this evening, local time."

"I've actually been to that place," replied Stefania. "This guy I dated in college was from New Jersey and we went there while I visited his parent's home one summer. It is pretty, at least in the summer. It's in an isolated area. Do you think I should try to catch a flight to go there and see what this is all about?" she asked.

"*We* should go to the States for the appointed place and time, as much as I loathe the States, it seems the logical next step. I'm still curious as to why this chap was coming to London first, when he could have flown direct from Sao Paulo to the States."

"He said 'we.' That's what I wanted to hear," thought Stefania.

"How will we get there in time?" asked Stefania, knowing full well the answer to the question.

"Obviously we'll fly on my plane. I flew it down from Norwich to Gatwick. If we leave this morning we'll get to the States this afternoon, local time. As I recall, we'll have to fly into someplace called Teterboro Airport. I'll alert the pilots and have a car rental arranged."

"Thanks Thomas," she responded.

"No thanks needed. I'll pick you up at your hotel at half-past eight. You can eat breakfast at the airport's VIP lounge while the jet is readied. Bring warm clothes though. This time of year on the east coast of the States is a bit chilly."

March 4, 40,000 Feet above the Atlantic Ocean

Sitting across from each other, the two settled into the plush leather seats of the Falcon 6X as it cut through the wispy thin clouds above the Atlantic Ocean for the seven plus hour flight to Teterboro, New Jersey.

Stefania wore tortoiseshell yoga pants, with a black sweater and scarf, her black mane held back by a pony-tail. Thomas dressed for comfort in blue denim jeans, a blue sweater and a camel hair blazer.

The attendants served French red wine and some artisanal cheeses, fresh fruit, nuts and olives.

"So Thomas, have you had any contact with that Svetlana woman from Russia after the meeting at the Vatican two years ago?" Stefania asked.

"Well the day you left the hotel in the rain she popped up at the hotel bar and we shared a cocktail," responded Thomas. "Her being at the bar was apparently no coincidence. I pressed her for information regarding the incident at the Vatican and she responded with nothing more than a smile. Other than that, I've met her at the Vatican in an official capacity in connection with the attempts to lift the UK sanctions against Russia. Several times in fact. I've seen her socially a couple of times. Why do you ask?"

"She saved our lives in Rio. You seemed taken with her at the meeting at the Vatican. She was the star of the show," Stefania responded.

"Our dealings have only been on a professional level. I haven't heard from her in months, in fact."

"Oh," Stefania responded.

"I've rented a Jeep SUV when we get to Teterboro," remarked Thomas. "You'll have to drive as you know I detest driving on the right side of the road, although we may encounter some winter weather."

"Yes, well as long as the SUV has all-wheel drive, we'll be fine," responded Stefania. "Remember, I went to university in New England. Despite my preference for Brazil and Rome, I've experience with winter weather."

"It hadn't slipped my mind," commented Thomas.

"You don't mind do you, I'm going to type up my notes so far, and finish up another piece I'm working on for Rodolfo," said Stefania.

"No, not at all," replied Thomas. "I brought some paperwork to go over, and I downloaded some articles on my tablet."

From time to time Stefania peered over the top of her laptop and observed Thomas's every movement, every letter he typed, and every time he mouthed a word.

Finally, she folded her laptop up, closed her eyes and reclined back in her seat, ear buds in her ears, her green eyes facing the window. Her eyes opened, then closed, then opened, then closed.

Just before falling into unconsciousness, through the thin slits of her heavy eyelids she saw Thomas get up and gently place a light blanket over her, making sure she was covered up to her chin. His soft lips planted a kiss on her forehead.

March 4, Near Walpack Center, New Jersey, USA

"Thank you for dinner," said Stefania, still wearing her sweater, scarf and yoga pants, as she drove the beige Jeep Grand Cherokee north on U.S. Route 206 towards the border with Pennsylvania. The sun had set on the cold overcast March day, and snowflakes flew through the beams of the headlights glowing like fireflies. A thin dusting of snow covered the roadway, but blew about like beach sand when a car passed going south.

"Hah," replied Thomas now wearing a blue ski jacket and black ski hat to complement his blue jeans. "No thanks needed because I would hardly characterize it as 'dinner.' A burger *deluxe* at a diner in New Jersey with chips isn't exactly my idea of fine dining. Where are we anyway?"

"We're near a place called Culver's Gap, according to the GPS. We'll be there soon, but it looks like lonely country," noted Stefania.

"To say the least," replied Thomas. "I've always believed New Jersey to be wall to wall people. This is like wall to wall nothing, trees and fields, and snow. Hopefully we don't see too much of the stuff."

"The Jeep is all-wheel drive, and it has a four-wheel drive option, so we'll be okay," Stefania replied. "I thought I noticed a small SUV following us for maybe the last eight miles or so, but maybe I'm just paranoid from our last project together."

Thomas turned around and looked back. "I see headlamps but can't tell what it is. Are you sure it's the same SUV?"

"No," Stefania said and laughed. "Okay, here is the turnoff to the left."

"Stefania, we are in the middle of a no-man's-land," stated Thomas. "This is about as dark as it gets in Scotland."

Stefania made a left turn, crossed a bridge, and came to an intersection.

Stefania pressed the seat warmer button for her car seat, the defroster button, and turned up the heat in the SUV.

"We are now officially in the Delaware Water Gap National Recreation Area. GPS says to make a right, and the sign says the road to Buttermilk Falls is to the right, so here we go," noted Stefania.

She proceeded slowly down a dark narrow deserted road passing an old cemetery.

"Be careful Stefania, the road is not paved and has ruts, holes and ice," Thomas cautioned.

"Oh Madonna, I've got eyes in my head Thomas. I'm not blind."

"Someone's coming," he said.

Out of the dark headlights came barreling down the road. A red pickup truck passed the Jeep, narrowly avoiding sideswiping it.

Thomas looked back.

"Oh Madonna, that pick-up truck almost hit us!" Stefania exclaimed.

"Yes, God knows what that person is doing up here this time of night. Interesting tag number though, Uncle Robert's initials and Granny's birthday. Quite a coincidence."

"Didn't you once tell me there is no such thing as coincidences?" Stefania asked.

"Sounds like something I might say," Thomas replied with a chuckle.

"The parking area is just ahead as I recall. It's almost 1930," Stefania replied with a smile.

The Jeep pulled in the deserted unpaved parking area as the snow, now coming down steadier, blew about. The crusty ice covering the lot crunched under the car's tires. The headlights reflected off of a parked black four door sedan.

"What's that on the ground next to the car?" asked Stefania.

"Blimey, it looks like a body. Pull up closer and let's get out."

Stefania put the Jeep in park, turned off the ignition, leaving the headlamps shining on the sedan. She threw on her red parka, and managed to get out before Thomas and ran the twenty feet to the body.

"Oh Madonna!" she exclaimed.

On the ground in front of her lay a man, dressed in a long wool olive-drab overcoat, blue jeans, and wing tipped black leather shoes, face down in the snow, with a small bloody gash in the back of his head. A patina of blood covered his dark hair.

Thomas rushed up from behind Stefania. He paused a moment. The rushing water of the nearby falls echoed through the snow covered woods.

"What the hell?" he asked, the mist of his breath clear now in the SUV's headlamps.

Thomas took his gloves off and felt the man's neck.

"He's still warm," Thomas said calmly. "Dead, but not dead that long."

"Do you think the red pick-up truck may have something to do with this?" asked Stefania.

"My thoughts exactly. Although some tracks are covered in snow, the tire tracks for this car are fresh, as are several leading out of the lot and turning from where we came. There are boot prints into the woods as well. The question is whether this was the priest's contact or was it the pick-up truck?"

Thomas rifled through the man's coat pockets and then his pant pockets.

"Nothing; no identification, no money, no phone, just the keys for the car. It's a rental."

Thomas put his gloves back on and picked the dead man's head up by the hair to get a look at the man's face.

"He's Asian, hmm," Thomas observed. "Looks like he got clobbered in the back of the head. Let's check the car. Put your gloves on though."

Stefania looked in the back seat, while Thomas looked in the front seat and glove box. He popped the trunk. Simultaneously they both ran to it.

"Nothing in the boot either," Thomas reported.

"Which means he's either a local or he's staying at a hotel. I doubt he's local with a rental. The rental agreement is probably electronic. The thieves likely have his hotel key, but if it's a card key, they have no idea what room he's in, assuming they are that smart," surmised Stefania

"I love it when you come up with deductions like that," commented Thomas.

"Thank you, your grace."

Thomas took out his phone.

"No bloody service, we must be too remote here."

Stefania bent down and looked at the jacket label.

"It's an Asian label, not that it means anything."

The two got back into the Jeep and Stefania started driving back the way they came. The Jeep slid and fishtailed a bit in the deepening snow.

"It's going to be slow going because of the snow," Stefania noted.

"Yes, I see," responded Thomas.

"We are not going to report this, are we?" Stefania asked.

"What do you think, given my position. Can you imagine the headlines, 'English Duke Involved in Death of Vatican Spy,' or some such thing. I was going to call Harry and have him run the plate number of the pick-up. It's late in the UK, but Harry's either up watching the tele, asleep in his armchair, or at the local pub. Either way he won't mind," responded Thomas.

"Well then, let me know as soon as you have cell service and I'll pull over."

Headlights suddenly appeared in the rear view mirror.

"That car came out of nowhere," she said.

"I've got service, pull over," Thomas ordered.

Stefania pulled over into a flat area near a corn field, the headlights illuminating old cut stalks all sticking out of the freshly fallen snow, all in rows stretching into the darkness beyond the reach of the headlights. The car from behind now whizzed past the Jeep, blowing snow up around as it flew by.

"Hmm, that was an SUV, similar to the one I thought was following us, but at least it's not the red pick-up," she noted.

"Harry, yes, it's Thomas. I know it's late, sorry about that. Any chance you have any connections with any of the American law enforcement authorities? Why? I need you to run a plate number. Great. It's, Romeo, Foxtrot, Mike, two, five, zero, seven, two, seven. It is a New Jersey plate which should belong to a late-model red Ford pick-up truck. Let me know as soon as you can, and any information on the owner. Thanks."

"What'd he say?"

"Harry said getting a plate identification is easy. He should be back to us shortly. Let's drive back to the hotel and we'll see if we hear back from Harry."

"What was the significance of the plate number again," Stefania asked.

"Uncle Robert's initials, 'RFM,' and Granny's birthday, twenty-fifth of July, nineteen twenty seven," Thomas replied.

"Quite a coincidence," Stefania said with a smirk.

"Yes, quite," replied Thomas.

Chapter 2
March 4, Near Blueberry Lake, New Jersey, USA

The wet snow came down heavier, sticking to the road and everything else for that matter like glue. The night became a winter wonderland, with snow covered trees and frozen lakes. The Jeep barreled over a rise, and around a corner southbound on U.S. Route 206. Stefania's hands gripped the steering wheel as the Jeep lumbered down the deserted highway. Every turn of the SUV, now in four wheel drive, brought a slip or a slide. Stefania concentrated on driving. The windshield wipers going back and forth, and the heater fan working overtime could be heard, but little else.

"Crud," Stefania exclaimed, "red light." She slammed on the breaks. The ABS did its job, and the Jeep slid through the vacant intersection in a straight line ultimately slowing on the other side of the junction.

"Fortunately we appear to be the only ones on the road," said Thomas rather nonchalantly.

"That's easy for you to say, you're not driving."

Stefania pressed the gas and the Jeep lurched forward.

Thomas' phone rang. Stefania jumped.

"Ah Harry, okay, please hold on."

Thomas put the phone on speaker, stuck it in the cup holder, and took his tablet out of the glove box.

"Okay, Harry. I'll type as you tell me the information."

"The pick-up truck is registered to a Wanda Dlorto with an address of eighteen Lenape Trail, Blueberry Lake, New Jersey. She's got a criminal record," said Harry. "It lists her occupation as exotic dancer, and she's got priors for drug possession, distribution, driving while intoxicated, prostitution, and petty theft. She's never really served any serious time."

"Thanks Harry," responded Thomas.

"I may be able to get you more information come morning your time. That's the best I can do on short notice," replied Harry.

"That's good enough for now. I'll let you know if we need more. Any word on our mysterious priest from the plane crash?" asked Thomas.

"I'm having a difficult time, but should be back in touch in a day or two on that."

"Thanks Harry."

"Stay safe mate. Although it doesn't sound like this Wanda bird is dangerous, my guess is she hangs out with unsavory characters," warned Harry.

"Good night," responded Thomas.

"Blueberry Lake," piped in Stefania. "I think we passed it on our way up here. Put the address in the GPS."

Thomas complied.

"Says it's ten minutes from here, although it may be more given our slow going," said Thomas. "I'll bet this Wanda person robbed our friend, dispatched him, and probably has what was destined for our mysterious priest."

"Agreed. I think our plan should be to stake out the place and then decide how to proceed," she said.

Thomas smiled and his eyes cut to Stefania.

"You've really become quite the investigative reporter since our last adventure, haven't you?" asked Thomas rhetorically.

"Well, I cut my teeth on that project. You and Rodolfo taught me everything I know."

"GPS says to make a right in one-hundred feet. Looks like this Lenape Trail is right off the main road," noted Thomas.

"Hold on. I'm going to make a nice slow turn," warned Stefania.

The Jeep skidded into the turn and after turning the steering wheel back and forth Stefania righted the vehicle.

"That frozen pond over there must be Blueberry Lake," said Thomas. "GPS says eighteen Lenape is up here on our right. Drive past it initially."

"There it is. Looks like an old bungalow. Lights are still on, and maybe the flicker of a television. And a red pickup truck in the driveway to the right of the house," commented Stefania.

Stefania scanned the narrow rural road for room to pull over and park. "I'll pull over here," she said.

"Brilliant," said Thomas.

"Why don't I go to the door. Claim I'm lost, ask for directions. I'll bet her guard will be down with a woman. You'll stand outside and enter when appropriate," said Stefania with a grin. "I think I can handle her if she tries anything."

"Yes, your *capoeira* training might come in handy, but let's case the lorry first, and then the shack," noted Thomas.

The two walked over to the pick-up truck. Fresh snow caked the windows. Thomas wiped some snow away from the passenger side window.

"As far as I can tell, there's rubbish in the cabin, but nothing that looks particularly inviting," he whispered to Stefania who stood behind him.

The old white clapboard bungalow had a windowed porch which appeared to be converted to a sitting room, with a wooden stair leading up to the front door. As Stefania and Thomas crept through the snowfall to the front of the house they could hear a television.

Stefania peeked into the front window. A skinny blonde woman sat on a battered blue sofa in a dimly lit room. She wore an oversize white tank top which hung below her pant-less waist, her pierced nipples protruding from the shirt. Vaping non-stop, the woman flicked the channels back and forth with the remote control, watching a large flat screen set up on a couple of plastic milk crates against the wall. Empty beer cans and liquor bottles littered the wood plank floor in front of the sofa. Stefania stepped back into the shadows where Thomas waited behind a snow covered spruce in the front yard.

"She's alone watching TV," said Stefania softly. "I'll go to the door, make my play and then you enter say you have to go to the bathroom and snoop around and see what you can find. I'll keep her occupied. If she gets uppity, I'll subdue her somehow."

"Right," whispered Thomas.

The gray wooden front door had three small slanted windows on an angle at about eye level. Stefania walked through the snow and up the rickety wooden front steps and knocked on the front door.

Upon arriving at the threshold, Stefania could see through the window on the door that the woman, whom she assumed was Wanda, get up from the sofa, slowly walk across a ripped and torn green area rug covering hardwood floor to the door. To Stefania's surprise she opened the door all the way.

"And what do you want?" Wanda grumbled, oddly turning her back to Stefania and flopped back down on the sofa.

"I'm sorry, I've gotten lost, my phone died, and I need directions back to the main road," Stefania said as she entered the room.

Wanda didn't reply.

"And my friend has to use the bathroom," Stefania continued.

Thomas then appeared at the doorway.

"Shut the door, do I look like I own the gas company," Wanda barked hardly audible over the high volume of the TV, turned to re-runs of an old American sit-com.

Thomas turned and shut the door.

Just then an unshaven twenty-something man with shiny long brown hair wearing a stained white wife beater and black track pants appeared in the doorway leading to the rear of the house next to the sofa. His tribal neck tattoos framed his sharp jaw and dilated brown eyes. Two inked teardrops adorned his worn cheek. He held a handgun at his waist which he raised to eye level with one shaky hand.

"Wanda, go in the back and get me some of those zip ties out of my pack," he said. "You two, keep your hands where I can see them."

Wanda got up from the beaten old sofa, with a brief glimpse of black hipsters covering a portion of a tattoo of a snake which started at her ankle and wound its way up her calf, to her thigh and beyond.

"Sure Duce," she replied. Wanda disappeared through the doorframe into the back of the ramshackle bungalow.

"I think we're going to have some fun with these two," he said.

I want to get into position to kick that pistol out of his hand, Stefania thought, as she shimmied toward him. *I need him a few feet closer.*

As far as Stefania knew, Thomas stood behind her, hands in the air, in his blue down jacket and black wool hat.

"Just my luck," commented Thomas from behind Stefania. "I'm going to die in a rundown old shack at the hand of some philistine named Duce in a place with the dubious moniker of Blueberry Lake, New Jersey."

"Shut up blue eyes!" Duce yelled.

"I'll be just another victim of America's gun violence," Thomas said. "My God, does everyone in this bloody country run about armed?"

"I said shut up you fuzzy foreigner!" Duce shouted again, seeming to come slightly unhinged. He took a few steps toward Stefania, and turned the handgun sideways. "Now you, with the dark hair, green eyes, and yoga pants, I've got some plans for you."

And I have some plans for you, Stefania thought. *Just a few steps closer please. I've been in this situation before jackass.*

Sweat seeped out of every pore in Stefania's five foot five inch frame.

Duce's eyes narrowed, and he gave Stefania the once over from head to foot.

"Yeh, I've got some excellent ideas," he said, followed with a cackle. "Wanda, where the hell are you with those ties?" He yelled as he took two steps closer to Stefania. He looked back slightly toward the door frame, "Wanda?" he shouted.

Stefania leapt into the air her right foot hitting his right hand knocking out the gun, skipping across the stained hardwood floor. Duce collapsed, his head hitting the old floor planks, taking a bounce in the process. Like road kill he lay there motionless, blood seeping out of the back of his skull onto the floor.

"Oh Madonna," yelped Stefania with a gasp.

"Jesus Christ!" exclaimed Thomas.

She looked up. In the doorframe where Wanda had disappeared stood a figure holding a smoking revolver equipped with a silencer. The fortyish woman wore tight blue jeans, and a tight black sweater, and a black wool winter hat, which she pulled off exposing her shoulder length brown tresses. Despite her rather modest attire, it accentuated her athletic physique, all the way down to her black military style boots.

"You!" Stefania exclaimed.

"Svetlana Greschenko, what in God's name are you doing here?" Thomas followed.

"I could ask the same of you two," Greschenko replied in accentless American English. "But let's clean this mess up, get the hell out of here, and then we can talk."

"If you are on official business, I find it hard to fathom a Deputy Director of the Russian SVR is working stakeouts these days," said Thomas.

"Yeh," added Stefania, "shouldn't you be in like, the Ukraine?"

Greschenko scoffed. "Like I said, let's clean-up, get out of here and we'll talk. The girl is dead in the back bedroom." Her eyes cut to Stefania. "Put your gloves on and drag this piece of trash back there too," she ordered pointing to Duce's lifeless body with her pistol, "and shut the door to the room. Don't touch anything with ungloved hands. The blinds are drawn. Otherwise, take care not to get any blood on yourself, don't step in the blood, and don't bother trying to clean anything up. I'll set the thermostat at forty something degrees Fahrenheit, I think that's about five degrees Celsius. Leave the lights on. I suspect what we are both looking for is in a black duffle bag in the back bedroom."

"Why'd you kill him?" blurted Stefania. "Didn't you want to question him?"

"This isn't the movies DiMaggio," snapped back Greschenko. "I don't banter with morons I'm about to sanction. I interrogate on my terms and where I'm safe. Who knows who could walk through that door next. Plus, he could identify us. He was expendable. Now are you going to get rid of the stiff or do I have to do it myself?"

Stefania dragged Duce's body through the doorway and shut the door to the bedroom as instructed. She rejoined the other two in the front room carrying the black duffle bag she found in the bedroom.

"Why is there no exit wound?" Stefania asked, "just a big bump on his forehead."

"It's the equivalent of about a thirty-two caliber, anything larger you would have taken the shot in the head after I blew his brains out," Greschenko responded, "although given how short you are, it might have missed you," she said and laughed briefly.

"And you used a revolver so no bullet casings would be left for the police to find," Thomas added.

"Of course, and I use subsonic rounds, the less noise and evidence the better," said Greschenko, as she pulled the throw rug over the blood stain on the floor, turned the television off, and wiped down the front doorknob.

"But I didn't think you could use sound suppressors with revolvers," replied Thomas.

"It's a Nagant M1895, given to me as a gift by my mentor Vasily," she replied. "It's my pistol of choice when I'm out in the field, and silencers work very well with it."

"That gun's a bloody antique," said Thomas.

"It's my calling card," replied Greschenko.

"I'd say, the bullets are quite unique," noted Thomas.

"Don't worry about it, that's my problem Thomas. There's enough crystal meth, molly, and fentanyl in the back for half the country. The local police will think the killing was drug related," she continued.

She picked up Duce's pistol from the floor and handed it to Thomas.

"Why are you giving me his gun?" asked Thomas.

"Let me put it this way, it's a forty caliber semiautomatic. You never know when it will come in handy if things go sideways, and unlike me, I doubt you have guns stowed away in half the places around the globe and you won't be able to purchase one, at least in New Jersey you won't," Greschenko replied. "Plus the serial number has been defaced, it's likely untraceable, other than the bullets and the shell casings of course."

Greschenko engaged the safety and released the clip.

"You've got ten in the clip and one in the chamber."

She jammed the clip back into place.

"I'd suggest you look around for more ammunition but we don't have the time to search this garbage dump. I'd keep it concealed, in the glove box or some other hidden spot in your Jeep. I've already purloined about three-thousand dollars in cash these clowns had in the bedroom. One never knows when it will come in handy."

Thomas took the pistol and put it into his jacket pocket.

"Any other questions?" she asked.

"How did you get a gun into the States," Stefania asked.

Greschenko rolled her eyes.

"None of your business," she curtly retorted.

She then walked up to Thomas, put her left hand on his cheek, and planted a long messy kiss on his mouth.

At that moment, Stefania's stomach fell through the floor like lead.

"I wondered when we would meet again duke," said Greschenko.

"I hadn't particularly, but this meeting isn't a coincidence Svetlana, is it?" he asked.

"Hah!" Greschenko exclaimed and then laughed, "but it's an incredible coincidence. What else could it be?"

March 4, Radcliffe Township, NJ, USA

Back on the snowy road, Stefania drove toward a twenty-four hour diner on U.S. Route 206 where they were to meet Svetlana Greschenko, a woman who they both met before. The duffel bag was in the back seat, and Greschenko followed in an SUV. Snowplows flew by in the other direction throwing snow onto the windshield.

"So what was all that about?" asked Stefania.

"I'm assuming you mean the kiss?" replied Thomas.

"Yes, the kiss, and did you know the Greschenko woman was going to be here?"

"I had no idea," he answered. "Her presence is an incredible surprise to me as well. As to the kiss, after the Vatican affair, you and I both were caught in a Gordian knot. You did me a favor I can never repay. Unfortunately, the Russians now know a great deal about me, my grandmother, my family, the Catholic Church, that I'd just assume not see the light of day."

"So there's nothing between you and Greschenko?" Stefania asked.

"No," replied Thomas.

"*Was he lying?*" Stefania thought. Although she'd never known Thomas to lie, it didn't seem part of his idiom.

"The sign we just went by said entering Radcliffe Township. Isn't that your title?" asked Stefania.

"Yes, in the late 1600s the king gave one of my ancestors, the sixth Duke of Radcliffe, a charter for acreage in New Jersey for the harvesting of timber for ships, particularly for masts, mining for iron ore, and the production of corn and potentially tobacco. I'll bet the hills here have iron deposits. I understood they named a town in the vicinity after the sixth Duke of Radcliffe. My guess is this is the town."

"I'm surprised you didn't preempt my question with one of your history lessons, your grace," Stefania teased.

"I must have missed it," Thomas replied sarcastically.

"Must be nice to have a town named after oneself," snapped back Stefania.

"There's quite a few, take Braselton, Georgia, for example," responded Thomas. "Look there's the diner ahead on the left," he said pointing. "Pull in."

Stefania carefully negotiated across a lane of traffic on the slushy road into a parking spot in the nearly empty parking lot at the white brick diner, with glass windows facing the parking lot. Greschenko's SUV parked next to them. Stefania grabbed the black duffle bag and the three walked into the vestibule. Stefania carried her ever-present black shoulder bag, and Greschenko, now wearing a waist length fur coat over her sweater, carried her bag as well, except Greschenko's appeared to be a very high end designer type. A row of booths lined the front of the little diner, with tables in the middle and a counter in the back.

There was a sixtyish bald portly man at the cash register, with a black button down shirt exposing his black chest hairs, thick as a rug, nesting a gold orthodox crucifix on a chain around his neck. His tight gray dress pants were covered by a white apron.

"Can we have a booth in the back," Greschenko asked.

"Yes, most certainly," he replied, it what sounded like Greek accented English. He showed them to the booth with three menus.

The group took a booth in the nearly empty diner looking out onto the snow covered roadway in front. Thomas let the two women sit first, and then he sat next to Stefania. Each ordered a coffee, and the man took their order, as it appeared there were no waiters or waitresses to be found in the place.

"The bag, all of its contents, on the table," Greschenko ordered.

Stefania rolled her eyes, picked up the bag and emptied its flotsam in the middle of the table. There wasn't much.

"Looks like we've got a passport, from Singapore," she observed. "A clear plastic case containing a flash drive, a wallet with a Singapore identification. Looks like two-hundred fifty dollars in cash, a credit card, not much else. No cell phone."

"And a hotel card key for his hotel in New York City," noted Greschenko. "It's still in the key jacket and someone wrote what looks like a room number on the outside."

Greschenko took out a small laptop from her shoulder bag, snatched the USB drive from Stefania, and plugged it in.

"It's bound to be encrypted," quipped Thomas.

"Then I'll unencrypt it," snarked Greschenko.

"How'd you get that technology into the country?" asked Stefania. Greschenko ignored Stefania's inquiry.

"Who's this man and why were you there at Blueberry Lake?" inquired Stefania.

"Alright, if it's going to shut you up. He is someone I'm following," Greschenko replied, pecking the keys on her laptop. "At this point I'll just say that much. I followed him from New York City to New Jersey. At some point I lost him, but I did have a GPS device planted on his car. The two brigands got to him at the parking lot in Walpack before I got there. I'm assuming he was a target of opportunity. I parked in the cemetery and trekked through the woods to the parking lot just as they left, confirmed he was dead, and followed them back to their shithouse. While you two were occupying them in the front I got in through the back which was unlocked by the way, shot the bitch between the eyes, with a second for good measure, and you know the rest."

"His passport and identification says he's Stanley Wu from Singapore," Stefania said.

"That's him," responded Greschenko.

"I wonder why there was no cell phone or watch?" asked Stefania.

"Probably those two idiots realized such electronics could be traced, so they threw them out the car window into the woods and snow somewhere between Walpack and Blueberry Lake," responded Greschenko as she scanned her laptop screen. "It's not worth the time and effort trying to find them. They're covered by snow and ice by now, plus there's little to no service in that area, even if we're able to triangulate the location."

"Well what's on the flash drive then?" asked Thomas.

Greschenko put the screen down as the coffees were served. After the man left, she put the screen up and showed the screen to Stefania and Thomas.

"Not much," said Greschenko. "One document in Word format."

"It looks like three times, dates and locations. 1300Z 0503 I92MM41.8E, 1430Z 1203 with a GPS coordinate, and 1900Z 1503 and a GPS coordinate," commented Stefania.

Stefania took out her phone and took a photo of Greschenko's computer screen.

"The last two are locations with GPS coordinates, I have no idea what the first one is," said Thomas.

"Me neither," agreed Greschenko.

"What, the two international geniuses don't have an answer?" teased Stefania.

"Is she always so tedious?" asked Greschenko.

"Why did this guy need such a large bag for this stuff?" asked Stefania.

Greschenko raised her eyebrows. "Not a bad question at all, for a novice," she said. "And what were you two doing stalking Mr. Wu?"

"Maybe we can coordinate and assist each other," chimed in Thomas. "A thumb drive was found by the Brazilian Navy in the possession of a Vatican official who died in the Air San Paolo disaster a few weeks ago. All that was on the thumb drive were the GPS coordinates and a time and date, 0030 Zulu, March 3, that's 1930 hours local time on March 4. The GPS coordinates were for Buttermilk Falls in Walpack, New Jersey. The Vatican denied all knowledge of this person. He was on a flight back to London when he died, and he had travel documents indicating he was flying here to meet with someone at that location on this time and date."

"Mr. Wu is Chinese," commented Greschenko, taking a sip of her coffee.

"Tell us something we don't know," shot back Stefania.

Greschenko tipped her head. "He's an ethnic Chinese living in Singapore, not a Chinese national, get it," Greschenko snapped.

"Are you going to go through his room at the hotel?" asked Stefania.

"I guess that's for me to know and for you to find out," replied Greschenko. "My, she's a quick study Thomas."

"Svetlana, we should all go to the room together. Why should we race to get there?" said Thomas.

"You've got a point. Of course I could dispatch both of you, take this stuff and be on my way, but fortunately for you Thomas, you're a little too important to kill. The Duke of Radcliffe, related to the royal family, a member of the House of Lords, your prominence saved your skin last time. Plus given current circumstances you are much more valuable to the Russian Federation alive and breathing than dead in a bullshit diner in rural New Jersey," noted Greschenko.

"Thanks Svetlana, your self-restraint is refreshing," Thomas replied snidely.

"Also, I saved both your skins in Rio, I'd hate to have done all that work for naught," commented Greschenko, now finishing her coffee. "God awful coffee."

Greschenko picked up the hotel card key.

"Here," she said as she slid it across the table to Stefania. "Frankly, I'd rather you two go through the room. The lobby, the elevators and hallways are all covered by CCTV. I'd rather not be seen entering his room, especially since I'm staying there myself."

"How do you know we'll share what we've found with you?" asked Stefania.

Greschenko looked at Thomas with a raised brow.

"I think I can trust Thomas," she said. Now staring at Thomas she continued, "He knows what can befall him and his family if he crosses me. You knew eventually there'd be an ask? The time has come."

"That certainly makes perfect sense," said Stefania, looking at Thomas and frowning.

The blood seemed to rush out of Thomas' face, now as pale as the new fallen snow.

"Text me when you've finished and you are out of the hotel," said Greschenko. "We should meet in New Jersey. I'll text you the location. The streets of Manhattan are covered by CCTV. I suggest you get to the hotel tomorrow. It won't be long until Wu's body is discovered. It may take a day or two to identify him, but once it hits the news, others may come looking for him."

"The MSS?" asked Thomas.

"Let's put it this way, Wu's not MSS," replied Greschenko. "The encryption on this thumb drive didn't take much effort to solve. An MSS encryption would have taken days to unencrypt."

"What's the MSS?" asked Stefania.

"The Ministry of State Security, the Chinese version of the Russian SVR, CIA, MI6, all the same," replied Thomas.

"Except the MSS isn't as sophisticated as the SVR," Greschenko said, grinning, wiping the last drip of coffee off her lips. "So text me after his room is gone through, okay?"

"Right, we'll be in touch tomorrow," said Thomas. "What about the cell phones of Duce and the girl?"

"I've got them," barked Greschenko. "If there's anything, I'll let you know."

"Aces," snarked Stefania with a scoff.

Greschenko grinned slightly, got up and walked out of the diner into the snowy night.

Turning to Thomas, Stefania took a long hard stare into his baby blues and shook her head.

Chapter 3

March 5, On the Way to New York City, Northern NJ, USA

The snow had stopped, but the day started gray and the roads' wet and slushy, as Stefania drove the Jeep down Interstate 92 toward New York City in the middle of the morning rush hour.

"This traffic is horrendous," commented Thomas. "We should have left earlier."

"Yes, the GPS shows bad traffic almost all the way to the City," replied Stefania. She turned on the radio to one of the local New York AM stations.

"Why did you do that?" asked Thomas.

"See if I can get a traffic report, might assist us in knowing when things will clear up," she responded. "Sometimes it's more accurate than GPS."

"Because of my high profile, I think you should go through Wu's room," said Thomas. "I'll park myself at the location Svetlana identifies."

"Oddly, I was going to suggest the same thing. However, I expect you to rescue me if I take the fall for it," Stefania replied.

"Naturally, I'd hate to see you in an American jail, although I'd wager petty theft doesn't merit jail time in New York City nowadays," responded Thomas with a smile. "The City might actually reward you."

The radio traffic report droned on for a few moments.

"Thomas," piped up Stefania, "pull my notes from my bag. What was the first item on Wu's thumb drive?"

"1300Z 0503 I92MM41.8E," Thomas responded.

"What did the traffic reporter just say, an accident on Interstate 92 East, mile marker 56.8?" asked Stefania.

"Yes, what's your point?" asked Thomas.

"What if I92MM41.8E means Interstate 92, mile marker 41.8 east bound, and the time converted from Zulu is 0800 and 0503 is March 5th?" she asked.

"It's quarter to eight now, and we are at mile marker 40.4," commented Thomas. "Despite this traffic, we'll be at mile marker 41.8 by 8 o'clock."

"This area is like a canyon, with these high walls on either side of the highway," noted Stefania.

"Yes, these are noise barrier walls I believe, twenty feet tall, designed to keep the noise from the cartway from escaping to the nearby residences, but they also act as a barrier from keeping persons and wildlife from entering or leaving the cartway area," responded Thomas rubbing his chin.

"Okay, what's the relevance of that?" asked Stefania.

"Looks like there's about thirty feet or so of evergreen landscaping between the edge of the cartway and the walls on either side. The large median is full of trees and also provides cover. My SAS training tells me that this is a perfect spot for an ambush," said Thomas.

"That seems a bit of an overreach," responded Stefania. "Well here we are, mile marker 41.8 on Interstate 92, just a few minutes shy of 0800."

"Go up a bit and pull over here," said Thomas, pointing to a rather well plowed area of the interstate shoulder clear of ice and snow just east of mile marker 41.8.

"What now?" asked Stefania.

"We sit, wait and see if anything happens, I suppose," responded Thomas.

Just then Stefania heard the unmistakable sounds of vehicles crashing into another; glass breaking, plastic crunching, and tires screeching.

"What the hell is that?" asked Thomas.

Stefania turned and looked to her rear.

"That semi-trailer behind us has plowed across the interstate blocking all eastbound traffic!" she exclaimed.

Then came the unmistakable sounds of rapid gunfire.

"Crikey," exclaimed Thomas.

"Someone from the truck is shooting at the cars stopped on the highway!" Stefania exclaimed as she crouched down in the front seat of the Jeep. "They are all sitting ducks."

"Look, there is gunfire coming from the brush on the side of the road as well," said Thomas, "all in the direction of the cars in traffic."

"State Police," said Stefania pointing to the westbound lanes, "they didn't take long to get here."

A white New Jersey State Police SUV, with its trademark blue and yellow chevrons on the front doors, pulled across a path in the median just west of where the truck had jack-knifed, and the trooper immediately started firing into the cabin of the truck with his service pistol. The man in the truck fell out onto the pavement, covered in blood, assault rifle in hand. A high pitched whistle screamed over top of Stefania's head.

"What was..."

Before she finished her sentence the police SUV launched into the air, flipped over, and landed on its roof. Fire engulfed it and dense black smoke rose from the scene.

"Christ, they've got bloody RPGs," said Thomas as calmly as ever. "Whomever they are, they mean business."

"Looks like the cavalry is here," said Stefania, pointing to two helicopters approaching from the east.

The thud thud of the helicopter rotors made the Jeep shake back and forth and the rotor wash from one of them bounced it from side to side.

Thomas looked up.

"Well one's a news traffic copter, he better watch out or he'll draw fire. The lower one is police. I'll bet they are attempting to determine where the shooters are specifically. I'm surprised they aren't firing at them already."

Just then two high pitched whistles screeched over Stefania's head.

"Well, they've got MANPADs; why wouldn't they?" said Thomas sarcastically.

Following a short trail of white smoke with her eyes, first the police helicopter burst into flames, crashing down out of the air like a fire covered log onto some of the disabled and bullet ridden cars on the westbound lanes. Then the news copter blew up, falling slightly more gracefully out of the sky, like a flame covered wet feather, bouncing a couple of times on the deserted westbound pavement, and rolling over. The dense black smoke from the burning police SUV and the two copters now obscured the whole area.

"Well, it will be a while before a copter comes around here again," remarked Thomas still huddling in the Jeep passenger seat next to Stefania.

Automatic rifle fire erupted again from the underbrush near the wall in the direction of the stranded morning commuters, ripping the stuck cars to shreds.

"I hate to ask, but what's a MANPAD?" asked Stefania.

"It's an acronym for man portable air defense system. Similar to RPGs, they can shoot down low and slow flying aircraft, like drones and helicopters," Thomas replied.

"Good to know," said Stefania.

"We've got to do something," said Thomas.

"Like what?" asked Stefania.

Thomas took the forty caliber pistol out of the glove box, cocked the slide and released the safety.

"I think they are concentrating on the cars to the west. They're not looking in our way, plus the smoke is drifting in our direction. It may obscure our approach. Follow me," he said.

"Why is it that every time I'm with you I end up in at least one gunfight?" Stefania asked.

The two bounded out of the Jeep and Stefania followed Thomas through the snow, through the brush up to the wall.

"There they are." Thomas pointed to two persons dressed in white and gray camouflage with white campaign hats hiding in the evergreen shrubbery. "They are about twenty to thirty feet away. I think we can sneak up on them along the wall."

Ordinarily Stefania would be petrified, but after her last adventure with Thomas, she oddly become more accustomed to dramatics and life and death situations.

"I'll try to dispatch them by bullet, but you stand by in case I need you to spring into *capoeira* mode," said Thomas.

"Got it," replied Stefania.

Oh Madonna, please get me out of this alive, she halfheartedly prayed.

"They are wearing body armor, so we are both going to have to aim for the head," said Thomas over the din of gunfire. "They are crouching down, so we may be at an advantage."

Hunched down and approaching from the rear, a few feet away Thomas stood and aimed the pistol at the back of one of their heads. Stefania stood and watched as Thomas pulled the trigger, but nothing happened.

One of the two, a woman, turned around, her braided ponytail snapping back as she moved. Stefania quickly kicked her in the face with the heel of her knee length leather boot knocking her over into the other woman. Thomas re-cocked the slide and an unspent bullet ejected. The first woman, now bleeding from the nose and mouth, wasn't doing much, so the other turned to confront Stefania, assault rifle in hand, but Stefania knocked the other woman flat in the face with her boot heel. The woman's campaign style hat flew off. The first woman started moving and Stefania kicked her again in the mouth, knocking a few of her teeth out in the process, and finished with a final blow to the throat.

"Well, that was effective," said Thomas, raising his eyebrows as he pistol whipped the second woman, who seemed to be groggy, knocking her out cold.

"Is that any way to treat a lady?" asked Stefania rhetorically.

"Let's get the hell out of here," ordered Thomas, as he looked around the sniper's nest, the two women incapacitated for the time being. Sirens could be heard blaring in the distance and closing quickly.

Stefania nodded.

Thomas put the gun in his jacket pocket and the two ran to the Jeep. Stefania sped the Jeep onto an unguarded exit ramp onto a local road.

"Did you notice something about the shooters?" asked Thomas.

"Yes," responded Stefania, "they were both Asian, like central Asian."

"Indeed," replied Thomas.

March 5, West New York, New Jersey, USA

Stefania entered the small galley style Cuban restaurant. Everyone watched the news coverage of the day's events on the wall mounted TV turned to a Spanish language channel.

Standing just inside the doorframe, Stefania's red down parka hugged her waist. Her tight blue jeans accentuated her voluptuous figure, only to be highlighted further by her knee high black leather boots she used to kick the daylights out of the women in the roadside machine gun nest earlier.

Two flat screens above the liquor racks faced the lacquered hardwood bar. A couple of store front windows faced the snowy sidewalk as light faded from the early March day. The interior brick walls gave the place a subdued look, although wood tabled booths with bright colored seating lined the wall facing the bar. Dimly lit art-deco wall sconces above each table provided some illumination. The back of the place housed a small seating area with five or so tables.

Thomas sat at the bar, his back to the door, gazing up at one of the two flatscreens. Stefania sidled up behind him. He swished back and forth what looked like his favorite drink, gin and tonic, the ice clinking against the glass, and then took a sip.

The bartender, a slim twenty-something Latina with a charming smile, and thin black sweater and matching tight black leggings, made eye contact with Thomas.

"We are characterizing the attack today on Interstate 92 as a terrorist attack," the FBI man on the TV said, surrounded by police and other officials. "We have one terrorist, a male, dead at the scene, and two female suspects, severely wounded, undergoing medical treatment at Saint Joseph's Medical Center in Paterson. We are still going through the wreckage on the highway, but we've accounted for approximately eight dead civilians, another seventeen wounded, five deceased state police, four from a helicopter and one highway unit, and two members of the press from a helicopter. Identities are being withheld pending notification of next of kin. We have no further comment at this time. Next press briefing will be at 10 o'clock this evening. Thank you."

"*Spot on*," Stefania thought. She scanned the restaurant for anyone suspicious. No one looked out of place. Most were talking Spanish, which she understood verbatim.

"Good afternoon," she said in Italian, startling Thomas.

Thomas jumped in his seat, and turned to his rear.

"Am *I* happy to see you," he replied in Italian.

"And me you," replied Stefania in Italian.

"Where's our Russian friend?" she asked.

"Oh, she'll be here, I'm confident of that," Thomas replied in Italian. "Let's speak in Italian, given the topic at hand I'd just as soon not publicize things."

"Certainly Thomas, and you haven't gotten rid of me," Greschenko said in Italian, as she walked over to the two and sat down next to Thomas. She grabbed her knee length fur coat, which covered a black patterned wool skirt, and flapped the fur over her black leggings as she sat. "Your best vodka on the rocks please," she barked at the barmaid in Spanish. A black fur *ushanka* capped her head.

"So what did you find?" Greschenko asked in Italian.

"First, you should know, that this attack," said Thomas in Italian pointing at the television screen, "happened at the first location from Wu's flash drive, mile marker 41.8 on Interstate 92, east."

"What, how do you know for sure?" Greschenko asked skeptically.

"We were there," responded Stefania in Italian. "We figured it out and waited. The terrorists were central Asian. I wouldn't say Chinese, maybe Uzbek."

The barmaid set down a tumbler of vodka with ice on a white bar napkin sitting on the polished wood bar countertop.

"How do you know that?" Greschenko asked incredulously, still in Italian.

"Stefania took them out," replied Thomas.

"What?" Greschenko said.

"The pistol jammed, and Stefania used her Brazilian martial arts skills to knock them out. They were definitely central Asian," Thomas noted, "and well prepared, they had RPGs and MANPADs."

"Not Uzbeks, they were Uyghurs," muttered Greschenko, hardly audibly, in Italian. "Well, what did you find in the room?" she asked.

"He's been there for a few weeks, based on the amount of clothes that were there, the receipts from around town," said Stefania.

"That I know," said Greschenko with irritation in her voice, "the question is why?"

"The room safe was open and nothing was in it, and there was little of intelligence value in the room. I found a bill of lading and I did filch his tablet, but if he left it in his room, unattended, I doubt there is anything of value on it even if we had his password,"

Stefania continued in Italian. "I'll bet his phone had a treasure trove of information."

"My my, you have very good observational skills. Thomas, I'm reevaluating my opinion of this one," said Greschenko, pointing to Stefania with her tumbler of vodka, and taking a sip.

Stefania rolled her eyes. "Why did you say they were Uyghurs?" she asked.

"Did I say that?" Greschenko asked.

Stefania tilted her head and looked at Greschenko.

"A hunch," she responded. "Just a hunch," she repeated under her breath.

"Well what's our next step?" asked Thomas.

"I'll have my people take a look at the tablet," replied Greschenko. "Let me see the bill of lading," she demanded.

Stefania handed it to her.

"It relates to a cargo container from Italy, I'll have it checked out," said Greschenko.

"I've taken a photo of it in case it goes missing," chimed in Stefania.

"Please," Greschenko said with a huff. "What about that dead priest of yours?" Greschenko asked.

"I haven't heard back from my investigator yet, but I would think our next step might be to check out his flat in Whitechapel," responded Thomas.

"What was his name again?" Greschenko asked.

"Charles Smith," Stefania volunteered.

"Where was he living in Brazil?" Greschenko asked.

"Nowhere, the papal nuncio there denied he ever was assigned there," said Stefania. "The Brazilian Navy could find no trace of him in Brazil."

"Well there must be a connection to Brazil somehow," pondered Greschenko.

"Agreed," chimed in Stefania.

"You agree with me. I'm starting to like this upstart more and more Thomas. Perhaps she *is* worth a few minutes of your time," snapped Greschenko.

"Right, so what's the plan?" asked Thomas.

"I'll have the tablet and the bill of lading checked out by our agents here before I leave New York," said Greschenko. "I suggest we meet in London and pay visit to Whitechapel. Maybe your investigator may come up with something by then, and I'll have answers too. Find out ahead of time if this priest's flat is surveilled in any way. I, for one, don't want to be videotaped breaking into it."

"Stefania and I should be able to leave this evening, I'll text you when we land tomorrow, and we'll meet and visit Whitechapel."

"Can't wait," Greschenko replied as she got up and walked toward the bar door. "And you better not be holding anything back."

"Good evening," Stefania said in Italian.

Greschenko turned and smiled, her long brown locks flipping back with her head, as she pushed open the door and stepped into the chilly March evening. A cool blast of air rushed in from the noisy street blowing Stefania's long black tresses back. They settled down as the door slammed shut.

"Dearest, please text me the photo of the bill of lading. I'm going to have Harry check it out," said Thomas.

"I deliberately did not volunteer that I've been to Smith's address already," whispered Stefania. "Can she be trusted?" Stefania asked, watching Greschenko disappear into the cold dreary New Jersey night.

"Not in the least," Thomas replied and drank the last of his gin and tonic likewise watching Greschenko's exit, "but what choice do we have."

"And she left you with the bill for her drink," replied Stefania with a smirk.

"She did indeed," added Thomas.

Chapter 4
March 6, London, UK

Well rested after the flight from Teterboro to Gatwick on Thomas' Falcon 6X, Stefania sat in the airport's VIP lounge while Thomas spoke to Harry on the phone. During the flight she and Thomas slept most of the way. A little chilly, she stood and donned a gray wool sweater over her white cotton shirt, which hung down below the beltline of her tight blue jeans. She sat back down and kicked back in her chair, crossing her knee high black leather boots.

Facing the broad windows overlooking the wet tarmac below and the private jets lined in a row she contemplated the immense wealth that some people have, including Thomas, compared to the vast majority of the world's citizens. The fact that she lives in a two bedroom flat in Rome with her father before he died from COVID had not escaped her. Thomas lives in a vast country house on thousands of acres, had a castle in Scotland, a townhome in London, and properties elsewhere. She didn't own a car. Thomas had many, mostly BMWs and Range Rovers. Although, she came from Brazil, and passed for upper class there, her life experience paled in comparison to Thomas's.

Phone in hand, Thomas paced back and forth in a secluded area of the lounge, wearing a smart maroon cashmere sweater and gray trousers, occasionally looking back and smiling at Stefania. Stefania reflected on her month long adventure with Thomas two years previous. She started out not liking him much, fell in love with him, and at the end he split her heart in two. He saved her life, and she agreed to deep six a story that would have destroyed his family, and probably the Catholic Church. Now the Russians held all the cards and were Thomas' puppet masters.

What a difference two years make, she thought.

Thomas finally finished his call and strode over to Stefania, sweeping his blond hair back from his forehead with his right hand.

"Well," she asked.

"Harry reported he could find no information on this Charles Smith, other than his address in Whitechapel which is on his UK passport," he said. "Harry checked it out and it's in a kind of grimy tenant house above a restaurant, there is no CCTV in the halls, the entryway or on the street nearby. His UK passport had no activity, probably because he used his Vatican passport."

"We should try to get into that room," Stefania responded.

"Yes we should," responded Thomas. "Svetlana called just as I finished with Harry. She's going to meet us here in a few minutes."

"Delightful, wonderful in fact," responded Stefania sarcastically. "There's no one alive I'd rather see."

"Now, now, she saved both of our lives in Rio last time," Thomas replied.

"Yes, how convenient," said Stefania as she looked up at Thomas.

"I've asked Harry to look into Stanley Wu as well," said Thomas.

Greschenko strode into the VIP lounge attired in black leggings and leather boots which bore a striking resemblance to Stefania's. Her navy wool jacket with oversize wood buttons was opened exposing a clingy see-through black sweater with a black lace bra underneath. Like Stefania, she clutched her ever-present large leather shoulder bag.

"What, you're now copying my wardrobe?" asked Stefania, looking at the boots.

"You're delusional," replied Greschenko. "These are quite practical in the wet weather, and don't have patterned soles or heals, so they don't leave tread marks or tracks."

"Which reminds me," Thomas interrupted, "Harry said the authorities in the United States are aware that two persons, a male and female, took out the two terrorists on Interstate 92, based on eyewitness accounts from survivors stranded in their cars on the cartway, of course."

"Any chance of them identifying us?" asked Stefania.

"I don't think so," responded Thomas. "Harry said the news feed from the copter before it was shot down did show a tan Jeep Grand Cherokee on the shoulder near the scene, but the vehicle tag numbers were not visible due to dirty snow, and it is a common vehicle and common color. For the same reason plate scanners didn't catch them. They found our footprints in the snow, but your boot left no tread patterns, so other than your size, they are somewhat difficult to identify. My boots are more identifiable by their patterned soles, but they are a common brand so hopefully nothing will come of it. I'll discard them. In any event, they found an abandoned vehicle on the shoulder closer to the sniper's nest which they've concluded belonged to the two culprits. So it's unlikely they'll pursue the Jeep angle."

"What's the status of the two women?" asked Stefania.

"They are still in hospital," interrupted Greschenko. "Their identities are unknown. One's in a coma. Their vehicle had been reported stolen. All of the weapons were of the type commonly available on the black market, both Russian and American weapons. So tracing their origin will take time. I'll bet the two won't talk, and will likely try to commit suicide as soon as they can, if they aren't dispatched by assassins."

"They are under guard?" asked Thomas.

"Of course, but that's irrelevant in today's world," responded Greschenko. "They can be gotten to somehow. Look what happened to Jeffrey Epstein. He was in a prison and they got to him. So what's the story with this priest?" asked Greschenko.

"My investigator could find nothing on him, other than his flat in Whitechapel," responded Thomas. "There are no CCTV cameras near the location, so I suggest we take care of business. I have a car waiting on the tarmac below."

"Of course you do," responded Greschenko.

The three walked down the outside stairs, dodged light drizzle and hopped into a hunter green Range Rover driven by Thomas' driver John, a non-descript twenty-something with a blond buzz cut, gray overcoat and nothing else particularly distinguishing. Stefania sat in the back seat with Greschenko, and Thomas sat in the passenger seat next to John.

"Hey John," said Stefania.

"Miss DiMaggio, nice to see you again," he responded.

Greschenko rolled her eyes.

"Where is your hometown John, your accent is different from Thomas's," asked Stefania.

"I'm from Yorkshire, Miss DiMaggio," he responded as the SUV sped off the tarmac, out of the airport area and presumably toward Whitechapel.

"Mother of God," Greschenko muttered under her breath.

"So did you uncover anything from the bill of lading or the tablet," asked Thomas.

"It was for a shipping container from the Port of Rome, Italy, shipped to the Port Newark-Elizabeth Marine Terminal, where it was picked up by truck and delivered to a warehouse in Union City, New Jersey, unloaded, and it now sits empty at a container storage area in Newark," she responded.

"That's consistent with what my investigator turned up," said Thomas.

Stefania turned to Greschenko.

"Well any idea who was at the warehouse and what was in the container, or were you going to leave us to guess?" asked Stefania.

"My, you're tediously inquisitive," noted Greschenko with a scoff.

"The manifest was for Italian luxury goods for delivery to upscale American retailers or to a supplier for purchase over the internet," remarked Greschenko.

"Why would Wu have a bill of lading for Italian luxury goods?" asked Stefania.

"He wouldn't," responded Greschenko. "My people are still looking into it but we suspect that the delivery was for the weapons used in the terrorist attack, probably hidden amongst a legitimate delivery."

Stefania crossed her arms and stared at Greschenko from her seat.

"Don't they check the containers, or scan them or something?" asked Stefania.

"Oh my, that little mind of her's picks up tidbits here and there," shot back Greschenko.

"Svetlana, there's no need for all of the sarcasm, really," piped in Thomas.

"I can handle myself Thomas," shot back Stefania in Portuguese. "I'm just not used to dealing with a sharper intellect I guess."

"Whatever, so you picked the one language I don't understand well. To answer your question, thousands of containers come into the Port of New York. If they are from a specific locale, or courier that has been problematic, they are either scanned, searched, or gone over with drug sniffing dogs. Otherwise, containers are scanned at random, maybe one in one-hundred or one in fifty. If the manifest contained items from a legitimate supplier, then it may not have raised concerns by customs officials. It was probably a one to five percent chance that this container would be scanned or searched."

"Why wouldn't they just ship the materials direct from China?" asked Stefania.

"Well," responded Greschenko with a smirk. "That would be easier, but containers from Asia are received in ports on the west coast and are subject to greater scrutiny than containers from say the European Union. About twenty-five percent of containers from China are scanned at the Port of Los Angeles, one in four is a higher risk than one in one-hundred in Newark, especially when you are shipping MANPADs and RPGs."

"But still, wouldn't that risk be too substantial?" asked Stefania. "If caught the arms could be traced easily, or at least the bill of lading would leave a trail to the money behind the shipment."

"There is notorious corruption in the ports in Italy and in New Jersey," she replied with a shrug. "The docks and ports of entry have long time been controlled by the Mafia. One could surmise that there were payoffs on both ends of the shipment to keep this particular container from getting any attention. Once the container was unloaded and shipped out by truck, it would be tough to find out where the cargo was delivered if it wasn't legitimate. We know that, at least optically, the cargo was shipped to stores in the tri-state area from the warehouse."

"What was on the tablet?" asked Stefania.

"My, you *are* thorough," cooed Greschenko. "It contained nothing of consequence. Oddly it was configured for English not Mandarin. The cached searches included restaurants in New York, escort services, pornography, and the directions to Buttermilk Falls, and some news websites, little else."

"He probably wanted to visualize the location. His car had GPS," noted Stefania.

"Anything of value was likely on his phone," noted Greschenko.

"Didn't I already say that?" asked Stefania.

"I hadn't noticed," shot back Greschenko. "Oh, and the FBI found a single unspent forty caliber bullet near the snipers' nest. The firing pin struck the shell casing but it didn't discharge. The FBI is comparing the firing pin mark against known marks in its database."

"But the pistol cannot be traced back to me," shot back Thomas.

"True," responded Greschenko. "I find the criminal element rarely take proper care of their weaponry, hence the misfire."

"What about Wu?" asked Stefania. "Have *you* turned up anything on him?"

"His body was found by some park rangers yesterday evening. He's been identified through the FBI database," responded Greschenko.

Stefania's eyes narrowed and cut to Greschenko.

The Range Rover bounced after hitting a bump as it sped toward Whitechapel.

"That's not what I meant. What is the story with Wu? You are hiding something. Why were you following him?" Stefania shot back.

The Range Rover slowed down and stopped.

"We're here," announced John.

"Harry said the flat is number two, just above the Indian restaurant at this address," noted Thomas. "Looks like a door to the side leads up the stairs to the flats. He said he saw no CCTV."

"I'll be the judge of that," snapped Greschenko. "Have your driver drive around the block, I want to check for cameras.

"Fancy a drive around the block John?" Thomas asked.

"Satisfied?" asked Thomas, after John drove past the location a couple of times.

"At this juncture, yes," responded Greschenko. "There are some cameras nearby, just go straight to the door, don't turn your heads."

"John, drive around or find a place to park and I'll call you when we need pick up," said Thomas.

"Put your phones on airplane mode," barked Greschenko.

The trio got out of the Range Rover into the overcast dank misty morning air.

Greschenko put on her sunglasses and stood on the sidewalk, strode across and entered the doorway. Thomas walked straight ahead and entered the doorway behind Greschenko, and headed up the narrow gray painted wooden stairway. Stefania followed closely behind, also holding the strap of her shoulder bag, the yellowing and grimy walls seemed to be closing in on her.

These walls were probably white once, Stefania thought.

The stairway led to a dim narrow hallway with dirty yellowing white walls and beaten wood plank floors. Apartment two was on the left, facing the back of the building. The shiny black door had the number two under the peep hole. A baby cried in an adjoining room, and foreign voices could be heard down the hallway.

"Bengali," said Thomas, "my guess is many of the tenants are Bangladeshi or Indian."

"You can smell the curry from the restaurant downstairs," chimed in Stefania.

Greschenko crouched down in front of the door and took out what appeared to be a lock picking device from her coat pocket.

Stefania whipped a set of two keys from her shoulder bag, inserted a key into the dead bolt, turned the lock with her right hand and the knob with her left, and the door opened with a long squeak.

"That was easier than your way, don't you think," said Stefania with a grin, gawking at Greschenko, still crouching in the hallway in front of the door. "Smith's key."

Thomas followed Stefania into the room, with Greschenko entering last.

The deadbolt clicked to the lock position.

"Why did you lock the door?" asked Stefania.

"Never leave a door unlocked," sneered Greschenko.

The gray walls of the small flat caged in one small space an iron frame bed covered with a gray striped comforter pushed against a side wall, a small kitchenette on the other side, a chest of drawers, next to the doorway, topped with a small television, and an old brown fabric armchair against the far wall in front of a window with a footstool in front of it. The closed back window looked out onto an interior courtyard which led to a roof below. Dusty white venetian blinds covered the window. Behind the front door was a door to the bathroom. A commode and rust stained pedestal sink could be seen through the door, and farther in floral patterned shower curtain surrounded an old free standing tub.

"This is perhaps one of the smallest flats I've ever been in, I must say," remarked Thomas. "If this Smith was a priest, it's odd that there are no items of religious significance here."

"It's rather cool in here, the heat is off," noted Stefania. "That pantry over there is the only storage space here."

Greschenko went to the small closet or pantry next to the kitchenette and opened the accordion doors to the space.

Footsteps approached in the hallway.

Greschenko stepped out of the pantry, closed the doors, and produced a revolver with a silencer from her shoulder bag and pointed it toward the door.

"Do you always walk around armed to the teeth?" snipped Stefania.

"Yes," Greschenko whispered matter of factly. "Shhh."

The footsteps stopped, seemingly in front of the door.

"Into the loo, all of us," Thomas quietly said.

The three crammed into the small bathroom. The last into the confined space, Greschenko closed the door softly. Thomas stood in the tub, Stefania straddled the toilet, and Greschenko in front of the sink with her pistol at the ready, pointed at the door. Other than the light which seeped in from under the door, the loo was dark.

Someone fiddled with the lock to the door to the flat. Stefania heard a click, and the grate of the door as it slowly opened. Silence permeated the cramped bathroom. Whoever opened the door must have stood in the doorway for a moment.

Stefania's heart pounded, she breathed heavily and sweat seeped out of every pore, despite the relative cool of the room.

Footsteps entered the room and the door creaked shut. The footsteps went by the closed bathroom door. The door to the pantry opened. Rummaging could be heard and then a loud clunk.

Someone's looking for something, Stefania thought.

The noises stopped. The footsteps moved away from the pantry.

And they've found it.

In that instant Greschenko swung open the bathroom door with her pistol drawn.

Standing there was a slim thirtyish Asian woman with a blonde bob cut, in a red leather overcoat, gray yoga pants with green sneakers, and a brown shoulder bag.

She immediately pivoted and kicked the pistol out of Greschenko's hand onto the bathroom floor, knocking her down in the process against the open bathroom door. Stefania jumped out and landed a kick to the woman's chest, sending her onto the bed, and knocking her bag to the floor. Stefania hesitated for a moment. The woman leaned back on the bed, jumped back up, pivoted to the left and landed a kick on Stefania's right shoulder. Falling to her left, Stefania saw a muzzle raised above her chest, and the tell-tale sound of a gunshot muffled by a sound suppresser.

The Asian woman crumpled to the floor, her back against the edge of the bed's foot board, with a bullet hole between the eyes, leaning slightly to her right. Bright crimson blood dripped down her left cheek like a tear. Her brown eyes gazed absently, and blood collected on the lip above her open mouth before falling onto the wood floor like a rain drop.

Greschenko, who had been crouching when she took the shot, got up, stepped over Stefania's legs and hovered over the Asian woman. She raised the Nagant M1895 again, and put another bullet into the woman's head.

Greschenko placed her gun into her shoulder bag and took some latex gloves out of the bag and put them on. She threw a pair of the gloves at Stefania as she got up off the floor.

Thomas emerged from the bathroom.

"Blimey!" he exclaimed.

"Do you always carry latex gloves with you?" asked Stefania, now standing.

"Yes," responded Greschenko, as she tossed a pair to Thomas, who caught them mid-air.

"You seem to be rather relaxed for a novice. Death doesn't bother you?" asked Greschenko.

"Let's see *chica*, two years ago I survived a terrorist attack in Rome, nearly got killed in a bathroom by a hit-man in a concert hall also in Rome, came within a hair of being run over by a car in Rio, also by an assassin, almost got run off the road near Haverford Hall by killers, and survived being held at gunpoint by some d-bag named Duce in New Jersey. Under the circumstances, I think I can handle it," responded Stefania, her hands straddling her hips.

"If I knew I was going to get a dissertation I wouldn't have mentioned it," said Greschenko. "Anyway, adequate job in occupying her until I could recover. One piece of advice, don't hesitate, if she had a gun handy, you'd be on the floor with a bullet in your brains, not her. Luckily we caught her by surprise."

"Adequate job," Stefania mumbled with a huff.

Greschenko grabbed the woman's bag and dumped its contents on the bed. Out fell a manila folder, a UK driving license, some makeup, spare tampons, birth control pills and other odds and ends, keys, and a turned-off cell phone. Greschenko patted the bag down again, and out of a side pocket pulled a pistol.

"I don't think she was expecting anyone in the flat," commented Thomas. "She wasn't prepared for your assault."

"Agreed," said Greschenko. "Hmm, looks like a Walther PPK, specifically a type S, thirty-eight caliber," reported Greschenko looking at the deceased. "Now what would a nice girl like you be doing with a gun like this?"

Greschenko rifled through the woman's coat pockets.

"Let me see the key you used to gain entry," Greschenko demanded.

Stefania took them out of her pocket and put them in Svetlana's hand.

"These two keys are identical to the keys she's got," noted Greschenko. "One is to this flat, the other is to who knows what. Here take these back, I'll keep her set of keys."

Greschenko slipped the woman's keys into her shoulder bag.

Stefania picked up the driving license from the bed.

"Says here she's Lucia Chen, from Vauxhall, London," she reported. Stefania placed the driving license on the bed and took a quick photo of it.

Thomas picked up the manila folder.

"This must be what she found in the pantry. Well let's see what we have here," he said handing the manila folder to Stefania.

She carried the folder to the wood countertop in the kitchenette and opened it. There appeared to be four or five pages of handwritten notes.

"These are money transfer instructions," Thomas said.

"No names or amounts, just account and wiring information," added Stefania.

"It should be easy enough to find the identities of the banks," replied Thomas. "The account holders and amounts transferred may be a different matter."

"What else is there?" asked Greschenko.

"Some phone numbers it looks like," said Thomas, "but no names."

"Several of these phone numbers are in Singapore and China, but also in the UK and Europe," said Greschenko.

"This one phone number in the UK looks extraordinarily familiar," observed Thomas. "Let me dial it on my phone."

Thomas fiddled with his phone, and then paused.

"Well who is it then?" asked Stefania.

"Yes, well Thomas?" followed Greschenko.

"It's the personal mobile number of my friend, Artie," Thomas muttered hardly audibly. "I have it saved on my mobile."

"Why would this nobody priest have the phone number of your friend Artie?" asked Stefania.

"Well, he's actually Albert, the Duke of Shropshire," Thomas replied.

"Okay, still, what's the significance of this Duke, I mean you're a Dukc too, right?" Stefania asked.

"He's a royal Duke," chimed in Greschenko. "His Royal Highness, Prince Albert George Victor Arthur, Duke of Shropshire, Earl of Wright, second in line to the throne behind his sister, Princess Mary. Known to his friends and relatives as 'Artie'".

"How do you know this stuff?" queried Stefania.

"It's my business to know *this stuff*," responded Greschenko snidely. "He was third in line until a ski accident last year in Gstaad killed the second in line, Prince Frederick."

"I think it's safe to say we can take these documents. Chen is dead, it's not like we can undo that," urged Stefania.

"You make a good point, if you weren't so irritating," said Greschenko. "My people can find out the bank account information and who the phone numbers belong to, so I'll take the file."

"Not before I photograph every page," responded Stefania, as she started taking photos of pages in the folder.

"Forward to me everything you've photographed," whispered Thomas into Stefania's ear.

"Are you done yet?" asked Greschenko from across the room.

"Yes, here's your file," replied Stefania with a huff, walking over and slapping the file on Greschenko's gloved palm.

"Why would this guy keep this information written down instead of on an electronic device?" pondered Stefania to no one in particular.

"Maybe he did and the paper was his back-up," said Greschenko. "My phone will destroy all confidential data if someone attempts to hack it. He clearly thought he had the paper file well hidden."

"Except she knew where to find it," said Stefania pointing to the dead woman with her chin.

"Here," Greschenko threw two towels from the bathroom to Thomas and Stefania.

"Wipe down everything you may have touched before you put the gloves on including the floor where you fell, but don't wipe up the blood. Put the towels in my bag. I'll take care of the doorknobs," directed Greschenko.

"What do we do about her?" asked Stefania.

"We put her in the tub," responded Greschenko holding onto Chen's forearms. "Thomas?"

Gazing at his phone in hand, Thomas was clearly preoccupied.

Stefania stepped up and grasped Chen's ankles. The two dragged her into the bathroom, lifted her slight body, and laid her into the tub.

"And don't walk through the blood on the floor," Greschenko directed.

"What about her things?" asked Stefania.

Greschenko looked at the detritus strewn across the old gray comforter on the bed. She quickly picked everything up and stuffed it all into Chen's bag.

"I'll take her phone and other things and get rid of them. The phone can probably be traced and the longer it takes someone to find and identify her body the better," said Greschenko. "Now let's get the hell out of here. Lock the door when we leave, and Thomas I need your driver to drop me off at Ludgate Circus."

"Certainly," replied Thomas absently, his head bowed down looking at his phone, "of course."

Chapter 5
Morning, March 7, Kensington, London, UK

Stefania arrived in a taxi at Thomas' Notting Hill residence for the first time. She'd been at Haverford Hall, his country estate in northeastern England, and at his family's castle in Scotland, but never here in London. She stopped on the wet sidewalk and looked up at the Victorian style edifice. White pillars held up a balcony on the second floor which served as a portico. Difficult to tell from the street, Stefania figured the white brick and stone townhome was at least four stories, with maybe a fifth story with dormer windows.

The cool dreary March morning didn't seem to do the building justice.

It probably looks less imposing in bright sunshine, she thought.

She stepped off the sidewalk, climbed a step or two to the front door, and rang the bell. The door opened and there stood a butler, traditionally dressed in a black butler's outfit and matching tie.

"Good morning, Ms. DiMaggio I presume?" he asked.

"Yes, good morning, yes, I'm Stefania," she responded.

"His grace is expecting you. Follow me."

The bright foyer had white and black marble floors with an elevator in front of her with a stairwell to her right. The stairwell led to a balcony which surrounded the large foyer and had several doors leading off to other rooms.

Stefania followed the butler into what looked to be a small library, certainly smaller than Thomas' library at Haverford Hall. Other than the wooden shelves stuffed with books, hardwood wainscoting covered the walls, and the floor was hardwood covered with a blue and beige Persian carpet.

Two matching red sofas were on either side of a large travertine fireplace with bookshelves on either side. Marching hardwood nesting tables with Chinese vase lamps were at the end of each sofa.

To the back of one of the sofas was Thomas' desk, with a brass desk lamp. Behind the desk and chair were three high backed chairs in a semi-circle around a glass-topped tea table.

"Please do sit down. I'll inform his grace that you are here," the butler said.

"Thank you," responded Stefania as she sat on one of the large red sofas positioned perpendicular to the fireplace.

This is quite odd. Every other time I've been to one of Thomas' residences, I've been with him. I've never had to wait for an audience.

Stefania took in the room, which had a street view window, several statuary and traditional artworks interspersed among the bookshelves, including some with religious themes.

Makes sense, she thought, *Thomas is devout.*

Thomas walked in, dressed somewhat casually for him, wearing a red wool sweater and khaki slacks. He sat on the sofa next to Stefania, throwing his arm up on the sofa back.

"My dear Stefania, how does it go?" he asked in Italian.

"It goes well, and you?" she responded, also in Italian.

"Well," he responded, then changing to English. "What are you doing tonight?"

"I don't have any particular plans, why?" she responded.

Maybe Thomas is going to take me out for dinner, she hoped.

"Well, I've invited my friend Artie and his wife Esperanza for dinner tonight here, and I thought you might join us, maybe do some fact finding," said Thomas.

"You figured I could speak with Esperanza in Spanish, and maybe find out why this priest from Whitechapel had Artie's phone number. Her being a Spanish duchess and all," Stefania replied.

"My God, you have done your homework, haven't you," said Thomas.

"Svetlana was correct. Artie is his Royal Highness, Prince Albert George Victor Arthur, Duke of Shropshire, Earl of Wright, second in line to the throne behind his sister, the Princess," Stefania revealed. "He married Duchess Esperanza of Malaga of Spain, and a devout Roman Catholic. The marriage was opposed by many in the UK because of her religion, but the Queen gave her consent because Artie agreed not to convert to Catholicism and to raise their children in the Anglican Church, and he was third in line at the time."

"You're quite thorough," commented Thomas.

"In the past, by virtue of the marriage Artie would have been taken out of the line of succession for marrying a Catholic but the Succession Act of 2013 solved that problem," added Stefania.

"Yes, and despite the marriage, Artie is the more popular of his majesty's two remaining children," said Thomas. "The Princess Mary is a bit awkward, not terribly outgoing. She's not taken to the public duties of the monarchy well. Her unconventionality is perceived as arrogance, hence her unpopularity. When she was younger she was the 'wild child' of the monarchy. She married a successful Scottish footballer, which one would have thought would have made her more popular, but oddly it had the opposite effect."

"Yes, I gather she is not as popular as your friend Artie," said Stefania. "I see Artie and Esperanza have two toddlers, but the Princess hasn't any children," noted Stefania. "Do you know Mary?" asked Stefania.

"We're acquainted. As you can imagine, we travel in much different circles," responded Thomas. "As you know we are distant relations through my mother."

"How did you become such good friends with Artie then?"

"We were at Sandhurst together, and served in Afghanistan as well in the SAS. Granny is his godmother and I believe she had a hand in setting him up with Esperanza. Artie is more down to earth and more my type."

"How many godchildren *does* your grandmother have?" asked Stefania.

"Many," Thomas replied with a shrug.

"Why didn't she set you up with Esperanza?" Stefania asked.

"Well, I think Esperanza was looking for a husband whose status eclipsed a non-royal duke of modest precedence in the peerage of England," replied Thomas with a grin. "Plus Artie is a great fellow. Top notch."

"Maybe she should have gotten to know you she would have liked you," Stefania added.

Thomas grinned and blushed slightly.

"Perhaps," he said.

"Has your grandmother made it her job to arrange marriages for all the protestant aristocrats in the UK to nice Catholic girls?" asked Stefania in a sarcastic tone.

"It would seem that way, wouldn't it," replied Thomas.

"So I researched Prince Frederick's death," added Stefania.

"And," said Thomas. "I assume you are getting at something. It wasn't a suspicious death at all. Frederick was an itinerant skier. He was last in his group as night fell on a double black diamond slope. Something happened and he went off trail and collided with a tree head-on."

"That's what the reports said," replied Stefania. "So what's the plan for tonight?"

"Artie and Esperanza will be arriving at about 7 o'clock. We'll have cocktails and then dinner. Artie and I haven't seen each other for a while so he and I will have a lot to catch up on. He knows I've been serving as a secret emissary between with the Vatican to resolve all the thorny issues that have come up, including sanctions instituted by the UK against Russia, so my guess is he'll want to discuss those matters."

"And I'll engage Esperanza in conversation in her native Spanish, lull her into a sense of ease after a cocktail or two or three, and see what I can find out," added Stefania.

"Spot on," said Thomas. "I was very lucky to get them this evening. They had a cancellation a couple of days ago for tonight, which I engineered actually, and when I reached out he was delighted to hear from me. I owe my cousin James for this one."

"Have you heard from Greschenko?" asked Stefania.

"No," responded Thomas, rubbing his chin, "which is a bit disconcerting. I've reached out, but she hasn't answered. I've asked Harry to get me what information he can obtain on Wu and Chen, and on the bank account and phone number information we found in Whitechapel. Harry called a few moments before you arrived, and said he would be paying me a visit in a few minutes, so he should be here any moment now. For whatever reason, Harry didn't want to talk on the phone."

"You know I checked out the two GPS coordinates we found on Wu's flash drive," said Stefania.

"And?" replied Thomas.

"One is to a remote area of the United States border with Mexico in Arizona, and the other is in a remote area of the Arizona desert," said Stefania. "Neither locale seems to have any particular pertinence, at least from the satellite map view. Both locations are barren wasteland."

"Hmm, perplexing," said Thomas. "Also interesting is that when I perused the chest of drawers in Smith's room there were some clothes, but not many. It seemed more like a place to crash temporarily, rather than a permanent flat."

"And I got a look at the pantry before Svetlana closed the door," interrupted Stefania. "Not much food. Some dry and canned goods, but very little."

"I should have liked to give the place a more detailed inspection, but that is out of the question now," replied Thomas.

The butler entered the room with Harry in tow.

"Major Harry Foster," the butler announced.

Harry walked wearing dark blue slacks, a button down shirt, cardigan sweater and herring bone blazer which draped over his large figure like a thick blanket.

Thomas stood up and shook his hand.

"Good morning Harry, thanks for meeting us this morning," said Thomas.

"Hello Thomas, Stefania," replied Harry looking at Stefania. "Frankly, given what I found I didn't want to report it to you other than in person and in a location without prying ears or eyes."

"That's intriguing," noted Stefania. "Now I'm captivated."

"Please do sit down Harry," said Thomas. "Would you like some tea?"

"Normally I would, but not today," responded Harry.

"So what have you?" asked Thomas, sitting back on the red sofa across from Harry who sat on the matching opposite sofa.

"First a question mate, where did you come upon the name Lucia Chen?" asked Harry.

"Stefania came across her name in connection with one of the stories she's pursuing," responded Thomas. "Just a name mentioned in passing, nothing more. Why do you ask?"

"Well if it's the same Lucia Chen, her full name is Lucia Rita Chen, she's an MI6 analyst, assigned to the China desk at Vauxhall Cross. Chen is single, no siblings, and her parents are deceased. Her parents immigrated to London from Hong Kong in 1990. She's gone missing, that is why I asked you the question," replied Harry.

"Crikey!" exclaimed Thomas looking at Stefania.

"Frankly, the less I know the better," said Harry. "Although I focused on Lucia, her father, Francis Xavier Chen, was a real estate developer type in Hong Kong in the 1980s and 1990s, and liquidated his portfolio before the 1997 transfer back to China. He was very influential in Hong Kong, and a staunch anti-communist. He purchased Endeavey House in Somerset and lived there until he passed several years ago. His wife predeceased him, and his estate was quite large. After he died Endeavey was sold to pay the taxes and death duties. Still, after taxes Lucia inherited a significant sum, in excess of twenty-million quid. She's independently wealthy, and really didn't need to work. You can imagine when I asked my usual contacts about Lucia Chen, some eyebrows were raised. I had to make excuses."

"I'm sorry Harry if this put you in a difficult position," responded Thomas.

"No matter Thomas, it's all part of a day's work," said Harry.

"Anything else about Chen?" asked Stefania.

"Also both her and her father had reputations as being monarchists, extremely so," said Harry. "You know she lived in Vauxhall, it's an expensive flat. I checked it out. There are plenty of CCTV cameras on the street, and her building lobby has a doorman and CCTV."

"What about Stanley Wu?" asked Stefania.

"Ah, Mr. Wu. He's a financier from Singapore, or *was* a financier from Singapore, sorry, with significant connections in China. To say he's a shady character wouldn't be a stretch. MI6 pegs him as a middleman between Chinese interests and others. He'd finance projects or investments outside of China, some legitimate, some not, with Chinese money."

"How sure are you of this?" asked Thomas. "That would suggest he's not MSS."

"Very," replied Harry. "He's not MSS."

"Right," said Thomas.

"I'll bet Greschenko knows more than she's telling us," blurted Stefania. "A great deal more."

Thomas looked at the ceiling, apparently in thought.

In that moment all Stefania could hear was the ticking of the mantel clock above the fireplace.

"What about the bank accounts?" asked Stefania, interrupting the lagging silence.

"The bank account numbers were three, one to an account in the Cayman Islands, one to a Singapore account, and one to an account in Rome," said Harry. "I've written down all the information here, I didn't want to transmit it electronically or have it saved on a computer hard drive," continued Harry, producing a folded white piece of paper from his jacket pocket. "We know the bank identities, but banks are not typically eager in revealing account holders, but based on what we found, the Singapore account is probably Wu's, or he had access to it. The others, who knows? The Rome account was a placeholder account, money was transferred in and transferred out from tax havens."

He handed the paper to Thomas, and Thomas handed it to Stefania.

"You also have the phone information here as well," said Stefania.

"Yes," Harry said, shifting as he sat to look directly at Stefania. "I've written down that information also on the paper. One, as Thomas knows, is to his Royal Highness, the Duke of Shropshire, the second is to a burner in Rome, so no identity."

"Does that suggest a Vatican connection?" asked Thomas.

"Maybe," Harry said shrugging.

"What of the others?" asked Stefania.

"The Singapore number was for Mr. Wu, the number in China I haven't been able to determine who it belongs to and probably never will, and one of the other numbers in the UK was for a burner," said Harry. "The last UK number was for Alistair Hough. Do you recognize the name?" asked Harry.

"Bishop Hough?" asked Thomas.

"Right," said Harry.

"That's not unusual, a Vatican representative having a Bishop's phone number," observed Stefania.

"It is, because Bishop Hough is an Anglican Bishop," noted Thomas. "He's high church, rumors are that he's next in line for the Archbishopric of Canterbury."

"Is that relevant?" asked Stefania.

"I'm not sure," responded Thomas. "So this Smith person, whomever he was, had contacts with the Duke of Shropshire, Mr.

Wu, Bishop Hough, and maybe the Vatican," remarked Thomas rubbing his chin.

"About your Charles Smith," said Harry. "It's like he never existed. I can't find anything on this specific Charles Smith, although there are many Charles Smiths out there. Now Lucia Chen worked for MI6 domestically at its China desk. She needed a driving license and credentials domestically, and she inherited a large estate. I'll wager Charles Smith was an alias. He either worked for MI6 or a foreign intelligence agency, or an organized crime syndicate. Very few entities can create a completely new persona out of thin air. The UK and Vatican passports *are* genuine, although he apparently used his Vatican passport almost exclusively."

"I've spoken with one of my contacts with the Vatican Secretariat of State," added Thomas. "He denies there is any record of a Charles Smith holding a diplomatic from the Holy See or even been with the Vatican diplomatic corps. Stefania, you said nothing else was found with his body?"

"That's what my cousin Hércules told me, although he did say his body had been in the sea for a while and if there was anything on his person, that could have easily fallen out or been ejected during the violence of the crash," replied Stefania.

"Logical," commented Harry. "Of course, I doubt the burner number is for his phone. Why would you write down your own phone number?"

"True, and there was nothing of religious significance in his flat," replied Stefania. "That's odd for a priest, based on my own and Thomas's prior experience."

Harry sighed and stood.

"I'll show myself out mate. I didn't bring a coat. Let me know if you need anything further," said Harry.

Thomas rose and shook Harry's hand.

"Thanks Harry," said Thomas solemnly. "Hopefully, this Chen inquiry doesn't cause you problems."

"I think I'm fine," replied Harry. "I can take care of myself, and as ex-MI5, I've many friends in and out of the service."

"Yes," said Thomas softly. "The service *is* a bit like a fraternity or club. You know you can always call on me if need be."

"Good'ay mate," Harry said as he walked out of the library and shut the door behind him.

"The question I have is why did this so-called priest, if he was a priest, have your friend Artie's phone number?" asked Stefania.

"Yes, all this is very peculiar. Maybe we'll find out more tonight," replied Thomas, rubbing his face with his hand. "I'm very bothered that Chen was MI6. If she was at Smith's flat on official business, my God, being involved in her death means we may be party to treason."

"We had no reason to know she was MI6," added Stefania. "Is it possible that she was acting outside her authority?"

"Let's hope so," responded Thomas softly. "Let's pray so."

Evening, March 7, Kensington, London, UK

Stefania arrived early at Thomas' townhome for cocktails and dinner with Artie and his wife Esperanza. More than anything she wanted to make an impression on Thomas. She wore a snug black lace dress with spaghetti strings, slightly above the knees, with a plunging neckline bearing a bit of cleavage with a hint of her black lace bra, and her nicest and shiny black pumps, the most expensive ones she owned.

"Ms. Stefania DiMaggio," the butler announced as Stefania was ushered into the library for cocktails prior to dinner.

Scotch on the rocks in hand, Thomas waited in a dark dinner jacket and pants, with black tie and matching shoes.

"My God, you look heavenly," said Thomas.

"Thank you your grace," replied Stefania.

"There are many protocols when speaking with a member of the royal family, but most of them will not apply here," said Thomas. "Artie and I are close friends. You'll have to curtsy."

"I see."

"What can I get you to drink?" he asked.

"Some red wine would be nice," she responded.

Stefania noticed a footman of some sort standing in the corner of the room. Thomas signaled to him with his hand.

"A glass of whatever red wine we have decanted for Ms. DiMaggio," Thomas ordered. "I think we've got a Tignanello decanted."

"Thank you," said Stefania.

"I've told Artie about you," said Thomas. "I had to create a pretense for tonight, you'll have to play along..."

The door to the salon opened and the butler interrupted Thomas mid-sentence, "His Royal Highness, the Prince Albert, Duke of Shropshire, Earl of Wright, and her grace the Duchess of Shropshire, Countess of Wright, Duchess of Malaga, Dame of Malta."

Artie dressed similarly to Thomas, had brown hair, but sported a close shaven beard. At about six feet tall he and Thomas were nearly the same height. Unlike Thomas, Artie sported a modest tan. His hazel eyes were set off by his dark close cropped beard and tan skin.

Thinner than Stefania expected, Esperanza wore a red sequined dress, with black trim, with a hemline well above the knees, a plunging neckline which accentuated her ample breasts. A gold cross with diamonds hung between her two bosoms, creating a focal point for the eyes. Well tanned, like Artie, Esperanza's shoulder length blonde highlighted brunette tresses hung over her shoulders. Her red soled black glittered pumps could be Louboutins. On her ring finger flashed a massive diamond engagement ring next to an elaborate rope designed gold wedding band.

"May I introduce my friends Artie and Esperanza, this is my friend Stefania," said Thomas while shaking Artie's hand.

Stefania curtsied.

Esperanza hugged Stefania and kissed her on the cheek.

Her dark brown eyes are comforting, thought Stefania.

"Thomas has told me so much about you Stefania. It is wonderful to finally make your acquaintance," said Artie.

"And yours as well your Royal Highness," replied Stefania.

The footman brought a tray of three glasses to the group. Two glasses of red wine, and what looked to be a tumbler of scotch.

"Thank you Herbert," said Thomas. "Especially for remembering our guests' tastes."

"If you ladies won't mind, Thomas and I have some catching up to do," said Artie.

"Not at all," said Esperanza. "I'm sure we'll have a lot to talk about."

The two men walked across the room and relaxed on the high backed chairs behind Thomas' desk around the tea table and started speaking in hushed tones.

Esperanza and Stefania sat on the red sofas in front of the fireplace, where a small blaze was making its way through a few hardwood logs.

Esperanza took several deep sips of her wine.

Stefania immediately noticed two tattoos on Esperanza's wrists, just above her hands. On her right wrist was a Christian cross, and on the left was a scallop shell.

"I see you have some inkings, what's their significance," she asked in Spanish.

"Well spoken Castilian is music to the ears," responded Esperanza also in Spanish, now smiling. "The cross is worn by our Coptic brothers and sisters on their wrists, and I wear it in solidarity with them due to their persecution, and the scallop shell is the sign of Saint James. I got the scallop shell tattoo after I finished the camino for the first time when I was nineteen. All in our camino group got the same inkings."

"Wow, quite symbolic," said Stefania. "So how have you adjusted to living in the UK?"

"I love my husband deeply, so wherever he is, life is wonderful," she replied matter of factly.

Esperanza took a lengthy sip of her wine.

"Wow, you two must have some connection," said Stefania.

"I would say so, yes. We are both old souls. We married but a year and a half after we met. Would have been sooner, but the Queen had to grant permission, and she thought long and hard about it because I'm Catholic," she responded. "At the time Artie's siblings hadn't married, and the Queen wanted heirs, so she gave in. Princess Mary still hasn't had children, and shows no inclination."

"You are obviously devout, has that caused any friction?" asked Stefania.

"None whatsoever," Esperanza responded. She took several additional sips of wine, the glass now almost empty. Her lips now wet and shiny with leftover wine, she added "Artie is a devout high church Anglican, we share much in common. This is excellent wine by the way."

"What about your children, does it bother you that they are not baptized Catholic?" Stefania asked.

"It doesn't matter. The Catholic church recognizes their baptisms, which will be helpful when the time comes," noted Esperanza.

"What about you, Thomas told Artie so much about you. It's almost like he's obsessed. I frankly couldn't wait to meet this mysterious Stefania."

"Well there is not much mystery to me. I'm just a nice Catholic girl from Brazil," Stefania responded with a slight grin and a shrug.

Her eyes cut to Thomas, who was speaking intently with Artie across the room. She hoped to catch a glance, or recognition from him. He turned and their eyes met. He smiled and went back to his conversation.

The butler opened the door to the library, which meant a short walk through the hall to the dining room. The couples walked into the dining room for dinner. Stefania never dined at Thomas' London townhome. The dining room was much smaller than at Haverford Hall. A crystal chandelier hung over the polished hardwood table set with a linen tablecloth, blue cobalt china, silver service, linen *serviettes*, crystal candelabras with candles alight, and a rust patterned Persian rug which ran the length of the room covering the hardwood plank floor.

The crimson walls complement the hardwood and rug nicely, Stefania thought.

Dinner, desert, and after dinner drinks back in the library kept the couples up and talking well past 1 o'clock. Artie and Esperanza left at half-past one.

Thomas and Stefania settled on one of the red high-backed sofas by the fire with a couple of cognacs in etched crystal *cordial* glasses.

"So were you able to find anything out?" asked Thomas.

"Other than she's a mega-Catholic and your friend Artie has a wife who worships him, no, nothing of significance as far as I can tell," Stefania replied.

"Disappointing then, but not all for naught," said Thomas. "I enjoyed seeing them."

"They were very interesting people. Certainly they're much more down to earth than I expected. I think Esperanza and I could be friends," Stefania said, adding a grin thereafter. A long yawn overtook her. "Sorry I'm exhausted. What does 'high church' mean?"

"Why do you ask?" asked Thomas.

"Well Esperanza mentioned that Artie was 'high church' and you referred to Bishop Hough in that way," she replied.

"Well a high church Anglican is about as close to being Catholic as you can get with still being a protestant," he replied. "Sometimes they are referred to as 'Anglo Catholics,' but that can apply in many contexts. The liturgy in high church Anglicanism is very similar to the Roman Catholic liturgy. The Anglo-Catholic vestments are essentially pre-Vatican two Catholic."

"Don't you think it's a coincidence that both Artie and the Hough are 'high church'?" she asked.

"I hadn't thought of it," Thomas responded. "Good point but there are many 'high church' Anglicans, especially in the aristocracy. It may very well be a coincidence."

"I hate to sound like a broken record, but if there is one thing you've taught me Thomas, is there are no such thing as coincidences," said Stefania, followed by another yawn.

Thomas laughed and took a lengthy sip of his cognac.

"Well then you'll be happy to know that Greschenko called me during dinner, which is why I stepped out for a moment," said Thomas. "She wants us to meet her at 8 o'clock tomorrow morning at Richmond Park."

"Why there?" She asked.

"She specified to meet on a path in the wood just beyond White Lodge," he responded. "I know the spot more or less. I'm guessing the location was picked due to the lack of video surveillance, and if she or we were being followed, that would be easy to detect. That park will be deserted at that time this early in the year, especially given the cool dreary weather we've been having."

"Makes sense," replied Stefania.

"Why don't you stay the night rather than go back to your hotel?" asked Thomas. "You'll have your own room. It'll be just like two years ago at Seil Isle and Haverford Hall."

"Not exactly like then, given what's transpired," said Stefania. "I've no change of clothes anyway."

"Can't blame me for trying," said Thomas. "I'll have John collect you and drop you off at your hotel. I'll accompany you for the short drive."

"Thank you Thomas."

"Don't thank me, thank John, he'll be doing the driving."

The Range Rover picked up the two at the sidewalk in front of the townhome, and they settled into the leather rear seats.

Stefania gazed out the mist and rain drop covered rear window at the streetlights of nighttime London passing by, and the glare of car head lamps here and there. She liked that Thomas asked her to stay. She wanted to stay, but at the same time, didn't want to get hurt again. Her feelings for Thomas lingered. Esperanza's revelation that Thomas spoke about her often made her heart flutter.

"Well here we are," said John, as the SUV came to a stop in front of the hotel. He got out and opened the rear driver's side door for Stefania.

"I'll pick you up at 7 o'clock tomorrow," said Thomas.

"Yes, see you then," said Stefania.

She leaned across the seat and placed one hand on Thomas' cheek. She kissed him softly on the lips for a moment and lingered, their lips hardly touching. Warmth permeated her body and it tingled from head to toe. She jumped out of the car in her bare feet, holding her expensive pumps in her left hand, strode quickly across the shiny wet sidewalk toward the hotel entrance.

I should have stayed the night, she thought

Chapter 6

Morning, March 8, London, UK

Stefania bundled up her gray wool overcoat and green plaid scarf over her red sweater, tight fitting jeans, and knee high black leather boots, as she stepped off the wet curb into the waiting back seat of Thomas' Range Rover. John closed the door after she got in.

"Good morning Thomas, John," she said, adjusting her gray crochet hat.

"Good morning," he said, adjusting his own cashmere scarf and Canada goose down coat with his olive drab hunting pants and brown boots.

"How many pair of hunting pants do you own?" asked Stefania with a devilish grin.

"A few," responded Thomas, also grinning. "Although I don't often hunt, except by invitation from friends, they're practical."

"The seats are warm," she said.

"I took the liberty of engaging the seat warmers, and here's a *latte* for you," said Thomas, handing Stefania a take-out cup topped with a plastic cap.

"Thank you. You remembered," she replied as the SUV lurched forward, narrowly avoiding a dollop of the coffee which leapt out of the small hole on the cup cover.

"Cute hat," noted Thomas.

"Thanks, it keeps my head warm on these chilly damp London mornings," replied Stefania. "My *avó* knitted it for me when I was a teenager. So what do you think is on the agenda for today?"

"I suspect that our friend Greschenko will have an update either on Wu, Chen, the phone numbers, bank accounts, or all of the above," said Thomas. "Or she'll probe information from us."

"I think she already knows everything there is to know about Wu, but is holding back," said Stefania. "And who knows if the information she gives to us will be accurate."

"I imagine you are correct on all counts," responded Thomas.

Stefania took a sip of her *latte*.

"Aren't I always?" asked Stefania, smiling from cheek to cheek.

"My, someone has a high opinion of oneself this morning," responded Thomas also smirking mischievously.

Stefania took another sip of coffee.

"So, under what circumstances would your friend Artie be heir to the throne, hypothetically speaking of course?"

"Well, Princess Mary would have to die with no issue, as they say, that is no children, hypothetically speaking, of course, and Artie would have to survive her, or Mary could abdicate after her mother dies," responded Thomas. "Why do you ask?"

"After last night I was just thinking about it. I mean Artie and Esperanza seem so dedicated to the UK, to the monarchy and to public service, more so than I would expect for someone who's eventually going to be fourth, fifth or sixth in line if Mary has children," said Stefania. "Eventually they'll be nobodies, relatively speaking."

"Artie has always been that way, and Esperanza knows the drill from her experience in the Spanish court. The titles are mere window dressing. It is a full time job being a member of the royal family in the UK," replied Thomas.

"Unlike your titles?" asked Stefania.

"My titles derive from my family's service to the crown and country hundreds of years ago. It has brought myself and my ancestors' great wealth. However, other than my position in the Lords, it is not a job. I can do what I want, go where I please, and I don't have to answer to the taxpayers," explained Thomas. "The royal family, they serve at the will of the people, and the people can get restless. Our friend Svetlana can explain what happened to Russia's royal family when the people got restless. I think the royals' biggest fear is the declaration of a republic."

"So what could possibly be the link between Wu, Chen, Smith and Artie?" asked Stefania. "I mean Wu and Chen are both of Chinese decent, but Chen is MI6, and was Smith really a priest? It sure doesn't look like it."

"I've been thinking about it. I'm going to see if I can find out more on Chen's background. Her father's name was Francis Xavier, which is a very Catholic name, after Saint Francis Xavier, one of the co-founders of the Jesuit order who did missionary work in China. Chen's name, Lucia Rita, is probably after Saint Lucy, or Lucia as the Italians call her, one of the first female martyrs of the church and her middle name after Saint Rita of Cascia. It would seem improbable that a protestant, or non-Catholic would be named Francis Xavier or Lucia Rita," explained Thomas.

"Finally one of your history lessons, I missed them so," said Stefania nodding her head.

"Really?" asked Thomas with a raised brow.

"I do, *really*. I always enjoyed your digressions when we were together during our last adventure," said Stefania. "So if Chen and her family is Catholic, it could be just a coincidence, and have nothing to do with anything," responded Stefania.

"Possibly, but what else do we have to go on?" asked Thomas. "And, as you've pointed out, there are no such thing as coincidences."

"I see your point," replied Stefania smiling. "Now that I think of it, one thing about Esperanza caught my eye. She had a scallop shell tattoo on her right wrist. She said she got it when she completed the camino for the first time."

"I've not heard of that tradition, but the scallop shell is the sign of the camino and it is associated with Saint James the Greater," responded Thomas.

"Well I could swear I saw the same tattoo on Chen's wrist, but I can't be certain of it," said Stefania.

"Hmm," Thomas said, rubbing his chin. "If true, that would be something pertinent. Chen and Esperanza are about the same age. I wonder if they were associated in any way?"

"Unfortunately we cannot ask Lucia Chen," Stefania said followed by a huff.

"I'm texting Harry now to do more research on the Chens. I'd like a full biography," said Thomas.

"Looks like we're pulling into the parking lot," said Stefania.

"John, please park and wait for us until we return," directed Thomas.

"Yes sir," said John.

The two left the comfort of the Range Rover into the damp March morning.

"I know the way," said Thomas. He led Stefania toward a pea gravel path into the forest in the park.

The morning mist rose from the adjacent meadows as glimpses of sunshine shown through the clouds. The fog seemed to hover over the treetops, deflecting the morning light in all directions. Still chilly Stefania's breath hung in the air as they walked into the woods. The two had the path to themselves. Although the leaves were still off the trees, the path darkened as they entered into the forest. The shadows of the tree branches created a camouflage quilt over the path and nearby forest floor.

"Well this is kind of spooky," said Stefania.

A few birds here and there chirped. A squirrel or two scurried about, and a hare crossed the path in the distance. A magpie chattered on a high branch.

Thomas stopped, and looked in both directions.

"This is the spot, or should be the spot," he said. "We should see her coming. The path is straight in both directions."

"I don't see anyone," said Stefania.

"It's almost 8 o'clock," said Thomas looking around.

A rustle in the underbrush ahead of them led their eyes to a small herd of deer leisurely walking across the path. Thomas' phone rang, interrupting the quiet and solitude of the deserted park.

"What," he said as he picked his phone out of his pocket and looked at the screen. "Svetlana," he said as he answered the phone.

"Yes," he said. "Right."

"Well?" asked Stefania.

"She said to go down this path toward White Lodge maybe a hundred yards, and take the path to the left," reported Thomas.

"Ugh," uttered Stefania.

The two quickly strode down the path and turned left, and there about fifty feet ahead was Greschenko sitting on a park bench.

Upon getting closer, Stefania noticed Greschenko was wearing a navy pea coat with large wooden buttons, a fur *ushanka*, black leggings, and knee high black boots. Sunglasses shaded her eyes. They looked to be top line designer types. Her black leather high-end tote clutched tightly in her right hand.

Greschenko rose to greet the two.

"I see you dressed down for the occasion," sniped Stefania.

Greschenko's eyes looked Stefania over from head to toe. "Nice hat," she replied.

"Now ladies," said Thomas. "So what have you found out?"

"Wu was the procurer," Greschenko replied.

"What do you mean Wu was the procurer?" asked Stefania curtly.

"My my, you're particularly tedious today," said Greschenko. "Whatever they are up to, and I'm referring to the three dead bodies, Wu, Chen and Smith, Wu procured the weapons."

"How do you know that?" asked Stefania.

"Well based on the bank account information we discovered at Smith's apartment, money was wired from a Hong Kong account to Wu's Singapore account, the equivalent of ten-million pounds sterling. Money was also wired from a Cayman Islands account to Wu's Singapore account, the equivalent of ten-million pounds sterling. Lastly, an equivalent amount in Euro were wired from an account in Rome to Wu's Singapore account."

"Well what was all that money used for?" asked Stefania.

"As much as I loathe your tedious nature, I admire your curiosity," responded Greschenko. "We haven't figured that out yet. Some of the money was for the weapons, their transport, and getting the terrorists into the United States."

"Well the money from Hong Kong, we can only assume it came from a Chinese state enterprise," said Thomas.

"Reasonable assumption," replied Greschenko.

"So why would the Chinese be smuggling Uyghur terrorists into the United States," asked Stefania. "And arming them."

"I'm floored. Another excellent question from the peanut gallery," said Greschenko.

"A false flag operation," responded Thomas. "What else could it be?"

"That is the only plausible explanation," responded Greschenko.

"I think I understand this, but unless I'm missing something, that terrorist attack would not have cost even close to approximately thirty million pounds," said Stefania.

"You are on the mark this morning," replied Greschenko. "And Wu's account balance is now zero, so all the money was spent. That little operation may have cost a few hundred thousand, half a million Euro at most."

"So why were you following Wu?" asked Stefania. "You've not answered that question. We've told you why we sought him out, but your appearance in New Jersey was quite convenient."

Greschenko smiled.

"Let's just say we became aware of someone purchasing MANPADS on the black market as well as other Russian weapons," said Greschenko. "We didn't want them used against Russian interests. We had terrible experience with MANPADS in Ukraine. We traced the money back to Wu. He was not particularly careful in covering his tracks, although he really didn't have to be careful given the Chinese have protected him for years. We wanted to see what the MANPADS were going to be used for. Now we know."

"Yes, but aren't you interested in where that money came from, and if there are going to be more attacks?" asked Stefania.

"If this is part of a false flag operation to blame terrorist activity on the Uyghurs, then it is possible there will be other attacks attributed to them," said Greschenko. "If you haven't noticed Russia has a little problem with our native Muslims in Chechnya."

"So the assumption is that the Chinese are funding Uyghur terrorists so they can justify their persecution of the Uyghur minority in China," said Thomas.

"Maybe," said Greschenko.

"Maybe?" asked Thomas. "It all adds up."

"That part makes sense," interrupted Stefania. "But some of the money came from China, but not all of it. We know Chen was MI6, and we suspect Smith was either MI6 or working for the Vatican. But the phone numbers in Smith's possession included the Duke of Shropshire and Bishop Hough. Why would they be involved with the Chinese in a false flag operation?"

"Thank you for that information by the way," said Greschenko. "We were pretty certain Chen was MI6, but you've confirmed it. Her phone was a burner. It yielded little information, other than the fact that she'd been in contact with Smith and another burner number in the UK."

"There's no reason any of these people except Wu would be involved with the Chinese, unless..." responded Thomas.

"Unless there's more here than meets the eye," said Stefania. "What if Wu was running the false flag operation as part of some other operation with ulterior motives. The false flag operation is nothing more than a smokescreen."

"As much as it pains me to agree with the Brazilian beauty, that is the most logical answer. It's a ruse, and elaborate ruse, but a ruse nonetheless," said Greschenko, kicking some pebbles on the path. "The Chinese may be unwitting participants in a plan where the false flag operation is a cover."

"So what is the ultimate objective?" posited Thomas.

"Perhaps the next attack will shed some light," said Greschenko. "The question is where and when will that occur?"

"Well we've got two GPS coordinates and dates, March tenth and March fifteenth," said Stefania.

"Both for remote locations in the middle of nowhere in the southwest American desert," replied Greschenko. "Those dates and coordinates could be a diversion."

"And a burner number here in the UK, and some phantom bank accounts who have owners who've invested ten million Euro and twenty million quid in something," said Thomas.

"And why did Smith have the phone numbers of the Duke of Shropshire and Bishop Hough?" asked Stefania. "And what about this other key? I've been looking at it. It doesn't look like any key I've ever seen. What was the address on Smith's Vatican passport?" asked Stefania.

"It is the address of the Apostolic Nuniciature in Brazilia," responded Thomas.

"Well who did Wu purchase the MANPADS and other munitions from?" asked Stefania.

Greschenko smiled slightly, turned and walked a few steps down the path, turned again and walked back.

"We know the identity of the supplier," Greschenko reported.

"Well," said Stefania, "who is it?"

"Emek Gerasimovich Souchev," she responded. "He's a notorious black marketeer for weapons, among other things. All kinds, it just depends on the price."

"Emek Souchev," muttered Thomas while rubbing his chin. "Hah."

"You know him?" asked Stefania.

"I've heard of him," replied Thomas. "I thought he was a myth, every good-guy's bogeyman."

"Given your answer, my guess is he's not easy to find," said Stefania.

"Oh he's easy to find," said Greschenko. "He's in Ashgabat, Turkmenistan. He's protected by the government there. He shares his profits with the ruling government apparatchiks, who aid him in procurement, shall we say."

"Is it possible we could get a meeting with him?" asked Stefania. "Maybe he can provide valuable information."

"Normally I would laugh at your question, because men like Souchev are corrupt and ruthless," replied Greschenko. "To suggest that Souchev would provide information on Wu, a client, would be a ludicrous suggestion. But..."

"But now because Wu is dead, maybe Souchev will open up," said Thomas.

"Souchev will do anything for money," replied Greschenko. "He has few scruples. Once he delivers the weapons his buyers are on their own. He only has to share his profits from arms sales with his government contacts. Payments for money laundering, contract hits, human trafficking, drug trafficking, bribes, or other endeavors he can keep to himself. Arms sales, he prefers to be paid in a hard currency, easier to share with his protectors that way. Everything else, he's paid in bitcoin, because it's harder for the government to track it. He's got a wife who likes expensive things, large homes, several mistresses, bodyguards, bribes to pay. All of that costs money."

"So you are saying that he'll speak to us for a price," said Stefania.

"You're delicious," responded Greschenko with a smile. "Absolutely luscious." She looked at Thomas. "He'll meet with us for eighty bitcoin, forty transferred before the meeting and forty at the time of the meeting."

"At today's rate that's about one-million quid," responded Thomas.

"Correct," replied Greschenko. "My government is willing to front forty bitcoin. You front the other forty and we have a deal. That's a pittance for you given your net worth."

Thomas walked down the path for a moment and turned to his right, staring into the underbrush, and crouched down for a second.

"Will it be safe to meet with Souchev?" whispered Stefania.

"As long as you are with me, it should be," replied Greschenko. "Let's put it this way, a trip to Ashgabat will be a real eye opener."

"What's Ashgabat like?" asked Stefania, as she watched Thomas contemplating Greschenko's offer.

"Kind of like Las Vegas without the gambling," responded Greschenko.

"What's he like, this Souchev?" asked Stefania.

"What he does for a living would make most cringe," replied Greschenko. "However, he's extraordinarily intelligent. Some would say charming in fact. Souchev speaks Russian, English, Turkmen, Kazakh, Uzbek and Mandarin. He was educated in the States, Texas I believe, he received a degree in petroleum engineering there. His father expected him to grow the family oil and gas business. By the time his father passed, Souchev was into other things. He mostly uses his legitimate businesses to launder money and to transport contraband."

"It sounds like you know him well," said Stefania.

"Let's just say I've had business dealings with him over the years, mostly pleasant enough and mutually satisfactory," said Greschenko.

"I can't let Thomas do this," Stefania said, as she walked over to Thomas. "Thomas, I can't ask you to pay this money, not for me anyway."

Thomas rose and turned to Stefania with a blank expression on his face.

"As with your last project, I fear this will impact me personally," he said softly with little emotion. "Somehow this implicates my friend Artie and therefore my monarch and my country. I must see this through. I'm meant to be involved. This is no coincidence."

Stefania followed Thomas as he walked toward Greschenko.

"I'll do it," he said. "I'll have my accountant purchase forty bitcoin later today."

"Good," responded Greschenko. "I'll arrange for the visas. I'll be in contact regarding travel arrangements. Good day."

Greschenko turned and quickly walked away from the two, and made a quick left down a forest path, clutching her black leather shoulder bag in her right hand, and disappeared into the haze.

The partly cloudy morning gave way to clouds which seemed to be lowering by the second. Drizzle started to fall. The stillness of the moment enveloped Stefania. A shiver went down her back, and goose-bumps ruffled her forearms.

"I've got a bad feeling about this," said Stefania leaning toward Thomas as they looked down the now deserted path. Her eyes cut back to Thomas, "Do you think we are being set up?" she asked.

"No," Thomas replied softly. "No," he repeated again, this time more confidently. "If the Russians wanted me dead or worse, they could easily do so, although my death would result in a great deal of scrutiny. The Russians also have plenty of material at their disposal to blackmail me. I'm much more valuable to them alive, at least at this point. Despite my misgivings, I suspect Svetlana's being genuine. For what purposes, I know not."

"I think she likes you," said Stefania with a smirk. "If a woman has affections, she might do extraordinary things for a man. She obviously wants you around."

"But to what end?" asked Thomas softly.

Thomas and Stefania took a few steps down the path toward the parking lot where Thomas' Range Rover waited to speed them back to Kensington from Richmond Park. The gravel crunched beneath their feet. The mist enveloped the barren treetops, a dense fog slowly crept to the ground, and a steadier rain fell. Thomas pulled the hood from his jacket over his head, which Stefania adjusted for him. The occasional flutter of wings could be heard as birds flew occasionally from tree to tree.

"I meant to tell you, I paid Bishop Hough a surprise visit this morning at 6 o'clock at Lambeth Palace, for about twenty minutes," said Thomas. "He's visiting the Archbishop of Canturbury and an early riser."

"What," asked a surprised Stefania. "Well what did he say?"

"Well obviously I couldn't interrogate him, but I delicately beat around the topic and got nowhere," responded Thomas. "Nothing perturbed him, he was indomitable."

Thomas's phone rang interrupting the relative silence of the forest. The two stopped mid step.

"It's Harry," he said. "Yes Harry," he said as he answered the phone, putting Harry on the speaker.

Stefania huddled next to Thomas to listen to the conversation. Both now stood in the middle of the walkway, the rain dripping off Thomas' hood, and Stefania's hat hardly keeping her head dry.

"Good'ay mate," said Harry. "I've got the additional background information on the Chens you asked for. It was relatively easy to come by."

"Well, let's have it then," said Thomas.

"The Chen family has been very influential in Catholic circles in Hong Kong for decades. Lucia Chen's grandfather, John Houghton Chen, was instrumental in arranging Pope Paul VI's visit to Hong Kong in December, 1970. Her father Francis Xavier Chen was involved in the 2011 transfer of relics of the late Saint John Paul II to Immaculate Conception Cathedral in Hong Kong. Both John and Francis Chen were Knights of Malta. Lucia was baptized at the same Cathedral in 1987."

"Thomas, why was Chen's middle name Houghton?" asked Stefania. "That's your surname."

"Anything else Harry?" asked Thomas.

"No, that's about sums it up," responded Harry.

"Thank you Harry," Thomas said with some apparent absence as he hit the hang-up button on the phone.

"Well Thomas, why does this John Houghton Chen have your surname as his middle name?" insisted Stefania.

"John Houghton was an ancestor of mine," responded Thomas with a little more energy in his voice. "He was the fourth son of the third Duke of Radcliffe during the Reformation. He was a Carthusian monk, I believe. In 1535 he refused to take the supremacy oath recognizing Henry the eighth as the supreme head of the church in England, was sentenced to death, hung, drawn and quartered. John Houghton was made a saint by Pope Paul VI in 1970, but not at the urging of our family, and frankly it came out of the blue at the time so I'm told."

"So Chen was named after this English monk?" asked Stefania, with some disbelief.

"Apparently so," responded Thomas with a shrug. "I mean John Houghton was beatified in 1886, but he was an obscure figure. It would have been odd to name someone after a beatified person not yet a saint. I wonder if there was meaning behind his parents' name choice?"

"Would there typically be?" asked Stefania.

"Well, traditionally Catholic first names contain at least one saint name, and often there is some meaning attached," responded

Thomas. "I'm named after both Saints Thomas More and Thomas Becket, perhaps two of the most prominent later-day English saints, both of whom died for their faith."

"Seems like an incredible coincidence that this Lucia Chen's grandfather was named after one of your ancestors who was executed for his loyalty to the Catholic church," added Stefania."

"Yes, it does," responded Thomas rubbing his chin with his gloved hand. "What is also particularly odd is that the Chens were supposedly fierce monarchists. I would say that's unusual for a devout Catholic family whose patriarch was named after a martyr from the Reformation."

"A little off-topic, but before I forget," interjected Stefania. "If Wu was a Chinese intermediary big shot, why was he meeting personally with Smith in New Jersey. Don't people like that have flunkies to do their dirty work?"

"Yes, indeed," replied Thomas with a raised brow.

"Unless of course unless what Wu and Smith were involved with was so secret he couldn't entrust it to anyone else," added Stefania.

"Excellent point Stefania."

"And what if Wu's death wasn't opportunistic as Greschenko said, but that Duce asshole and his girlfriend Wanda were in on it somehow?"

"Another excellent point," added Thomas with a nod. "About last night..."

"What about it?" asked Stefania.

"Well, you laid a snog on me, which after your refusal to stay the night, was quite perplexing," said Thomas.

"I felt like I wanted to kiss you, that's all," said Stefania with a smile, wiping the rain from her face. "Can't a girl show affection when it suits her?"

"That's all, hmm," said Thomas with a crack of a smile. "I must apologize for not bringing a brolly, but I didn't expect the rain."

Thomas's phone rang again. As he took it out of his coat pocket it slipped out of his hand onto the pathway.

"I'll get it," said Stefania.

Stefania bent down to pick up the phone. Her hand clutched it. Through the sounds of the raindrops she heard a soft cracking sound. Gravel from the path sprayed up onto Thomas' boots.

"Did someone throw a rock at me?" she asked.

Thomas immediately grabbed her forearm and yanked her off the path into the underbrush. The two crouched in a bed of some wet needles under pine fronds behind a thicket next to the path, now hardly visible.

"I think someone took a shot at either you or us," whispered Thomas. "You were saved by bending over to pick up my phone. The fog also helped. Otherwise, you'd have been hit."

"Are you sure?" whispered Stefania.

"I know the sound of a missed shot hitting dirt, and that was it," said Thomas softly.

"I didn't hear a gunshot," whispered Stefania.

"They were likely using a sound suppressor," whispered back Thomas.

"What's that?" Stefania whispered, pointing to a ribbon thin red stream of light peaking through the foliage hitting the needle covered ground in front of them.

"It's a laser sight, a gun's laser sight," whispered Thomas, as he pulled her behind the trunk of a rather large pine. "Someone's looking for us. The fog and thickets are causing problems for the assassin."

"What do we do?" asked Stefania.

"Let's try to make our way through the wood to the path we originally came in on. It's well travelled," responded Thomas. "Finding company may help us escape."

"Won't they see us try to get away?" asked Stefania.

"Maybe," said Thomas. "But I'm counting on the underbrush, fog, and the fact that our clothes may blend into the surroundings to assist."

Thomas led Stefania by the hand through some thick underbrush and what seemed like after a quarter-mile of slow walking while crouched through forest and undergrowth they came upon the pathway they sought. They arrived at the edge of the path where two constables in uniform on horseback walked toward the parking lot.

Thomas and Stefania bounded onto the path out of a hedge.

"Good morning officers," said Thomas.

"Good day to you," said the one constable, a woman with a blond ponytail sticking out from her helmet. "You were off the path?"

"Yes, we had lost something and were able to find it," replied Stefania.

The female constable stopped and gave the two a once over.

"Well, it doesn't look like you were poaching mushrooms," she said.

"No mushrooms here," said Stefania, opening her bag and showing the officer.

"Right," she said, giving her horse a slight kick to get it moving again.

"Let's walk with them to the parking lot," whispered Thomas. "They will provide cover."

"All right, and by the way, here's your phone," said Stefania. "Who called you?"

Thomas looked at his phone.

"It was Greschenko."

Stefania rolled her eyes.

"Blast, she saved my life yet again."

Afternoon, March 8, London, UK

The Range Rover flew over the Putney Bridge crossing the foggy Thames toward Kensington.

"John, please keep an eye out to see if we're being followed," directed Thomas.

"Yes sir," replied John. "So far, I'm not noticing anything."

"Are you going to call Greschenko back?" asked Stefania.

"Yes," replied Thomas. "My understanding is that it's probably safe to call from my mobile. They would only be able to hear conversations in real time with a mobile intercept assuming there is one close-by. But they'd know who I called and where I called from. Just in case however, John, can you please hand me your mobile?"

John passed back his phone to Thomas.

Thomas dialed a number on John's phone and put it up to his ear.

"I see you called," said Thomas. "I believe our communications have been compromised. We need to meet. Call me back at this number," he responded.

He pressed the hang-up button on the phone and put it in his jacket.

"So you left a message," asked Stefania.

"Yes," replied Thomas. "She probably didn't take the call because she didn't recognize the number."

"Now that I think of it, it was awfully coincidental that we were shot at shortly after Greschenko left us in the Park," said Stefania. "And wasn't she the one who picked the locale?"

"True," said Thomas somewhat pensively. "But it could also be an attempt to frame her, she being the last person who saw us. The trajectory of the shot concerns me."

"Why?"

"Well, it would have appeared to come from above, like someone climbed a tree. Of course they could have used a self-climbing tree stand of the type deer hunters use."

"What does that mean?"

"Well it means whomever it was could have followed us there, or followed Greschenko. She may be compromised as well."

John's phone rang. Thomas looked at the phone.

"Greschenko," he said as he accepted the call. "Yes," he answered. "We believe that our communications are compromised, this phone may well be as well," he said. "Right, understood." Thomas hung up.

"Well?" asked Stefania.

"We are to go to Trafalgar Square," replied Thomas. "There is a political demonstration going on. She instructed us to walk up the stairs of the National Gallery at 1 o'clock."

"That's it?" asked Stefania.

"Yes," replied Thomas. "John, please detour toward Trafalgar Square, and drop us off a block or two away, and here's your mobile," continued Thomas as he handed the phone to John.

"Yes sir," replied John.

Thomas took his phone from his jacket pocket, scrolled through a few numbers and called a number.

"Herbert," said Thomas. "Yes, please have dinner ready at seven for myself and Ms. DiMaggio. I'm taking her to the National Gallery to see the Renoir exhibit, and then we'll be back to dine. We may be delayed due to a demonstration in the area," he continued. "Right," concluded Thomas as he hung up the call. "Just a little diversion in case someone is listening in. It makes our trip to the National Gallery look more innocent."

"Do you think she's setting us up?" asked Stefania.

Thomas opened his mouth then paused.

"No," he replied. "As I said before, killing me would do the Russians no good, and killing you would eliminate any cooperation I give them. We must assume there are different actors involved."

"What are we to do once we get to the National Gallery?" she asked.

"I...don't... know," Thomas responded slowly. "I don't know," he repeated. "I assume we'll find out."

Is it a mistake to place all of my trust in Thomas? thought Stefania. *Perhaps the Russians had so much control over him, he cannot be trusted. I refuse to believe that's the case.*

"There'll be too much going on for anything to happen," reassured Thomas. "There are literally thousands of people in the square. My guess is she will try to contact us clandestinely using the crowd as cover."

"Or the crowd will be cover for our deaths," responded Stefania.

"I don't think so," said Thomas.

"I know Thomas," said Stefania. "It doesn't make sense. Why would she reveal all the information regarding the bank accounts, money and arms transfer and Souchev, if she was going to have us killed?"

"Quite," replied Thomas.

"Unless she changed her mind," replied Stefania. "That is always a woman's prerogative."

Suddenly the Range Rover stopped. Stefania looked out the front windscreen. They were stuck in traffic. People with placards and signs were walking by the SUV.

"I'm sorry sir, we can't go any farther," said John.

"Then this is where we get out," said Thomas. "John, I'll be in touch."

The two hopped out of the Range Rover and got caught up in the rope of humanity converging in the direction of Trafalgar Square. From the looks of the signs it appeared to be some kind of environmental demonstration. Other than Thomas and Stefania, everyone's hair was dyed green. Thomas grabbed Stefania's hand.

His ungloved hand touching her's gave Stefania a feeling of relief and comfort. She had once heard that human hands touching each other arguably provided as much sensation as a kiss. A physic once told her that energy passed when hands were held. Whatever the case, Thomas' hand holding her's sent a tingling feeling from her toes to her head, the kind she got when she took her daily dose of niacin.

How funny, she thought. *I'm the feeling I get when Thomas touches me is akin to that of a dietary supplement.*

The rain had stopped, to be replaced again by a cold drizzle.

"We are on Haymarket Street," said Thomas, looking around. He stopped Stefania at a corner. "It's almost 1 o'clock. Let's go this way."

Stefania could see the dome of the National Gallery and a church spire nearby. Chanting, shouts and screams reverberated throughout the area. Someone balked through a megaphone exhorting the crowd, which then cheered. Thomas and Stefania struggled to walk up the sidewalk adjacent to Pall Mall to Trafalgar Square and the National Gallery. The stairs to the entrance of the National Gallery were crowded but not wall to wall people like the raucous din of humanity in the square below. As the two ascended the stairs a non-descript man in a trench coat and duffer flat cap bumped into Thomas, nearly knocking him down. Still holding his hand, Stefania pulled him toward her so he didn't tumble down the stairs.

"Crikey," said Thomas, steadying himself, hardly audible.

Stefania looked down the stairs toward the square below. The man had disappeared into the demonstration.

"Are you alright?" asked Stefania.

"I think so," responded Thomas, patting himself down. "Let's go."

Thomas grabbed Stefania's arm and led her back the way they came until they got to a not-so-crowded spot. Thomas stuck his hand in his coat pocket and pulled out a manila envelope.

"What's that?" asked Stefania.

"I assume the gentleman who almost knocked me over placed this in my pocket," responded Thomas.

He opened the envelope and pulled out two phones held together by a rubber band. Thomas released the rubber band. Each phone had a yellow post-it note attached with a six-digit code. One post-it read "Thomas" and "call me, S," the other "her's."

"Here," said Thomas, handing Stefania the phone which said "her's." "I gather this one is yours and that's your security code."

"Thanks," said Stefania. "'Her's' huh, I suppose that beats the myriad of alternatives she could've called me."

Thomas pulled something else from the envelope.

"Here," he said as he handed a wire to Stefania. "These are the rechargers and probably Wi-Fi adaptors."

"Why do these phones have an antenna?" asked Stefania.

"These are satellite phones," responded Thomas. "Probably linked to Russian satellites. Let's walk this way," he said as he put the new phone in his right jacket pocket and took out his old phone and pressed the call button.

"Yes, John, can you pick us up at Piccadilly Circus, we'll be waiting next to the tube station entrance on Coventry Street," said Thomas.

"You told her that your communications were compromised so she gave us phones," said Stefania with a huff. "I wish I could solve all of our problems with a snap of a finger. They are probably encrypted or some such thing so we can't be followed and our calls can't be monitored."

"Well you've been doing your homework," responded Thomas. "You're likely correct. You don't like her much do you?"

"Not so much that I don't like her, as much as I loathe her," barked Stefania.

"Interesting distinction," remarked Thomas with a slight grin.

The rain fell heavier again. Stefania adjusted her knit cap.

"John's here," said Thomas with some excitement pointing to the Range Rover approaching.

The Range Rover stopped, Thomas opened the rear passenger's side door and the two jumped in the back seat.

"Drive on," said Thomas.

"Where to?" asked John.

"Drive back to Kensington for now," directed Thomas.

"What now?" asked Stefania.

"First I'm going to put the seat warmers on and then I'm going to call our friend," responded Thomas.

Thomas took out the new phone and entered the security code.

"Hmm, her number is the one of only two numbers in the contacts list, the second number is yours," said Thomas. "You should check your phone, and probably engage the facial recognition security feature."

Stefania did as she was told.

"Yep, two numbers in contacts, her's and yours," she acknowledged. "How convenient."

Thomas pressed the call button on his phone to Greschenko's phone number.

"Yes," he said. "Thanks for the phones. After you left someone took a shot at one or both of us in the park," he added. "Laser sights, I'd say it was a .223 round or thereabout," he continued. "It was no coincidence. I see, thank you. Right, we'll meet you there tomorrow at Noon."

Thomas ended the call.

"Well?" asked Stefania.

"She wants us to meet her in Malta at 1900," Thomas responded rubbing his chin. "She's still arranging the visas for entry into Turkmenistan, but she should have it all done after a brief layover in Malta. Svetlana thinks we'll be safer outside the UK."

"Why would that be?" asked Stefania excitedly. "Wouldn't we be less safe elsewhere? That doesn't make sense. It will be easier to make us disappear outside the UK."

"I'm not sure whoever is after us cares where they kill us," replied Thomas. "If it were the Russians, I'll wager they'd use a nerve agent or poison rather than a bullet to the brain in Richmond Park right after we met with one of the Deputy Heads of its foreign intelligence service."

"I suppose that makes sense, but if not the Russians, who?" asked Stefania.

"I don't know, but as I've said, the fact that Chen was with MI6 very much concerns me," said Thomas. "Perhaps Svetlana may have answers."

"Why Malta?" asked Stefania.

"Svetlana knows that I have business interests in Malta, so flying there wouldn't be suspicious. It's also notoriously corrupt there," responded Thomas. "My guess is Svetlana probably has paid off officials, and we can probably fly directly to Ashgabat from Valetta without attracting much attention, at least officially."

"Seems like a lot of work just to visit Souchev," noted Stefania.

"Given the visa requirements to enter Turkmenistan, a visit there may seem suspicious," Thomas responded. "And you were correct about the phones. They are encrypted, untraceable, and all data will be destroyed if someone tries to hack them. I suggest we go to your hotel and you pack your things. I'll have the plane ready to takeoff from Gatwick in ninety minutes. As I recall, it's about a three hour flight to Valletta."

"What will be the accommodations once we get there?" asked Stefania.

"It sounds like we may be there for a day or two, plus a few days while we're away, so I'll get my usual suite in Valletta. Given what transpired today, I suggest we stay together. It'll be safer. You'll have a separate room, of course."

"Of course," responded Stefania with a nod. "I accept your offer and thank you," she said with a grin.

"Jolly good," said Thomas with a grin. "John, please detour to Stefania's hotel."

"Yes sir," responded John.

"So you're my protector again?" asked Stefania.

"Stefania, it seems like you've been my protector over the last few days, but I've never stopped love," replied Thomas with a glance.

Stefania sighed, and tingles went up and down her spine.

Chapter 7
March 8, 42,000 feet over France

Stefania woke from a short nap as Falcon 6X dashed through the high thin air toward Valletta. She rubbed her eyes, and swept back her luxurious black tresses. Stefania's chin leaned against the portal window, her breath causing an immediate fog on the window, which she wiped away with her hand. Now she caught a glimpse through the clouds below of the snow capped Alps dotting the terrestrial horizon. As she usually did for air travel, she dressed for comfort. An oversize red sweater hung over her frame down below her waste covering her black leggings to just above the knees. A pair of high heeled black leather knee high boots kept her feet warm.

"We are over France," whispered Thomas with a grin leaning slightly toward her and seated across in his tan slacks, navy cashmere sweater, brown leather Bruno Magli loafers, and two-button beige camelhair sports jacket.

The table between them was set with lunch service including wine glasses.

"Thanks," responded Stefania. "No need to whisper, I'm full awake."

"I wanted to wait until you woke before having luncheon served," said Thomas. "We rushed to leave, and I don't know about you, but I'm famished."

"Yes, thank you very much Thomas, you are so kind," responded Stefania with a smile. "Don't you think the time for wining and dining me has come and gone?"

"I've ordered Italian fare," said Thomas ignoring Stefania's question. "The VIP chef at Gatwick is excellent. I think we've *salumi* and cheese for antipasti, *cacio e pepe* as a *secondi*, fresh fruit or biscotti for *dolce* with espresso."

A female attendant with blonde hair held back in a ponytail, wearing a short blue skirt, white stockings, and white blouse approached.

"Red or white miss," she asked. "And would you prefer flat or mineral water?"

"Red and flat please," Stefania responded.

"Red and flat for me as well," added Thomas.

The attendant returned, and poured the wine and water and brought over a *salumi* plate with *prosciutto de parma*, hot and sweet *sopressata*, various olives and cheeses.

Stefania stabbed a hunk of parmesan, matched it with a bit of ham and nibbled.

"After what we've been through this makes the day," she said pointing at Thomas with the harpooned cheese and ham. "On our last adventure I always felt the safest high up in the air, with you, leaving all our troubles behind."

"Unfortunately, I suspect we are flying into the jaws of the devil this time, not escaping it," responded Thomas, wiping his mouth with a white linen napkin after gobbling down some cheese and salami.

"Yes, I see your point," responded Stefania. "But truly what is going on here? We've obviously gotten someone's attention, but who? I mean Greschenko is the only person who really knows what we've uncovered."

"As Svetlana put it, Wu is, or was, 'the procurer'," said Thomas. "And he's dead. There are many moving parts to this. The façade is that Wu financed a terrorist attack by the Uyghurs."

"But once you pull back the façade, there are many layers," said Stefania after taking a sip of wine. "There's Smith, a Vatican diplomat that the Vatican disclaims. Second, there's Chen, an MI6 analyst who was involved with Smith somehow. She comes from a background of devout Catholics from China and had a key to his room. How does that figure into all this or is it just a coincidence? Third, your friend Artie's number turns up in Smith's room, as well as the Bishop's. And I think Greschenko knows more than she's letting on."

"Fancy that," remarked Thomas in a sarcastic tone. "I don't think Chen's Catholicism is a coincidence. I suspect all of these facts are related somehow."

"Won't the Chinese come looking if they think their money was expropriated?" asked Stefania.

"Not necessarily," responded Thomas. "Ten million pounds sterling, in the big scheme of things for the Chinese, is petty cash. But what about the information Wu was going to give to Smith, the GPS coordinates?"

"If it was meant for Smith I suspect it's something completely different," said Stefania. "It identified the attack in New Jersey, but the other two GPS coordinates are mere points on the map in the desert. You and Greschenko agreed that of the thirty million Wu had in his account only a few hundred thousand would be needed to fund the New Jersey attack."

"Right," said Thomas. "Artie's number is the one odd fact that doesn't fit into any of this. I've known him for years. He aligns himself politically with the Tories, but other than that, there is nothing in his background which would suggest a role here."

"His wife is Catholic," interjected Stefania. "And I'm pretty sure Esperanza and Chen both had the same scallop shell tattoo on their wrists."

"Yes, but you yourself said she didn't make a point of it when you spoke to her, and Artie, although high church, doesn't really speak of his religiosity," said Thomas. "Maybe Chen and Espiranza both went on the camino at some point."

"Another coincidence?" asked Stefania. "Remember there are no such things as coincidences. Who did you quote to me last time, Saint Julian of Norwich, who said that everything happens due to God's divine providence?"

"My Stefania, you have an excellent memory," responded Thomas.

The attendant removed the now nearly empty *salumi* plate and served the pasta dishes.

"This looks delicious," added Stefania.

"Let's hope it tastes as good as it looks," said Thomas. "After Malta, it may be the last good meal we have for a while. I have no idea what to expect in Turkmenistan."

Stefania twirled a bit of her pasta on her fork and shoved it into her mouth.

"Oh this is divine," she said. "Almost as good as I've had in Rome."

She patted down her now greasy lips with a linen napkin.

"But why silence us?" asked Stefania. "What do we know and who knows it other than Greschenko?"

"I'm afraid that by asking Harry to check out Chen, it may have tipped someone off," said Thomas, after gulping down a forkful of pasta. "Look at it this way, let's say MI6 is involved. Harry often drops my name in asking for information. In any event it is well known among certain circles that he is my fix-it man. If there is one entity which can monitor my communications or travels it is MI6."

"You're saying MI6 knew of your meeting with Greschenko and followed us to Richmond Park?" asked Stefania.

"Yes and no," responded Thomas. "We may have been the targets, and MI6 could have followed us there. The meeting with Greschenko could have been serendipitous."

"But why try to kill us and not Greschenko?" asked Stefania. "She knows what we know, or maybe more."

"Maybe whoever did it was trying to pin the hit on Greschenko?" replied Thomas.

"But why?" asked Stefania. "If MI6, why? Is it revenge for Chen's death or something else?"

"Frankly, I don't think anyone knows Chen is dead or have even found her body yet," said Thomas. "Her phone was turned off at Smith's flat. And believe me, if the chief of secret intelligence wanted us dead, we'd be dead. At the very least we'd be prohibited from leaving the UK."

Stefania finished swallowing another forkful of pasta and licked her greasy lips clean with her tongue.

"Well then none of this makes sense," replied Stefania, after taking a sip of wine.

"Unless this is all a ruse for something completely unexpected, and a different actor or actors are pulling the strings," said Thomas.

"That's an incredible theory, if true. But why?" asked Stefania.

"Indeed, why?" asked Thomas. "That inquiry may be answered when we find out what Wu used the rest of the money for."

"It sounds like Souchev may have the answer," responded Stefania.

"By the way, you haven't informed Rodolfo of any of this, have you?" Thomas asked.

"No," responded Stefania. "He just knows I'm on an assignment with you relating to the Air Sao Paulo crash. That's all I've told him at this point."

"Good," commented Thomas softly after a nod.

"So what's the plan for Malta?" asked Stefania.

"We land, get settled in the hotel, and meet Svetlana at 6 o'clock at the Rotunda of Mosta," responded Thomas.

"What's the Rotunda of Mosta?" queried Stefania.

"It's basilica in the town of Mosta, Malta," answered Thomas. "It's about seven and a half miles inland from Valletta."

"A basilica, I assume you picked the spot?" asked Stefania.

"Actually not, although I've been there before," responded Thomas. "Svetlana chose the spot. Don't know why. It's actually a wonderful church modeled after the Pantheon in Rome, dedicated to the Assumption of the Virgin Mary. I've found it to be a very spiritual place. Legend has it that a NAZI bomb fell on the church during mass in 1942 but did not detonate. The locals perceived the event to be a miracle."

"What are we to do specifically when we get there?" asked Stefania.

"We are to sit in a pew and she will sit behind us," replied Thomas. "I gather there is a mass at half-past six and that will be the cover for the meeting."

"Why all this cloak and dagger stuff?" asked Stefania. "Can't we just meet with her in a secluded place and have a chat."

"Unfortunately I'm not in a position to control Greschenko," whispered Thomas slowly with a smile, leaning forward toward Stefania.

The attendant collected the plates and glasses.

"Please prepare for descent, we will be landing shortly," she instructed.

"Oh, how I hate this part," said Stefania softly. She put earbuds in her ears and tightened her lap belt.

"Indie?" asked Thomas as he settled back into his seat.

"Yes, of course, it speaks to me, especially when I'm anxious," replied Stefania.

"I'd prefer opera," said Thomas.

"I know, but I've found going to the opera to be somewhat dangerous these days, wouldn't you agree," whispered Stefania with a slight grin.

"*Touché*," whispered Thomas. "The worst thing that can happen at an Indie concert is you might get a residual high from the couple smoking cannabis behind you."

Stefania laughed and turned up the volume on her phone and closed her eyes as the plane descended into Valletta.

March 8, Mosta, Malta

"I'm not happy that I didn't have time to change," said Stefania as her and Thomas crossed the square toward the immense beige limestone columned and domed basilica in front of them.

"You look as beautiful as ever," replied Thomas. "I didn't change either. At least I got to repay your chauffeuring me around in the States. The Maltese drive on the shady side of the road, like us Brits."

"I'm more concerned about what Greschenko thinks," snapped back Stefania with a frown.

The two stopped walking for a moment and gazed up at the basilica in front of them. The sixty degree air seemed cool as the sun set so she cuddled up next to Thomas.

"This is absolutely wonderful," remarked Stefania as the two approached the basilica. "The setting sun casts a yellowish glow on the church, kind of like a blessing from above."

"It's quite striking I agree," replied Thomas. "Whenever I'm in Malta I make a point to visit this church and of course the co-cathedral of Saint John in Valletta."

"For the Caravaggios I presume?" asked Stefania.

"You know me all too well," responded Thomas.

"You're not that difficult to figure out," said Stefania with a devilish grin.

"I'm not sure how to take that," said Thomas smiling.

"Take it as you like," shot back Stefania as she climbed the stairs and entered the open doors of the edifice.

"How marvelous is this," she exclaimed as she dipped her hand in the holy water and blessed herself.

Stefania stood still, bent her neck skyward, and took in the coffered dome with its oculus, and the arches of the side-chapels.

"This compares easily with the greatest churches of Rome," she continued.

"Harrum," uttered a short pudgy man entering the church behind her.

"Oh, excuse me," Stefania said in Italian, as she moved aside to let the man through."

"People are coming in for mass," whispered Thomas. "Let's take an innocuous seat in the back and trust Greschenko finds us."

The two found a couple of empty seats in the rear of the great basilica. Echoes of people walking on the marble floor and whispers bounced back and forth from the dome and back down.

The spiritual nature of the place infused Stefania. At peace with herself she breathed in and out rhythmically, and knelt to meditate. Sunlight graced her face from the setting sun, glowing through a window from one of the side chapels. Her mind cleared of all clutter she closed her eyes and surrendered her consciousness to God. Calmness pervaded her being, and happiness filled her soul. She opened her eyes and sat down.

Thomas turned and smiled at her.

"Remember our last adventure?" she whispered. "The Sheikh said to follow the path of the Holy Mother. This church is dedicated to the Assumption."

"True," whispered back Thomas.

Stefania grasped Thomas' left hand and held it in her right. The warmth and tenderness of his hand recalled a time when they were closer; a time when she had surrendered her heart to him, only to have it torn to pieces. She released her grip and put her hand back into her coat pocket.

"This is an impressive dedication to the Assumption, but is dwarfed by the Assumption Cathedral at the Kremlin," a familiar voice whispered from behind.

Greschenko, thought Stefania.

"Don't look back, just listen," Greschenko continued in a whisper. "Thomas, your activities are being monitored. Leave your personal phones in your rooms connected to chargers, only bring the phones I gave you. I will pick you up on the southeast corner of St. Lucia's Street and Old Bakery Street at 2115. Walk there. Make sure you're not followed. We'll be leaving in my plane together at 2200. We'll need to fly together. DiMaggio, you'll travel under your Italian passport. I've obtained a letter of invitation based on that. Thomas, I have obtained an Italian passport for you since you speak the language fluently. Leave your UK passport in the hotel safe. There's a missal under your seat. Your passport is in it. There will be visas waiting for both of you in Ashgabat as well, although I'm hopeful we'll not spend too much time in customs based on my connections. We will arrive in Ashgabat at about 0830 local time. We've an audience with Souchev at 0930. Also, be ready to order the transfer of the bitcoin at the meeting. We won't get the information we're looking for until you make the transfer. I've already completed the transfer of our bitcoin as a deposit. Bring one piece of luggage each but don't expect that we'll be there long."

"What about accommodations and the return?" asked Stefania in a whisper. Hearing no response she whispered "Greschenko?"

"She's gone," whispered back Thomas looking behind him.

Stefania reached under his seat and picked up a missal from the floor. She opened it and an in the order of mass for August fifteenth was an Italian passport, with its characteristic red cover.

"Greschenko has a sense of irony," whispered Stefania. "The passport was placed in the order of mass for the feast of the Assumption."

She opened the passport cover.

"Very funny, very funny," she now said in a louder sarcastic tone provoking several churchgoers to stare back at her.

She handed the open passport to Thomas.

"Tommaso DiMaggio," he whispered. "It appears we are travelling as husband and wife."

"Except you've taken my name," said Stefania. "I'm sure that was intentional, a subtle dig by Greschenko."

"My guess it was a matter of convenience," replied Thomas as he closed the passport and placed it in the breast pocket of his camel hair jacket.

"That's how you rationalize it?" snarked Stefania.

Thomas looked at his phone. "We'll have two hours from now to get packed and get to Saint Lucia's Street, we'd best get a move on."

"It's 2115," said Thomas looking at his phone as the two stood in the dark on the somewhat deserted southeast corner of St. Lucia's Street and Old Bakery Street at the appointed time.

"I'm chilled," said Stefania holding on to the strap of her trademark large black bag slung over her right shoulder. "I don't think I anticipated it being this cool in the evening here this time of year. I wish I had time to change clothes."

"Yes, it is quite chilly. I would have liked to change as well," responded Thomas, looking up Old Bakery Street.

Stefania took a glance in that direction as well toward the deserted law offices and businesses lining the small boulevard.

"I see headlamps approaching," she exclaimed.

A dark colored SUV came into view and screeched to a halt in front of them. The rear lift-gate opened as a man with crew-cut brown hair in a dark suit, white shirt and dark tie jumped out of the front passenger seat grabbed their bags. The passenger side rear door opened. Inside sat Greschenko, illuminated by the dim interior light of the SUV.

"Well are you just going to stand there or get in?" she yelled with a cock of the head.

Stefania got in first and sat in the middle next to Greschenko, and Thomas followed shutting the door. The rear hatch closed, the man jumped back in the passenger seat and the SUV accelerated.

Stefania looked Greschenko over. She wore a black skirt over black lace stockings with her single breasted navy pea coat with large matching buttons, and floral print scarf knotted around her neck. Her brown locks were tucked behind her ears, accenting a pair of sapphires dangling from her earlobes from gold clasps.

I saw that coat a month ago in a catalogue, she thought. *I'll bet it's cashmere, probably cost a thousand Euro.*

"Cashmere?" Stefania asked.

"Of course," replied Greschenko. "I prefer fur, but outside of Russia, you know," she said as she shrugged. "People get crazy when you wear fur."

"Fur would be too much, don't you think?" asked Stefania. "It's not that cold out."

"Fur works for me whenever it is chilly," responded Greschenko snidely. "I trust you took all of the necessary precautions?" asked Greschenko.

"We did as you said," replied Thomas cutting his eyes across to Greschenko. "Except we took a cab here. Seemed ridiculous to walk all the way with our bags and potentially be seen by CCTV all over the city."

"It's your hide, not mine," she responded in a sarcastic tone.

"Who are your friends?" asked Stefania snidely, motioning to the front seat with a tilt of the head.

"The driver is from my embassy," replied Greschenko. "Anatoly, sitting next to him, is my personal assistant."

"So what did you mean that I'm being followed?" asked Thomas.

"I didn't say you were being followed, I said your activities were being monitored, there's a difference," Greschenko shot back.

"What's the difference?" asked Stefania.

The SUV stopped for a moment. The driver spoke to someone outside in Maltese. The SUV lurched forward.

"We are here," said Greschenko.

A gate and fence passed by. Now on the tarmac, the SUV flew by parked planes and came to a stop at the foot of the stairway leading to the door of a corporate style jet.

"An Antonov 148-300?" asked Thomas as he stepped out of the SUV. "I'm impressed."

"It suits my purposes," responded Greschenko shrugging.

The trio climbed the stairs and entered the luxuriously appointed jet cabin. A center aisle separated tan leather covered single seats by each portal. Anatoly followed with their luggage. A male steward with dark slacks and a white shirt and red tie took their coats.

"Hmm Thomas, I think she's got you beat. The light wood trim and tan leather appointments seem higher grade than in your jet," teased Stefania with a mischievous grin.

"I think not," Thomas responded tersely.

Stefania took stock of Anatoly as he strode down the aisle. Tall, a sharp chin and chiseled features, short cropped brown hair, he appeared about her age. His smartly pressed dark suit and white dress shirt, seemed a little tight, but presaged an athletic build. His slightly askew thin gray striped tie looked like he never made an attempt to tighten it.

Thomas and Stefania sat abreast of each other on either sides of the aisle, with Greschenko facing Thomas. Anatoly parked himself toward the front of the jet near the steward. Almost immediately the cabin door closed and the plane started moving. The cabin bounced as the jet taxied over the tarmac. An announcement came over the intercom in Russian.

"We are about to take off," said Greschenko. "Make sure you are appropriately buckled in."

Stefania began perspiring and pulled her lap belt tight. Her eyes cut to Thomas, who simultaneously turned to his right and grinned at Stefania.

Having Thomas beside me is all that I need. God how I hate flying.

"Does he speak?" asked Stefania.

"Who Anatoly?" responded Greschenko. "Hah, he's one of those silent types whose actions speak louder than words. Maybe when he gets to know you better."

Anatoly turned back, expressionless, and then forward again.

Stefania glanced at Greschenko staring out the portal. The engines roared and the jet tore quickly down the runway. Aloft in a few seconds, it seemed like an eternity to Stefania. Stefania peered out the window as the jet banked. Lights outlined the shoreline against the dark sea, and in seconds the lights were behind them as the plane rose into the night sky over the Mediterranean.

"So, what did you mean when you said Thomas' 'activities were being monitored,' to use your phrase?" Stefania asked.

Greschenko seemed to ignore Stefania's inquiry and looked across the table between them at Thomas.

"Someone at MI6, specifically, someone at MI6's China desk, accessed MI6's file on you," said Greschenko. "We are not sure whom."

"What does that mean?" asked Stefania in a raised tone.

Greschenko turned to Stefania.

"That means that it is likely that a person or persons at MI6's China desk are interested in Thomas," replied Greschenko. "Our other operatives within MI6 indicate no other interest in Thomas within the agency."

"Then it is likely an isolated few," chimed in Thomas.

"Yes," responded Greschenko. "We believe without official authorization from higher echelons."

"Chen's position was at the China desk," murmured Thomas rubbing his chin.

"I'm aware," replied Greschenko. "We've reason to believe that those persons are misusing their authorization to electronically track you and perhaps monitor your communications."

"So whomever they are, they're sidestepping the legal procedures under the Investigatory Powers Act," responded Thomas.

"Oh please, imagine that," barked Greschenko with a laugh slapping her hand on the table. "You westerners with your legal protections!"

"How do we know you're not lying," interjected Stefania.

"You don't, but as I said, it's your hide, not mine," snapped Greschenko. "It already appears someone is out to kill you and it's not me because I could've easily made you two disappear already."

"I thought it ironic that you had us meet you on Saint Lucia's street when Chen's first name was Lucia," commented Thomas.

"Now that *was* a coincidence," said Greschenko with a laugh. "But the question to me is why would someone at MI6 want to either monitor you, or kill you?"

"Maybe for the same reason you were following Wu," interjected Stefania snidely.

"MI6's China desk would care about the negative effects of terrorists acquiring Russian military hardware," responded Greschenko. "But why would they be interested in you?" asked Greschenko looking at Thomas and pointing at him with her index finger.

Thomas opened his mouth as if to answer.

"The only connection," interjected Stefania. "Is that Thomas asked Harry to check out Lucia Rita Chen and her family."

"This Harry should have been more circumspect," said Greschenko.

"How was he to know that the inquiry might have adverse consequences?" asked Thomas. "Due to my time in the service I have many chums in MI6 and MI5, using my name typically helps obtain information easier, and having Harry as an intermediary insulates me as well."

"So what did you uncover about Chen, other than she worked at MI6's China desk domestically?" asked Greschenko.

"She is single, inherited a substantial sum from her father, who made millions of quid in Hong Kong real estate prior to the turnover, and her grandfather and father were devout Catholics," noted Thomas. "Presumably she was as well."

"What about your friend Artie?" asked Stefania. "His number was on Smith's list. Could there be a connection?"

"I think it's safe to assume that no one knows we were at Smith's flat, and that we were responsible for Chen's demise," said Greschenko sarcastically. "Therefore, no one knows you know that Artie's name was on Smith's list. Frankly, we don't even know its pertinence."

"I hate to agree with her, but she's got a point," added Stefania.

"Thank you," Greschenko replied with a smirk. "As far as we've been able to determine, Chen's body has not been discovered, and Smith was presumed dead in the plane disaster."

"So then, we're left with Harry's inquiry," said Thomas.

"And you can't contact him, other than in person," added Greschenko. "And even that might be perilous. Whoever is involved is likely monitoring your communications, and Harry's. Who knows, your residence may be bugged."

"It's Chen's disappearance coupled with Harry's inquiry, that's the problem," added Stefania.

Greschenko's eye cut to Stefania.

"Precisely," said Greschenko. "They haven't heard from Chen, but she's presumed compromised."

"What's the protocol for our meeting with Souchev?" asked Thomas.

"Souchev likes to mix it up," said Greschenko. "Don't forget, he's an international felon, so he's an asshole. He'll either have his henchmen meet us at the airport and shuttle us directly to him, or he'll make us go through customs, get to our hotel, and then summon us, or he may just show up. Just be ready to transfer the bitcoin."

"Sounds a bit mysterious," added Stefania.

"Not really, it's just Souchev being Souchev," responded Greschenko. "He'll put on a show."

"Are we in danger?" asked Stefania sheepishly.

"*I'm* not in danger," barked Greschenko. "I've vouched for you two, so you'll likely be fine. I just hope you're not easily offended."

"Why?" asked Stefania.

"You'll see," answered Greschenko.

Anatoly sidled up to Greschenko's seat in the aisle, holding a few manila folders and a tablet.

"I assumed you might want to get some rest during the flight," said Greschenko looking at Thomas with a smile, and then turning to Stefania. "If you are hungry we have some kasha and tea for breakfast in a few hours. In the interim, ask the steward if you require anything. Now, you must excuse me, I've got some business to attend to," said Greschenko as she got up from her seat and headed to the back of the jet with Anatoly.

Stefania looked out the portal and saw the dim lights below outlining the Turkish coast. She dimmed the light above her and reclined her plush leather seat.

"Tired?" asked Thomas.

"Yes," replied Stefania, as she moved about in her seat to get comfy.

Her eyelids became heavy. They opened and then closed several times.

In bright sunlight Stefania sat on the sandy ground, her back against the rear tire of a large white SUV. She turned to Thomas.

Greschenko sat next to Anatoly, their backs to the truck's front tire.

"Will we be alright?" she asked.

"Yes, just close your eyes," he said.

She reached for Thomas' hand at the same time he reached for her's. She held it tight.

Thomas held a large panting black long haired dog tight against him with his other arm. A bandana covered the dog's eyes.

She could hear Thomas whispering, "Hail Mary, full of grace, the Lord be with thee."

Stefania joined in, "Blessed art thou..."

Greschenko also joined in "among women..."

Then a bright light pierced her closed eyelids.

"Ahhh!" Stefania exclaimed, sitting up in her seat. She pivoted her head around. Her whole body clammy from a cold sweat. She wiped her soaked palms on her leggings.

"Stefania, are you alright?" asked Thomas. "You must've had a bad dream."

"Yes, I'm fine," she responded. "It was so vivid, like a premonition of some kind."

"Well, what was it about?" asked Thomas.

"We were in a desert, a barren landscape, sitting on the ground next to an SUV, all four of us. Your dog was there too. Something bad was about to happen," replied Stefania softly. "I don't know what. I was terrified. We were all reciting the *Ave Maria*. Then a bright light, and I woke up. I think the dream involved this project."

"You were talking in your sleep," said Thomas. "It *did* sound like you were praying to the Holy Mother. I can't imagine it's a premonition. It's just a coincidence. You're obsessing about this."

Stefania raised her brows and cut to Thomas. Her eyes met his.

"I'm reminded that according to you, there is no such thing as coincidences," snapped Stefania. "Papa always said I had a second sight."

"Well, Greschenko is an atheist, as well as narcissist," whispered Thomas. "I can't imagine she ever prays to anyone other than herself."

"Did I hear my name mentioned?" asked Greschenko walking up the center aisle.

"Stefania had a dream and you were in it," said Thomas.

"We were all in the dream," added Stefania.

"I don't have time for dreams, only reality," snapped Greschenko as she sat back down in her seat. "Anatoly briefed me on some recent developments."

"What kind of developments?" asked Stefania

"Confusing developments regarding Wu," responded Greschenko. "Our sources in the MSS tell us that the Chinese have no idea who was responsible for the terrorist attack in New Jersey. In other words, it's not their false flag operation."

"Well, who else would want to cast blame on the Uyghurs?" asked Stefania.

"Someone who probably wants to avoid detection," responded Thomas. "If they make it look like the Uyghurs, they implicate the Uyghurs or China, but not themselves, whoever 'they' are."

"Also," added Greschenko, "our sources indicate that Wu was a fentanyl dealer. He was responsible for some smuggling operations of fentanyl into the United States through an elaborate network. The Chinese know nothing about the importation of the weapons used in the attack."

"Is it possible that Wu used the fentanyl smuggling operation to get the weapons into the United States?" asked Stefania.

"You're surprising me anew all of the time," stated Greschenko sarcastically. "Either that or you're getting smarter."

Stefania rolled her eyes.

"We are operating under the assumption that Wu used the opioid smuggling operation to get the weapons into the United States," said Greschenko.

"Didn't you say you found opioids in the shack in New Jersey?" asked Thomas.

"Yes," responded Greschenko. "Uncut and enough for a country."

"The bag we found at the shack was likely Wu's," said Stefania. "Those two hoodlums probably emptied the drugs out of the bag. Which means they *were* meeting with Wu in New Jersey. It was no accident. "

Greschenko clapped.

"But what about Smith?" asked Thomas.

"Our guess is that Wu was going to dump the drugs with the two scum, and then meet with Smith," said Greschenko. "The two got greedy, and killed Wu for whatever reason, maybe over money."

"Think about it," noted Stefania. "Wouldn't Wu know Smith died in the plane crash?"

"Maybe, maybe not," said Greschenko nodding her head. "He may not have known Smith's true identity. But we found no information indicating that Wu was meeting with someone else. Of course we never recovered his phone. The Chinese are scrambling to contain the damage. They don't want to be fingered as complicit in the terror attack. If they didn't know about the weapons import, what else could've Wu been up to?"

"What about the money they paid to Wu?" asked Stefania.

Greschenko clapped again.

"Excellent, you are catching on," she said with a laugh. "The money was Wu's commission for the fentanyl import and delivery, but he obviously paired it with monies from other sources to fund the operation."

"But we all agree that the thirty million was significantly more than enough to cover the cost of the weapons and their importation," commented Thomas. "There had to be something more significant Wu used the money for."

"Which is why we are seeing Souchev after all," added Stefania.

Greschenko bit her lower lip.

"I hate relying upon degenerates for information," muttered Greschenko. "Who knows whether he will tell us the truth, or just send us on some wild goose chase."

"Why would Wu fund an operation out of his own commission?" asked Stefania.

"Wow, you have all the questions, but unfortunately none of the answers," said Greschenko.

"Well most people don't part with millions of quid just for the fun of it," snapped Thomas.

"True," said Greschenko.

"And we know that Wu transferred the thirty million before his death," noted Stefania.

"Regrettably, I suspect Souchev probably knows what the money was used for," said Greschenko. "He's one stop shopping for all of your criminal needs."

"Will he risk not being truthful to you?" asked Thomas. "I mean you have leverage, don't you?"

"Souchev is arrogant and protected in his country," responded Greschenko. "But believe me if he lies, after the bitcoin we've paid him, as soon as he leaves his country, if he ever does, he's a dead man. I'll do it myself if I have to."

"Remind me not to get on your bad side," said Stefania.

"Let's put it this way, you've never been on my good side," said Greschenko with a smirk.

"Nice to know," replied Stefania.

"You're making positive progress, much to my surprise," said Greschenko laughing. "Let's have some kasha and tea. We may not eat for some time once we get to Ashgabat, and when we do eat, let's just say I'm not particularly fond of mutton."

"Hah, mutton is virtually all we eat in Scotland," added Thomas with a grin. "That and venison."

"You're kidding yourself if you think it's the same," responded Greschenko with a scoff.

The small jet bounced and weaved, and the engines whined as it descended into Ashgabat airport. An announcement came over the intercom in Russian.

"The pilot says there are some heavy cross-winds, so the landing may be turbulent," announced Greschenko.

The blood drained from Stefania's face and she began perspiring. She tightened the lap belt. She looked out the portal as the plane got lower and lower. The wings swung up and down, side to side, then the noise of the landing gear being deployed. She gripped the armrests tightly. Finally a bounce, and another, and the engines roared as the jet finally slowed and came to a stop and taxied off of the runway. The plane seemed to be going away from the terminal. A second announcement came in Russian.

"We are being diverted to an isolated area of the airport," reported Greschenko. "I'm assuming Souchev is up to something."

The jet came to a stop. Outside the window Stefania saw two white SUVs with tinted windows, with four large young men in black suits with white shirts and dark ties standing at the ready. Pistol holsters were visible on a couple of the men. The jet's engines powered down.

"The welcoming committee," said Greschenko with a frown and a shake of the head. "Souchev is annoying, if he weren't such a valuable source of information I'd, well never mind."

The attendant opened the door.

"Let's go. The staff will take care of the luggage," said Greschenko who went out the doorway first and down the stairs to one of the men who seemed in charge.

Stefania stepped out into the bright sunlight. The breeze caught her hair and whipped it around. Chilly, she wrapped her arms around her chest, keeping her sweater closed. Thomas followed her down the stairway to the tarmac.

"The SUVs will bring us and our things to Souchev's penthouse at one of the luxury hotels in Ashgabat where we will be staying," announced Greschenko. "Apparently our entry visas have been issued and are awaiting us at the hotel. Souchev will receive us immediately upon arrival."

The guards opened the rear doors of the SUVs and Greschenko and Anatoly got into first SUV, and Stefania and Thomas got into the one behind. The rear hatch shut after their luggage was stowed. Almost immediately the SUVs sped across the tarmac and out a fenced-in area of the airport and headed down a grand boulevard bounded by palm trees but nearly devoid of other vehicles.

"Greschenko said Ashgabat was like Las Vegas on steroids," said Stefania. "Now I know what she meant. All of the buildings are over the top white marble, fountains everywhere, rising from the desert like a mirage."

"A Stalinist Las Vegas," responded Thomas.

"Clean as a whistle, that's for sure," added Stefania.

The driver and his guard companion sitting in the front seat started speaking in another language, presumably Turkmen.

"I suggest we keep our comments to a minimum for the duration of the ride," whispered Thomas into Stefania's ear in Italian.

Stefania nodded.

The SUVs slowed and pulled up a circular driveway to the *porte cochere* of an imposing high-rise white marble building with reflective glass windows.

"We must be here," whispered Stefania.

Thomas nodded.

The men in the front got out and opened the rear doors for Stefania and Thomas who met Greschenko and Anatoly next to their SUV.

"I am Amit. Mr. Souchev will see you now. Your things will be brought to your rooms," announced one of the slimmer dark suited men wearing dark sunglasses from Greschenko's SUV.

The group was paraded through a large lobby with white marble floors covered with red Persian style throw-rugs, with a reception desk along the far wall manned by two female attendants. The few people in the lobby didn't seem to notice the group or seem to care. Led to bank of elevators they were herded into one. Anatoly stayed behind in the lobby. Once inside the dark wood paneled elevator, Amit swiped a security card and pressed the button for the twentieth floor. The elevator shot skyward.

Looking up, Stefania spotted a CCTV camera. Her eyes shot to Thomas and pivoted up toward the camera. Thomas winked back at her. In less than a minute the elevator stopped. The doors opened into a small vestibule, with white marble floors, beige walls with soft light from wall sconces. Twenty feet away in front of them were ornate dark wooden double doors with brass fittings. A camera above the door watched their every move.

One of the men in the black suits started patting down Thomas. He held his arms wide part.

Greschenko said something in Russian and the man replied also in Russian.

He turned to Stefania. His strong hands pressed hard against her side, all the way down to her feet. He did it again, from behind and reached her breasts.

"Hey," she said as the man pressed hard against her breasts. He continued to do the same all the way down and to her buttocks.

"I feel like I just got molested!" she exclaimed.

"I vouched for you two but he doesn't seem to care," said Greschenko nonchalantly, shrugging. "He said he has orders."

The man turned to Amit and said something, presumably in Turkmen.

Amit walked toward the doors and swiped his security card again. After a sound of a faint click, he opened the right door and then the left one.

The group proceeded through the doors into an expansive room with hardwood floors and a white marble staircase going up in front of them and a wall of windows along the far wall.

"Please follow me," said Amit in soft voice.

They walked to the left of the staircase into a sunken sitting area which was furnished with several brown leather sofas and low backed leather chairs. A glass topped brass table was in the center in the middle of the sofas and chairs. An off-white Persian style throw-rug softened the hardwood floor in the sunken area.

"Mr. Souchev knows you are here and will be with you momentarily," said Amit, again in a modest tone. "You are welcomed to some tea while you wait."

Shortly after those words exited Amit's mouth, a twenty-something Asian woman with shoulder length dark hair, wearing a clingy sleeveless white top and similarly high-waisted clingy tan pencil skirt, entered the room from the right and placed a Russian tea set on the glass table.

"My I offer you some tea?" she asked in slightly accented English.

"Yes, thank you," said Greschenko. Her eyes cut to Thomas and Stefania and her head motioned to the tea set.

Stefania got the message.

"Yes, thank you," she replied.

"Yes, please," added Thomas.

The three all stood as the woman poured black tea into traditional glass Russian tea glasses and served the group. She then stood by the side wall next to Amit.

Stefania examined the ornate Russian tea glass holder.

These are wonderful, bronze I'll bet, she thought. *The glass is probably Crystal. What's that?*

She noticed a folded stamp size piece of paper stuck between the holder and the Crystal glass. She righted her head quickly. Thomas and Greschenko seemed to be preoccupied with the view from the wall of windows on the far side. Ever so delicately she took the paper out between the holder and the glass.

Footsteps could be heard coming down the stairs. Into her legging waistband the paper went.

Around the right side of the staircase appeared a slim tanned fit man. Maybe in his mid-thirties, slightly less than two meters tall. Well groomed, he sported a dark mane of hair with touches of gray, longer and curly in the back, slight razor stubble, and bulging biceps accentuated by a tight fitting blue and white striped polo shirt. He wore blue jeans held up by a brown leather belt. His matching loafers clicked on the hardwood floor as he strode over from the staircase. A hint of men's cologne wafted in Stefania's direction.

"Svetlana Sergeyevna!" he bellowed in English. "As always, I'm charmed by your presence."

"Emek Gerasimovich!" Greschenko said excitedly in response. "It's always nice to see you when I visit your country."

"Please, Kiko to my friends," he replied as the two exchanged kisses on each cheek. "You and I have always been on a first name basis."

If this guy is Souchev, he's not what I expected, thought Stefania. *He isn't bad looking, quite handsome in fact. Not what an international arms dealer and criminal should look like. No scars, no tattoos, quite presentable. He looks like he just walked out of a country club after golfing a round or two.*

"Let me introduce..." said Greschenko.

"The Duke of Radcliffe," said Souchev, turning to Thomas, shaking his hand. "It's a pleasure to make your acquaintance Duke. Don't worry, although I know your identity, your visa has been granted under your alias passport name Mr. DiMaggio."

"Thomas, please, no need for formalities," said Thomas.

"And you must be Stefania DiMaggio," said Souchev now turning to Stefania and looking her over from head to toe. "I agree Lana, she *is* quite fetching."

"Lana?" said Stefania, glancing at Greschenko.

"We've known each other for years," said Greschenko under her breath followed by a shrug, giving Stefania a stark stare.

Souchev took a seat in one of the leather chairs with a glass topped brass end table adjoining it. The Asian woman quickly poured a cup of dark black tea and handed it to Souchev in a Russian tea glass.

"Thank you Nalia," said Souchev, who then took a sip.

"This is quite a place you have here," said Thomas.

"Oh yes, thank you," responded Souchev. "I own the hotel, so living on the top floor let's me keep an eye on things. I understand you've come all this way for some information?"

"Yes, Kiko," said Greschenko. "We believe a gentleman, who you knew, Stanley Wu from Singapore, purchased some MANPADs, RPGs, automatic weapons, and other things, and we were wondering if you could assist us in providing the particulars of the purchase."

Souchev smiled slightly and put his teacup down on the table and crossed his legs.

"Typically I would be hesitant to discuss an arms deal, but since I understand Wu is deceased, well its academic isn't it," said Souchev softly in a monotone. "Except he didn't purchase the MANPADs, RPGs and automatic weapons, they were thrown in as part of the deal, for a nominal amount. A bonus if you will."

"Well what was the deal?" asked Greschenko.

"Aren't we forgetting something? asked Souchev in response. "I have one-half of the bitcoin," he said softly with a smile after taking another sip of tea. "I'd like final payment."

"Thomas," said Greschenko.

Thomas took out the encrypted phone provided by Greschenko and dialed a number.

"It's me," said Thomas. "Make the transfer, Thanks."

Souchev took another sip of tea.

Amit stood by with a tablet in hand.

"Ms. DiMaggio if you have an interest in employment in Turkmenistan, I can find a position for you and quadruple your income," noted Souchev in a soft voice with a grin. "I'll provide free housing and travel."

"Thank you, but I'm fine," said Stefania.

"Suit yourself," responded Souchev.

"The transfer has been made," declared Amit looking at a tablet.

"Thank you," said a barely audible Souchev.

"So if the deal with Wu wasn't for the MANPADs and RPGs, what *was* the deal?" asked Stefania.

"You *are* impetuous," said Souchev, shifting in his chair with a drop of tea hanging on his lip soon wiped off with a napkin by Nalia. "Keep in mind, I'm a businessman. I make money off of what I sell, but I frankly care little what my buyers do with their wares, as long as it doesn't involve me, and I'm safe and sound here in officially neutral Turkmenistan."

"Kiko," interrupted Greschenko, "darling, what was the deal?"

"One RA-115," responded Souchev, drinking more tea.

"Yield?" asked Greschenko.

"Six KT," responded Souchev.

"Operable?" asked Greschenko.

"Yes, arming box and code fob included," responded Souchev. "It has an uninterrupted power source battery backup."

"The price?" asked Greschenko.

"Twenty-nine million dollar down payment," responded Souchev. "Plus incidentals, as I said the MANPADs, RPGs and automatic weapons were thrown in."

"What incidentals?" asked Greschenko.

"Delivery of certain contraband to the United States, which yielded me well more than a hundred times Wu's deposit," responded Souchev quietly as he placed his tea glass on the table. "I was paid handsomely by third parties for the delivery. All told, the deal netted me and my colleagues here over three-hundred million dollars, *net* of payouts to our silent investors, in various currencies of course. Mr. Wu was due to get a kick-back, but, oh well, circumstances have changed."

"So Wu funneled your drugs to the United States using his transport network for free in return for the weapon, and he was to take a kick-back?" asked Greschenko.

Souchev smiled and took another sip of tea.

"Who were the investors?" demanded Stefania.

Souchev ignored the question and said something to Greschenko in Russian.

"I see, but how did you get the RA-115, the contraband, and other arms to Wu?" asked Greschenko.

"That I'm not prepared to share with you, let's just say I have a reliable and secure shipping network," Souchev said with a shrug.

"You know I can find out," said Greschenko.

"Then, by all means, try," replied Souchev softly.

"What's an RA-115?" asked Stefania.

Greschenko ignored the question.

"Kiko, how did you come upon a RA-115?" asked Greschenko.

"That will cost you one-hundred more bitcoin," said Souchev with a smile.

Greschenko took her phone out of her bag and made a call, speaking in Russian with someone on the other end.

This guy is so underwhelming. Calm, collected, not overbearing, thought Stefania.

"It's being taken care of," said Greschenko. "Amit can confirm when the transfer takes place."

"I'm aware," said Souchev.

"Well what's an RA-115?" Stefania again asked.

"An RA-115 is a modest sized portable tactical nuclear weapon," snapped Greschenko. "This one apparently has a yield of about six kilo-tons. An RA-115 can fit in the trunk of a car, or maybe even a duffle bag if someone could carry it. Depending on yield, it could weigh anywhere from one-hundred twenty to three hundred kilograms."

"Transfer has been made," declared Amit.

"Excellent," added Souchev. "This is becoming a profitable day for me."

"Well Kiko, how did you come upon an RA-115?" asked Greschenko again.

Souchev turned to Thomas.

"Thomas, do you recall the name Gregori Orloff?" asked Souchev.

"Yes," responded Thomas. "He was a notorious double agent. He was a colonel in GRU and at the same time worked for MI6. He ultimately was found out and assassinated by GRU in the UK with a nerve agent a few years ago, as I recall."

"Well your information is accurate to a point," said Souchev, recrossing his legs. "Orloff was originally stationed in Turkmenistan, and took a wife here, a wife who wasn't particularly loyal to Orloff. A wife who could be bought."

Souchev's eyes shot to Nalia.

"He also had some interesting habits, of which I doubt GRU would have approved, not the least of which was his side job with MI6," Souchev continued in his typical soft monotone. "GRU had RA-115 devices stashed in various locales, including Ashgabat. The one in Ashgabat went missing."

"Crikey, that's a story I've not heard," blurted Thomas.

"Lana, you can confirm this all with your General Stasevich," added Souchev. "Orloff provided the manual authorization code fob. Oh, and the tamper resistant measure was removed by Orloff as part of the deal at the time so the device could be moved, and the GPS locator beacon was disabled."

"So you blackmailed Orloff into releasing the RA-115 to you?" asked Greschenko.

"Given what Orloff was into, he didn't take much convincing," said Souchev softly with a smile. "Had GRU found out, life for him wouldn't have been pleasant or lengthy for that matter. Spies, particularly double agents, make excellent black-mail targets. When you speak to Stasevich you'll learn that GRU paid me generously for information on Orloff. Orloff proved extremely profitable. Let's say it's my experience that double agents have a short shelf life. His days were numbered anyway. I just hastened the process. Nalia, more tea please."

Nalia poured more tea into Souchev's glass.

"Where is the RA-115 now?" asked Stefania.

"How should I know," responded Souchev. "I delivered it to Wu. Where it went after that, is none of my concern, as long as it left Turkmenistan, which it did."

"What about timing?" asked Greschenko. "Timing is important," she repeated somewhat loudly and forcefully.

"Lana, I'm not pleased by your tone," responded Souchev in his typical monotone.

"I'm sorry, but can you please give us an idea of the timing of the shipment," asked Greschenko calmly.

"That's better. I don't know the particulars, only that it had to reach its final destination by the fifteenth of March," replied Souchev.

"Beware the ides of March," said Thomas quietly, followed by a frown.

"That doesn't give us much time," noted Stefania. "I wonder what Wu's remaining funds were for?"

"The remaining funds were probably Wu's cost of shipping," theorized Thomas.

"Correct," replied Greschenko. "However, a RA-115 could not be shipped through a typical port of entry, at least in a developed country. Most ports have radiation detectors."

Souchev smiled again and took a sip of tea.

"Kiko, I think we've taken enough of your time," said Greschenko.

"Always a pleasure Lana," said Souchev as he rose from his chair and exchanged kisses with Greschenko on both cheeks. "Amit, the visas."

Amit walked over and handed an envelope each to Thomas and Stefania.

"You each have a three day entry visa to Turkmenistan and two night's stay at my hotel here, on the house," said Souchev. "Make the best of your time. Perhaps visit the Monument to Neutrality, truly striking."

"Thank you Kiko for your hospitality," said Greschenko. "My government is extremely appreciative, as always, of the information you've provided and your cooperation."

"Of course," replied Souchev. "I'm always at the Russian Federation's disposal, provided the compensation is agreeable."

Souchev turned to Stefania, and his eyes started at her feet and moved slowly to her breasts.

"And Ms. DiMaggio, Lana knows how to reach me if you change your mind with regard to my invitation for employment," said Souchev. "It would be nice to have you here."

"Thank you for the offer, but I must decline," said Stefania, with a frown looking back as they made their way out of the room to the vestibule where they were met by the men in the black suits and ushered into the elevator.

Stefania's eyes cut to Greschenko. Greschenko always seemed perpetually perturbed. Now she looked more perturbed than usual.

Greschenko said something to one of the men in Russian.

"*Da*," he said in reply. He pressed the button for the lobby.

"What's going on?" asked Stefania.

"We are leaving," said Greschenko. "I've asked them to gather our luggage and to drive us back to the airport."

Anatoly met the group in the lobby.

"Inform the pilots we are on our way, have the jet readied, we are leaving with haste," announced Greschenko. She also said something in Russian to Anatoly.

I heard her say "Stasevich," didn't Souchev just mention that name to Greschenko? Stefania thought.

"Certainly," replied Anatoly.

Greschenko's head turned to Thomas and Stefania.

"Don't say anything of importance until we are on the plane," instructed Greschenko to Thomas and Stefania in Italian.

Thomas and Stefania nodded.

A couple of minutes later their luggage appeared in the lobby. It was loaded into the two waiting white SUVs which took off toward the airport, down the broad empty boulevards of Ashgabat, passing all of the white marble buildings.

"I must say, I'd have liked to do some sightseeing here," said Stefania.

"As would I," replied Thomas. "I doubt we'll have occasion to return any time soon. It's certainly a curious place."

*Again he said "we," * thought Stefania.

The SUV's sped onto the tarmac through a gate and up to the waiting jet. Stefania and Thomas hopped out of the SUV and scurried up the stairway to the jet cabin, followed by Greschenko and Anatoly. Shortly thereafter the attendants stowed their luggage.

Greschenko barked some orders at the pilots in Russian. The door closed and the jet engines revved. The jet jerked and started moving across the tarmac. The pilot announced something over the intercom.

"We have been cleared for departure," said Greschenko. "We will be airborne momentarily. Prepare yourselves for departure."

Suddenly the jet stopped.

Greschenko got up, walked up to the flight deck, and spoke with the pilot, and walked back.

"Something's wrong," she said. "We've been ordered to hold in place here on the tarmac."

"Why?" asked Stefania.

"If I knew I'd tell you," snapped Greschenko. "If Souchev holds us for improper reasons there will be hell to pay from my government."

Stefania looked out the portal and two white SUVs blocked the jet's progress on the tarmac. Stefania began to perspire, and her stomach pulsed with the air of anxiety.

I hope this doesn't have anything to do with the note that came with the tea, she thought. *I haven't even read it yet.*

After a few minutes, another white SUV pulled up next to the jet and Amit got out of the SUV with a package.

"Open the door," growled an agitated Greschenko.

"Amit is coming up," announced Greschenko. "Let's see what he has to say."

Stefania slouched down in her seat.

Try to act cool.

Amit entered the cabin and walked up to Stefania.

"Mr. Souchev did not expect you to leave us so suddenly," he said with a hint of disappointment. "He had hoped to have another opportunity to speak with Ms. DiMaggio. I have gift from him to you, Ms. DiMaggio."

Amit handed her a package with red and white striped wrapping paper and a bow. The bow held a note, folded in two, in place.

"Thank you," said Stefania.

"Farewell," said Amit, as he turned and left the cabin.

"For the love of God!" exclaimed Greschenko with a frown, turning to Stefania.

Stefania let out a sigh of relief.

"Well, what does it say?" asked Thomas.

"It says," started Stefania, "'something sweet for someone sweet,' and it's signed Kiko. There apparently is a phone number."

Stefania unwrapped the box and opened it.

Greschenko looked inside and rolled her eyes.

"He stopped to give you halva, unbelievable!" Greschenko exclaimed. "Typical Souchev. Close the cabin door and let's get the hell out of here," she ordered the attendant.

"What's halva?" asked Stefania.

"It's a sweet delicacy in the middle east and central Asia," responded Thomas examining the box's contents. "This looks like it has pistachios in it. I've had it before, quite tasty. He's obviously taken with you."

"Souchev likes pretty things," said Greschenko. "Don't be fooled. Nalia is one of his concubines. You'd have a job with him, you'd live a life of luxury, for a price."

"He's not what I expected," declared Stefania. "He didn't seem that threatening."

"He's a wolf in sheep's clothing," responded Greschenko. "He's a ruthless thug. A sophisticated one, but a gangster nevertheless. And he's the most dangerous kind, he's intelligent, he's got money, tons of it, power, and government protection. He's not a man that can easily be gotten to. He typically holds all the leverage. He doesn't drink, smoke or do drugs, and he has so many women he can't be tempted. He can only be bought, for a price."

Stefania picked up a slice of the white confection mottled with pistachio nuts and tasted it. The sugary halva melted in her mouth.

"Tasty and sweet," she said, passing the box to Thomas.

"Don't mind if I do," responded Thomas taking a piece of the halva.

The jet jerked forward and sped across the tarmac.

The pilot announced something in Russian.

"We are finally cleared for takeoff," said Greschenko. She then said something to Anatoly in Russian. Stefania again understood one word, a reference to "Stasevich."

Stefania took a deep breath, tightened her lap belt, and sighed.

God how I hate flying, she thought, *especially take off and landing.*

The jet turned and stopped. Its engines revved and started rolling down the runway. After a few seconds it ascended into the cloudless blue sky. As soon as the jet leveled off, Greschenko and Anatoly went to the back of the plane into a separate compartment.

"The fact that Souchev sold Wu a nuclear device is disturbing to say the least," said Stefania to Thomas. "What does six kilotons mean?"

"To provide context, as I recall, the Hiroshima blast was about sixteen kilotons and total destruction was about one square mile with a conflagration extending maybe four square miles from ground zero, but that was a very inefficient and relatively primitive device," replied Thomas. "I'm by no means an expert, but destruction from an atomic weapon of six kilotons or less depends a great deal on the terrain and altitude of the blast."

"I'm assuming that the nuclear device is part of this terrorist operation that Wu was apparently involved with?" asked Stefania.

"That's a reasonable deduction," responded Thomas. "The question would be where to employ the device?"

"Greschenko said it would be difficult to ship it through a typical port of entry due to radiation detectors," added Stefania.

"She's right," agreed Thomas. "It would be difficult to get the device in through an airport or port in most developed countries. Not something you'd want to risk for the amount Wu paid for the thing. It would have to be brought in covertly either by sea, or by land in the case of a country with porous borders."

"Would the logical locale be the United States, since that's where Wu was, Smith was headed, and where the attack took place in New Jersey?" asked Stefania.

"Yes," responded Thomas. "It would be, especially if we have no way of tracking the device."

"She slipped me a note," whispered Stefania.

"Who slipped you a note?" asked Thomas quietly.

"I assume Nalia," whispered back Stefania, "with the tea."

"Dear God, what does it say?" asked Thomas.

"Hold on, I'll get it out of my waistband," whispered Stefania.

Just then the door to the compartment in the rear of the plane opened and Greschenko's voice could be heard as she approached from behind with Anatoly in tow. Stefania stuffed the note back in her waistband.

"Well?" asked Stefania.

"Well what?" replied Greschenko.

"What did Stasevich tell you?" asked Stefania.

"You *are* droll aren't you," said Greschenko with a huff. "It doesn't much matter, I was probably going to tell you anyway, but if you repeat it, I'll have you both killed, and that's no empty threat."

"You are ever so comforting," chimed in Thomas.

"Apparently as long as they keep the RA-115 hooked up to an uninterrupted power source, it's good to go," Greschenko reported. "It will run on one-hundred and ten volts or two-hundred twenty volts, all you need is an adaptor. It also has a back-up battery which lasts for forty-eight hours."

"It seems easy then, just cut the power, right?" interrupted Stefania.

"Not so quick little miss genius," replied Greschenko sarcastically. "Once the thing is armed, if the power source is cut, there is a capacitor, it automatically detonates."

"What does the bloody thing look like?" asked Thomas.

"It's in a metal container, about the size of a footlocker or steamer chest," said Greschenko running her hands through her hair. "Although the container is probably disguised to look somewhat innocuous, albeit with a power cord. The chest contains a key lock, but an ordinary looking one, nothing peculiar."

"Seems risky," added Thomas.

"Not really," said Greschenko. "There *was* a built-in booby trap, a grenade type antipersonnel explosive if someone attempted to open the box without the key, it also disabled the device. The key disabled the trap."

"What do you mean, *was*?" asked Stefania.

"You *are* observant," said Greschenko. "But didn't you hear Souchev, he said the tamper resistant device was removed."

"How would this device be able to bypass the radiation scanners at ports?" asked Thomas.

"It wouldn't," said Greschenko. "The amount of lead lining required to avoid the scanners would have made the device immobile."

"So it's unlikely that the device will be smuggled in by air or sea through a major port," posited Stefania.

"You're getting the hang of it," said Greschenko, rubbing her chin again. "Not in a first world country anyway."

"How is it armed?" asked Thomas.

"It has a digital timer which can be set to go from any amount of time from entry of the arming code," replied Greschenko. "There is a twelve digit code key which is typed in on a key pad, letters and numbers, which is taken from a fob, then press enter. The code on the fob changes every minute."

"Can't GRU just deactivate or change the fob?" asked Thomas.

"No," replied Greschenko somewhat dejectedly. "Apparently the fob is synchronized to each device. GRU trusted its agents implicitly. Once a valid order was received, the GRU officer would place the RA-115 in proximity to the intended target and arm it, and enter the time for detonation."

"There must be a way to deactivate the bloody thing," said Thomas loudly.

"No," shot back Greschenko. "Once armed, it cannot be disarmed."

"Seems a bit reckless, wouldn't you say?" asked Thomas sarcastically.

"Each device *had* a satellite tracking system," shot back Greschenko. "Except Souchev said Orloff disabled it."

"So this thing could be anywhere?" asked Stefania.

"Anywhere but apparently Turkmenistan," replied Greschenko. "I'll bet Souchev could tell us where it's not."

"Bloody hell," snapped Thomas. "What a cock-up."

"We are looking into Wu's smuggling network," said Greschenko. "Perhaps it will lead us to the RA-115."

"It sounds like we only have until March fifteenth," said Stefania. "Then boom."

"You have a penchant for stating the obvious," snapped Greschenko.

"Who's Stasevich anyway?" asked Stefania.

"Colonel General Stasevich is the head of GRU," replied Greschenko. "It's no secret, and you met him two years ago at the Vatican, remember."

"Oh, yes," said Stefania.

"I have more business to attend to with Anatoly. Make yourselves comfortable for the remainder of the flight to Malta. If you need anything, ask the attendants."

Greschenko and Anatoly disappeared into the back of the jet and shut the door behind them.

"Well, what does the note say?" whispered Thomas.

Stefania slipped the paper out from her waistband. She unfolded it.

"It says Cesária Bolo, Praia," whispered back Stefania.

"Praia is a City in the Cape Verde Islands," noted Thomas. "I can only assume Cesária Bolo is a woman's name."

"What does it mean though, and why leave it with me?" asked Stefania.

"I think you can assume that Nalia isn't so happy being Souchev's concubine, either that or she's got a conscience," replied Thomas.

"Or both," said Stefania.

"I'll call Harry when we get to Malta. I'll take that chance but I can't call Harry on his mobile or land line, I'm sure they're being monitored by whomever, but I'm going to try one of his usual spots," said Thomas.

"So our next stop after Malta is going to be the Cape Verde Islands?" queried Stefania.

"Yes, we are lucky that you speak Portuguese, and I'm serviceable in it."

"At least finally we'll be seeing some warm weather. Can we at least stay the night in Malta?" asked Stefania. "It seems like I've been in these clothes forever. I'd like a change and a fresh bath."

"Certainly," replied Thomas. "No word of this to Greschenko. "Let's see what Harry finds out about this Cesária Bolo. She might be a dead end."

Stefania tilted her head and looked Thomas in the eye.

"Really your grace, really?" she asked sarcastically.

Thomas laughed.

Chapter 8
Late Evening, March 9, Valetta, Malta

Stefania walked with Thomas down the carpeted hallway of their hotel in Valetta. Her legs felt like lead as they walked by a wall sconce with soft lights after every other door. They finally reached the double doors of their suite.

"I'm so tired, I'm going to take a bath and go to bed," said Stefania as Thomas fiddled to find the card key to open the doors to the suite.

"You don't want to get some room service, anything to eat?" asked Thomas.

"I'm spent," she replied. "Hopefully they've brought our bags up already."

Thomas swiped the card key and turned the brass door knob, and opened the doors. The two walked in and Stefania closed the doors behind them.

"Lights are on, they must have brought up our bags," said Thomas.

The sitting area between their two rooms had tan marble floors, a white throw rug with a blue sectional sofa facing a large screen television on top of a cabinet. Brass lamps were at either end of the sofa. There was also a desk, and a table and chairs for dining, as well as a wet bar completely stocked. French doors led out to a balcony.

"If you would wake me when you get up," asked Stefania as she proceeded to the door on the right of the living area to her bedroom.

"Certainly," replied Thomas as he walked to his bedroom door to the left of the living area.

Stefania turned on the lights, but left the door open.

No bags, hmm, she thought.

The soft king size bed with a hardwood canopy awaited her tired bones. The marble floored bathroom off to the side promised a hot bath with jets of water and bubbles. She paused for a moment.

This hardly seems the time, but should I address my lingering feelings with Thomas, she thought. *Maybe he shares my feelings. We may not be alone if we venture out with Greschenko again.*

All of a sudden a crash came from Thomas' room.

Sounds like glass breaking.

"Thomas?" she shouted.

He didn't answer.

Then a large thump came from his room, like luggage falling to the floor.

She ran through the sitting area and opened the door to Thomas' room, a mirror image of her's.

An Asian man wearing a dark pin striped suit, blue dress shirt, no tie, pinned Thomas to the carpeted floor. His left hand grasped Thomas' neck, while the other hand gripped a handgun which Thomas tried to dislodge with his left hand. Thomas' right hand pushed up on the man's chin. Thomas gasped for air.

Instinctively Stefania's *capoeira* training kicked in. Still sporting her boots, she spun around and landed a solid kick to the man's head knocking him off Thomas and sending his gun skipping across the floor underneath the bed. He jumped up quickly. She spun around again, landing a kick to his midsection. He fell to the floor.

Stefania turned to Thomas as he rolled on the floor gasping for air.

Her eyes cut to the man again just as he lunged for her. She jumped back, spun around and landed a solid kick to his face. He staggered back against the wall as bright red blood gushed out of his nose and down his face like a waterfall.

Thomas managed to pull himself up, sitting on the floor with his back to the bed. The man staggered quickly to the door from Thomas' room to the hallway and disappeared out the door.

Stefania went to the doorway and looked down the hallway. The man was gone. She shut the door, switched the security bolt closed, as well as the manual latch.

"Oh Madonna, are you alright?" asked Stefania.

Thomas still gasping for air, tried to speak. Stefania snatched a bottle of water from the bar and gave it to Thomas, who slaked some water down.

Thomas finally caught his breath.

"I think so, I walked in after we parted and he jumped me," said Thomas in a raspy voice, now standing.

Stefania now noticed that the room was a mess. The bed had been taken apart, the drawers were hanging out of the chest, the night stands were tipped over, the armoire was open and clothes were strewn all about.

"He was looking for something, that's for sure," said Thomas, his voice returning to normal. "He must have been here when we got back. I think our arrival surprised him. He didn't have time to leave."

"Why is it that when we are together I'm always escaping with within a hair of my life?" asked Stefania sarcastically.

"My thanks and apologies," replied Thomas with a smile.

"Don't mention it," replied Stefania. "It's disturbing that I now feel safer when we're with Greschenko."

"Quite," replied Thomas, as he looked under the bed, and grabbed for something.

His hand emerged with the handgun, which he held with a white handkerchief.

"A Walther PPK," said Thomas. "Looks to be a thirty-eight caliber."

"What does that mean?" asked Stefania.

"It's a very popular weapon, especially for undercover work," replied Thomas.

"Did you notice if he took your phone?" asked Thomas.

"Mine is still attached to the charger in my room, where did you put yours?"

"I attached it to a power bank and placed it behind the draperies next to the balcony in the living room. Please check it for me," said Thomas as he stood up, rubbing his neck.

"It's still here," reported Stefania. "I say we get the hell out of here, ASAP."

"Agreed," said Thomas. "I'm afraid your shower and clean-up will have to wait. You can change on the plane. I'll maintain our reservations here for appearances sake. Please go on line and make a reservation for a suite at the Hotel Pérola in Praia. Make it in your name, I'll reimburse you. I'm going to call the pilots and let tell them to get the plane ready. We are leaving tonight."

"That sucks, I haven't showered in days. Now I'm all sweaty and sore."

"Bring your mobile when we leave, just keep it on airplane mode," directed Thomas.

"OK, but what about Harry?" asked Stefania.

Thomas picked up the Russian satphone and dialed a number.

"Yes, is Harry Foster at the bar?" asked Thomas. "Right, tell him it's Thomas."

"What are you going to ask him?" inquired Stefania.

"Harry, it's Thomas. I have no time to explain. Find out whatever you can on a person named Cesária Bolo, I think she's located in Praia, Cape Verde Islands. How will you reach me? Do you still have that burner that no one knows about? Right, I'll call you on that number tomorrow morning at 7 o'clock, but don't be near your house at the time. Also, any word on Chen? Right, thanks Harry."

"What did he say?" asked Stefania.

"No word on Chen, which is curious," said Thomas.

"Why do you say that?"

"Because we know she was MI6, not a field agent, but assuming she was on MI6 business, they would've known she was going to Smith's flat," posited Thomas. "Her body would have been discovered by now."

"Which means whatever she was doing at Smith's flat wasn't in connection with MI6 business, not official business anyway," noted Stefania.

"Greschenko said the phone she had was a burner."

"So she didn't want MI6 to know she was at Smith's flat," concluded Stefania.

Thomas looked at Stefania with a raised brow.

"Oh Madonna," mumbled Stefania putting her hand on her forehead.

"Why did you tell him not to be at home when you called?" asked Stefania.

"If we're being monitored, it's likely Harry is too, although they'd have to be more careful with him, given his background," responded Thomas. "They might have bugged his flat, or set up a mobile intercept in his neighborhood."

"I get it," said Stefania.

"I'll call Harry tomorrow from Praia. Let's turn the satphones off," said Thomas. "Cesária Bolo will have to remain a mystery until then."

Early Morning, March 10, 40,000 feet above the Atlantic Ocean

"Now that we've leveled off, I'm going to change," declared Stefania. "All the clothes I have are for March weather in the UK," she said with a frown.

"The high temperature in Praia should be in the twenty-five to twenty-six degrees range I would think, so it will be much warmer," responded Thomas. "I'll wait until we arrive to change."

"What time will we be landing?" asked Stefania.

"Because it took longer than I thought to get the pilots and plane ready, we took off pretty late. I don't think we'll land until eight-thirty local time," responded Thomas. "I'll have to call Harry from the plane."

Stefania walked down the aisle to the rear bedroom compartment and closed the door. She changed her underwear and bra, threw on a pair of tight fitting jeans and replaced her sweater with a looser fitting red blouse, and she walked out of the compartment.

"That was quick," said Thomas.

"Not by design," she replied. "I've got few choices, so my fashion decisions were limited."

"I see you kept the boots."

"Yeh," she responded. "Other than my runners, this is all I have."

Thomas smiled.

"You look 'fetching' as Souchev would say."

"Thank you your grace," Stefania said as she felt the blood rush to her head.

"You're blushing."

"Maybe," Stefania said as she smiled back.

"No, you're definitely blushing," teased Thomas.

"You're just jealous because Souchev showed interest and gave me halva."

"I'm no such thing, although not to acknowledge your comeliness would be impolitic under the circumstances," he responded.

"What a sweet thing to say, I think, after I dissect the diction of that sentence," Stefania teased.

"It's almost 7 o'clock in the UK, and we are approaching the Cape Verde islands. I should be able to phone Harry."

Stefania sat down across from Thomas and sunk into the plush leather seat.

Thomas picked up the plane's satphone, dialed a number, placed it on speaker and set it on the shiny wood table between them.

"I hope I remembered his burner number, I'm dialing it by memory."

"Hello," answered Harry.

"Good morning Harry, it's Thomas."

"Thomas, bear with me because I'm in King's Cross station. The background noise may be a bit much, but I thought it the safest place to speak in public."

"No problem Harry, what have you?" asked Thomas.

"Cesária Bolo is a Cape Verde Islands shipping magnate," explained Harry. "She took over the family business on the death of her father. The company is Bolo Enterprises, you may have seen the name on the side of shipping containers."

"Yes, I think I have," said Thomas. "Go on."

"The company started shipping goods to and from Cape Verde, Portugal, and Africa, but then branched out into major trans-Atlantic shipping," responded Harry.

"Legitimate?" piped in Stefania.

"Hi Stefania," responded Harry. "Yes, except for one interesting aspect. Bolo also specializes in small lot shipping things of value, artwork, antiquities, things of that nature."

"Why is that interesting?" asked Stefania.

"Some of things which they've shipped were stolen, and on several occasions they've found contraband in the shipments," said Harry.

"Like what?" asked Stefania.

"Like exotic animals, ivory, purloined antiquities, and artwork," said Harry.

"Was Cesária Bolo prosecuted?" asked Thomas.

"No," responded Harry. "She declined knowledge and blame fell on the clients. The company was fined. If Bolo leaves Cape Verde at all, it's generally to Africa."

"Very interesting," said Stefania.

"Anything on Cesária Bolo personally?" asked Thomas.

"She's not gormless, let's put it that way," responded Harry.

"What does that mean?" asked Stefania.

"She attended university in the UK, speaks four or five different languages, and runs a billion quid shipping conglomerate," responded Harry. "She's clever."

"Did you find out anything about her personally?" asked Thomas.

"She's thirty-seven, Creole, single, pretty fit, baptized Catholic, lives in a walled villa outside Praia with her dogs," reported Harry. "She loves her dogs. She also spends a lot of her time in her offices at her shipping company in the Porto da Praia."

"So she speaks English?" asked Thomas.

"Yes, that Portuguese, Spanish, and several dialects of Creole," said Harry.

"Smashing," said Thomas. "What's Bolo's phone number?"

Thomas wrote the number down on a piece of note paper.

"Any word on Chen?"

"Nothing," said Harry. "They've no idea what happened to her."

"Thanks Harry," said Thomas. "And don't call me, I'll call you on your burner."

"Right," responded Harry. "G'day mate."

The call ended with a click.

"Seems like we should speak to Bolo," said Stefania. "But how?"

"I've got an idea," said Thomas as he dialed a number.

"What have you in mind?" asked Stefania.

Thomas put the phone up to his ear.

"Yes, may I speak to Ms. Bolo?" he asked in choppy Portuguese. "Thomas Houghton. No. I have a very expensive piece of artwork I need shipped from the UK to Bermuda, and I would like to schedule a meeting with her as soon as possible to discuss the particulars. I will pay substantially for the consignment. Time is of the essence. No, I'll call back in an hour or so. I'll be in Praia today and would like to meet with her late this morning or this afternoon if at all possible. Because of the nature of the shipment I only wish to discuss it with her. Right. Thank you."

"Okay, explain," said Stefania.

"Harry said she attended university in the UK," said Thomas.

"So?" asked Stefania.

"If she's spent any time in the UK whatsoever, despite my low profile, she's bound to have heard of me. At the very least she may Google me," said Thomas.

"...and you set a trap," murmured Stefania rubbing her chin.

"Maybe," Thomas replied softly sitting back in his seat with his phone in hand rubbing his chin.

"What happens if she calls your bluff on the artwork?" asked Stefania.

"I've got plenty of artwork at Haverford Hall, some valuable, some rubbish, but my guess is all she'll care about is the fee," responded Thomas. "And I've got a house in Bermuda I never use. If she checks me out, she'll know all of this."

"Excellent," said Stefania excitedly, now sitting back in her seat.

"Not so fast," responded Thomas. "It's clever only if it gets us an audience with Bolo today."

Stefania laughed. "A house in Bermuda, hmm..."

"Yes," Thomas replied. "On a bluff overlooking the sea with its own private beach."

"Why are you never there?"

"I used to bring Granny and Aunt Josephine, when they were healthy, but it's not the kind of place one goes by oneself."

"I see," said Stefania softly.

"By the way, how'd you know someone would be at Bolo's office this time of the morning?" asked Stefania.

"Longshoremen and stevedores are early risers," responded Thomas with a smile. "Many ports open early and close late. Remember, I was in the SAS."

"I haven't forgotten that tidbit about your grace's background," replied a beaming Stefania. "I bet you looked great in uniform."

"Looks like we're getting ready to land," said Thomas ignoring the compliment.

"Oh boy," uttered Stefania followed by a long sigh as she put on her lap belt and tightened it snuggly.

Chapter 9

Late Morning, March 10, Porto Da Praia, Cape Verde Islands

The taxi pulled through the gate and stopped at the open two story sliding door to a blue corrugated warehouse building with "BOLO" in red capital letters splashed on its side. The bright sunshine sparkled off the bay to the right, and several large freighters were tied up on an adjoining quay. Beyond the warehouse stood a small mountain of blue shipping containers, all with "BOLO" on the sides in big red capital letters.

Thomas, having changed into khakis, with a white button down madras shirt and brown leather loafers, got out the driver's side rear door. Stefania followed, in her red blouse and jeans, out the passenger side rear door, with her ever present large black shoulder bag.

Thomas leaned in the driver's side window.

"Please wait for us to return," he said in choppy Portuguese.

The driver nodded saying "yes."

"Thank you," said Thomas as he handed the driver two twenty Euro notes.

"Where do we meet her?" asked Stefania.

"The woman on the phone said proceed through the large door to the stairs along the wall, and go up into the office area," said Thomas.

They walked through the large doorway onto concrete flooring. The open interior contained a few forklifts parked about, yellow industrial shelving going back as far as the eye could see and up twenty feet or so, stacked with pallets upon pallets containing various boxes and barrels, many wrapped in clear plastic.

"Cleaner than I expected for a storage warehouse," said Stefania.

"Those must be the stairs," said Thomas, pointing to blue painted metal stairs against the far right wall leading up to a windowed mezzanine.

"Must be," agreed Stefania.

The two trudged up the stairway and opened a metal door with a window. A young Creole woman with glasses sat at a hardwood desk in the small outer office.

"Can I help you?" she asked in Portuguese.

"I am Thomas Houghton, I have an appointment with Ms. Bolo," replied Thomas in Portuguese.

Stefania noticed that on the other side of the office, next to a door presumably to the inner office, sat a beefy muscle bound Creole man on a sofa watching a football match on a flat screen television. He wore a red t-shirt with tan shorts, and constantly switched the television channels.

What a stark contrast the hardwood floors and wood paneled walls of the outer office were to the warehouse below, she thought.

"Yes, I'll let her know you are here," the woman said as she picked up the phone and uttered a few words, too low in tone to be heard.

"Thank you," replied Thomas, now looking around the outer office and apparently noticing the man in the red t-shirt.

"Bodyguard?" Stefania said in Italian.

"Probably," Thomas replied.

"Ms. Bolo will see you," the woman said in a soft voice. "Follow me please."

The woman took the two through the doorway past the man in the red t-shirt. They entered a much larger office, with hardwood floors and wood paneling. A row of windows on the right overlooked the port. A slim Creole woman, slightly less than six feet in height, who had been sitting at a large writing desk behind a computer screen, got up and walked toward the two. She wore a low cut yellow floral print blouse, which exposed her cleavage, and matching yellow lace brassiere. Her tight tan slacks looked like they were painted on, and her high heels made her look even taller. Ruby red lip gloss covered her full lips, which only accentuated her high cheekbones.

Again, not what I expected, thought Stefania. *I'm always expecting the bad guys, or in this case bad girls, to look the part.*

"I'm Cesária," she said in a somewhat high pitched voice in British accented English. "You must be the Duke of Radcliffe?"

"I am, and Thomas is fine," he replied. "This is my colleague Stefania DiMaggio."

The three shook hands.

"Pleased to make your acquaintance. Please, do sit down," she said, pointing to two brown leather chairs which sat across from her table desk. She glanced at her computer screen. "Your internet photo does not do you justice, you look much younger in person."

"Thank you," replied Thomas.

Stefania heard panting, and looked to her right. Laying on a dog bed next to the right wall was a large German Shepherd.

"Don't worry, Emy won't bother you unless I tell her to," said Cesária.

"The craftsmanship of that table desk is extraordinary," remarked Thomas. "It is truly one of the most beautiful pieces of furniture I've ever seen."

"It's a Louis XIV writing desk," Cesária replied as she sat back down behind it.

"My, I didn't know the craftsmanship of reproductions was that intricate," marveled Thomas.

"It's not a reproduction," Cesária replied in monotone. "It's an original."

Why do all these villains speak in monotone, like nothing bothers them, thought Stefania.

"So you want my firm to handle an art shipment from the UK to Bermuda," Cesária asked.

"Yes," responded Thomas. "That and another matter."

"And what would that be?" Cesária asked with no expression.

"I have another item I need shipped to the United States, but it cannot be shipped through normal channels," said Thomas.

"And why is that?" Cesária asked.

"Let's say it is a piece of artwork which came into my father's possession years ago," said Thomas. "I have a buyer in the States, and don't want anyone to know the nature of the shipment."

"What is it precisely?" Cesária asked somewhat forcefully.

"A painting," replied Thomas.

"Which painting?" asked Cesaria. "It does make a difference."

"Caravaggio's Nativity," replied Thomas.

"The *Nativity with Saints Francis and Lawrence*," said Cesária with a grin. "That *would* attract attention. Missing since 1969, it was stolen by *la cosa nostra* from the Oratory of Saint Lawrence in

Palermo. I'm familiar with its history. Where in the United States is it to be delivered?"

"Hollywood area," replied Thomas.

"Naturally," said Cesária. "That will cost two and one-half million quid payable up-front."

"The painting is very delicate," said Thomas. "How will you ensure its safety and delivery without being discovered?"

"It will go through Mexico," she responded. "The southern border of the United States is porous. Everything that travels across the southern border goes through the cartels. I pay them as couriers. Nothing ever happens to the cargo, you can be rest assured of that."

"I would want to know the particulars of the route and handling," said Thomas.

"That is my trade secret," replied Cesária forcefully. "It will get delivered. Who you referred you to me by the way? You are not one of my usual customers, although I probably handle unique shipments for half the peerage in the UK."

"Stanley Wu," replied Thomas.

The poker face expression on Cesária's face suddenly changed ever so slightly. Her voluptuous lower lip dropped a millimeter, and her cheeks tightened.

"Stanley Wu," she repeated the name in her monotone. "Staaaanley Wu," she said his name again slightly slower and louder.

"I think our business is concluded," she said. "It's time for you to go."

Her hand moved under her desk.

Stefania turned around as the door opened behind her.

The burly man in the red t-shit stepped in.

Thomas stood up.

"You handled a shipment for Wu to the States, we need to know where that shipment went and where it is going," declared Thomas.

"I don't think so," she replied with a grin. "Marcos, show our guests out," ordered Cesária in Portuguese. "Emy!"

The shepherd rose up and started growling at Stefania.

"Not so fast!" a familiar voice barked in English. "At least until *I* get some answers."

"Greschenko!" exclaimed Stefania. "Why does this not surprise me."

"Crikey, you *do* always seem to pop up," added Thomas.

Greschenko, in pink yoga pants and matching athletic top stood behind Marcos with her trademark Nagant pistol pressed snuggly to the back of his head. Her hair pulled back in a pony tail, beads of sweat rolled down Greschenko's forehead. Behind her, Anatoly walked in wearing a dark suit, white shirt, dark tie, holding a semi-automatic handgun at his waist.

"On the sofa big guy," ordered Greschenko.

Marcos did not move.

Stefania's eyes rolled.

"She said get on the sofa you big oaf," snapped Stefania in Portuguese.

Marcos finally sat on the sofa. Anatoly trained his pistol on Marcos. Greschenko pointed her Nagant at Cesária. Thomas sat back down and crossed his legs, seemingly satisfied in watching the whole episode unfold as a spectator.

"I want some answers regarding Wu's shipment," snapped Greschenko, her voice trembling. "Now, where's my fucking box?"

On all fours between Cesária and Greschenko, Emy the shepherd dog, now snarled, showing her teeth.

"I'm not sure you are in as good a position as you suspect," answered Cesária in her brutal monotone.

"Oh yes," said Greschenko. "You mean the other bodyguards in the warehouse? They're under control. I've got plenty of support, more than you can imagine Ms. Bolo."

Stefania motioned with her eyes to the shepherd.

"If I don't start getting answers, the bitch gets put down," snapped Greschenko, now training her pistol on the dog. "First a shot to the leg, then a shot to the other leg, and so on, ending with a shot to the head. It will take a good twenty minutes."

Cesária grimaced.

"And if that doesn't do the trick, I'll take you back to Russia and you'll never be heard from again," said Greschenko, raising her eyebrows.

"Alright," answered Cesária, "I'll have to check my computer."

"Never mind, I'll just start making the fur-ball into mincemeat," barked Greschenko, now lowering the pistol toward the dog's foreleg.

"I said alright," responded Cesária, now finally with a bit of stress in her voice. "Emy, go lay down."

The canine strode over to its bed and flopped down.

"Wu had two shipments," Cesária continued, "one went by container from Italy to the Port of Newark, New Jersey, but I suspect you are asking about the special shipment, one stainless steel steamer trunk."

"That's the one," said Stefania.

"It went by private yacht originally from Italy, which docked off the gulf coast of Mexico near La Pesca, where the trunk was picked up by launch by the *Cartel del Norte*, taken up the *Rio Soto La Marina* and transported over land to a location on US Mexico border where it is to be handed off to persons on the US side at that spot. That's my part of the operation. Where it goes from the border, I haven't a clue."

"Where is it now?" barked Greschenko.

"It is somewhere in Mexico in transit, I don't know where, I just know that the transfer took place," responded Cesária. "The cartel has been paid and is in the process of transport."

Greschenko walked up to Cesária, her pistol now at her side.

"Identify the border location," Greschenko demanded.

"I'll have to look at my computer," Cesária responded.

"DiMaggio, make sure she's not doing anything stupid," barked Greschenko.

Stefania walked around to the other side of the table desk and watched Cesária peck on the computer keyboard.

"It's all in Portuguese," said Stefania. "But I can read it."

"Well?" asked Greschenko.

"All I have is a GPS coordinate for the transfer location," reported Cesária. "It's at the end of a dirt track east of Agua Prieta and west of Casa de Madera, Chihuahua State, near someplace called Guadalupe Canyon."

"What is the time for the transfer?" demanded Greschenko.

Stefania pushed Cesária aside.

"It says March twelfth at 1130 Zulu," replied Stefania, looking at the computer screen.

"In that time zone it's probably 3:30 a.m.," added Thomas. "The witching hour."

"We don't have much time," said Stefania.

"No, we don't," added Greschenko. "Is there anything else on the computer?"

Stefania scanned the information on the screen.

"Nothing pertinent that I can tell," responded Stefania. "Everything she's said is consistent with what's on here."

"Let's move," said Greschenko.

"Nice making your acquaintance Ms. Bolo," said Thomas as the foursome left the room and walked down the stairs.

Waiting in front of the warehouse was a caravan of four gray SUVs guarded by obviously Russian men in various types of dress, most with khaki pants and polo shirts covered with flak jackets, all gripping automatic rifles at waist level. Five local men were sitting on the floor next to a fork lift being guarded by two of the Russians in khaki pants.

Greschenko's eyes cut to Thomas and Stefania. "You're coming with us," she said.

"Oh boy," muttered Stefania.

Thomas walked up to the waiting cab and said something to the driver who then drove off.

The trio got into the back seat of one of the SUVs. Anatoly shut the door behind them and clambered into the passenger seat. The truck took off.

"And where are we going?" asked Thomas.

"To your hotel," responded Greschenko. "What the hell did you think you were doing here?"

"Following a lead," responded Stefania.

The SUV flew by the bay on the left shimmering in the equatorial sun. The sun kissed white washed buildings of greater Praia flew by to the right.

"I'm keeping tabs on you both," said Greschenko, now calmer than her agitated demeanor at the Bolo warehouse.

Greschenko then spoke to someone in Russian on a satellite phone for a few minutes.

Stefania took her tablet out of her shoulder bag and looked through her notes as they sped toward the hotel.

"You'd better have that thing on airplane mode," snapped Greschenko.

"Yes, and the GPS coordinates Bolo gave us are the same coordinates which were on Wu's thumb-drive," reported Stefania.

"So Wu is importing a nuclear device to the United States," pondered Thomas. "Won't it be difficult to get around with the radiation detectors they have on roadways?"

"Maybe," replied Greschenko. "Unless they avoid the interstates and use local or secondary roads."

"How long can they do that?" asked Stefania. "The target must be close by, in the southwestern United States."

"I so hate it when you make sense," blurted Greschenko with a smirk.

"I love it when you make sense," replied Thomas with a grin.

"We are going to Mexico and will try to recover the box," declared Greschenko.

"Whoa *chica*, what do you mean *we* are going to Mexico?" asked Stefania.

"I can't leave you two alone, you are liable to run off again," responded Greschenko. "Frankly I'm considering making you disappear but I'd need the president's permission to kill you," as she pointed at Thomas, "and..."

"And of course you have so much on me and my family, I wouldn't dare cross the Russian Federation," exclaimed Thomas.

Ignoring Thomas, Greschenko smiled and continued, "You're both just going to have to tag along so I can keep tabs on you, and..."

"And then what?" asked Stefania.

"Let's just say we'll play it by ear," responded Greschenko.

"That's comforting," said Thomas.

Greschenko's eyes cut to Thomas.

"Until we recover the RA-115 I can't risk it getting out and you two are security risks," said Greschenko. "Someone's trying to kill you both and unfortunately it's not me. Somehow MI6 is involved, and I can't figure out why or how. I'll address that issue after we recover the box. You're both safer with me, whether you like it or not."

"Again, comforting," said Thomas.

"Would you rather be dead at the hands of MI6, or worse yet, tortured for information and then killed," snapped Greschenko mockingly. "DiMaggio here would probably take the worst of it."

"Hah," scoffed Stefania shaking her head. "What about Bolo," asked Stefania. "Will she talk?"

"Don't worry about Bolo," said Greschenko, "my government will make sure she stays quiet. Blackmail is a wonderful thing."

"How am I going stay under MI6's radar on a trip to Mexico?" asked Thomas.

"Easy," responded Greschenko with a smirk. "You're going to make a week long reservation at a resort in Monterrey for you and Ms. DiMaggio here. You'll be two young lovers continuing your winter holiday in warm weather locales, Malta, Cape Verde, and now Monterrey."

"Two lovers," mumbled Stefania under her breath.

"What was that DiMaggio?" snapped Greschenko.

"I said 'good covers'," responded Stefania.

"Of course they are," responded Greschenko. "You'll travel under your own passports which provide automatic visas into Mexico. Anatoly and I will travel under our diplomatics."

"Why don't we just fly into Chihuahua City?" asked Stefania.

"No one goes there for holiday," barked back Greschenko. "It would immediately raise suspicion."

"But what'll we do when we get to Monterrey?" pondered Thomas.

"You'll both be with me," added Greschenko, now in a softer tone. "I'm enlisting a Zaslon special operations group of Directorate S who'll assist us in recovering the RA-115. I'm under strict orders to take whatever steps are necessary to recover the RA-115 before it gets into United States' territory."

"What if you can't?" asked Stefania it a bit of a loud tone.

"What was that?" barked Greschenko.

"What if you can't recover the RA-115 before it gets into the United States?" barked back Stefania with a raised brow. "I mean it's possible you won't get to it in time. We've got less than forty-eight hours to get to Mexico and track this thing down."

"You've got no intention of informing the American authorities of this potential threat, do you?" asked Thomas.

Greschenko glared at Thomas. "Don't concern yourself with the external affairs of the Russian Federation," Greschenko responded softly. "It can only get you into trouble."

"For starters, you have no idea where the box is," noted Stefania. "There's over a thousand kilometers between Monterrey and the border spot, fifteen to sixteen hours by car at least."

The SUV hit a bump jerking her forward as she spoke.

"Plus northern Mexico is lawless," added Thomas. "What makes you think you'll be able to locate the box, and if by some stretch of luck you do, that the couriers will just hand it over."

"Leave that to me," Greschenko snapped back.

"Wouldn't it make sense to just wait for the delivery at the Mexican side of the border at the appointed time?" asked Thomas.

"While the location is remote, the Americans monitor the border with drones, electronics, satellites, and other methods, even the Mexican side of the border" added Greschenko. "Too much activity will attract unwanted attention. I'm under orders to intercept the box well *before* it gets close to the border, and to use all resources at my disposal to do so. I follow my orders."

Thomas poked his finger into Stefania's leg.

"My guess is the Deputy Director, SVR Directorate KR, is operating on orders from the top," whispered Thomas to Stefania in Portuguese, "with little knowledge of her immediate superiors, and she probably cannot commit significant assets in the United States without higher approval."

"Since when do you know so much about our friend here?" asked back Stefania in a Portuguese whisper, followed with a frown.

"I've learned a lot since our time in Rome," whispered back Thomas.

"I'll bet you have," said Stefania snidely in English.

"I know you are speaking of me in Portuguese," said Greschenko. "It doesn't matter, I'm holding the trump cards."

"I can only assume that you have intelligence you are not sharing with us," noted Thomas as the SUV screeched to a stop in front of the hotel.

Greschenko grinned and her eyes cut to Thomas.

"Just pack your bags, and check out of the hotel," said Greschenko, now in a steadier tone. "I'll wait here. My two friends in the accompanying SUV will go with you to make sure you don't take any unnecessary detours. We'll take your plane to Monterrey. Anatoly is an expert pilot in case your pilots try anything funny."

"Aces," grumbled Stefania with an eye roll.

Chapter 10
March 10, 40,000 feet above the Gulf of Mexico

Stefania propped her shoeless feet up on the polished wood table in front of her exposing her blue and red stripped socks. She sank her slim frame into the plush leather seat. Across the aisle sat Thomas napping, and facing him Greschenko kept an eye on both of them while listening to something through her earbuds. The loud monotonous hum of the jet engines was the only sound in the dim cabin.

"So what do you know that you're not telling us?" asked Stefania.

"What's that?" asked a clearly irritated Greschenko.

"You must have intelligence in Mexico, why not share it?" demanded Stefania. "Who are we going to tell?"

"What makes you think I have intelligence?" barked back Greschenko.

Stefania huffed and tilted her head back.

"Well let's see," she continued, now making eye contact with Greschenko. "Everything you are doing makes no sense, therefore, there must be a reason. We are not going straight to the border, which is the most logical thing to do. So what's your game?"

"Your good looks belie the fact that there's apparently a brain in that head of yours," snapped Greschenko. "A small one, but a brain nevertheless."

"So what's the deal?" again demanded Stefania. "I'm a captive audience, who am I going to tell and to what end? Like you I'm not interested in seeing innocent people being incinerated by a nuclear bomb."

"Naturally I have intelligence," responded Greschenko. "We've got information from our people on the ground as to the cartel transporting the box, timing, and the like."

"So you think the cartel couriers will just hand the box over to you?" asked Stefania.

"You are insatiably tedious," barked an irritated Greschenko. "The cartel is arrogant. They will not expect anyone to challenge them in their own territory. Unlike you westerners the Russian Federation gives two shits about sensibilities of the Mexican government or the cartels. We can be ten times as ruthless."

"I just hope it all goes to plan," responded Stefania. "Because if it doesn't, and the box gets across the border, you'll have some major splainin' to do."

"The box won't get across the border," Greschenko said loudly. "It won't get close."

"How can you be so sure?" asked Stefania, again smiling.

"I know," barked Greschenko.

"Ah huh," sneered Stefania with a hint of sarcasm.

"I can't understand how he can possibly tolerate you?" snapped Greschenko looking over at the sleeping Thomas.

"I can ask the same question about you," responded Stefania grinning.

"He has no choice *but to* tolerate me," replied Greschenko with a long drawn out smile, tilt of the head and raised brow.

"Huh!" grumbled Stefania, turning to the portal and gazing out into the night.

Unfortunately, she's right on that one, she thought.

Night, March 11, on the road North from Monterrey, Mexico

Stefania woke up from a brief nap. Her awakening didn't change the fact that she was still living something short of a nightmare. She sat imprisoned in the rear seat of a white SUV with tinted windows, as part of a three SUV caravan flying at high speeds up a road in rural Northern Mexico. Next to her sat Thomas, and in the front passenger seat Greschenko, next to Anatoly, the driver. They had been on the road for a good fifteen hours or so, heading north from Monterrey, stopping only for bathroom breaks and fuel. Inside the other two SUVs, one in front and one in back, five Russians each, eight men and two women.

Thomas and Stefania had to check into the resort in Monterrey for appearances sake and were able to clean up and change clothes. Expecting the arduous drive, Stefania changed into a new pair of comfy skin-tight black leggings, with a pink athletic top covered by a gray hoody, with sneakers. Her pony tail popped out of the back of a blue baseball cap she bought at the resort, with her trademark black shoulder bag at her side. Thomas dressed practically also, with khaki cargo pants, a light tan sweater, hiking shoes he purchased at the resort, and a tan windbreaker type jacket.

Despite being there against her will, Stefania looked on the bright side. The whole affair would make a great story, if she could tell it. Of course being with Thomas all this time reminded her of her last adventure with him, and the love which came and went, and her affection which lingered like fog over a valley at sunrise.

Other than the monotony of the drive, the whole ordeal excited her after all. They were picked up at the resort just after sunrise by the SUVs which were apparently driven up from the Russian Embassy in Mexico City. Occasionally Greschenko or Anatoly would break silence and talk in Russian on her satellite phone and on a small hand-held radio with the other SUVs.

Stefania took off her aviator style sunglasses and rubbed her eyes. The bright Mexican sun had now set and the filtered light of a half moon shown through light clouds, illuminating the barren mountains to the distant west. The headlamps reflected off dust blowing across the endless road in front of them.

Greschenko seemed ready for anything, wearing jeans, a white tank top covered by an oversize pull-over gray sweat-shirt, and what looked to be combat boots. Anatoly, likewise wore cargo pants, a pull-over windbreaker, combat boots, and a campaign hat. Greschenko had her signature Nagant, with an AK-47, its stock folded, wedged next to Greschenko's seat. Stefania saw Greschenko sneak an automatic pistol into the center consol.

Stefania poked Thomas's leg, and leaned her lips into his left ear.

"Remind me why we couldn't take a helicopter?" she whispered in Portuguese. "I mean I'm no spy, but wouldn't that be more practical. She must have a helicopter at her disposal."

Thomas smiled.

"Only she knows," he whispered back in Portuguese leaning towards Stefania and pointing to Greschenko. "What, you don't like road trips?"

"I heard 'helicopter,'" said Greschenko, looking back at Stefania. "While you two were doing nothing particularly relevant on the flight I was learning Portuguese on this app I found."

"So why are we driving hundreds of kilometers when I'm sure we could just fly by plane or helicopter?" asked Stefania. "The Russian Federation must have such resources at its command," she stated snidely.

"Who said I don't have a helicopter?" replied Greschenko. "A helicopter flying toward the border from the south would arouse the attention of the Mexican and the American authorities, who are constantly looking at drug and cartel operations in Northern Mexico. Also, depending on the terrain, we'll need a vehicle to transport the device. I'll bring in a helo for pick-up if and when necessary."

"See, she's got her reasons," said Thomas with a raised brow.

"So how do you figure we're going to get the box?" asked Stefania. "I mean if they are traveling as we are, they must have hours on us."

"Your tedious questions again," growled Greschenko looking up at the SUV's ceiling. "None of your God damned business!"

"I would surmise," whispered Thomas, "that if the couriers have no reason to be suspicious, they will stop for food, and probably rest for the night. I'll wager we are probably an hour or so from the border, but still a couple hours from the exchange time."

"It's just past midnight, so officially March twelfth," murmured Stefania. "So she probably figures we'll catch up to them at some point, probably tonight, since we've hardly stopped moving."

"There is probably a *hacienda* ahead where the couriers have camped for the night before embarking on the short trip to the border for the exchange," whispered back Thomas. "That's where she intends to get it. I'll also bet the Russians have surveillance at the border."

"I thought she said that would arouse suspicion?" asked Stefania softly.

Thomas pointed to the sky.

"Satellites," he whispered. "I'll bet she's getting nervous however. It clouded up before sunset."

"What about drones?" asked Stefania softly.

"I can't imagine that Russia has those assets close by, and Cuba's likely too far off," responded Thomas in a whisper. "Plus American radar would likely pick up a drone, especially a large one hovering over the border. They may have a mini-drone in one of the other SUVs if we get close."

"This all assumes she knows who and where exactly the couriers are," said Stefania softly with a snicker.

"Spot on," whispered Thomas.

"She seems awfully confident though," responded Stefania in English, loud enough for all to hear.

"I've got ears you know," barked Greschenko.

"Does one usually wear designer clothes to a confrontation with the *Cartel Del Norte*?" teased Stefania in Portuguese.

"One wears what one finds comfortable," replied Thomas in Portuguese with a smile, his silhouette illuminated by the dim dashboard lights from the front seat. "Why do beautiful women wear skin tight yoga pants knowing full well that any red blooded male will give them a look over, but then they get offended when that happens?" Thomas whispered in Portuguese.

"They're comfy," responded Stefania in Portuguese. "And some of us, assuming I fall within that category, don't mind the attention."

"Hmm," uttered Thomas.

"So I guess I'm a beautiful woman then?" said Stefania softly in Portuguese with a grin.

Thomas smiled.

"I *do* know that all the women were ogling at me at the *Sala Santa Cecilia* in Rome," whispered back Thomas.

"I don't remember that," murmured Stefania with a mischievous grin, her lips now barely touching Thomas' ear. "I *do* remember a certain duke eying me from top to bottom."

Thomas leaned into Stefania's ear. The warmth of his lips next to her lobe made her spine shiver.

"Yes," whispered back Thomas. "How would it have looked if I was the only man in the hall not giving you the once over?"

Stefania slid closer to Thomas, facing him, and placing her index finger on his cheek, slightly turning his head toward her. Her lips were now millimeters away from his.

"I do believe that's what you said then," she said softly.

"Sounds like something I might say," he whispered in reply, grinning. "Depending on the circumstances, of course."

"Of course," she whispered back.

Stefania looked beyond Thomas' face out the window of the SUV. The sky had darkened, the moon was gone, and no stars were visible. All that could be heard were the occasional bumps in the road.

Facing Thomas, Stefania leaned in a millimeter closer to his lips.

"So it only depends on the circumstances then?" she again whispered with a smile.

Her eyes closed and her lips moved to within a hair's width of Thomas'.

The truck started slowing, and then voices from the radio in Russian could be heard. The SUV screeched to a halt.

Stefania lurched forward and looked out the windshield. In front of the leading SUV two dark pick-up trucks blocked the road. Four dark clothed men stood in the road, with automatic rifles drawn at the lead SUV. Two others stood out the moon roofs of the pick-ups, and another two in the truck flat beds, all with weapons at the ready. The lead Russian vehicle pulled across the road, perpendicular to Greschenko's SUV.

"What's going on?" asked Stefania.

Greschenko did not answer.

"They don't appear to be *Federales*," said Thomas. "My guess is they are *Cartel del Norte*, and they mean business. Your lead driver is trying to block us from the line of fire."

Anatoly snatched the AK-47, unfolded the stock, and pulled back the slide. Greschenko took out her Nagant. Greschenko's radio telegraphed additional excited banter in Russian.

"Shit!" Greschenko yelped.

Thomas looked back.

"Crikey, they're behind us as well," he said.

"Aces," said Stefania sarcastically.

"You bloody well couldn't have assumed you'd make it through their territory without encountering them, did you?" asked Thomas excitedly.

More agitated Russian squawk blasted from the radio.

Greschenko yelled something to Anatoly in Russian.

Thomas put his hand on Stefania's shoulder and pushed her down. She looked between the seats, over the center console, out the windshield.

One of the cartel men walked over to the lead SUV.

"They're having a parlay," said Thomas.

A shot rang out.

The passenger side doors to the lead truck flung open and the Russians started shooting using the SUV as cover. Two of the cartel men dropped where they stood. Greschenko rolled her window down and opened the door. She leveled her pistol and took out one of the cartel men standing out of the moon roof of the pick-up truck to the right with a head shot, his upper torso now slumped onto the roof of the pick-up. Anatoly opened his door, crouched on the ground and started firing his AK-47 in short bursts at the closest truck.

Stefania opened the center console, took out the automatic pistol, and hid it under the back seat.

Like firecrackers, automatic weapons fire continued back and forth. The leading SUV sank to the left as its driver's side tires were shot out. A woman in the lead SUV jumped out of the rear passenger compartment, ran to the rear and fired something at one of the pickup trucks. Like a rocket it whistled through the night. She immediately collapsed onto the road, sprawled out. Glass shattered as the lead SUV was peppered with gunfire. An explosion rocked the pick-up truck to the left. Flaming debris fell around the roadblock. Three more cartel men fell, and a Russian from the lead SUV who had been firing over the hood hit the ground. A gunman jumped from the bed of one of the pickups and fled into the darkness. Another Russian from the lead SUV lobbed something over the hood at the pick-up on the right. A second later the pick-up's bed lit up, flipping the truck on its side. Now a raging blaze brightened the road in front. To the rear, a similar firefight could be heard, obscured by gun smoke.

Gunfire ended up front, but continued to the rear. Two Russians ran toward the rear with their AK-47's at the ready. Ahead the shot-up hulk of the lead SUV illuminated by the orange glow of the burning pick-up, the bodies of the cartel men littered the road around the roadblock. Thick black smoke from burning tires lofted into the night sky. An explosion in the back reverberated through the area.

"Another RPG," said Thomas.

Greschenko and Anatoly jumped back into the truck. She barked something at him in Russian. The truck swerved to the left side of the road into the desert, and lumbered around the burning and shot-up pick-ups and back onto the road. One of the Russian men walked around the site to each cartel men lying on the road, pumping short bursts of automatic gunfire into their bodies. A body stuck out of the sunroof of one of the enflamed pick-up, slumped over, black, charred and smoking, as the truck burned beneath him. The combined wretched stench of burning rubber, plastic, gasoline and flesh, wafted into Stefania's nose.

Greschenko gave another order into the radio in Russian. The truck accelerated and sped up the road.

"You're just going to leave those men and women behind?" asked Thomas.

"They know their duty," she responded calmly. "Hopefully the rear vehicle will be serviceable and they'll be able to catch up. Otherwise, they're on their own."

"Now I know why the Ukrainians referred to the Russian soldiers as 'orcs,'" responded Thomas. "They act as cannon fodder."

"We've lost time," said Stefania. "Will we be able to make it to the border in time?"

"Let me worry about that," responded Greschenko.

Greschenko took out her satellite phone. Words in Russian were exchanged.

"Shit!" Greschenko exclaimed.

"The clouds have obscured your satellite surveillance of the border exchange locale?" asked Thomas. "And the mini-drone was in one of the SUVs?"

Greschenko did not respond.

The radio squawked in Russian.

Greschenko yelled something in Russian and threw the radio onto the dashboard.

"I gather your troop didn't do so well and won't be rejoining us," snarked Thomas.

Greschenko scoffed.

"Left them behind to stave for themselves just like in Ukraine?" asked Thomas.

"Here?" interrupted Anatoly.

"*Da*," said Greschenko.

The SUV turned to the right on a well worn gravel road and accelerated up the road for about a mile when it came to a large adobe mission style dwelling. The SUV stopped several hundred feet from the home. Fifty or so feet ahead, the road turned into a paving stone driveway entering a compound through an ornate steel gate which was open. A fountain spewing water sat in a deserted courtyard in front.

"Stay here," ordered Greschenko.

"And where're we going to go exactly?" asked Stefania sarcastically.

Greschenko replied with a stare.

Anatoly turned the headlights off and shut the engine.

Greschenko and Anatoly stepped out of the vehicle, guns drawn, and walked up toward the *hacienda*.

"A safe house," said Thomas. "Lights are on, but I'll wager no-one's home."

"How far are we from the border?" asked Stefania.

"Not far," responded Thomas. "But my guess, having served in Afghanistan, is that the road to the border will likely be a tough and slow drive."

"Why is that?" asked Stefania.

"Because if it were easy, they wouldn't have chosen it," replied Thomas. "The Americans would monitor the location and it would be risky. On such roads it could take an hour to go a few miles, hiking might be quicker, but of course, we can't bring out a nuclear weapon in a steamer trunk on our backs."

Greschenko and Anatoly appeared out of the dark and jumped into their seats. Anatoly managed a quick k-turn and the SUV accelerated down the gravel track back to the main road.

"I gather they're not receiving guests?" asked Thomas.

Greschenko barked something Russian into the radio.

With a bump the SUV jumped back onto the main road with a jerk, and accelerated.

"It's 2 o'clock, we've got ninety minutes to make it to the border," said Thomas.

"I can tell time," snapped Greschenko.

"What road are we on?" asked Stefania.

"I believe we're on Mexico Federal Route 2," replied Thomas.

"It's getting mountainous," noted Stefania.

"Stop stating the obvious," barked Greschenko.

"Does Anatoly ever speak," asked Stefania.

"Yes, but mostly I observe," Anatoly retorted in perfect American English.

Greschenko said something to Anatoly in Russian. The SUV slowed.

"Turn right now," said Greschenko, pointing to a hardly visible dirt road to the right.

The truck took a slow turn onto the narrow rugged track.

Immediately Stefania noticed the bumps and jolts.

Thomas poked her side.

"Speed?" he whispered.

Stefania looked over Anatoly's shoulder.

"About twenty kilometers per hour," she whispered back.

Thomas nodded his head.

"This road is unforgiving," she said.

"So am I," sniped Greschenko.

Greschenko uttered something in Russian to Anatoly.

"*Nyet*," he responded.

The SUV plodded along up the road, seemingly taking forever to go a few hundred feet at a time, up steep hills, down through ravines and up along ridge lines. The light of the headlamps bounced off bushes and brush on either side of the track, some larger trees and cacti, some so close to the SUV that branches could be heard scratching the sides.

"This is treacherous country," said Thomas. "There is probably no border wall at this locale because it's so remote and difficult to get to that the Americans don't see much activity in this vicinity."

"It's 0320," whispered Stefania.

"Yes," whispered back Thomas. "We won't be there in time."

Greschenko looked up at the sky through the sun roof.

"Still cloudy," said Thomas.

"Can't satellites see through clouds?" asked Stefania softly.

"Not generally," whispered back Thomas. "Even if they did, I don't believe it could be done in real time."

"Won't we come face to face with the couriers on their way back out?" asked Stefania softly.

"Maybe," responded Thomas. "Unless..."

"Unless what?" asked Stefania.

"Unless there is another way out," replied Thomas with a shrug.

The SUV hemmed and hawed, seemingly taking hours to crawl its way up a steep ridgeline.

Stefania's cell phone showed it was 0342. She showed it to Thomas. He nodded.

The SUV stopped. Anatoly and Greschenko looked at each other.

"Shit!" she exclaimed, banging her fist on the dashboard.

Illuminated by the headlamp was single six foot tall white concrete obelisk. The trail split. One way veered to the left back toward Mexico, and the other straight.

"A border marker," whispered Thomas to Stefania.

"We've missed the exchange and the courier left that way," Greschenko said with some agitation, pointing to the left. "Let's get out and see if we can find anything."

It felt good to get out of the SUV. Stefania hadn't stretched in hours. Her kidneys had taken a beating. The cold night air hit her like a brick wall and shocked her into attention.

Whew, that's refreshing, she thought

She took a deep breath, a long stretch, and then turned on the flashlight on her phone and walked a few yards past the border marker. The headlights of the truck also lit up the area, the SUV's exhaust lingering in the chilly still night, as if a mysterious fog enveloped them all.

Shining her phone light on the ground in front of her, she noticed some impressions in the sandy desert pavement.

"Look here," she said. "Looks like quad tracks leading north."

Greschenko, Anatoly and Thomas ran over.

"I see," said Greschenko. "There are two sets of footprints leading to where the quad must have been parked. By the size, I'd say men's."

"And what are those?" asked Thomas, pointing his phone light at some other tracks. "They look like dog tracks, I'd say a medium size dog, between sixty and seventy pounds, but there are only three paw prints, and what's this odd fourth track?"

"I know what that is," exclaimed Stefania.

"Do share," said Greschenko, her hand on her hip.

"It's a dog with a brace on its hind leg," she said. "The brace has a rubber pad that slips under the hind paw and has ridges for traction. So you've got three paw prints and one brace print."

"Now how the hell do you know that?" demanded Greschenko.

"My college roommate's dog tore his Achilles tendon," said Stefania. "We had to take her to a special clinic in Morgantown, Pennsylvania, to have a brace fitted and constructed. The dog's injury was inoperable, and she couldn't have walked otherwise."

"And I thought I've heard everything," snapped Greschenko. "So we are looking for two men with a quad and a dog with a brace, in possession of a tactical nuclear device."

"Shouldn't be hard to locate," said Thomas with a snicker.

"I'll bet they took the quad to a larger vehicle, farther up the road across the border," said Stefania. "It would take them forever in an SUV, but faster by quad."

Anatoly grinned and then walked off.

Greschenko scoffed.

"Well what's the plan?" asked Stefania.

"Take a look," said Greschenko pointing to Anatoly.

Anatoly was busy removing the Mexican license plate from the SUV and replacing it with an Arizona tag.

"I guess we're going stateside," said Stefania.

"Seems like you've got a knack of guessing correctly DiMaggio," barked Greschenko.

"I'd call it more than a knack," said Thomas, smiling.

Stefania turned to Greschenko.

"Looks like you've got a 'Plan B,'" she stated.

"I've always got a 'Plan B," admitted Greschenko as she walked over to the SUV, opened the front passenger door and pulled out a small brown satchel from the glove box.

She unzipped the bag and handed Stefania a New York driver's license.

"What's this?" asked Stefania.

"Since we didn't enter this country legally, it's a New York driver's license identifying you as Stefania DiMaggio, with an address in a rental unit in New York City," said Greschenko matter of factly. "Thomas is again Mr. DiMaggio," she continued, handing him a New York driver's license.

"What if we get stopped and the police check these identities out?" asked Thomas.

"They'll check out," added Greschenko, again matter of factly.

"Right," said Thomas. "I dislike Americans and now I'm masquerading as one, how ironic."

"What about you and Anatoly?" asked Stefania.

"That's not your concern," responded Greschenko. "We're covered."

"So you figured that even if we didn't catch the couriers before they managed to get to the border, you'd have satellite information on their vehicle or you'd be able to launch a mini-drone to surveil the border," said Thomas.

"Yeh," chimed in Stefania. "But you didn't get that satellite data due to the overcast skies and the drone, well it got shot up by the cartel."

Greschenko scoffed.

"I've buried the Mexican plates, we're ready to go," piped in Anatoly now wearing a shoulder holster with his pistol in it. "Here," said Anatoly handing Greschenko a belt holster.

She took off her belt and adjusted the holster.

"Get in," ordered Greschenko.

The four got in and the SUV proceeded slowly past the border obelisk into southern Arizona, bouncing over a particularly large rut in the dirt trail.

Greschenko folded the stock of the AK-47, wedged the long gun between the front passenger seat and the console, and strapped her pistol into her holster.

"Don't you think it's a bad idea having your weapons in plain view?" asked Stefania.

"Hah," bellowed Greschenko, slapping her hand on the dashboard. "Something miss know-it-all doesn't know. Arizona is an open carry state, and Anatoly and I are law abiding citizens of the State of Arizona."

"Oh," responded Stefania with a smirk.

The radio squawked in Russian again, and Greschenko responded. She then turned the radio off and threw it in the glove box.

"Won't be needing that will you now?" asked Stefania.

"Just keep an eye out for a spot along the road where a larger vehicle could pull over and take delivery of the box," said Greschenko.

The SUV continued bouncing and plodding on the dirt road, sometimes barely larger than the width of the truck. Finally it went down a steep grade and crossed what appeared to be an *arroyo*.

The dim rays of sunlight started to creep above the eastern horizon.

"It looks like the overcast has moved to the east of us," noted Thomas.

"When do we get to a real road?" asked Stefania.

"We will be coming up on Guadalupe Canyon Road shortly," said Anatoly, looking at the SUV's satellite GPS system.

Sure enough, after crossing a dry creek bed the SUV came to an unpaved tan colored gravely road.

"This must be it," said Thomas.

"Look, there is a little sandy clearing to the left where the two roads meet," noted Stefania.

"Stop here," said Greschenko. "Let's see if there are any tracks in the clearing."

The foursome got out and walked over to the clearing. The cool morning air crept through Stefania's creaky bones after the jarring ride.

Greschenko stood a few feet away, her hands on her hips, the fog of her breath illuminated by the dim morning light.

"There are the quad tracks," said Stefania.

"And there are two sets of other tire prints," said Thomas pointing to the ground.

Greschenko and Anatoly walked up about twenty or thirty feet examining the tire impressions.

"It would appear to me that there was a larger vehicle towing a smaller trailer," she said.

"They must have put the quad on the trailer," said Stefania. "There are two sets of footprints and the three paw prints and the brace print."

"Yes, but they end mid-vehicle," said Thomas. "Very strange."

"It was an RV," said Stefania.

"What?" asked Greschenko.

"Think about it," she responded. "They've got a large trunk size box with a nuclear weapon in it. It has to be hidden."

"What better place to hide it than inside one of those big recreational vehicles Americans are so fond of," retorted Thomas.

"The only vehicle you enter midsection is an RV," added Stefania.

"An RV towing a quad would not attract much attention," agreed Greschenko. "But which way did it go?" she asked as she walked toward Guadalupe Canyon Road looking at the ground.

Stefania followed her, and crouched down, as the early morning sunlight cast shadows over the dessert terrain, enhancing the impressions in the sand.

"It went west, see," Stefania exclaimed pointing to the faint outline of the tire tracks exiting the lot and turning to the left.

"So they went back toward Arizona, as opposed to New Mexico which is just to the east," declared Greschenko rubbing her chin.

"What, no sarcastic remark?" asked Thomas.

"She's observant, that's all," responded Greschenko with a smirk.

"And she happens to be correct," said Thomas grinning at Stefania.

The breeze picked up and tossed a crumpled piece of paper by Stefania's feet. Instinctively, she snatched the paper before it blew away.

"What's that?" Thomas asked.

Stefania unfolded the paper.

"It's an internet printout of someplace called the Santa Maria Ranch Museum," replied Stefania. "Looks like it's not too far distant."

Stefania stuffed the paper in the side pocket of her ever-present large shoulder bag.

Greschenko picked up a piece of gravel and tossed it across the road and squatted down, her elbows on her knees, holding her forehead in her hands.

"What is to the west of consequence?" asked Stefania gazing to the west as the rising sun cast its early glow over the barren mountains, the sun now warming her back.

"Nothing," answered Greschenko, "and everything."

Chapter 11
Early Morning, March 12, East of Douglas, Arizona, USA

On the cloudless bright sunny day the SUV sped west on Guadalupe Canyon Road, kicking up torrents of tan mist in its wake.

"Not a car, not a soul, for thirty minutes," blurted Stefania.

"This *is* lonely country," said Thomas. "But remarkably beautiful."

"I've been taking photos when I can," responded Stefania. "The stark contrast between the mountains and the meadows is wonderful. And what was that herd of animals we saw?"

"Pronghorn," interrupted Greschenko. "A type of antelope I believe. I'm surprised you didn't know that DiMaggio."

Thomas turned to Stefania and grinned with a raised brow.

"Well there's a sign you don't see every day," noted Thomas, pointing to a brown sign, with white lettering, ahead.

"'Travel Caution Smuggling and Illegal Immigration May Be Encountered in this Area,'" read Stefania. "Well we're proof of that I suppose."

Stefania reached back into the well of the SUV and pulled out a bottle of water from a flat of water Anatoly had stowed there.

"You want?" asked Stefania, showing Thomas a bottle.

"Thank you," he responded taking the water.

"I've been drinking all the time, but haven't had to wee, unusual for me," remarked Stefania.

"Way too much information DiMaggio," said Greschenko in monotone. "There is very low humidity here. You raise a good point though. Good to keep hydrated. Pass me a bottle."

Stefania handed up a bottle to Greschenko.

"A vehicle is coming," said Anatoly in a monotone.

"I see," replied Greschenko.

Stefania looked over Anatoly's shoulder. Ahead a dust cloud got larger by the second. A white SUV barreled toward them.

Anatoly said something in Russian.

"Border patrol," said Greschenko, as if for Thomas and Stefania's edification.

The white Ford Explorer with a green chevron on the side slowed and drove by.

"Border patrol alright," said Thomas. "Two officers."

Stefania looked back. "They're turning around."

"Shit!" exclaimed Greschenko.

"Is that your trademark pejorative?" asked Stefania sarcastically.

Thomas smiled, and Anatoly grinned slightly.

"Lights on," said Anatoly.

Stefania looked back. The light bar on the roof of the Border Patrol SUV flashed red and blue, the headlamps flashed on and off as well.

The truck slowly stopped and the Border Patrol SUV pulled up behind. A male officer, tall, dark hair, tan skinned, mustache, emerged from the driver's side. A female officer, lighter skin, shorter, jet black hair, got out of the passenger side. She pulled out a large black dog from the back of the SUV. The two walked up to the respective sides of the SUV.

The male officer got to Anatoly first. "License and registration sir," he asked in what sounded like a south Texas drawl.

The female officer walked the dog around the SUV. It sniffed the outside of the vehicle. The officer then peered inside the cabin of the SUV, giving Greschenko, Stefania and Thomas a head to toe examination.

Anatoly handed the officer his license and vehicle registration.

"A bit far from Tucson this morning, aren't ya'll, ah, Mr. Anthony Harris?"

"Yes, officer," Anatoly replied, "we are sightseeing officer, ah, officer Ramos," obviously reading from the name tag on the officer's gray uniform.

"Sightseeing?" he laughed.

"We are from New York, we are visiting our friends here in Arizona," interjected Stefania. "We left early, drove down here and are on our way to see the Santa Maria Ranch Museum."

"You must've taken a wrong turn," said officer Ramos.

The female officer tapped Greschenko's window.

"Can I see your identification?" the female officer asked Greschenko.

Greschenko rolled the window down and handed her driver's license to the female officer.

"Mrs. Lana Harris from Tucson," she said. "How long have you lived in Tucson?"

"Ten years or so, ah, officer Gutierrez," Greschenko answered.

"I see ya'll are carrying," officer Ramos responded.

"Yes," Greschenko said.

Officer Ramos handed the license back to Anatoly and walked around the front of the SUV to Greschenko's side.

Stefania's heart started beating what seemed like a thousand times a second. Even though the open windows let in the cool March air, the sweat beaded on her forehead and under her arms and breasts. Her eyes and Thomas' eyes made contact. She wanted to ask, "what should we do?"

As if he knew she needed consoling, Thomas nodded.

"It'll be all right," he mouthed.

"I'm a collector," said officer Ramos. "What'd ya'll have there?"

"A Nagant M1895," said Greschenko somewhat proudly.

"Serviceable?" he asked.

"Of course," she responded.

"Mind if I take a gander?" he asked.

"Not at all," responded Greschenko.

She got out of the SUV, unclipped her holster and produced the revolver.

"Sweet," he said. "And I'd say in excellent condition. I've only read about these."

Greschenko smiled. "It was a gift from my grandfather. He fought in the great patriotic," she paused, "he fought in World War Two, and traded for it from a Soviet soldier."

"Do you two mind producing your identification?" asked Gutierrez, now talking to Stefania and Thomas.

"Not at all," Stefania and Thomas handed Gutierrez the New York drivers' licenses Greschenko had given them.

She stood looking the licenses over.

Stefania noticed that with all the activity on the passenger side of the vehicle, Anatoly slowly released the safety on his holstered pistol.

"Why all the firepower?" asked officer Ramos, pointing to the AK-47 next to the front seat.

"We wanted to show our friends here some of the sights in southern Arizona," said Greschenko. "But this is wild country, you never know who or what you are going to bump into whether it be man or beast."

"That's an understatement," said Gutierrez, handing back the licenses to Stefania and Thomas.

"Can we take a look in the back?" asked Gutierrez.

"Darling, can you open the hatch?" Greschenko asked Anatoly.

The back hatch popped open. Officer Gutierrez looked in. The dog sniffed the back of the SUV.

"Only a flat of bottled water and a backpack with a tool kit and first aid kit," she said and then closed the hatch.

Officer Ramos handed the revolver back to Greschenko and she got back into the SUV.

"Everything seems to check out," said Ramos to Gutierrez in Spanish in earshot of Stefania. "Just two *gringos*, and their wives."

"Sparky hasn't found any drugs, but I've got an uneasy feeling about these four," responded Gutierrez in Spanish. "I can't say what it is. The girl looks Latina. What kind of name is DiMaggio anyway?"

"Being she's a Yankee from New York, I'd say it's Italian," responded Ramos in Spanish. "Wasn't Joe DiMaggio Italian? That's her married name anyway. Oh hell, let's let'm go. We've got another half-hour and then we're off-shift."

Gutierrez looked at Stefania again.

"I'd like to arrest them just for being from New York," Gutierrez said in Spanish followed by a laugh.

Ramos laughed back.

Stefania struggled not to make eye contact.

"They're carrying a lot of heat," followed Gutierrez again in Spanish.

"Look where we're at," whispered back Ramos. "In Arizona, let alone in the middle of nowhere, plus her pistol's a God damned antique. It's not that unusual."

"I'm still skeptical," muttered back Guttierez in Spanish.

Stefania looked at Thomas. She understood them verbatim, knew they were close to being detained, and if that happened, a gunfight would surely ensue.

"You look like you're about forty, does your license have your birthday correct?" Gutierrez asked Stefania in Spanish.

"I'm sorry officer, I don't understand Spanish," Stefania responded.

"Never mind," Gutierrez replied waving her hand.

"Let'm go," Gutierrez told Ramos in Spanish. "She's clueless. Any Latina woman her age would challenge my statement assuming she understood it, especially with her looks. Let's lead them to the ranch, just to make sure that's where they're going."

"Sure, it's on our way," Ramos responded in English.

"A few miles up ya'll come to a 'T' in the road," said Ramos to Greschenko leaning on the passenger side door. "That'll be Geronimo Trail. Make a left and that'll take ya'll to the ranch museum. Ya'll have to leave the weapons in the car at the ranch, can't carry there. We're going that way so just follow."

"Thank you officer," said Anatoly.

"No problem," Ramos responded. "Ya'll have a nice day now, you hear."

Ramos and Gutierrez got into their SUV with the dog and pulled alongside the SUV. Gutierrez made a motion to follow them and the Ford headed west followed by a wall of dust.

"The oldest trick in the book," said Greschenko with a huff. "I'm shocked you handled it so well."

"What's that?" asked Stefania.

"She was testing you," said Greschenko. "She asked you a question in Spanish. Good thing you played dumb, although I'm sure it comes naturally."

"Yeh," snapped back Stefania. "And you almost said Great Patriotic War instead of World War Two. The officer didn't catch that gaff. Are you really a spy or is that just your day job?"

Greschenko scoffed.

"Unfortunately we have to waste time following the officers to this museum," said Greschenko. "I do have to thank you for coming up with an excuse, it probably not only saved us, but also saved the officers."

"Leaving two officers dead by the side of the road would not exactly maintain our cover," snapped back Stefania.

Greschenko scoffed again and folded her arms.

"Ladies," said Thomas. "Let's keep our collective minds on the task at hand. Unless you know something I don't, finding this RV was always going to be by a stroke of luck anyway."

"Yes," responded Greschenko. "But we know it went west, and based on the GPS, I'm betting it went west on Geronimo Trail toward Douglas."

"Why, pray?" Thomas asked.

"Just a feeling," Greschenko replied. "Why go back east toward New Mexico when they could have gone east on Guadalupe Canyon Road in the same direction?"

"Maybe Guadalupe Canyon Road is impassible or closed farther east," interrupted Stefania. "This is rough country, and RV might not be able to traverse the terrain."

"Perhaps," responded Greschenko. "But RVs use a ton of petrol. They don't know we're after them. They're not suspecting they're being followed. If I were them, I'd go back to Douglas, get petrol, maybe something to eat, and move on to wherever they are going."

"That's quite a wager," said Thomas. "You never struck me as the gambling type."

"I'd say, using my logic it's better than a seventy-thirty chance," responded Greschenko confidently.

"Time will tell," replied Thomas.

The Border Patrol SUV veered to the left at the intersection with Geronimo Trail.

Anatoly turned to Greschenko.

"Follow them," she said.

Anatoly nodded.

The border patrol SUV slowed as they came to an intersection. Ramos' arm protruded from the driver's side window and pointed toward the left toward a gravel road leading back east. High desert surrounded them.

"Give him a wave, and turn," ordered Greschenko.

Anatoly did as he was directed. After a few minutes they came to the ranch museum and Anatoly parked the SUV.

Anatoly said something to Greschenko in Russian.

"Let's step out and go through the motions," directed Greschenko. "In case the border patrol comes back, or we bump into them on our way out."

Anatoly and Greschenko got out of the SUV and started stretching. Thomas and Stefania followed suit.

The chill of the morning air now gone, the bright sun of the southwest desert warmed Stefania's face.

"Looks like we're right on the border," said Thomas, pointing to the border wall across a pasture area.

Stefania nodded.

Greschenko and Anatoly walked in the direction of the border wall for a closer inspection.

"It's like an oasis," said Stefania. "A beautiful oasis in a barren wilderness."

"Yes," agreed Thomas as they both walked toward a pond surrounded by trees and green grass. "I'm exhausted. Unlike you I didn't catch any sleep on the ride up to the border. It seems like I haven't slept in twenty-four hours."

"Try to sleep on our way out of here," she suggested.

"Easier said than done," he responded.

Stefania took her phone out.

"Let's take a selfie," she asked.

Her and Thomas merged with the pond in the background for a quick snap.

She turned her head toward Thomas for a moment, lingered, peering into his blue eyes, and smiled.

"This is a wonderful isolated place," said Thomas returning the smile. "It reminds me of the delightful solitude of the Seil Island."

"Other than the fact they are completely different, I kind of see your point," replied Stefania.

"I so miss Aunt Josephine," said Thomas solemnly.

"I'd only known her for an hour or so," replied Stefania quietly. "But I held her hand as she left this world, and I felt a strange sense of calm in her. She knew where she was going, and it didn't bother her. She passed with a smile on her face and a tear down her cheek."

"I remember," whispered Thomas. "Thank you for comforting her in her final minutes."

The two walked for several moments in silence.

"What are you thinking?" asked Stefania.

"Ha, that's a loaded question," replied Thomas. "It must be destiny that we seem to come together for these adventures. If they weren't so serious and potentially deadly, I'd say they were enjoyable."

"Thank you Thomas," said Stefania. "I enjoy your company too."

"I wonder how we'd get on under normal circumstances," pondered Thomas.

"We'd certainly have a lot of shared experiences," said Stefania with a laugh.

"That's an understatement," countered Thomas also with a laugh. "Let's check out the ranch buildings, shall we."

The couple walked towards the buildings.

"Greschenko and Anatoly are busy taking photos of the border wall," noted Stefania. "Figures."

The one-story white stucco ranch buildings, with green trim around the windows and doors, were clustered a stone's throw from the pond.

"The incredible natural beauty of this place makes up for its loneliness," remarked Stefania.

The two entered the main ranch building. Inside wood plank floors, and whitewashed walls greeted them, as well as a fieldstone fireplace.

A thin boney woman stood guard. She wore a red checked pattern flannel shirt and faded blue jeans held up by brown leather belt with a large turquoise and silver belt buckle. A black felt cowboy hat covered her head, and beat up cowboy boots made her seen a few inches higher than her short frame. Her short gray hair peaked out from under the brim of the hat, with a long braided pony tail down past her neck. A packet of cigarettes stuck out of her shirt pocket. Her tan, but wrinkled face, disguised her age.

She must be in her sixties, thought Stefania.

"'Mornin'" she said with a smile, nod, and tip of the hat.

"Good morning," replied Thomas for the both of them.

"The ranch is quite isolated," commented Stefania. "How many visitors do you have daily?"

"This time of year, not many, unless a tour group comes by," she responded in a raspy voice and a slight drawl. "It's early, today maybe ten or so cars in a day. You're the second group this mornin', although the first wasn't interested in much."

"Why do you say that?" asked Stefania as Thomas examined a cabinet with period mementos.

"A couple of fellas in an RV with a dog," she responded. "They let their pooch out to take a run and a shit. They filled their bottles from the well, and left. We get some who are just pass-throughs. I had to clean up for the pooch. Don't like to leave the dog shit lyin' around." The lady shrugged.

"What color was the RV?" asked Stefania.

"I donno," responded the lady. "Tan with some kind of stripe. They were haulin' a quad on a trailer. Why?"

"We might know them," responded Stefania. "What color was the dog?"

"She was a blackie," responded the women. "Cute thing, looked like a retriever dog, seemed friendly enough too. She had some kinda contraption on her hind leg."

"What about the owners?" asked Stefania.

"Darlin', you *sure* do ask a lot of questions," replied the lady shaking her head. "But I don't mind the conversation. Anywho, two fellas, one kinda looked, you know, Indian. Short hair cuts. They'd tattoos on their arms."

"Age?" asked Stefania.

"I can't tell age on young folks anymore darlin', maybe late twenties, early thirties?" she said with a shrug.

"When did they leave?" she asked.

"Less than a half-hour or so ago," the lady responded.

"Did they say anything?" she asked.

"Not much," the lady responded. "They did ask for a good place to get some grub in Douglas. I told 'm about the Gadston Hotel."

"Is that where they went?" asked Stefania.

"Can't imagine," the lady replied. "It's a fancy place, you know sit down, and they just didn't seem the type."

"Do you mind me asking how old are you?" asked Stefania.

"A hair shy of eighty-eight," said the lady.

"You look maybe twenty years younger," responded Stefania. "What's your secret?"

"Kept away from men," she said. "That's my advice," pointing to Thomas. "I've got no use for 'm. Kill ya every time. Heartbreakers, every single one of 'm. Oh, and a shot of Black Jack before bedtime, home cooked meals, home grown beef, church every so often, thank the Lord for what I've got, sleep with a pistol next to my pilla, and hard work on my family's ranch a few miles up the road. That's what I call clean livin'."

"Thomas," said Stefania in a loud voice. "Let's go out and look at some of the outbuildings."

"Right," said Thomas.

"So nice to speak with you," said Stefania to the lady. "Thanks for your advice."

"Pleasures all mine," she replied with a slight wave. "Thanks for stopping in y'all. *Adios*."

After they exited the door Stefania walked quickly a few feet on the wrap-around porch toward one of the other ranch buildings and rounded the corner.

Thomas caught up.

"My, you're eager to view the place," said Thomas.

"That's not it," Stefania whispered. "As much as I hate to admit it, Greschenko was right. According to the lady inside they left here about a half-hour ago. Two dudes, a black dog in a tan RV with a quad in tow."

"That'll make Greschenko go bonkers," whispered back Thomas. "We had best tell her. Let's hit the loo first though. She's liable to leave in a rush and who knows the next time we'll stop."

"Okay, let's meet by the truck," said Stefania.

Stefania bumped into Thomas as they exited the bathrooms.

"Greschenko and Anatoly are already in the truck," said Stefania, looking at the parking area. "Let's go."

The two trotted up to the SUV. Stefania jumped in the back seat followed by Thomas.

"Let's move," barked Greschenko. "Drive toward Douglas."

The SUV backed quickly and sped down the gravel road west, kicking up small stones and huge clouds of dust in its wake.

"Ah, Greschenko," said Stefania.

"What DiMaggio?" she replied curtly.

"The odds *are* in your favor," she said.

"What do you mean?" asked Greschenko.

"I spoke with the lady in the museum," responded Stefania. "They were here."

"What?" asked Greschenko, now turning around in her seat looking at Stefania.

"We're looking for two men, one possibly Asian, tattooed arms, in a tan RV, stripe down the side, hauling a quad, with a black retriever dog," said Stefania. "Left here about a half-hour ago. They were asking about a place to eat and the lady referred them to the Gadston Hotel in Douglas, but she didn't think they went there."

"So they've got a little more than thirty minutes on us," said Greschenko, rubbing her chin. "Anatoly, speed it up."

Stefania looked at her phone.

"Looks like it's going to take about thirty minutes to get to Douglas from here," said Stefania.

"Shit," mumbled Greschenko.

"You know," said Stefania with a grin. "There are several other equivalent pejoratives in English, including 'piss,' 'crap,' and 'damn it.' You might want to change it up a bit."

Greschenko grumbled something in Russian.

"You don't want to know what that means," said Anatoly with a smile.

"I can hazard a guess," said Thomas, winking at Stefania. "I must say, you are handling this whole situation rather lightly."

"After our adventure last year, I'm toughened up a bit," retorted Stefania. "Also, I think Papa is watching over me. I pray for his intersession."

"I didn't know he'd passed," responded Thomas.

"He died during the COVID epidemic in Italy," replied Stefania with a slight frown.

"I'm so sorry," said Thomas softly, touching Stefania's arm ever so slightly.

"It's okay," said Stefania in a low voice. "I've come to grips with it. Papa got sick, and two days later he left us. The worst part is I couldn't be with him when he passed in the infirmary. He couldn't receive the last rites. I still live in the flat we shared. I've never touched any of his things. They remain where he left them. Not a day goes by without being reminded of him."

"I know how you feel," said Thomas. "Although I never knew them, I feel my mum and dad watch over me, and Aunt Josephine as well."

"The passing of your Aunt Josephine was a dramatic event for us all," said Stefania. "That day will be etched in my memory forever."

Anatoly said something in Russian.

"Go straight to the hotel, but drive around the block, let's see if we see the RV," said Greschenko.

"Buildings," said Stefania.

"And people," said Thomas. "We've reached civilization."

"My phone says we are in Douglas," said Stefania.

Anatoly made a right here, and a left there, and then turned down a boulevard.

"'G Avenue,'" said Stefania. "What an anonymous street name."

"Here it is, on the right," said Anatoly.

A large tan and brown three story building stood at the street corner. A green awning welcomed visitors.

"The Gadsden Hotel," said Anatoly, pointing to the building. "I'll go around the block."

"No sign of an RV with a trailer, or any RV for that matter," said Stefania.

"We'll go in to make sure they're not here," said Greschenko. "DiMaggio, you and I will go in."

"Why me?" Stefania asked.

"Why not?" Greschenko replied.

Stefania turned to Thomas and shrugged.

"Let us out and drive around the block again and then wait for us in front," directed Greschenko.

The two got out of the SUV and entered the old hotel.

"Wow!" exclaimed Stefania. "This is not what I expected."

She now stood in a brown marble columned lobby, with brown marble floors and a grand white marble staircase. A stained glass skylight filtered the sunlight into the elaborate space, with room-wide stained glass scene from the old west just at the top of the stairs.

"I find that small town America holds many hidden gems like the ranch and this hotel," replied Greschenko. "The Americans on the coasts would rather travel abroad than visit the wonders of its interior."

"Here," Stefania pointed toward a restaurant.

The two walked into a nicely appointed dining room, with marble floors and wine racks along the walls. The restaurant bustled with diners, and wait staff dodged around Stefania and Greschenko.

"He must be the *maitre d'*," said Stefania pointing to a short older balding gentleman with a gray mustache, wearing a gray suit, blue shirt and striped tie standing next to a podium.

"Hello," said Stefania.

"Would you like a table?" he asked. "There's about a thirty minute wait."

Stefania looked at her phone.

"It's only 1130," she said. "Is it always this crowded for an early lunch?"

"Not typically," he responded. "A lot of folks are in town for the musical festival outside of Tombstone, north of here."

"This is the only place to stay?" Stefania asked.

"They either stay here, in Tucson or Bisbee, or in Tombstone at one of the two hotels there or at the RV park," answered the *maitre d'*.

"The RV Park," Stefania said looking at Greschenko.

The two rushed out through the marble lobby and out the front door and jumped into their respective seats in the SUV.

"Well?" asked Thomas.

"There's an RV park in Tombstone apparently," said Greschenko. "They might be there."

Stefania typed in "music festival in Tombstone" on her phone.

"Hmm" said Stefania.

"What makes you go 'hmm'?" asked Thomas.

"The *maitre 'd* said that the restaurant was crowded because of a music festival outside of Tombstone,'" answered Stefania.

"Right," said Thomas. "And."

"It's a three day musical festival outside of Tombstone in the desert starting later today," responded Stefania. "Thousands of people attend, apparently in costume. Many camp in one square mile of flat sandy desert for three days, in tents, campers, and RVs. My favorite Indie band will be performing on the last day with many other headliners. Many celebrities make appearances at this thing."

"So you think the RV is going to this festival," responded Thomas.

"Yes, but," said Stefania.

"But what? asked Thomas.

"What if they are going to detonate the nuclear device at the festival?" Stefania pondered in a soft voice. "What if they are going to detonate the nuclear device at the festival?" Stefania repeated louder, more confidently.

Anatoly turned to Greschenko. Greschenko turned back to Stefania. Her face evinced shock.

A tingling sensation ran up Stefania's spine to her neck and down her arms.

"An RA-115 device is a tactical weapon, most effective in close proximity to hardened targets," said Greschenko solemnly. "It would be incredibly deadly detonated in an open landscape, with few if any hardened structures, against thousands of people congregated in two square kilometers of flat, featureless desert."

"Would they be able to get it in?" asked Stefania. "Wouldn't the RV be searched?"

"Maybe," said Greschenko. "But probably not searched with a Geiger counter. It would be the perfect camouflage. If it were discovered, they could easily dispatch any officers and then set it off, still killing thousands. Like the highway attack in New Jersey, it's probably a suicide mission anyway."

"My God," murmured Stefania.

"Indeed," whispered Thomas with a rub of the chin.

"How do we get to this festival?" asked Greschenko.

Stefania looked at her phone.

"Says take Route 80 north through Tombstone and then make a right on East Yacenda Road just outside of town," said Stefania. "It's several miles down East Yacenda in the middle of the desert. The RV park is just before East Yacenda on the left. One minor thing we ought to be aware of, though."

"What's that?" asked Greschenko.

"There's a border patrol checkpoint just north of Yacenda at the intersection of Routes 80 and 82," said Stefania. "Let's keep that in mind."

"Right," said Thomas.

"What did Souchev say?" asked Greschenko. "The delivery needed to be made by March fifteenth."

"The last day of the festival," said Stefania. "That's when all the headliners perform."

"That must be when they intend to detonate it," added Thomas.

"Unless they're forced to take action sooner," uttered Greschenko softly.

"Anatoly, step on it," she ordered. "We need to find them before they're forced to set it off."

"We need to stop for petrol," he said.

"Find the next petrol station then," barked Greschenko.

"Shouldn't we notify the American authorities?" asked Stefania prior to realizing the preposterous nature of her inquiry.

"DiMaggio, if you are right about this musicfest attack, I'll take back everything I've ever said about you," said Greschenko with a raised brow. "We'll whipe the slate clean. But your last statement, oh yes, that'll work. 'Hello 911, I'm a Russian spy illegally in the country, and I think there may be two dudes in an RV with a nuclear weapon and a crippled dog who want to blow up a concert venue.'"

"I guess that's not going to work," replied Stefania.

"You think?" blurted Greschenko.

After topping the gas tank off, the SUV flew west on Highway 80 toward Tombstone.

"We should be in Tombstone in less than an hour," said Stefania.

No one replied.

Stefania glanced toward Thomas. His head lie against the interior window, his eyes tightly shut and his dirty blonde hair slightly askew. His deep breaths were followed by long exhales. Thomas' arms crossed, as if frozen in time, stubbornly resisting a point of view during a robust conversation. Beyond his silhouette, out the window the desert terrain flew past. Drab tan moonscape interrupted every so often by sagebrush, an errant cacti, agave, or a lonesome homestead in the middle of nowhere.

Somehow this brought Thomas down to her level, thought Stefania. *Here's a British Duke, important and rich beyond belief, held prisoner to exhaustion like the rest of us, being held captive on the threat of blackmail.*

Stefania always put Thomas on a pedestal. After the events of two years ago, she resolved he couldn't be forgiven for that transgression. Yet, she thought about him from time to time. Every once in a while he'd pop up in her dreams. Those feelings, kept at bay on purpose, percolated to the top every now and again. Like now.

She stood on that windswept heath at Haverford Hall that warm June day two years ago when he expressed his undying love for her.

What did he say, "my heart will always be yours," or something equally as romantic.

I hesitated, she thought. *Why did I hesitate?* She asked herself. *Insecurity, vanity, pride, maybe; then it all fell apart.*

She let out a long deliberate sigh.

Greschenko turned around.

"Not up to the task DiMaggio," she asked in her usual snide way.

"I'm fine, as long as you are," Stefania responded.

"I'm alright," responded Greschenko. "I'm just not that keen on getting vaporized in a nuclear conflagration. Anatoly, how about you?"

Anatoly shook his head and said "*Nyet.*"

"What's the plan?" asked Stefania.

"What do you mean?" hissed Greschenko.

"What's the plan once we get to Tombstone?" repeated Stefania sarcastically. "Don't you have one?"

"We'll check out the RV park first," said Greschenko condescendingly. "Then proceed to the musicfest and see if we can find this RV."

"What if we do find it?" asked Stefania.

"We'll incapacitate the occupants, get the key to the box, terminate them, and deactivate the bomb if possible, and dispose of it," responded Greschenko. "It may have to be buried in the southwestern America desert temporarily, or taken back across the border into Mexico. I'll obtain orders for certain when the time comes."

"You say it with such a sterile tone," said Stefania. "What if we don't find it in time?"

"Then we'll see a brief flash of light," responded Greschenko with a shrug. "It'll be quick."

"Aces," said Stefania under her breath. "Looks like we're approaching Tombstone," she now said out loud.

"I see," responded Greschenko. "The RV park will be on the left after we leave town."

"Traffic," said Anatoly.

"Crap!" exclaimed Greschenko.

"At least you are changing it up a bit," Stefania said snidely. "All this traffic is because of the musicfest."

"Stick to telling me things I don't know," snapped Greschenko. "What time does this musical thing start?"

"The first concert is at 1900, but they start letting in attendees around 1400," replied Stefania. "It's closing in on 1300 now, so I imagine everyone is getting in line for admittance."

"Ah, finally, we're moving," said Greschenko. "There it is, turn here," she ordered.

The SUV turned left into the RV park, a gravely lot, interspersed with short trees, and RV slots.

"It's packed," said Stefania.

In one of the spots sat a detached trailer with a quad on it.

"Look there," exclaimed Stefania pointing. "That's an ATV two seater, with rear cargo deck. More than big enough to carry two men, a dog and a trunk size case."

"Shit!" exclaimed Greschenko pounding her fist against the dashboard. "The RV's gone."

"Back to 'shit' again," said Stefania. "It's probably on line to get into the festival, assuming we're following the right RV."

"Anatoly, step on it," shot Greschenko.

The SUV screeched out of the RV park back into the slow moving line of cars, RVs and SUVs heading toward the festival. In a couple hundred feet Anatoly made a right turn onto East Yacenda Road, a straight as an arrow flat gravel track through the desert seemingly heading to the gray mountains on the eastern horizon.

"So how do you know so much about quads?" asked Anatoly, in a rare breach of his perpetual silence.

"My cousin has a ranch in Brazil," responded Stefania. "They have quads."

Greschenko turned to the back seat and rolled her eyes.

After about five miles the slow moving caravan came to a dead stop.

"How far are we from the entrance?" barked Greschenko.

"According to the festival map, maybe a mile," replied Stefania.

After a few moments Greschenko took her revolver out of its holster, reloaded, and then checked the clip on the AK-47. Anatoly did the same with his sidearm. She opened the center console.

"Where the hell's my forty-caliber semi-automatic?" she yelled.

Thomas still sleeping, awoke. Groggy, he looked around.

"Where are we?" he asked.

"We're on the road to the festival entrance, stuck on line apparently," replied Stefania.

"Where's the forty?" Greschenko demanded.

"Oh that," responded Stefania. "I placed it under the seat for safe keeping. I wanted to be armed in case something happened with those border patrol agents."

"Yeh, and I've got some prime land to sell you in the Pinsk Marshes," responded Greschenko. "Give it to Thomas. Good thing it wasn't seen when the border agents stopped us, it's a ghost pistol. Everything else we have is legit. Owned by my husband here and me, law abiding citizens of Arizona," she said, looking at Anatoly.

"No identification, no serial number, untraceable," commented Thomas.

She grabbed a belt holster out of the center counsel and threw it at Thomas. It landed on his lap.

"Right," said Thomas. "What's the plan?" he asked as he strapped the holster to his belt, and holstered the pistol.

"Anatoly, pull over onto the side of the road," Greschenko ordered. "We could be in this queue for hours. We'll have better luck on foot."

"Wait, police," said Anatoly looking into his side-view mirror.

"They're coming up fast," added Thomas, straining to look back over his left shoulder.

Stefania jumped onto Thomas' lap and opened the window to get a better view.

A caravan of siren blaring SUV's, red and blue lights flashing, could be seen coming up behind them in the wrong direction in the vacant left hand lane.

First an unmarked black Tahoe, tinted windows, lights flashing flew by, followed by a white Cochise County Sheriff's pickup with a green chevron on the front fender. Then two black Range Rovers, tinted windows, with no lights, followed by another black Tahoe and a white Sheriff's pick-up truck.

"Must be VIPs," said Stefania.

The caravan disappeared into the distance.

"Anatoly," barked Greschenko.

The big SUV swerved to the right, and crawled up a small sandy berm on the side of the road. After a couple of large bumps, Anatoly parked the SUV in the desert about ten feet off of the roadway, between a large agave and a mesquite tree. A cloud of dust engulfed the truck as it stopped.

Greschenko grabbed something out of the glove box.

"Here," Greschenko said as she handed a cigarette pack sized black hand-held two way radio to Stefania. "Press the black button on the side to speak, release to hear." She then gave one to Anatoly.

They all jumped out of the SUV.

Stefania's lungs filled with the dry desert air, as a gust of wind tossed her pony tail about. She took a long stretch.

"It's possible the RV got behind us somehow," barked Greschenko. "By now there's probably forty or more vehicles back there. Anatoly you go back, and let us know if you find the RV. I'll be with these two and we'll go forward. Catch up to us if you don't find anything."

Anatoly ran off down the road behind the SUV.

Greschenko's satellite phone rang.

"Shit," she exclaimed. "I've got to take this."

Stefania raised a brow.

"She's really got to vary her pejoratives," whispered Stefania to Thomas with a grin. "She can't say I didn't give her some options."

Thomas laughed.

Greschenko blathered on in Russian into the phone and turned away from the two, toward the SUV.

Stefania jerked her head forward toward the long line of SUVs, cars and RVs in front of them.

"Common, let's go," she whispered again to Thomas, motioning forward with her head.

Thomas hesitated.

Sensing freedom, and an adrenaline rush, Stefania ran off along the long line of vehicles.

"Tan RV with a stripe, Asian dude, black dog with a leg brace," she repeated to herself.

"Wait," yelled Thomas who caught up to Stefania after about six vehicles.

Stefania slowed her pace to a fast walk.

"VW, Jeep, red van, gray RV, white RV, camper," she said as she trolled up the queue along the road.

"A tan RV with a stripe ahead," said Thomas pointing.

They approached the RV slowly.

"It's not ours," said Stefania. "No trailer hitch."

"Brilliant," responded Thomas with a smile.

"We must've gone by thirty or forty by now," said Stefania, as she stopped with her hands on her hips, catching her breath. She turned to her left at a red convertible Mustang with four college-age girls in costume bouncing around to loud music.

"Thirty-eight to be exact," said Thomas.

Something caught her attention out of the corner of her eye. She snapped her head forward.

"Did you see that?" she asked.

"See what?" replied Thomas.

"I thought I saw some guy with a black dog on a leash up ahead," said Stefania.

Stefania dashed ahead past ten more vehicles and stopped just behind a tan RV sporting a yellow and blue stripe down the side, with a trailer hitch. She walked over to the side of the road, bending down she examined the sandy dirt on the side of the road.

Footsteps from behind approached.

She turned.

Whew, it's Thomas.

"This is certainly the first RV which fits the description," whispered Thomas. "Even has a trailer hitch."

"Look," whispered Stefania back as she pointed to the sandy dirt on the road shoulder.

"Dog tracks," said Thomas. "One foot with a brace."

"What do we do?" asked Stefania. "Radio Greschenko?"

A metal latch opened behind her, then the creek of a door opening.

Standing in the doorway of the tan RV was an Asian looking man, clean shaven, muscled, mid-twenties, with a crew cut, black t-shirt, khaki shorts, sneakers.

His brown eyes caught hers. They lingered for a second.

This dude is up to no good.

His eyes shifted to Thomas, still examining the tracks, then to the door his left hand held open.

As if in slow motion he stepped back and started closing the door.

Stefania spun toward the man and landed a kick to his legs knocking him onto his back inside the RV. She fell back onto the roadbed. The RV door hit Stefania's leg and bounced open, now flush against the side of the RV.

"Crikey!" Thomas exclaimed.

The man scrambled to his feet, attempting to grab the doorknob from the inside of the RV.

Thomas jumped into action, ran in and tackled him onto the floor. The two rolled back and forth on the RV's blue carpet. The man tried to reach for Thomas' pistol.

Stefania clambered through the door. No sooner than she did, a figure jumped her from the right side. Now in a chokehold, she struggled. A hairy thick forearm wrapped itself around her neck. Heavy breathing, and warm moist breath coated her left ear. She kicked back. Her feet no longer on the floor, consciousness crept away.

In the center of the RV Thomas now held the Asian man in a full nelson. Stronger and bigger than Thomas, Thomas barely held his own.

"Thomas," she softly screeched with what seemed like her last breath.

She had another in her.

"Thomas," she rasped.

The arm pulled tighter. A scallop tattoo inked its wrist. It blurred.

Thomas released the Asian man and pulled out the pistol. With a blast from four feet away a bullet rocketed by Stefania's ear and into the cheek of the man who held her. His warm blood spattered onto her face and hair. The arm which held her so tight, seconds from choking the life out of her, suddenly went limp. The body with the arms fell to the floor with a thud. Stefania landed on top of him, her ears ringing.

Thomas turned.

The Asian man kneeled over an opened stainless steel trunk in the middle of the RV's floor to the left of the doorway. With a look of concentration, he put his right hand in the trunk, pulled it out, and then shut the lid with a click.

A muffled gunshot rang out, this time from the doorway. The man crumpled to the floor. A synthetic beep, like a muffled alarm clock being set, sounded. Only a second long, it seemed like forever. Blood trickled down a small hole in the back of his head. A shorter beep continued every second for ten seconds, like a stopwatch, then stopped.

Greschenko walked through the door, pistol next to her side with a silencer attached, shot him again in the head, kicked the Asian man in the ribs and checked the box lid.

"Shit!" she exclaimed. "It's locked."

Stefania stood up, still gasping for air, and staggered over to the box, peering at the key lock. She snatched a key chain from the pocket of her leggings, inserted one of the keys into the lock, and turned it to the left.

An audible "click" could be heard, and the lid popped, slowly rising to the open position like a car trunk.

Greschenko's head cocked slightly, a stunned look greeted Stefania.

"It's the unknown key from Smith," said Stefania in a raspy voice, with a shrug. "It looked like the right size so I tried it. You took the same key off Chen."

Greschenko looked into the trunk.

"It was pre-set for thirty minutes. He armed it," she declared.

"Aces," said Stefania followed by a hack.

Dispensing with the lecture Stefania would have expected, Greschenko barked, "Let's get this thing moving. Go back the way we came. Go across Route 80 onto West Yacenda. We've got to get at least twenty kilometers from here, and then we have to have enough time to get at least twenty kilometers away. Move now!"

She calmly closed the door to the RV and started barking orders into her radio in Russian presumably to Anatoly.

Thomas searched the Asian man's shorts' pockets.

"It's in the ignition," said Stefania now sitting on the floor next to the trunk, pointing.

"You know I'm horrible driving on the right side of the road," said Thomas.

Greschenko rolled her eyes.

Stefania gasped for breath, holding her neck.

"OK, I'll drive," she said righting herself, breathing heavily.

She started the RV, backed it up slightly, and then did a u-turn and headed back west.

Greschenko sat next to the steel trunk and spoke animatedly in Russian on her satellite phone.

She hung up.

"Once armed there is no way to disarm it," she said. "As I suspected, if we cut the power, it goes off. DiMaggio, I never took you for a slow poke, move it, all the traffic is in the oncoming lane."

Stefania turned for a second to reply and for the first time noticed a black long haired retriever dog, lying down in a crate behind the driver's seat, with its head on the floor next to a red and green rope toy, a red bandana around her neck.

"Thomas, that dog looks just like your Connie," she said.

"So she does," replied Thomas. "She's a flat coat, an English breed."

Thomas coaxed the dog out of the crate, and it immediately sidled up to the driver's seat next to Stefania, and sat down.

"The dog tag says her name is Carmen," said Thomas. "That's one of my favorite operas. She's taken a liking to you."

"There's no accounting for taste," murmured Greschenko.

As the RV flew west on East Yacenda, horns sounded and behind them emerged the SUV, with Anatoly behind the wheel, into the maelstrom of dirt whipped up by the RV.

"Good, Anatoly's following," said Greschenko. "He's our lifeline."

"What are you doing Thomas?" she demanded.

"I'm searching him," he said. "He's not Asian like the other one."

"Find anything?" asked Stefania.

"Yes, a UK driving license," responded Thomas. "Says his name is Devon Harrop from York, that's odd."

"Why is it odd?" she asked.

"Well Harrop is an unusual sir name, although I believe it does originate from Chesire," replied Thomas.

"This guy's name is Giles Manhire," interrupted Greschenko. "His driver's license says he lives in Sahuarita, Arizona. There's also an identity card saying he's a member of a reservation community, whatever the hell that means. I assumed he was Asian."

"It means he's a native American," interjected Stefania, turning back slightly from her duties as driver. "He's not Asian. The lady at the ranch said he was Indian, but I assumed she meant Asian Indian."

"I think these are genuine," said Thomas. "I don't believe they're traveling under assumed identities."

"Now why would nuclear terrorists do that?" asked Greschenko.

"Because they figured they'd be incinerated so what difference would it make," exclaimed Stefania from the driver's seat. "It's unlikely that anyone could trace the attack to them directly."

Thomas patted the dog on the head and under the ears, and took a look at her collar again.

"The dog's tag has an address in Sahuarita, Arizona, and has the owner as Giles Manhire," blurted Thomas.

"If we survive this, then we'll investigate," snapped Greschenko.

The RV sped west past the line of vehicles heading east.

"We're at Route 80," said Stefania. "I'm going across onto West Yacenda, but we've got a problem."

"We've got a lot of problems," barked Greschenko. "Be specific!"

"There isn't much gas left in this thing," responded Stefania. "Says it'll go another five more miles or so."

Stefania looked down at the GPS screen on the RV's console.

"That may be enough," responded Greschenko. "Just get us as far as it'll go."

"Where does West Yacenda go?" asked Thomas.

"Into the desert," Stefania said at the same time as Greschenko.

"It turns to the northwest and connects with Route 90 ultimately," said Stefania.

"These clowns weren't armed," said Greschenko. "Their phones are burners, and other than their id's there's not much here of significance, other than the dog and some beer and frozen tacos in the fridge."

Thomas saved me. Stefania thought, as if waking from a trance. *He could have left me to die. He risked his life for mine.*

She grinned from ear to ear.

The fuel gauge bounced at empty. The engine started to lose power. The RV bucked a few times.

"Pull it over if you can!" barked Greschenko.

Stefania pulled the gear shift to neutral and glided the RV to a stop on the side of the gravel road. Anatoly and the dirty SUV pulled in front.

Greschenko looked into the stainless steel trunk.

"DiMaggio start your phone's stopwatch now," she ordered.

"Done," said Stefania.

"We've got twelve minutes," said Greschenko. "Get out, quickly and get in the truck!"

Stefania instinctively put the RV keys into her pocket and with Thomas and Greschenko, jumped out the side door to the RV, with the dog in tow, on a leash held by Thomas.

Stefania and Thomas jumped into the rear seat of the SUV.

Greschenko banged on the rear passenger side window.

"What?" asked Stefania as she opened the window.

"Give me the keys," demanded Greschenko.

"Why?" asked Stefania.

"Just give me the damned keys," Greschenko hissed.

Stefania slapped the keys into Greschenko's right hand.

Greschenko locked the side door to the RV and got into the front passenger seat of the SUV.

"Always lock the door behind you," said Greschenko curtly.

The SUV sped off trailed by a storm of dust.

"Quickly Anatoly, as fast as you can go," said Greschenko. "We've got less than twelve minutes to try to get twenty kilometers away."

"Some vegetation ahead," said Anatoly.

"My phone says it's the San Pedro River," said Stefania.

The SUV slowly crossed the dry wash, shaded by small trees and shrubs, and picked up speed again and headed northwest.

"There's a slight rise ahead," noted Thomas.

"How much time do we have DiMaggio?" asked Greschenko.

"A little more than two minutes," replied Stefania.

"Pull off behind this slight rise, it may shelter us," ordered Greschenko.

"We've gone a little more than eighteen kilometers," Anatoly added.

The SUV turned right into the desert. Stefania bounced about as Anatoly went as fast as he could given the rough terrain.

After a minute, Greschenko declared, "This is about as good as we are going to get. Park parallel to this little ridge line, and let's get out. How much time?"

"Seventy seconds," replied Stefania.

They all hurried out of the SUV. Just east of them rose a craggy outcropping of tan and gray rocks, speckled with short cacti, and a few short shrubs and trees.

"Which way would you say the breeze is blowing?" asked Greschenko.

"Southwest to northeast, its light, but it's there," replied Thomas.

"Sit on the ground on the passenger side of the truck behind the tires, shut your phones off completely, and cover your eyes," Greschenko ordered.

Thomas took the bandana from around the dog's neck and wrapped it around her eyes.

"Won't the EMP fry our phones and the SUV's electronics?" Thomas asked.

"I'm not going to argue the matter with you Thomas, and what does it matter at this point," said Greschenko somewhat calmly. "With devices ten KT or less EMP is less effective, turning the phones off should work, and a ground blast is less disruptive than an airburst. The SUV should be safe."

"What's EMP?" asked Stefania.

"Electromagnetic pulse," replied Thomas. "No time to explain."

In the bright sunlight Stefania sat on the desert pavement, her back against the rear tire of the SUV. She turned to Thomas.

Greschenko sat next to Anatoly, their backs to the truck's front tire.

"Will we be alright?" she asked.

"Yes, just close your eyes," he said. "Although I don't find comfort in the fact that we're near a place called Tombstone."

Stefania grinned and reached for Thomas' hand at the same time he reached for her's. She held it tight.

Thomas held Carmen against him with his other arm, the bandana covering the dog's eyes.

She could hear Thomas whispering, "Hail Mary, full of grace, the Lord be with thee."

Stefania joined in, "Blessed art thou..."

Greschenko also joined in "among women..."

A bright light pierced Stefania's closed eyelids, every capillary visible like a work of abstract art. The ground trembled beneath her. The SUV shook side to side, squeaking as it did so. Shortly thereafter a thunderous roar rolled across the desert, echoing off of the small ridges and knolls. Then a warm breeze blew from the east, which lasted for a few seconds.

"Well there you have it," said Greschenko.

Stefania opened her eyes. Greschenko stood there looking to the northeast.

Stefania got up, brushing the desert dirt off her leggings.

"Wow," said Stefania.

A thin ominous mushroom shaped cloud towered over the higher rocky terrain to the northeast. The mushroom cap lit up like a lampshade, and slowly faded. The towering shape began to lose its configuration as the southwest breeze moved across the desert to the northeast.

"It's about five-thousand meters high, probably less," said Greschenko, now powering up her satellite phone.

"What about the fallout?" asked Thomas. "Shouldn't people in the area be warned?"

"I leave that to the United States government," said Greschenko.

"How can you be so callous?" asked Thomas.

"There were no dwellings or visible human habitation for at least five kilometers of where the RV was left," responded Greschenko. "In any event, the maximum dose of radiation from the fallout will be between ten and one-hundred rads per hour for a few hours northeast of the detonation site. The total fallout will be dissipated within forty-eight hours."

"What does that mean?" asked Stefania.

"I think what she's trying to say is that there is a minimal likelihood of negative health impact from the blast," replied Thomas. "Or at least none that's she's prepared to admit."

"Exactly," chimed in Greschenko. "The musicfest was due east, the fallout will travel northeast, likely missing the concertgoers completely."

Greschenko started speaking into the satellite phone in Russian.

Thomas grabbed a bottle of water from back of the SUV and a towel he found back there. He wet the towel down with water.

"What are you doing?" asked Stefania.

"Let's just say, I wouldn't look in the mirror if I were you," he responded.

He wiped blood splatter off of her face and her hair with the towel.

Delightful pin pricks scattered across Stefania's skin as Thomas delicately cleaned her face and hair.

"Hold still," he said, as he then poured water from the bottle over her face and hair. "There, I think I got the best of it."

"Thanks," she said. "But now I'm soaked."

"The humidity here is about fifteen percent, you'll be dry in minutes," he responded.

"We should get to this Giles Manhire's address ASAP," said Stefania.

"Yes, but she's got problems," said Thomas, motioning to Greschenko with his chin. "The Americans will know by the composition of the fallout that this was a Russian weapon."

Greschenko hung up the phone.

"Thomas is correct," interrupted Greschenko. "However, the Americans will think the attack had something to do with a nearby Army installation known as Fort Huachuca. My government will try to paint it as an attempted terrorist attack against that installation."

"Why would the Americans buy into that?" asked Stefania sarcastically.

"Because my government informed the American government a day ago about the missing RA-115," responded Greschenko. "Today we gave them Wu's name, and the identity of the target. It will just look like the morons who stole it detonated it by accident on the way to the target. Let's go."

Stefania shook her head and muttered, "What are you Russians trying to get on the Americans' good side given the Ukraine fiasco?"

"Touchy subject best to avoid," whispered Anatoly.

All four got into the SUV with Carmen on her leash, and Anatoly sped off westbound on gravely West Yacenda at high speeds, a gritty fog in its wake. The dog sat up and looked out the passenger side window, all the while Stefania stroked her long fur coat.

"Get us out of this area before it is cordoned off," demanded Greschenko.

Anatoly nodded.

"If Smith had the key to the trunk, how did one of these two get it?" asked Stefania.

"Obviously Orloff had more than one key, which means Souchev had more than one key when he sold the MA-115 to Wu," responded Greschenko in a matter of fact tone.

"But why more keys?" asked Stefania. "And why these guys?"

"Backup," said Greschenko. "Smith was Plan A these guys were Plan B. In any well planned operation there is always a Plan B. These two must have been the back-up."

"We still don't know why these two guys wanted to blow up musicfest," said Stefania.

"I think we've concluded that there is an ulterior motive here," interjected Thomas. "This isn't your garden variety false flag operation."

"No, there's more to it than that," said Stefania.

"Hopefully we'll find out," replied Greschenko. "We've got an address and a name in Sahuarita, and maybe someone who might want their dog back. I've got two password locked mobiles, but we won't be able to get these analyzed for a while."

"So I guess it's on to Sahuarita then," said Thomas. "You're going to miss the concert."

Stefania laughed.

"Dearest, let's just say you owe me a concert," replied Thomas with a smile.

"The fact that we got in line to a concert that I never got to attend, doesn't mean I *owe* you one," said Stefania still smiling.

Greschenko let out a loud scoff.

"*Pl-ease*," she snarled. "Drivel," she finished under her breath.

"West Yacenda dumps us off onto Route 90 just south of Route 82," said Stefania. "There's a border patrol checkpoint on Route 90 north of Route 82, so we should take Route 82 west to avoid that."

"Thanks DiMaggio," snapped Greschenko with a frown. "I know where we're going. We'll take Route 82 west to Route 83 north to East Sahuarita Road into Sahuarita."

"I thought you were going to take back everything you said about me if I was correct about the attack on the musicfest," Stefania asked.

"I have," responded Greschenko, smirking. "The slate is clean. We've started fresh."

"Aces," Stefania said sarcastically.

Thomas and Anatoly both smiled.

The SUV barreled down East Sahuarita Road toward Sahuarita. The flat featureless desert passed by, littered with cacti and small trees and brush.

Stefania leaned over to Thomas's ear.

"Thank you," whispered Stefania.

"For what precisely?" asked Thomas softly.

"For saving my life," whispered back Stefania. "That's twice."

"I can hardly say," murmured Thomas.

"You had him, but you let him go to save me," said Stefania softly.

"I suppose so, yes," whispered Thomas. "That's just once though."

"Two years ago near the *Via Archimede* in Rome, when they tried to blow up the Sheikh, remember," murmured Stefania with a raised brow.

"Oh yes, but you can't count that, can you," said Thomas, now slightly louder. "I mean we were both in peril and I saved yours and my own hide. Can't count that one, I'm sorry."

"I at least owe you one," whispered Stefania with a smile.

"You owe me a concert, that's all," replied Thomas.

"I checked out your Devon Harrop," said Stefania quietly.

"And," replied Thomas.

"His public social media indicates he's a seminarian at Saint Pancreas Anglican Seminary in York. See."

Stefania handed her phone to Thomas.

"The photo shows him with Bishop Hough," said Thomas quizzically.

"Hough's number was in Smith's possession," noted Stefania.

"Yes it was," replied Thomas in a low voice as he looked out the window. He quickly turned back to Stefania.

"That means there's a connection of some kind," he said.

"I would think it does," said Stefania.

"What is the identity card address again?" demanded Greschenko.

Thomas stared at the photo on Stefania's phone.

"Thomas," blurted Greschenko. "Check the identity card and read me the address."

"Oh, I'm sorry," said Thomas. "The identity card says 1950 West San Xavier Road."

"Hmm," said Greschenko. "We have to get on the freeway north. We first go by what looks like pecan groves and we come to it."

"Such a happy dog," said Stefania, stroking the panting dog's head and back.

The SUV turned right onto the freeway and Anatoly sped up.

"Looks like fifteen minutes or so and we'll be there," said Anatoly in his typical monotone.

The monotonous hum of the freeway beneath them, Stefania's weary eyes began to droop shut. They opened briefly and fell again. Light and sound disappeared into a subtle darkness. Suspended in air, she looked down on the four of them and Carmen, huddled against the SUV. A blinding light, a white-out, obscured the scene for a second. The flash subsided. From above she saw the four get up and watch a mushroom cloud glow like a starburst reaching for the heavens. Her eyes jumped open. She shook herself to consciousness and turned to Thomas.

"The explosion, that was it," she exclaimed.

"It was what?" he asked.

"It was the dream I had on the plane back from Ashgabat," she answered. "Remember I dreamt we were all sitting next to a white truck, covering our eyes, praying to the Madonna, with a black dog. That was the dream down to the last detail."

"It does sound like what you conveyed at the time," responded Thomas rubbing his chin. "I'm sure it was just a coincidence."

Stefania tipped her chin, raised a brow and poked Thomas in the ribs.

"Yes," she said with a smile. "But there are no such things as coincidences."

"Looks like we're here," declared Anatoly.

"But it's a church," said Stefania.

"DiMaggio, you're stating the obvious again," sniped Greschenko. "This is the address Thomas gave me."

Thomas took another look at the identity card.

"If this is 1950 West San Xavier Road, then we're here," declared Thomas.

Anatoly parked the SUV in an expansive parking lot.

Stefania got out of the SUV. Before her stood a Spanish style mission church.

She gazed skyward at the impressive edifice. Two bleach white bell towers set off the tan colored doorway surround. The deep blue sky background made the church seem surreal, as if heaven itself surrounded the place.

Leaving the others behind, she rushed inside only to be star struck by the elaborately gilded ornate altar stretching from floor to ceiling.

She gasped.

"Oh Madonna," she muttered.

Instinctively she made the sign of the cross and stood dumbstruck at the intricately carved statue of the Virgin Mary above the altar, as if the statue returned her gaze.

"It's wonderful, isn't it?" asked a man's voice from behind in Spanish accented English.

She turned and behind her stood a thin young priest, about her age and height, with jet black hair, slicked back, a goatee, wearing a black cassock.

"Yes it is," she replied in Spanish.

"I'm glad you are impressed," he replied in Spanish. "I'm father Luis. This must be your first time here."

"Ah, yes," she responded. "More or less by accident. My friends and I found a black dog and his tags said his owner was Giles Manhire at this address."

"Giles is a local," responded father Luis in Spanish. "He lives in his RV, which is why the church's address is on the tags. I would suggest you leave the dog with his sister though."

"Hello," said Thomas emerging from behind the priest with the dog on a leash.

"Father Luis, this is my friend, Thomas, who found Carmen," said Stefania.

"You're English," said the priest.

"Yes," responded Thomas.

"That's coincidental," said father Luis shaking his head, sporting a slight grin.

"How so?" asked Thomas.

"Giles is an Anglophile," responded father Luis. "His mother was English. His father married her in the UK when he was in the Air Force and he brought her back. Giles's a student of English history, particularly the Tudor period. More obsessed with it actually, you know, the reformation."

"What about it?" asked Thomas.

"Giles has theories," said father Luis. "He started in seminary, but didn't finish."

"What theories?" asked Stefania.

"He doesn't like the reformation in England," responded father Luis with yet another grin. "He believes that the monarchy's destiny is to become Catholic again. Oddly, for someone so conservative theologically, he recently considered joining an Anglican seminary. He's very complicated philosophically."

"How long have you known him?" asked Stefania.

"Several years," responded the priest softly. "He was born and raised here in the Indian community. His mother died in a car accident years ago, and his father of COVID during the pandemic."

The padre picked a phone out of his pocket and scrolled through his contacts and pressed dial. He put it up to his ear.

"Hmm, no answer on Giles' phone," he said.

"Where was his mum from in the UK?" asked Thomas.

"I don't recall precisely," replied the Father. "I used to know. He did go back and visit her family there."

He pressed dial again.

"Elizabeth?" he said. "Yes, it's father Luis. Some folks found your brother's dog and brought her here. Okay, no problem. If you don't mind me asking, where was your mother from in the UK?" After a lengthy pause, all the while nodding his head and smiling at Stefania and Thomas, he continued, "Oh yes, thanks for reminding me. Thank you."

"My apologies, it was a longer conversation than I anticipated. Elizabeth is a talker. She asked I take Carmen until she can come by to pick her up," said the priest. "Leave her with me. Oh, and she gave me the family history. She said their mother Mary was from Leeds. They met while her father was stationed as a communications specialist at a place called RAF Menwith Hill. Her surname was Harrop."

"Thank you so much father," said Stefania.

"Thank *you* for finding Carmen," responded Luis. "Giles loves that dog, I'm sure he's searching for her as we speak. I must be going. I have to prepare for holy mass."

The priest and the dog disappeared out a side door of the church.

"Give me a moment," said Stefania.

She genuflected, bowed at the altar, crossed herself and stood for a moment, collecting her thoughts and gazing up at the statue of the Virgin Mary for a few silent seconds.

"Let's not tell Greschenko that Giles lived here," whispered Stefania to Thomas. "She's liable to interrogate the pastor or worse."

Thomas smiled.

"Understood," he responded. "He had no permanent residence or family, hence the church address. He lived out of his RV. The priest took his dog. That's the narrative."

"Perfect," responded Stefania. "Plus she'll assume the relevant information is on his phone, and she's got that."

"I agree," whispered Thomas. "The UK connection is interesting though. Giles and Devon must be related somehow. Leeds is in Yorkshire."

"It can't be just a coincidence can it?" whispered back Stefania. "That this guy is an Anglophile ex-seminarian, his mom's from York, her surname was Harrop, Devon Harrop was an English seminarian, Smith was English, some of the money sent to Wu was from London, Chen was MI6, her family were monarchists, and last, but not least, Smith had the private phone numbers of your friend Artie and Bishop Hough."

"Agreed," said Thomas staring at the ornate altar. "But why blow up the musicfest? What is that connection? I do say, this *is* one of the most lovely churches I've seen in some time."

"Musicfest," mumbled Stefania, slapping her right hand on her right thigh.

Thomas looked turned and looked toward the back of the church. "Let's go and see what the other two are up to."

Thomas and Stefania exited the church. They lingered on the sidewalk outside the little church. Stefania plopped her buttocks on the railing to the left, crossed her arms, and gazed to the west.

The sun levitated above the western hills, slowly creeping downward, the sun's rays reflecting off a drapery of high misty clouds. The desert sky exuded hues of ochre and crimson.

"What an extraordinary sunset," remarked Thomas.

"It is," affirmed Stefania. "Arizona is famous for its sunsets."

"Is it?" asked Thomas.

"I visited the Grand Canyon with my friends in college," she replied. "Truly magnificent."

"I should like to go there," replied Thomas. "Despite my distain for America."

The church bell started tolling.

Stefania turned slightly toward Thomas. Her eyes caught in his baby blues. They lingered, slightly transfixed. The rays of the setting sun eclipsed only by Thomas' profile. Thomas moved closer.

The bell rang again.

Was this it finally? Thought Stefania. *Finally a romantic moment with Thomas with the incredible sunset and the bell tolling.*

"Hey, you two," a female voice yelled from a distance.

Stefania hesitated.

"Thomas, Stefania," a male voice barked. "Over here."

"Our two cohorts, I presume," said Thomas softly with a slight smile.

"Yes, our ride" replied Stefania, now looking out into the parking lot.

"That's the loudest I've heard Anatoly speak," said Thomas.

"Now that's a sight I didn't expect to see," commented Stefania. "Svetlana and Anatoly sitting on the tailgate eating."

The two walked over to the SUV, a few grains of desert sand in the parking lot cracking under their feet.

"What have you got there?" asked Stefania as she approached the SUV.

"Despite the fact that I despise America, I love its interior, and American local food, despite how health conscious I am," said Greschenko as she took a huge bite of what looked like a burrito. "Don't worry, there's some here for you, two pork, bean and cheese burritos, and two beef, bean and cheese burritos, take your pick. Fresh salsa, red and green, on the side. Nachos too. We have water, and we picked up some iced teas."

"I detest all things American," added Thomas. "Normally, I'd be aghast at this, but I'm famished," said Thomas, grabbing one of the burritos wrapped in foil.

"Don't be such a snob Thomas," snapped Greschenko. "The website says this comes from the best little taco stand in Sahuarita. What they call a 'mom and pop shop.' It's actually excellent."

Stefania unwrapped one of the burritos and took a bite.

"Mmmm, delicious," she said, wiping some leftover refried bean from her lips. "Thomas, you've got to broaden your horizons. This is some good stuff."

She washed the burrito down with some cold iced tea.

"So what'd you find out?" asked Greschenko. "I see the dog is gone."

"Manhire was a local native American kid, grew up in the native community, lived out of his RV, and listed the church as his address," said Stefania. "All of his family is deceased. He went to the seminary and left, and had an interest in English history. His parents are deceased, but his mom was from the UK. He was going to join an Anglican seminary. The priest agreed to take his dog. You can go in and ask the priest if you want to."

"Any idea what the hell this bumpkin was doing with my RA-115?" asked Greschenko.

"Not particularly," answered Thomas. "However, his interest apparently in the UK raises an interesting question. Also his companion, as Stefania noted, was an English seminarian from York."

"You think that's the connection?" asked Greschenko.

"It's all we've got," responded Stefania.

"I thought I asked him," snapped Greschenko. "Are you his mouthpiece now?"

"Oh Madonna, Greschenko!" sniped Stefania, her eyes cutting to Greschenko. "As much as I hate to say it, we're all in this together, until you are prepared to release Thomas from your blackmail threat."

Greschenko's eyes rolled.

"Okay little miss smarty yoga pants," barked Greschenko. "How do you think this all fits together? You've piqued my curiosity."

Greschenko stuffed the last bit of a burrito into her mouth and gulped down some iced tea. She raised her brows.

"Well?" she demanded.

"Smith had an apartment in London and was from the UK," said Stefania. "Chen worked for MI6 and was from a devout monarchist Catholic family from Hong Kong. Harrop was an Anglican seminarian, and Manhire was an ex-seminarian with a penchant for English history, particularly the reformation. Smith's apartment contained the phone numbers of the Duke of Shropshire, Anglican Bishop Hough, and a burner phone from Rome. The Duke's wife is Catholic."

"Agreed," said Greschenko. "What about Wu?"

"Wu obviously was just a conduit," replied Stefania. "He was paid by funds from Rome, China, and the Cayman Islands. He was nothing more than the procurement agent. He purchased and delivered arms for both the terrorist attack in New Jersey, and the RA-115 for the attack on musicfest."

"So far you haven't stated anything new," said Greschenko with another eye roll. "What are the common threads? Other than Wu all of these persons are English or Anglophiles, most are Catholic, other than the Duke of Shropshire and the Bishop. That's it."

The shadows on the parking lot became longer as the sun settled on the western horizon.

"But how are all these people connected?" asked Stefania.

"Maybe they're not," said Anatoly shrugging, sitting on the tailgate next to Greschenko finishing off his burrito.

Greschenko turned him with a wide grin.

"You don't truly believe that do you?" she asked.

"*Nyet*," he responded with a laugh.

"One thing is clear, this was meant to cast blame on the Uyghurs, and to utilize them in some sort of a false flag operation," piped in Thomas.

"Yes," responded Stefania. "The Uyghurs were intended to take the fall, but other than the Chinese, who would benefit from such a false flag operation?"

"No one," snapped Greschenko. "But as much as I'd like to blame the Chinese, GRU doesn't think it's the Chinese and frankly neither do I."

"And why might that be?" asked Stefania.

Greschenko's eyes narrowed and her cheeks tightened.

"Ugh, you're so tedious," snipped Greschenko. "I'll lay it out for you. If the Chinese were going to conduct a false flag operation to blame the Uyghurs for international terrorism, why would they utilize Wu, someone who is so obviously connected to them? They might as well be sending a formal letter to the CIA saying, 'hey guys, oh by the way, it was us.'"

"So it's a double false flag operation then," said Thomas quietly while rubbing his chin. "Someone's trying to finger the Chinese for pinning the attack on the Uyghurs."

"That's a reasonable assumption," said Greschenko, while putting some lip balm on her lips. "This dry air is killing my lips."

"But who would want to do this?" asked Stefania.

"MMO," barked Greschenko. "Means, motive and opportunity are always the keys. We know the means, but who had the opportunity and what's the motive. Once we determine that, we'll know who."

"And I'm no expert, but..." started Stefania.

"You can say that again," interrupted Greschenko.

"This was a well planned, highly complicated and expensive operation," continued Stefania. "Who would have the knowledge to undertake such a scheme and put it together?"

"Wow, now we're getting somewhere," yelped Greschenko with a slap to her thigh and a laugh. "Best question you've had yet DiMaggio."

"Chen," Stefania blurted.

Anatoly's brows raised and he turned to Greschenko.

"Someone at MI6 would have the knowledge and ability to put this together," said Thomas quietly. "Chen certainly had all the intelligence at her fingertips."

"Chen had crossed our minds, together with perhaps compatriots at MI6," said Greschenko with a grin.

"But again, why?" asked Stefania.

Greschenko's eyes rolled.

"So what's our next move?" asked Thomas, wiping his mouth with a paper napkin.

"By the way, how was the burrito?" asked Greschenko.

"Food always tastes better when one is hungry," said Thomas.

"I'll buy that for now," said Greschenko. "Our next step, unfortunately, is to attempt to go back to Mexico the way we came."

"Won't that be incredibly risky?" asked Thomas.

"Maybe," said Anatoly. "But we're law abiding Arizona citizens until we get to the border, and then we resume our true identities in Mexico."

"Plus," added Greschenko. "All border crossings into Mexico have been temporarily closed because of the bomb. We've no choice."

"What's our timing?" asked Stefania.

"We leave at first light," said Anatoly. "The area around the blast site has been cordoned off, so we'll have to take another route."

"And what's that?" asked Stefania.

"Really?" asked Greschenko. "Tonight, we're staying at a hotel near Tucson under our assumed names. Tomorrow we take Route 83 south to someplace called Parker Canyon Lake. From there we take a West Montezuma Canyon Road to the Coronado National Monument. I'm worried that there may be added security around Fort Huachuca, so we have to avoid that. We then head to Route 92, which we'll take to Route 80 into Douglas. Our story at that point is we're taking lunch in Douglas on our way to visit the Santa Maria Ranch Museum and the San Bernardino National Wildlife Refuge, and we try to make it back across the border the way we came. Starting tomorrow afternoon there will be a low overcast in the area and the potential for thunderstorms in the evening. If we are lucky, we should be able to make it out around dusk. If we have to ditch the SUV, we'll hoof it and I'll arrange for my people to pick us up on the other side."

She tipped her head and stared at Stefania.

"Do you approve?" she asked snidely.

"I like the change of clothes and hotel part," said Stefania. "I'm really feeling dingy and need a good shower."

"I'm glad our plan meets with your requirements," snapped Greschenko. "I'll make sure my directorate runs all operations by you for good measure in the future."

Anatoly and Thomas both grinned from ear to ear.

"What if we're stopped?" asked Stefania.

"It depends on when and where," barked Greschenko. "If it's at the very end, when we are close to the border, we're armed and we may have to take matters into our own hands. Otherwise, we'll improvise. With our documents and stories, I can't imagine we'll have any problems until we close in on the border."

"Best laid plans," muttered Stefania. "What are the hotel arrangements?"

"Because of musicfest the accommodations were few and far between," said Greschenko. "You and I will share a room at a cut-rate hotel we found, and Anatoly and Thomas will do likewise."

"So eight hours of torture then," snapped Stefania.

"I doubt it will be that long," barked back Greschenko. "And you don't know what torture is. I'd be happy to introduce you to some of my techniques."

"I'll take a pass," said Stefania.

"I thought you would," responded Greschenko.

"Shouldn't we best be getting on then?" asked Thomas.

"Saddle up," barked Greschenko.

Chapter 12

Early Morning, March 13, Montezuma Pass, Arizona, USA

The SUV pulled into the small parking lot at the top of a deserted ridge. A few agaves dotted the landscape, some residual snow stuck in the shadows, and the vacant skeleton of a tree loomed over an expansive view down into the desert valley to the peaks beyond.

The four exited the vehicle. Anatoly and Greschenko walked to the rest rooms located in a small brown hut.

Stefania stood in the brightening sunshine overlooking the vastness of the countryside with Thomas next to her.

"Some ride," Thomas quipped, still in the clothes from the day before.

"Yes, two hours not for the faint of heart," replied Stefania. "It's cool here."

"The sign says we're at about two-thousand meters," said Thomas.

"That high," said Stefania. "It's wonderful up here."

"The view *is* splendid," replied Thomas.

The cool March wind caught Stefania's hair and tossed it about. She sidled up next to Thomas. In the distance raptors circled in the thermocline. She took her phone out and took a few photos of the desolate beauty of the valley and mountains to the east.

"Say cheese," she said as she grabbed Thomas and they huddled for a quick selfie.

"Yes, this view is incredible," said Stefania in a hushed tone.

"The empty vastness of this region tickles the heart," responded Thomas.

"What else tickles the heart?" asked Stefania.

"I hesitate to inquire, but how was your night with Svetlana?" asked Thomas, dodging the question.

"She didn't talk much to me," responded Stefania. "She was on her sat-phone speaking Russian for a good portion of the time. She did purchase a couple of razors at the hotel desk and some hair remover. I don't think she's got any hair on her entire body. She's smooth as a dolphin. She looks good naked, and she's not shy about it, that's for sure."

"She's into fitness," replied Thomas.

"Yep, she did yoga in the room in her thong," replied Stefania. "She's insufferable. How about you with Anatoly?"

"He's surprisingly personable and accommodating," responded Thomas. "They have the BBC on the motel tele, and we watched the news from the UK. He was the perfect roommate, didn't even snore."

"I guess you have to be accommodating when you work for Greschenko," said Stefania softly.

"At the very least," replied Thomas.

Stefania turned around.

"There're out," she said, watching Anatoly and Greschenko head to the SUV, let down the tailgate and break out a couple of bottles of water.

"Right," said Thomas.

Thomas jogged up to the brown hut.

The shadows from the mountains to the east grew softer as the sun rose. Stefania's hoody absorbed the sun's warmth. She took it off tied the arms around her neck, revealing her pink athletic top. Her aviator style sunglasses shielded the strong rays as they crested the high peaks to the east.

Why is it that I don't tickle his heart, thought Stefania. *I blew it two years ago. He loved me and I let it slip away.*

"Always make the best of your circumstances," a male voice said.

She turned as a father spoke to his teenage daughter admiring the view about five meters away.

Thank God I'm not going crazy, she thought. *The vastness of this view is evidence that God created earth. It did sound like papa's voice though.*

"I will always protect you," the male voice said.

She turned again. The man and his daughter were still there.

Boy his voice carries, she thought.

She quickly blessed herself. Solitude and calmness overcame her.

Footsteps approached from behind.

"Right," said Thomas.

"I did some additional research last night on our Mr. Harrop using the hotel's Wi-Fi when our friend was in the shower," said Stefania softly still facing the rising sun.

"Indeed," whispered Thomas also gazing forward. "And?"

"Harrop was very vocal on social media about his views about the church and the monarchy," said Stefania. "There's a lot out there on him."

"Like?" asked Thomas.

"He believed that the monarch could not be the Supreme Governor of the Church because no temporal prince can fill that role," she murmured.

"There must be more to it," whispered Thomas.

"And the church can only be led by a descendent of the apostles, a validly consecrated bishop," she mumbled.

"That's radical for an Anglican," said Thomas softly.

"Yes, apparently they wanted to kick him out of the seminary but Bishop Hough interceded on his behalf," said Stefania quietly. "He believed only in apostolic succession."

"That's not orthodox Anglican theology," responded Thomas.

"No, sounds like something a Catholic or Orthodox Christian would believe," said Stefania under her breath. "How does that remotely relate to blowing up musicfest with a nuclear bomb?"

A slight shiver crawled up Stefania's spine and goose bumps erupted on her forearm. A slight breeze kicked up tossing her black tresses about.

"They weren't meant to survive," replied Thomas.

"They were dupes Thomas," whispered Stefania.

"Indeed, just the type who would give their lives for a cause," whispered back Thomas. "But what cause?" he pondered.

"Surely they weren't the organizers," said Stefania in a hushed tone.

"Certainly not," replied Thomas softly.

"Wu, Chen, Smith, what's the common thread?" asked Stefania quietly. "And there were some interesting news reports on the explosion."

A whistle pierced the air from the parking lot.

Stefania turned around.

"Speak of the devils," she said. "They're summoning us."

Stefania took one last look at the vermillion sunburst sliding beneath the clouds and rays of light beaming onto the valley floor.

"Spectacular," she said, barely audibly.

They walked slowly to the SUV where Greschenko and Anatoly were sitting on the tailgate, finishing a couple of bottles of water.

Greschenko pulled out her cell phone and thrust it into their faces.

"Do you know this man?" she demanded.

Greschenko showed them a photo. Stefania recognized it as the man who attacked Thomas at the hotel in Malta.

"It depends on your definition of the term 'know,'" replied Stefania with a smirk.

"Don't get funny with me," Greschenko snapped. "Do you or do you not know him."

"This man attacked me at my hotel in Malta upon our return from Ashgabat," said Thomas.

"You were attacked in your hotel?" growled Greschenko. "And you didn't think to tell me!"

"You never asked," replied Stefania with a smile.

"Obviously he got away," interjected Thomas. "Stefania saved the day."

Greschenko scoffed.

"So who is he?" asked Stefania.

"His name is immaterial, but it's John Gabriel Tsang," barked Greschenko.

"Relevance?" asked Stefania with a smile.

"You tell me Thomas," Greschenko snapped back. "He's MI6. My people photographed him snooping around the resort in Monterrey yesterday, including the hallway where your rooms are located. They ran his photograph through our database."

"We don't know him, or why he attacked me in Malta," Thomas said solemnly.

"He seemed to be going through Thomas' room when we got back," said Stefania. "We were able to disarm him."

"It's probably related to the attack on you in Richmond Park," said Greschenko.

"Reasonable assumption," responded Stefania.

"I'm glad you agree," snapped Greschenko with a grin. "If he's seen again, he may have to be apprehended and interrogated. I don't want to make that decision because that will open up a whole new can of worms."

"Why didn't you have him followed?" asked Stefania.

"Because he was just suspicious, and we didn't know who he was," hissed Greschenko followed by one of her trademark eye rolls.

"So MI6 is in Monterrey," said Thomas quietly.

"Obviously," said Greschenko curtly. "And there can be only one reason why, other than you two, unfortunately, there is no other connection."

"But what do we know that is so disconcerting to MI6?" asked Stefania.

"Or to certain persons at MI6," said Greschenko. "Our operatives have uncovered no agency-wide communications regarding Thomas. It seems to be limited to China desk. We do know that Tsang was born in Hong Kong."

"They're off the reservation as the Americans would say," said Thomas.

"What does that mean?" asked Stefania.

"Certain individuals at MI6 have gone rogue, they're operating without orders," replied Thomas.

"Which means you two are in true danger," barked Greschenko. "Under your preposterous western concepts of the rule of law, UK citizens, especially prominent ones, cannot just be targeted for investigation or sanction by MI6."

"Quite right," said Thomas solemnly. "There'd be hell to pay for killing a member of the House of Lords."

"This means that a cabal at MI6 is significantly involved in this whole affair somehow," said Stefania. "It's not limited to just Chen. But to what end?"

"Brilliant deduction," said Greschenko snidely. "Brilliant fucking deduction, and I suppose you're going to next tell me it gets dark at night."

"You may not like the question, but Stefania's inquiry goes to the heart of it," said Thomas. "What *is* MI6's involvement here?"

"More importantly, what is this all about?" asked Stefania. "It can't merely be about two disaffected seminarians wanting to blow up musicfest for shits and giggles. None of this adds up. You're telling us it's not the Chinese and it doesn't appear to involve any of your typical terrorist groups. Well who's behind it all?"

Greschenko scoffed.

Stefania's eyes narrowed and cut to Greschenko.

"Look, Wu was the procurer, Souchev was the supplier, but who were Smith and Chen working for, not to mention Tsang?" continued Stefania in a raised voice. "And who bankrolled this?"

"Svetlana, you don't like the questions because you don't have the answers," said Thomas.

Anatoly grinned slightly.

"No, but we'll find one, eventually, you can be rest assured of that" said Greschenko who gulped down the last bit of her bottle of water and through the empty into the back of the SUV. She licked her wet lips.

Stefania tipped her head in Greschenko's direction.

"It would be nice if you found out before Thomas and I get killed," she said. "One more thing," snapped Stefania. "The American press is reporting that the junior Senator from Arizona, Enedina Andrade Castillo was on her way to the musicfest at the time of the blast. She was nearby. There are conspiracy theories circulating on the internet that the purpose was to kill her."

"Why would anyone go to such trouble just to kill a US Senator?" asked Thomas. "When they could just shoot her anywhere."

"If they didn't want it to appear that she was the target," replied Stefania. "Hey, isn't she the Senator that backs increasing sanctions against Russia? She's an outspoken Russia-hater, and she's the deciding vote in the Senate on the issue."

"That's no matter," added Greschenko.

"Well," replied Stefania. "She's a young, attractive Latina, and a Republican, a rising star in a Senate where the Republicans have a one seat majority. In addition to the Russian sanction vote, there is a big vote coming next week to enhance penalties for human trafficking as well as an amendment to the kingpin law. She *may* be the deciding vote on that one too. Narcos and traffickers may want her dead. The Governor of Arizona is a Democrat and her successor would be a Democrat, presumably. There are rumors she may be the Republican's next presidential choice."

"Which may be why the cartel was so eager to get the bomb to the border, and to stop us from getting to it," said Thomas.

"Or it could be a complete distraction from the real purpose," said Stefania. "Theories intentionally planted to take everyone's eyes off the ball. Maybe to avoid this Senator's antagonistic attitude toward Russia which Ms. Greschenko here conveniently brushed off."

Anatoly smiled with a raised brow.

"'Disinformation works like cocaine,' so said comrade Andropov," Anatoly whispered just loud enough for Stefania to catch.

"You're starting to make sense DiMaggio," bellowed Greschenko. "But the Russia angle is a dead-end."

"Is it now?" replied Stefania sarcastically. "The American president desperately wants to curb the Russian sanctions to again tap into Russian oil."

"Time," said Anatoly, tapping on his wrist watch.

"We'd best be off," said Greschenko calmly. "We've got a schedule to keep."

Evening, March 13, Guadalupe Canyon, Arizona, USA

Under a dark overcast, the SUV sped in a blizzard of dust toward the unmarked tract which would take them to the border. Thunder could be heard in the distance. Flashes of azure light lit up the western horizon.

"Looks like a storm's coming," said Thomas.

"The forecast was for that possibility," replied Greschenko. "Hopefully the weather will cover our escape."

"So far we've seen one border patrol vehicle and it didn't stop us," remarked Stefania.

"How much farther to the dirt track?" asked Greschenko as the last shades of light waned away into darkness.

"We should be there in a few minutes," replied Anatoly. "I marked it on my GPS."

The sky lit up with a blue hue, and thunder cracked overhead. Large raindrops began pelting the SUV.

"Here it is," said Anatoly as he turned the SUV to the right onto the barely there trail that they used to enter the country. "Get ready for a long bumpy ride, and it'll be worse than when we came due to the weather."

Greschenko checked her Nagant, the AK-47 and the forty caliber semi-automatic.

The headlights reflected off of shrubs and brush lining the route as the rain poured down. Occasionally the lighting illuminated the surroundings, nothing more than desert hills and ravines and an unforgiving muddy track.

"Good thing we ate a hearty lunch in Douglas, otherwise, I'd be starving right about now," said Stefania to Thomas.

"That was the purpose of the plan," Greschenko replied. "I'm surprised how much you ate, given how skinny you are."

Stefania rolled her eyes.

One of these days I'll earn her respect, or I'll punch her in the face, one or the other, thought Stefania. *Not sure which would make me feel better.*

The SUV suddenly stopped.

"Look," said Anatoly.

Stefania and Thomas looked out the windshield. A stirring torrent of muddy water churned across the road in front of them.

"I don't remember this on the way in," said Stefania.

"It wasn't here then," countered Greschenko.

"What do we do?" asked Stefania.

"Go through it," ordered Greschenko.

"Go through it?" asked Anatoly.

"Yes, go through it," ordered Greschenko.

"I don't think it's safe," snapped Stefania.

"I concur," added Thomas.

"And I don't care what you two think," barked back Greschenko. "Go!"

The SUV lurched forward and quickly entered the rapids. About two-thirds of the way through the rear end started moving diagonally. Progress stopped.

"We're stuck," Anatoly uncharacteristically snapped. "The water is almost up to the door."

"Shimmy it," suggested Stefania.

"What?" asked Anatoly.

"Shimmy it back and forth," repeated Stefania. "Go back and then forward again until you get traction."

With a jolt the SUV went into reverse then tossed forward a few feet.

"Try it again," directed Stefania. "Go back a bit farther."

The SUV backed up, and then with a couple of hard bumps flew forward and up out of the wash.

Now in the clear, Anatoly rolled down his window and looked at the side of the SUV.

"It's caked with mud," he said. "Thanks Stefania, how'd you know how to do that?"

"My cousin in Brazil has a ranch," she said. "We drive all over the property, and go through the streams and water courses there. You learn a lot."

Greschenko scoffed.

Thomas smiled, and in the rear view mirror Stefania could see Anatoly grinning as well.

"Let's get moving," barked Greschenko.

After ten minutes of slow going on the muddy trail the rain stopped. Thirty minutes later the clouds cleared and shortly after that the SUV came to the border obelisk and pulled across into Mexico, bearing right in the fork in the trail.

"Why are we stopping," asked Thomas.

"To stretch and to let Anatoly replace our Arizona tag with a Mexican tag," replied Greschenko. "Anatoly, you remember where you buried them?"

Anatoly had already removed the rear Arizona plate.

"I'm on it," he responded as he disappeared behind some scrub.

Greschenko pulled out her satellite phone, speaking forcefully in Russian the whole time.

Stefania walked up a few yards up the road to the crest of a hill. The half moon illuminated the valley and she could see the road snake across the ridge line above it. It hadn't rained there, so the modest breeze kicked up some dust.

The howling of a coyote reverberated throughout the hollow. The hoot of an owl close by calmed her for some reason.

Footsteps approached from behind.

Thomas, she thought.

"I'm not looking forward to the lengthy drive back to Monterrey," said Stefania still gazing out into the darkness.

"I can't imagine that Greschenko intends to drive another sixteen hours to Monterrey," said Thomas softly, his breath visible in the cool night air. "There is no need for secrecy or surprise at this point.

I'll bet she'll have Anatoly drive us to the nearest small airport where a plane will be waiting."

"It's wonderful isn't it," said Stefania.

"I wouldn't call it wonderful, but flying back to Monterrey is a better option than driving there for the better part of a day," replied Thomas.

"Not that, silly," said Stefania. "The beautiful simplicity of the desert is what I'm talking about. This trip has given me a new appreciation for the American southwest."

"It's truly incredible," said Thomas leaning in to Stefania's ear and lowering his tone to a whisper. "Doesn't make me like Americans, but America, yes I'll agree."

Stefania's spine tingled. Thomas' whisper had a tranquilizing affect on her. She instinctively smiled.

Thomas stepped slightly in front of her and turned around. The moonlight glimmered off of his face as he swept his hair off of his forehead. Stefania moved forward slightly, leaning in toward Thomas. Their lips were so close she could feel the warmth of his breath. As her eyes closed a light approached. She quickly opened them.

"What's that?" she said, pointing to headlights on the trail heading in their direction.

"It's a vehicle of some kind," replied Thomas. "It's still a ways off. We probably have five minutes. Let's go."

Greschenko just finished her phone call, and Anatoly sat in the driver's seat, with the car door open, ready to get moving again.

"We've got company," said Thomas pointing up the trail.

"What," said Anatoly with slight agitation in his voice.

Greschenko ran ahead to the rise in the road, and then ran back.

"We can turn around and go back across the border, or go back to the fork and go out the way we originally came in," said Anatoly.

"I'm sure they've seen our headlamps," said Greschenko. "It's either coyotes, narcos, or *Guardia Nacional*, the new *Federales*."

"Either way, it's unlikely they'll let us just slip away," said Thomas. "If its coyotes or narcos, we're in their territory and it won't go well. If it's *Guardia Nacional*, we have no good reason for being here. If we go back over the border they'll notify the Americans."

"The road is on the ridge line, there's no way to avoid them," said Anatoly.

"If it's the police, why would they care if we are sneaking into Mexico?" asked Stefania. "I thought people snuck into Mexico all the time."

"They may be looking for nuclear terrorists," replied Anatoly. "Not your garden variety hoodlums."

"Exactly," responded Greschenko this time without her characteristic roll of the eyes. "And none of us can afford to get caught this close to the border."

"Thomas and I haven't done anything," said Stefania.

"DiMaggio we don't have time for a discussion," snapped Greschenko. "We could be held indefinitely in a Mexican jail. Concepts of due process mean nothing here. Diplomatic immunity may ultimately apply to us, maybe not, but definitely not to you. Not to mention the fact that the cops here are notoriously corrupt. They may be on the narcos' payroll in any event, bought and paid for, and if so, they could deliver us all to the cartel and in the best case we'll be held for ransom."

"Unfortunately, I'm afraid she's correct," added Thomas nodding.

"DiMaggio, have you ever used an automatic pistol?" asked Greschenko.

"Yes," she replied. "I've shot some at my cousin's ranch in Brazil."

Greschenko grabbed Anatoly's pistol out of its holster.

"Here, take this." Greschenko handed it to Stefania, releasing the safety and cocking the slide. "Put it in the back of your leggings like this. Thomas take the ghost forty from the center console. Anatoly, the AK-47 stays with you."

"What do you have in mind?" asked Thomas.

"Stefania and I will stand in the front. We'll act like we got lost on our way to Agua Prieta. Since we're woman and speak Spanish it may make them less suspicious. Hopefully that'll get one or two of our guests into the clear. You two duck down in the front seat. We'll leave the doors open so hopefully they'll think it's just us women. On my mark, I'll hit the dirt and shoot out the headlights to their vehicle. DiMaggio, jump behind that large rock to the right and take out anyone on that side of the pick-up. I'm going to try to roll under their truck to save my ass and I'll shoot at legs, feet and tires if I have to, or up into the truck bed. Anatoly, take out any open targets on the left and center, Thomas to the right."

"How possibly do you think this will work without us getting killed?" asked Stefania.

"I've seen you in action DiMaggio, you're quick on your feet," said Greschenko. "And we all know this isn't your first rodeo. Thomas was with the SAS, and Anatoly is an SVR trained sniper. Hopefully we'll be able to surprise them, and once their lights are out they may be blinded by ours for a moment and we'll have the advantage."

"That assumes there are not more of them than us," argued Stefania.

"We have to play the cards we are dealt DiMaggio," barked Greschenko. "Let's take our positions."

Stefania joined Greschenko in the front of the SUV, leaning against the hood. Six feet stood between her and the rock on the side of the road. The vehicle crested the rise and slowly approached them. Its headlights bouncing up and down as it hit bumps in the road. A cool breeze wafted by, evaporating the sweat that pooled on Stefania's forehead. Out of the dark it came into view. Difficult to make out due to the glaring headlamps, it appeared to be a black pickup truck. The truck stopped about fifteen feet in front of where they stood.

The shadow of one man with a cowboy hat, western style shirt, blue jeans and cowboy boots now stood outside the passenger door, a pistol holster dangling from his waist. Three men, also with cowboy hats, stood in the pickup truck bed with automatic rifles trained on Stefania and Greschenko and the SUV. A hatless driver, his long hair dangling to his shoulders, stood behind his door with a pistol trained on the women.

"We're lost," Greschenko said in Spanish. "We're on our way to Agua Prieta and we took a wrong turn."

"That's too bad," the standing man with the hat replied with a chuckle. "You are on my road, in my territory, and it's a toll road. You have to pay the toll."

"Let us through and we'll be out of your way in no time," yelled Greschenko in Spanish.

"I'm Juanita Peña from Monterrey," pleaded Stefania in Spanish. "My friend Maritza and I were on our way to Agua Prieta to visit my cousin Paco when we got lost."

There is no way they could believe this crap, thought Stefania. *We're miles off the highway.*

"You don't sound like you're from Monterrey," snapped the standing man in Spanish.

"*El Lobo*, that is one of the trucks," yelled one of the men in the flatbed. "From the ambush. I'm sure of it."

"Well that changes everything!" yelled back *El Lobo* followed by a cackle. "You not only owe me a toll, but a debt for killing ten of my men and destroying four of my trucks."

"*El Lobo*?" snapped Stefania.

"A drug lord," replied Greschenko. "A prominent one."

"Aces," muttered Stefania.

"Walk towards us, and when you get about five feet away, you bitches strip, everything off," demanded *El Lobo* now unzipping his jeans.

"In your dreams asshole," grumbled Stefania.

"The ones in the back of the truck are all wearing Kevlar vests," whispered Greschenko in English. "So aim for the head, neck, or legs. After ten steps, I'm making my move."

Shit, there is no way we're coming out of this alive.

Stefania kept her eye on the rock to the right.

One step, two, three, four, five, six, seven eight, nine, ten.

Shots rang out and the pick-up truck's headlamps went dark. Stefania dove behind the rock, scraping her elbow and knees in the process. A cavalcade of gunfire erupted. She peered out from behind the rock. The man on the driver's side lay on the ground motionless. The three gunmen in the rear of the pick-up directed non-stop automatic rifle fire at the SUV.

The SUV's headlamps now illuminated a fog of gun smoke. The sound of bullets striking metal and the smashing of glass reverberated between gunshots. A hardly audible slight hiss emanated from the front of the SUV, as a foggy gas escaped into the air.

I see Anatoly firing, but I don't see Thomas.

Stefania pulled out the pistol from the back of her pants. She stretched out prone on the ground like her cousin Hércules had taught her with both hands on the pistol. She leveled the gun site at the head of the man closest to her and squeezed the trigger. Two shots rang out, among the many, and the gunman collapsed like a wet rag into the back of the truck.

The SUV sank as its front tires flatted. The firefight turned dark as the SUV's lights shattered.

Only one remained. He turned and started firing at her. She lay flat on her back behind the rock. The bullets ricocheted off of the rock, and then he stopped. Silence enveloped the scene. Stefania peaked over the rock.

A shadowy figure crawled out from beneath the pick-up like a ghost in the night. A groan could be heard from the opposite side.

"My God," said a man's voice in Spanish softly, followed by a gasp.

Then a flash pierced the dark. The groaning stopped.

Greschenko's work, thought Stefania.

The shootout lasted less than ninety seconds, but to Stefania it seemed like hours.

She could hear Greschenko yelling something in Russian as she kicked the *El Lobo's* dead body. Anatoly emerged from the SUV with a flashlight in one hand, and the AK-47 in the other, and walked toward Greschenko.

Now all that could be heard were crickets chirping, and the fluttering of wings overhead. Maybe an owl, bat, or dove in the night. Compared to the crescendo of moments ago, quiet filled the darkness.

Where's Thomas?, thought Stefania.

Stefania stuck the pistol back in her pants, took her phone out, put on the flashlight, and ran to the passenger side of the SUV. In the dark, illuminated only by the glow of her phone Thomas lay on the ground, propped up against the rear door. A thin line of crimson blood trickled down from the right front of his sweater. Thomas held his left hand just below his right shoulder from where blood seeped out.

"Oh Madonna!" exclaimed Stefania. "Thomas, are you alright?" Stefania asked in Portuguese.

"Please dearest, Portuguese isn't my best language," he said with a grimace.

"I'm sorry, I revert to my native Brazilian when excited," she said as she placed her hand on Thomas's cheek.

"Good thing the bullets were full metal jacket rounds," replied Thomas with a slight smile. "It went right through me. I think it's just a flesh wound. Will you help me up?"

Thomas reached up with his right hand, holding his left over the wound.

"Gently," said Thomas.

Stefania pocketed her phone, grabbed Thomas' right hand and lifted.

Thomas gasped as he rose to his feet.

"Agh, that was more painful than I anticipated," he murmured.

Stefania took out her phone again to light the way.

Thomas and Stefania strode by the front of the SUV, pieces of the shattered windows crackling under their feet toward the pick-up truck.

"Doesn't look like we're going anywhere soon," said Thomas.

"Yes," replied Stefania. "Most of the windows are blown out, the front tires flat and the engine looks all shot up. What are we to do?"

"Greschenko said she always has a plan B," replied Thomas.

"There they are," said Stefania pointing to the pick-up truck.

A slight gust blew whatever remaining gun smoke off the road, and kicked up dust in the process.

Stefania and Thomas approached the pick-up, similarly shot up with its windshield shattered, at least one flat tire, and riddled with bullet holes. Greschenko and Anatoly were leaning on its hood.

Anatoly's left arm sported a small bloody gash, and his short brown hair caked with blood from a wound to his scalp. Her clothes dusty and soiled, Greschenko didn't seem particularly worse for the wear. She held her trademark Nagant pistol to her side.

"Anatoly, are you okay?" asked Stefania.

"Of course he is," snapped Greschenko.

"A bullet grazed my arm, and either a ricochet or flying debris sliced me in the head," replied Anatoly. "I consider myself lucky."

"Nice shooting everyone," said Greschenko. "We were outnumbered and outgunned and came out alive. Even DiMaggio performed admirably."

"I wouldn't consider narcos as professionals, but outgunned we were, yes," replied Thomas. "But I'll accept the complement nonetheless."

"Now what?" asked Stefania.

"Oh you of little faith," replied Greschenko with a smile as she walked back to the SUV.

"The pickup truck might be serviceable," said Thomas. "Looks like one flat tire, but without headlights we're getting nowhere until dawn, not on this road, and I don't think we should stick around all night."

"That wouldn't be a good idea," said Anatoly with a slight frown.

Greschenko emerged from the darkness with her shoulder bag and two bottles of water from the SUV. She rummaged around in her bag and plopped a small first aid kit on the hood of the pick-up truck. She then took out her satellite phone and started barking into it in Russian.

Stefania opened the small satchel kit which contained a few gauze pads, anti-bacterial ointment, some band-aids and medical tape.

"Let me clean your wounds, put on some anti-bacterial jell, and then cover them up until you both can get proper medical attention," she said to both Thomas and Anatoly.

Stefania removed Thomas' right arm from his sweater exposing Thomas' well hidden muscular build. She ripped open gauze pads, dabbed some water on each and cleaned the entry and exit bullet holes. Stefania smeared lotion on the wounds and placed gauze pads on both secured by medical tape and delicately put his arm back in his sleeve.

She did the same for Anatoly's arm.

"Anatoly, I don't know what I'm going to do about your head," she said. "I'm going to apply jell, but it seems to have stopped bleeding. I won't be able to secure gauze with all of your hair, and you may need a couple of stitches on your arm."

"Thank you Stefania," said Anatoly nodding with a soft smile.

Greschenko stopped talking for a moment, took a small pill container out of her bag and threw it to Stefania. Stefania caught it mid-air. Greschenko continued her phone discussion in Russian.

"What's this?" she asked showing it to Anatoly. The jar had no label.

"They're Vitamin K pills and cipro," said Anatoly. "Svetlana is always prepared."

"A coagulant and an anti-biotic," chimed in Thomas. "Nice to have with you, just in case."

"Here, take one of each," handing two pills and a bottle of water each to Thomas and Anatoly.

"You are very lucky," said Anatoly. "Those damned 5.56 by 45 millimeter NATO rounds can yaw and fragment upon hitting flesh."

"I know," replied Thomas, his brows raised. "It must have been the short distance and they were probably using carbines. Shorter barrel, less velocity. Doesn't make it hurt less though."

Meanwhile, Greschenko rummaged around in the cab of the shot up pick-up truck.

"Ah," Greschenko said. She pulled a paper map she found in the truck and spread it out on the hood next to Anatoly's flash light and continued to speak into her phone animatedly in Russian pointing to topographical features on the map and cross-referencing to the GPS on her phone.

Through her ripped leggings and hoody Stefania wiped down the scratches to her knees and elbow inflicted on her dive behind the rock, and added some jell and band aids to them. She walked around in the dark looking for her baseball cap which flew off in the fracas, and while doing so took her hair tie off, reorganizing her pony tail. Always self conscious, she now imagined that she looked like a beat up ragamuffin.

"We shouldn't linger long," said Thomas.

"Yes," added Anatoly. "Once they're missed, others will come."

Anatoly took out a cigarette, lit it up and took a drag.

There it is, thought Stefania as she picked up her hat brushing it off. From ten feet or so Stefania surveyed the scene. Two dead gunmen lay on the dirt road, and three more in the back of the pick-up truck with one hanging over the cab.

She stood looking back in a stupor.

My God, am I so heartless that I've gotten used to violence. Is this desensitizing me? Am I so invested in my story that it's blinding me to what I am doing?

She hardly noticed that Thomas had walked up to her.

"You did what you had to do," said Thomas softly.

"Pardon," said Stefania. "I'm sorry."

"I said you did what you had to do."

She put her right hand on Thomas' cheek, and Thomas grasped it with his left, and then kissed it.

Shivers ran up and down her spine.

"You could've walked out on this a while ago," said Thomas. "The Russians can blackmail me, ruin my life, my family's reputation, but you are free."

"I'm free as long as I'm alive," responded Stefania. "I baled on you last time after the Vatican fiasco. I don't want this to end in the same way."

"You two," barked Greschenko. "Come here."

Greschenko finished her call.

"We will be evacuated by helicopter," she declared. "But we have to get to a safe spot for extrication."

"Where's that?" asked Stefania.

"Here," replied Greschenko pointing on the topographic map to a flat area of terrain. "It's three kilometers from here. We go off the road here to the right, down the mountain following an *arroyo* here. At the bottom it flattens out and widens."

"I see, but where do we get picked up?" asked Stefania.

"There's a wide area of the wash which is sandy and devoid of trees," responded Greschenko. "Hopefully there's no water there. That's the pick-up spot."

"When?" asked Stefania.

"Under normal circumstances it should take us about thirty minutes to get there," said Greschenko. "I'm giving us forty."

"How can a helo get from Monterrey to that spot in forty minutes?" asked Stefania.

"It can't," responded Greschenko. "We were never going to make that long drive back to Monterrey. There was no need for surprise coming back, other than getting across the frontier. The helo was waiting for us at a rendezvous point. It is now going to pick us up here since we can't get to it. Got it?" asked Greschenko with raised eyebrows. "It will take the helo about thirty or so minutes to get here, and by then we'll be at the rendezvous."

Thomas turned to Stefania and nodded as if to say "I told you so."

"Yeh, I've got it," replied Stefania.

Ugh, I hate flying in a plane, I can only imagine I'll be terrified in a helo.

Greschenko hopped up into the bed of the pick-up.

"What are you doing?" asked Stefania staring up at Greschenko.

"I know what she's doing," replied Thomas. "Greschenko's wily, that's for certain."

Greschenko threw something to the ground with a thud, then a second.

"Two Kevlar vests," she said. "A bit bloodied, but serviceable. I suggest you put them on in case there's trouble on our way to the helo pick-up."

"But won't the narcos know that we're responsible for this if they catch us?" asked Stefania.

"Sure will," responded Greschenko with a huff, still standing in the pick-up truck bed. "But they'd figure that out anyway. Plus, we're also subject to running into other narcos, coyotes, and God knows who else."

"Point taken," said Stefania.

Greschenko jumped down from the bed of the truck sporting Kevlar vest, an ammo belt and an automatic rifle.

"What have you there?" asked Stefania.

"A FX-05 *Carabina*, in good shape too," replied Greschenko. She cocked the slide, held it up and took a shot into the darkness. "Still operable." She then ejected the clip and reloaded it with a new one. "How you on ammo with the AK?" she asked.

"I've got enough for another firefight, not much more," replied Anatoly. "I'm more comfortable with the AK."

"Then stick with it," replied Greschenko. "And get a vest for yourself, there's one left." Greschenko motioned to the dead driver on the ground.

Anatoly stripped the vest from the driver.

"How about for the forties?" asked Greschenko.

"We've got thirty or so rounds left, enough for a full clip for each," replied Anatoly looking up as he snatched the vest off the dead man. "She'll be fine with it," motioning to Stefania with his head. "Not sure he's going to be much help," now motioning to Thomas.

"Do you two want to take an FX each?" asked Stefania.

"No," replied Stefania. "I'm fine with the pistol. I've never fired a carbine before."

"I'm afraid in my condition I'm barely serviceable with the forty," replied Thomas dejectedly. "I'll do my best with it."

Stefania picked up a vest and delicately put it on Thomas.

"Agh," Thomas groaned.

"I'm sorry Thomas," replied Stefania.

Thomas's eyes caught Stefania. This time he gently placed his left hand on her cheek, caressing it slightly, and kissed her on the forehead.

Stefania's heart skipped a beat. Thomas withdrew with a soft smile. Stefania stepped back and strapped her vest on.

"This thing is heavy," she commented.

"They usually run around ten pounds or so," said Thomas. "It'll make the trek a bit tougher."

"DiMaggio, get your shoulder bag," ordered Greschenko. "You'll have to make do with it somehow. Anatoly, take the backpack. Be sure that we leave nothing behind of significance, and make sure your weapons are locked and loaded."

"Understood," Stefania replied.

"I've got the vehicle tags in my pack," added Anatoly.

"Alright," barked Greschenko. "Let's get a move-on. I'll take point, DiMaggio stay behind me, followed by Thomas. Anatoly bring up the rear. We'll precede single file down the *arroyo*, no talking, no phones, no lights. Understood?"

They all nodded.

"The helo's on route," she said.

No sooner than she finished speaking did Greschenko disappear behind a large agave. Stefania followed her.

"These sneakers aren't going to hold up going down this wash," Stefania whispered to no-one in particular.

"Shhh," snapped Greschenko.

Stefania stumbled over the rocks. The rugged gully illuminated only by the moonlight.

Her predicament finally dawned on Stefania.

I got Thomas into this mess, she thought. *God if anything happens to him I don't know if I could live with myself.*

She could hear Thomas behind her, his footsteps, his every breath, and an occasional moan.

Thoughts bounced around in her head.

What will the helicopter ride be like? What if it can't find us? Will Thomas be alright?

It seemed like they had emerged from the gully into a flatter sandy area, maybe even a trail. It made the going easier.

Greschenko suddenly stopped. Stefania almost ran into her. Greschenko crouched down and motioned for everyone to do the same. She raised the FX to her shoulder.

Through the silence of the night Stefania could hear faint voices, male voices, speaking in Spanish, getting louder by the second. Stefania didn't like her situation, but she'd learned one thing about survival. She removed the pistol from her bag and clicked off the safety. She heard Thomas and Anatoly do the same.

Shadowy figures emerged ahead from the brush, cowboy hats with presumably persons underneath. They stopped. They crouched, and guns were drawn.

They see us, we see them, now what?

"Let us pass and no-one gets hurt," blurted Greschenko in Spanish.

No response.

"I said, let us pass and no-one gets hurt," repeated Greschenko in Spanish. "Otherwise, we'll kill every single one of you mother fuckers where you stand."

Still silence.

"Yes," came a voice in Spanish. "Agreed."

"Step off the path two meters and let us pass then," ordered Greschenko in Spanish. She then said something in Russian, presumably for Anatoly's edification.

The shadowy figures stepped off the path.

"Let's go," she said to Stefania in Spanish. "Keep your guns at the ready."

As they walked down the trail Stefania could see two male figures with cowboy hats in front, one with a pistol, the other with an automatic rifle, followed by six or seven what looked like young females, and two armed men with cowboy hats bringing up the rear. After they went by, Stefania looked back and the group continued on their way.

"Human traffickers," whispered Greschenko. "The lowest of the low. Under different circumstances I'd have killed the bastards."

"Where were they going?" whispered back Stefania.

"Don't be naïve," responded Greschenko softly. "America has an insatiable appetite for drugs, sex, and material things. They were importing sex. The only reason they didn't engage us is that a gunfight may have killed or wounded their precious cargo. Now quiet."

How long has it been now? Stefania asked herself as she trudged along the now sandy *camino. Thirty-five or forty minutes?*

She dare not take out her phone and check the time and draw Greschenko's ire.

I don't know about Greschenko, but I actually think Anatoly is warming up to me.

Over her shoulder she caught a glimpse of Thomas. His left arm held his right. Still in the *arroyo*, the group surrounded by a low thicket, Greschenko stopped and squatted down. She took out the map, laid it on the ground, and used her phone flashlight. She then checked her satellite phone's GPS.

"Well?" whispered Stefania.

"We are about one-hundred meters from the pick-up point," Greschenko whispered back. She pointed ahead. "Let's go."

The last hundred meters took longer than Stefania expected. After trudging in the sandy wash they came to a flat clearing where the *arroyo* widened, keeping the area free from brush.

"We are here," declared Greschenko.

She took out her satellite phone and started talking in Russian. Thomas and Anatoly sat on a couple of rocks at the edge of the wash. Anatoly took a water bottle out of his pack and handed one to Thomas and one to Stefania.

"Thanks Anatoly, but I'm not thirsty," said Stefania.

"We should hear them any second now," said Greschenko.

Stefania scanned the sky. The slight thud thud of copter blades whirling through the sky could be heard from the south. It got louder by the second. She could now see the strobe lights from the chopper's underside.

"It's coming in very low," said Stefania.

"Yes," replied Greschenko. "When it lands, duck and run up to the door, we'll go in single file. They'll give you headsets when we get in. Hopefully they'll shut down to let us in, if not, cover your eyes as best you can, and hold onto your hat, it will be stirring up a lot of sand."

"Why aren't you telling Anatoly and Thomas this?" Stefania asked.

"They'll know what to do," replied Greschenko. "This is your first time in a helo, yes?"

"Yes," replied Stefania.

"Well then," said Greschenko. "Here it comes, follow me in."

The sleek white chopper came in low over the desert, and landed fifty feet in front of them. The wash erupted in a torrent of blowing dust. The engines powered down and the sliding door flung open. The rotor slowed. Greschenko looked back and motioned toward the copter.

The four ran toward the whirlybird, heads down and jumped into seats facing each other, Anatoly and Greschenko in the front facing Thomas and Stefania. A slim young woman, with short blonde hair, in jeans, combat boots, and a tight fitting olive drab shirt handed everyone earphones. The engines powered back up. The woman slammed the sliding door shut. Anatoly, Greschenko and Thomas strapped a harness over their chests. The woman pushed Stefania back and fastened Stefania into a harness. The helmeted pilot looked back and Greschenko whirled her hand around in a circle in the air. The chopper lifted from the ground in a bank of dust into the night sky.

A young man in a matching olive drab shirt, military style cargo pants, and campaign hat wearing combat boots, started looking over Anatoly's wounds. An olive drab duffle bag lay on the floor with medical supplies. As he looked over Anatoly's arm wound, Anatoly pointed to Stefania. The man gave Stefania a thumbs up and a smile. He then turned to Thomas, and immediately gave him an injection of some kind in his arm.

Stefania could hear a constant muffled whine through the headset and occasional banter in Russian. Sitting closest to the windows, she gazed out into the night. Anxious from her fear of flying, butterflies circled in her gut. As the helo rose into the sky she saw in the far distance what appeared to be several vehicles, headlights ablaze, illuminating the grizzly scene of the shootout on the frontier between Mexico and the United States. The copter banked sharply to the right away from the scene.

Exhausted and covered in sweat and dust, Stefania's mind raced. She couldn't help but wonder, *what's the common thread here? What am I missing? Was this Arizona Senator just another distraction?*

She turned to Thomas, who seemed more at ease, and in less pain. Stefania smiled, and Thomas returned her grin.

Where is this going? she thought. *Think, Stefania, think.*

Chapter 13

Morning, March 14, 40,000 feet above Mexico

"**D**o you love him?" asked Greschenko quietly, sitting back in the plush leather seat of Thomas' jet as it leveled off after take-off on its way to Mexico City. Greschenko seemed ensconced in comfort, wearing tight jeans with black knee-high boots, a revealing clingy black sweater, her brunette tresses flowing down to her pert breasts.

"Pardon," asked Stefania, sitting across from Greschenko. Greschenko having taken the facing seat after the group boarded the jet. The hotel store in Monterrey allowed some quick shopping. Stefania donned new black yoga pants and a white hoody complete with the hotel's logo. She kept her beat up sneakers, but cleaned up she figured they didn't look half-bad.

Thomas, his hair askew, slept on a couch two seats aft. Unfortunately he needed more than the store could provide. Anatoly, roughly his size and build, loaned Thomas a pair of camouflage cargo pants and an olive drab military style sweater with black shoulder pads, and his hiking boots.

I've never seen Thomas so mismatched and disheveled, Stefania thought. She smiled at the notion.

Greschenko took a sip from a Bloody Mary, and licked her lips.

"You heard me," responded Greschenko. "Do you love him?"

Stefania awoke from her daze.

"My feelings, whatever they are, are none of your God damned business," replied Stefania, looking over Greschenko's shoulder back to the slumbering Thomas. "Do *you* love him? I'm sorry, you're incapable of love, other than loving yourself."

"He's an interesting specimen," replied Greschenko. "But your characterization of me is unfair."

"How so?" asked Stefania.

"I'm dedicated to my job and my country," said Greschenko. "It's all I've ever known. I don't need a man or woman for that matter to complete me."

"Neither do I," replied Stefania. "But love isn't about completeness is it now. It's an esoteric feeling which manifests itself between two people, drawing them together as one."

"So you *are* in love with him," replied Greschenko with a grin.

Stefania rolled her eyes.

"Why don't you speak with his grandmother about it," snapped Stefania. "You'll have met your match in her, you might not survive the audience, and as I said, I don't think you know what love is," replied Stefania.

"I know about desire and lust," said Greschenko. "Two emotions which have made my job significantly easier."

"How so?" asked Stefania.

"Men are easy to play," said Greschenko. "Most want sex, and if not sex, money. So honey traps set with women, or other men depending on the circumstance, often do the trick. That's how I get most of my intelligence."

"How about women?" asked Stefania. "How do you get to women?"

"Straight women who are attached are the most difficult," offered Greschenko. "Those, we have to blackmail somehow, like men of conviction, such as Thomas. Gay women are the same as men. Single women can be gotten to with bait, usually men or women way above their level."

"So you're whole operation two years ago was to blackmail Thomas so he'd be your tool?" asked Stefania.

"No, but it worked out that way didn't it," replied Greschenko with a smile.

"What's the connection between Thomas' friend Artie and Chen and Tsang?" asked Stefania.

"How the hell am I supposed to know," replied Greschenko.

"I thought you knew everything about everybody," snarled Stefania.

"Your enhanced belief in my abilities is flattering," quipped Greschenko. "Other than Bishop Hough, as far as we can tell no-one else has a direct connection with the Duke of Shropshire, other than Thomas and his grandmother, of course."

The jet jolted, and then a second bump. The blood drained out of Stefania's face and she tightly gripped the armrests.

"You've gotten pale all of a sudden DiMaggio," Greschenko said snidely. "Can't take a little turbulence?"

"I reviewed his web biography when we were in Tucson and there doesn't seem to be any connection between Artie and Hong Kong, where Chen and Tsang are from," said Stefania.

"Maybe there isn't any," shot back Greschenko with a raised brow.

Anatoly walked up the aisle from the back of the plane in his trademark camouflage cargo pants, olive-drab sweater and combat boots, resembling Thomas, with the exception of his crew cut brown hair.

"Excuse me Stefania," he said and then said something to Greschenko in Russian, and she replied also in Russian.

"Excuse me," thought Stefania. *That's a first; he's getting polite.*

"So what's the plan?" asked Stefania. "Why are we going to Mexico City?"

"I'm going to have the burners we found on the two in Arizona decrypted, see if they turn up anything. Other than that, I've gotten pre-approval to detain, question Tsang, *et cetera*," answered Greschenko.

"*Et cetera* meaning *to kill* him?" asked Stefania in a raised tone.

"*Et cetera* meaning none of *your* God damned business."

"This likely isn't the end you know," said Stefania with a tip of the head. "We thwarted a nuclear terrorist attack. If there are others behind this, they may be persistent."

"Unfortunately, you are correct," replied Greschenko, taking another sip of her cocktail. "However, it is my job to make sure that the Russian Federation is not implicated. In that regard, my job is completed for the time being. We do, however, wish to know who was the money behind Wu as the buyer of our nuclear weapon. That individual, or individuals, will be terminated with extreme prejudice lest they try it again. A wet operation."

"And how do you intend to find that out?" asked Stefania.

"Individuals at China desk at MI6 are involved somehow, and I've got the bait," said Greschenko.

"The bait?" asked Stefania.

"Yes, the bait," repeated Greschenko. "You know, when you want to catch a fish you put a couple of worms on a hook and hope the fish bites."

"And Thomas and I are the worms?"

"Your words, not mine."

"Aces," said Stefania followed by a sigh.

Stefania glanced over Greschenko's left shoulder. Thomas stretched and yawned.

"What's this talk about going fishing?" he asked.

"Just small talk," replied Greschenko staring into Stefania's eyes. "Inconsequential."

"Thomas, do you know of any connection between your friend Artie and Hong Kong?" asked Stefania.

Thomas stretched again.

"That hurt," he said as he put his arm down. "I've got to learn to take it easy with my right arm. Your Russian medic did a nice job with it. Hopefully in a few weeks it'll be as good as new."

"How will you explain the bullet holes?" asked Greschenko.

"I'll just say it's an unreported wound from my service in Afghanistan," replied Thomas. "Once it's healed of course. In the interim, I'm going to say I've sprained it or some such thing."

"What's an 'unreported wound?'" asked Stefania.

"Many of us SAS blokes in Afghanistan wouldn't report minor wounds for fear of being taken off station," answered Thomas.

He paused for a few moments. His face lit up like a child's on Christmas day.

"Afghanistan, that's it!" he exclaimed.

"What about Afghanistan?" asked Stefania.

"Well that jogged my memory," replied Thomas.

"What about?" asked Greschenko.

"Lord Darby, the fourth Viscount, was a major player in the First Anglo-Afghan war in the nineteenth century," explained Thomas. "He was a British officer at the time, a colonel or general I believe."

"I'm not following, Thomas," said Greschenko, taking sip of her Bloody Mary.

"His great-grandson, the seventh Viscount Darby was part of the Crown Colony administration of Hong Kong before the handover in 1997."

"Still not following," added Greschenko with a frown, taking another sip of her cocktail.

"It totally slipped my mind, and it's a little known fact," said Thomas.

"What, what's a little known fact?" impatiently snapped Greschenko.

"It's not public knowledge, but Lord Darby acted as a sort of a mentor for Artie," replied Thomas. "Artie used to refer to him as 'Uncle.' A spare heir is a tough position. The heir gets all the attention. Lord Darby was good friends with the Queen's consort when they served together in the RAF. After he returned from Hong Kong, he became the then Princesses', the current Queen's, equerry, served in that position for years, which is when he took Artie under his wing, so to speak."

"We need to speak with this Lord Darby," said Stefania.

"I'm afraid that's impossible," replied Thomas. "He's deceased."

"What about his children?" asked Stefania. "Maybe they might have some information."

"He had no children," chimed in Greschenko.

"True," said Thomas. "But how do you know that."

"It's my business to know the details of the heir's equerry," snapped Greschenko. "Although I didn't know he was the Duke of Shropshire's mentor."

"Who is the current Viscount?" asked Stefania.

"The heir to the title was Lord Darby's first cousin, Harold," replied Thomas. "They weren't close, so I can't imagine speaking to Harold would yield any information. He's not close to his majesty."

"Isn't that similar to your predicament," said Stefania. "If you die without children your cousin James inherits your title."

"That's correct," replied Thomas quizzically, with a puzzled look on his face. "But I don't remember ever telling you that."

"I remember meeting James and his wife Katarina at Haverford Hall," replied Stefania. "I like her very much. She almost died with me when we were nearly run off the road near Haverford," said Stefania in a louder voice.

Stefania's eyes shot to Greschenko, her brows raised.

Greschenko rolled her eyes.

"As I recall James and Katarina were married Anglican, and their child was likewise baptized Anglican, but they were brought up

Catholic and James ultimately converted," said Stefania. "Another marriage arranged by your grandmother."

Thomas slapped his thigh with his left hand with a loud smack.

"He demanded the last rites from a Catholic priest," exclaimed Thomas.

"Who?" asked Greschenko.

"Lord Darby," replied Thomas.

"How do you know this?" asked Stefania.

"Grandmamma," replied Thomas. "My grandmother told me after his death."

"So he was Catholic," said Greschenko. "Him and a billion others. As I recall his funeral was at Westminster."

"Abbey or cathedral?" asked Stefania. "It makes a difference."

"I'm not sure," grumbled Greschenko.

"What!" exclaimed Stefania in feigned astonishment. "I can't believe my ears."

Greschenko retorted with something in Russian.

"Now I'm recalling it," said Thomas. "He was an Anglican convert to Catholicism. He converted while in Hong Kong."

"How would your grandmother know?" demanded Greschenko. "It could've just been a rumor."

Stefania smiled.

"His grandmother knows all things Catholic in the UK," said Stefania with a laugh. "It's a small community. If Elizabeth said it, it was true. She's probably responsible for most of the converts among the aristocracy."

Thomas scratched his head.

"What are you thinking?" asked Greschenko.

"I'll bet he's thinking the same thing I'm thinking," replied Stefania.

Greschenko rolled her eyes again.

"Which is what, precisely?" she demanded.

"If Lord Darby was in Hong Kong at the same time as Chen's father, Francis Xavier Chen, a real estate magnate, perhaps he knew him," said Stefania.

"It would seem plausible," murmured Greschenko, sweeping her brunette mane back with her hand. "Thomas, is it likely?"

"I would think so," said Thomas. "Lord Darby's lofty position in the administration would have given him access to Hong Kong's elite, of which Francis Xavier Chen certainly was one."

"Unfortunately that's speculation at this point," said Greschenko softly while running her hand through her hair.

Stefania's mind raced. Like a tape recorder she rewound and replayed memories locked away in her brain.

"How is it that James and Katarina's child was baptized Anglican, but raised Catholic?" asked Stefania.

"The Catholic church recognizes Anglican baptisms," replied Thomas. "It's the other sacraments that have to take place in the Catholic faith, reconciliation, communion, confirmation, holy orders, and matrimony being the big ones. In any event, I'm sure granny pulled some strings."

"Ahh," replied Stefania.

"Ahh what?" growled Greschenko.

"Nothing," said Stefania. "Is it possible this Catholic angle is leading us down a primrose path? A diversion, another false-flag, designed to lead astray."

"There is an old Russian saying," said Greschenko quietly, looking back at Thomas and then at Stefania. "Loosely translated it means 'Little thieves are hanged, but great ones escape.'"

"I know that saying," said Anatoly, walking down the aisle and standing next to Stefania with his hands on the head rests of the seats on either side. "The thief who stole three kopecks is hung and the one who stole fifty kopecks is praised."

"What's your point?" asked Stefania in a raised tone.

"So far Smith, Wu, Chen, the two rubes in New Jersey, the and the two ne'er-do-wells in the RV are dead, the alleged Uyghur terrorists captured," replied Greschenko, still in a soft monotone.

"Smith, Wu and Chen are mid-level, and the rest are bit players," added Anatoly nodding.

"Which means, according to the saying, and frankly my instincts, whoever is at the top of this, is someone of significant influence and power," said Greschenko in a monotone.

Stefania picked up her tablet, switched off airplane mode and entered a search for the seventh Viscount Darby.

Greschenko's eyes cut to her.

"What?" responded Stefania. "This cover story of yours is that Thomas and I are going to Mexico, it's not a secret."

Greschenko folded her arms and turned her head away.

"Holy crap," exclaimed Stefania. "Well that was easy."

"What DiMaggio?" asked Greschenko. "Spill the beans."

"Says here that Lord Darby converted to Catholicism while stationed in Hong Kong," replied Stefania.

Stefania saw Anatoly's reflection on her tablet screen. He read along as she reviewed the web biography.

"Well we've established that already," snapped back Greschenko.

"Interesting," said Anatoly, now smiling.

"Well what is it?" asked Greschenko excitedly.

"Says here that real estate magnate Francis Xavier Chen was Lord Darby's sponsor at his confirmation," replied Stefania forcefully, followed by an ear-to-ear grin. "And his funeral took place at Westminster Cathedral."

"Why are you grinning DiMaggio?" demanded Greschenko "Smiling for no reason is a sign of stupidity. You found information on-line. You didn't perform a miracle."

"You never answered my question, why we are going to Mexico City," demanded Stefania.

"Oh but I did," responded Greschenko softly, with a devious smirk. "I told you we were going fishing, and my sources tell me that Mexico City is the best pond to catch a bottom feeder such as Tsang. I've got the worms, now I just have to cast the line."

"What am I missing?" asked an apparently bewildered Thomas.

"You don't want to know," responded Stefania.

Early Afternoon, March 14, Mexico City, Mexico

Two black SUVs picked up the group from the airport in Mexico City. The truck in the lead carried the luggage. Stefania and Thomas took the back seat of the follow-up SUV, Greschenko took the front passenger's seat, and Anatoly took the driving duties. The original driver went with the lead SUV. The bright sunshine flowed through the long moon roof illuminating the entire cabin. The SUVs sped away from the airport on the *circuito interior* toward downtown Mexico City.

"I gather that Stefania and I are the bait in your attempt to locate Tsang," said Thomas. "But what is the plan exactly?"

Greschenko turned back from the passenger seat and her eyes cut straight to Thomas.

"In a few minutes you will check into the St. Regis and pay with your credit card," she said matter of factly. "Another stop on the whirlwind tour of exciting locales by you two lovers."

Stefania scoffed loudly, her eyebrows raised.

"That wasn't necessary," added Thomas.

Ignoring the interruption, Greschenko continued, "Your luggage will be brought to your rooms. You will take lunch at the hotel, and later you will then be seen leaving by private car to the Basilica of Our Lady of Guadalupe."

"Why did you pick the basilica as the location for the fishing expedition?" asked Thomas.

"Because it is eminently believable," replied Greschenko. "Your religiosity is well known. It makes perfect sense that you would make a pilgrimage to the basilica while in Mexico City. No one would believe you'd go clubbing."

"She's got a point there," added Stefania.

Thomas turned to Stefania with a frown.

"What?" Stefania asked as she shrugged.

"Assuming Tsang is using his MI6 authority to keep tabs on you, he'll know you've arrived in Mexico City as soon as you register at the hotel. He'll then follow you, and make his move, preferably at the basilica or on its grounds," said Greschenko.

"What makes you think he'll try to take us out there?" asked Stefania.

"Because there will likely be a lot of people around as it's a Lenten Sunday, you'll be there for Mass at 1800," she replied. "It'll be easy for him to melt into the crowd, and there are plenty of escape routes," said Greschenko. "Unlike the others, we don't think he's on a suicide mission."

"What makes you so sure he won't get away?" asked Thomas.

"We'll have the entire complex crawling with our agents," added Greschenko. "He won't get away."

"Just like the bomb wouldn't get across the border," snapped Stefania snidely. "That went well, didn't it."

In the rear view mirror Stefania saw Anatoly breaking a slight smile.

"You're still breathing DiMaggio, and your heart is pumping blood," barked Greschenko with a smirk. "You should count your blessings."

Late Afternoon, March 14, Tepeyac Hill, Mexico

With Thomas next to her, Stefania strode through the large cobbled square in the Guadalupe complex. The huge modern, circular green domed basilica loomed in front of them. The older, more ornate red brick church rose above them through the swarm of pilgrims filling the square. The warm mellow rays of the subsiding sun reflected off its golden dome and red brick made the old church seem more sedate and welcoming than the cold modern architecture of the new basilica.

Stefania turned in her black yoga pants and sneakers, for flats, white jeans and a low cut thin long blue cotton sweater which covered her tight derriere, but still exposed enough cleavage to peak Thomas' interest yet conservative enough for church. She noticed that Thomas wore khakis and a tight sweater which accentuated Thomas' athletic build and muscular upper body. The crisp leather soles of his brown loafers clicked on the pavers as they walked through the square.

She took out her phone. It was 1745. They had been walking around for twenty minutes and no sign of Tsang. Like a slow flowing river, the crowd of devout Mexicans inched toward one of the seven doors for the 1800 mass. Greschenko and Anatoly kept pace thirty feet behind them. More Russian agents were in the crowd looking for Tsang.

"During our last adventure, we ended up at Aparecida in Brazil," said Stefania. "I thought that was the largest shrine to the Holy Mother?"

"The basilica there is," replied Thomas. "But the Basilica of Our Lady of Guadalupe, is the most visited Marian shrine in the world."

Stefania instinctively turned around and took a selfie of herself with the old church in the background.

222

"The new basilica seems, from the outside at least, a bit sterile," said Stefania, hoping to coax Thomas into one of his history lessons which she desperately missed.

"I agree," replied Thomas pointing at the modern edifice. "It was constructed in the 1970s, but the old basilica has all the charm," he continued as he turned toward the right and the older church.

"What is the story of Our Lady of Guadalupe?" Stefania asked, even though after being confirmed into the church two years ago, she was well aware of the legend of the patroness of the Americas.

The two turned back toward the modern church, slightly jostled by the crowd, swept up by the quiet wave of humanity.

"It's actually very compelling," confessed Thomas as they walked toward one of the doors of the circular basilica. "Similar to Fatima, Lourdes and Medjugorje, the Guadalupe story involves several apparitions or visitations by the Holy Mother. In this case, to Juan Diego, an indigenous man, who she spoke to in his native Nahuatl language. According to the account, during the fourth apparition, the Holy Mother told Juan Diego to pick roses from the top of the Tepeyac Hill, near where we are standing, which he did and collected them in his cloak, or *tilma*. When Juan Diego opened the *tilma*, the flowers fell out, but on the mantle was a depiction of the Holy Mother as a pregnant indigenous woman. That *tilma* is housed in the basilica."

"Ah, Thomas, I so missed your history lessons," murmured Stefania with a sigh.

"What was that?" he asked.

"Nothing," she replied. "I'm sorry, you were saying."

"The mantle has great significance to indigenous Mexicans," continued Thomas. "It contains several relevant symbols which are significant only to them, everything from the color of her cape, her belt, the snake, and the rays of light surrounding her. The most unusual part of the image is that close analysis of her eyes indicate they contain reflections of people, tripled versions of the same reflections of the type found on the human eye."

By now the two entered the cavernous church.

"Let's take in mass," said Thomas.

Stefania stood for a moment looking toward the main altar with the green, white and red tricolor Mexican flag draped under the gold framed image of the *tilma* centered about thirty feet up, and then sat next to Thomas in the back of the huge church. Thousands of pilgrims crowded into the place, nevertheless, placidity and quiet created an air of calm. She forgot their purpose in being there. The choir began singing in Spanish. Her eyes drooped closed, and all the thoughts in her mind evaporated like the morning mist. The tranquil gaze of the image on the *tilma*, looking down upon the congregation, filled her with solemnity. Meditating while in a spiritual place had become one of her favorite coping mechanisms.

Now looking down from above, as if flying through the air, she saw herself and Thomas, thousands of others in the church, and Anatoly and Greschenko, busily searching for them. Thomas prayed while she sat there next to him, eyes shut, in a trance like meditation. She rose above the basilica. A motorcycle raced through the darkening streets of Mexico City toward them. A sense of foreboding filled her being. Her stomach sank.

"Everything will be alright," an androgynous voice said in Italian, or Spanish, Italian, French, Portuguese or English. "You know all the answers, but take care, danger lurks."

A young father sat behind them speaking into his young son's ear, and stroking his jet black hair.

"And your faith will guide you," said the voice.

"Stefania," she heard. "Stefania," a voice said again.

Her eyes opened.

"Stefania," said Thomas. "Time to go."

The crowd rose from their collective feet and proceeded to the exits.

"What happened?" she asked.

"Mass has concluded," said Thomas shrugging.

"Did I participate?" asked a somewhat astonished Stefania.

"Yes," replied Thomas. "More or less, although you seemed a bit out of it. You didn't go up for communion though."

"There you two are," said a familiar female voice.

"Greschenko," said Stefania. "I wondered when you were going to materialize."

"Tsang is not here," she declared.

"Maybe Tsang's found what he wanted, or has lost interest in us," said Stefania, now feeling content and at peace after her meditation.

"I doubt it," grumbled Greschenko.

The four exited the basilica into the dusk-lit square. With the sun slipping below the horizon, the spooky shadow of night crawled upon them. Subtle vermillion hints of the setting sun were giving way to a gray evening.

The four piled into a black SUV, with Anatoly driving, Greschenko riding shotgun, and Stefania and Thomas in the back seat. With a lurch the SUV began the nine minute trip back to the St. Regis through the now darkened streets of Mexico City. Presumably the other agents were already gone.

Emerging from a darkened area, street lights started passing by. Stefania turned and stared at Thomas. The sharp profile of his face illuminated on and off by the passing city lights. The inner placidity she felt suddenly evaporated, and anxiety gripped her. She moved her gaze an inch to the right. Out the side window a motorcyclist kept pace with the SUV. A woman sat behind him holding on to the seat rest. Her frame covered in a tight fitting leather riding vest, her head and eyes obscured by a black helmet with a reflective visor. Her black curls flowed down from underneath the helmet and blew back in the wind. The SUV stopped at red light. The motorcyclist stopped next to the rear door of the SUV. The woman unzipped her vest with her gloved right hand.

Stefania clutched Thomas' sweater just below the neck line and jerked him toward her. Thomas' gasped as he lay on top of Stefania, his breath warming her cheeks and lips. A millisecond passed. Time seemed to stand still. Small round pieces of tempered glass showered them like rain. Stefania closed her eyes. Her ears filled with the sound of the screech of a motorcycle accelerating. The smell of burning rubber combined with gun smoke wafted through the SUV.

Greschenko yelled something in Russian. The only words Stefania understood were *Avenida de los Insurgentes*. The SUV jerked forward, swaying from side to side as if weaving in and out of traffic. Stefania held Thomas close. The SUV made a sharp turn and the two fell onto the floor, Stefania now on top of Thomas between his upright knees. The SUV's engine revved as it sped up.

Stefania righted herself onto the seat and brushed the round pebbles of glass off of her clothes.

"What the hell just happened?" she yelped.

"We'd best to the hotel straight away," said Thomas.

"No," barked Greschenko over the sound of the wind rushing in the shot out rear windows and front driver's side window of the SUV. "We're going to the embassy, at least temporarily. We'll need a new vehicle."

"You didn't think Tsang would do the deed himself?" asked Thomas rhetorically. "There are so many contract killers in Mexico you can't toss a stone without hitting one."

"That wasn't Tsang," added Stefania. "Unless he grew breasts and long hair since we last saw him."

"My reaction was slow," said Greschenko, now in a monotone. "She used a sound suppressor. I managed to get a couple of shots off as they took off, but I doubt I hit either of them. Thank goodness I still had the silencer otherwise I'd have ruined Anatoly's hearing."

"You assumed that because Tsang was a lone wolf at MI6 he wouldn't have sought local help," said Stefania.

Greschenko scoffed and struck the dashboard with her right fist.

"Shit!" she exclaimed, striking the dashboard again.

"You know what you do when you assume," said Stefania. "And you've got to start mixing it up with your pejoratives already."

Anatoly smiled.

"Exactly like Rodrigo Lara," said Greschenko loudly. "Except a woman is less conspicuous but it was the same goddamned MO. Don't worry, we'll find out who she is."

"Don't these embassy vehicles have bulletproof glass and armor plating?" asked Stefania.

"Those are reserved for consular officials," piped in Anatoly. "We're not consular officials. We're expendable."

Now on her phone, Greschenko barked orders in Russian.

"We're bloody lucky is what we are," said Thomas excitedly. "She shot straight through, and missed us both. If you hadn't pulled me down, instead we'd be driving to the morgue."

"Just returning a favor owed," said Stefania.

Evening, March 14, Russian Embassy, Mexico City

"No thank you," said Stefania referring to an offering of caviar on dark crusty bread by a young slim blonde female servant in a white military uniform with gold buttons, matching braids and epaulets. Two other male servants in similar garb stood at each end of the table, removing dishes or refilling glasses of water, wine, or retrieving cocktails.

Stefania took stock of the white paneled dining room, with gold leaf trim, where she sat at a large oval square Russian imperial style mahogany table across from Thomas, with Anatoly sitting next to her, and Greschenko opposite him. The matching chairs were ornate, with gold trim and sea foam green cushions, but hardly comfortable. A crystal chandelier cast a soft glow over the room. Across from her, windowed French doors led into the wooded grounds surrounding the embassy. Feeling safe for the time being, she took a sip of white wine.

"You're crazy," whispered Anatoly into her ear.

"Pardon me," replied Stefania.

"You should take the caviar," he whispered again. "We are getting this VIP treatment because of Assistant Director Greschenko."

Greschenko, seeming distracted, fiddled with a tumbler of vodka and ice.

The waiter came back and served soup.

"What is this?" asked Stefania.

"It is *solyanka*," replied Anatoly. "A hearty soup served in the winter in Russia, and although warm here, it is the season for the dish."

Hesitant, Stefania dipped her spoon into the dish and took a sip of the soup.

"This is quite good," she replied.

"Of course it is," shot back Greschenko.

This is so filling, I can't imagine there is another course.

"The next course is *pirozhki*," declared Greschenko. "Then desert. Other than the caviar, when I have the chance to order what I want, I ask for the comfort food I remember from my *babushka*. It's been long enough without a proper Russian meal."

"She had a grandmother?" Stefania whispered into Anatoly's ear.

Anatoly smiled slightly and covered his mouth with his hand.

The female attendant entered the room from a doorway behind Stefania and brought a large manila envelope to Greschenko. She removed some papers, looked them over and stood up. She threw a photo of a modelesque thirtyish woman with full lips and long curly black hair on the table.

"Viviana Ortiz Cantú," she said.

"Who is she?" asked Thomas.

"She's the contract killer," replied Greschenko. "She's Venezuelan, and *Cartel del Norte's* best assassin."

"Was it in retribution for the battles with the cartel do you think?" asked Stefania.

"Unlikely," said Greschenko.

"Why is that?" asked Stefania.

"Because Tsang crossed the border into Guatemala using one of his alias passports less than ten minutes after the attempt was made on your lives," said Greschenko.

"That's no coincidence," said Stefania cutting into her pastry, and lifting a fork full of meat and cabbage into her mouth.

"Of course not," said Greschenko. "The Mexican authorities were kind enough to provide us with that tidbit of information. Where Tsang is now, is anyone's guess."

"What about Cantú?" asked Stefania. "Is she still lurking about?"

"The Mexicans aren't saying," replied Greschenko. "And we have no way of knowing, and we can't trust the Mexicans, half of them are on the payroll of the cartel."

"And the burners off the two in Arizona?" asked Stefania.

"No texts, unfortunately," said Greschenko. "Just phone calls to each other, and to another burner number, the one from the list in Smith's flat."

"Not unexpected," added Stefania rubbing her chin. "We knew there had to be a connection, and that makes sense. Whoever has that burner is their contact."

"Or was their contact," grumbled Greschenko softly with a shrug. "We're trying to find the location of that burner through the mobile network, but it appears to have been either turned off or disposed of. Last active location was in London, Trafalgar Square area, a few days ago."

"That narrows it," snarked Stefania, folding her arms.

Greschenko rolled her eyes and scoffed.

"I know you've been running the show Svetlana," said Thomas. "But let me contact my investigator Harry in London. He may be able to get inside information on Tsang that you don't have access to."

"We've infiltrated MI5 and MI6," bragged Greschenko. "I can't imagine this Harry may have access to information we don't."

"How high placed are your sources?" asked Thomas.

"That's a state secret," replied Greschenko with a huff.

Anatoly cut to Greschenko and raised his eyebrows.

"Alright," she responded. "You can call him just this once, but I must insist you both stay the night in living quarters on the consular grounds for your own safety more than anything else."

Thomas turned to Stefania.

"Much to my chagrin," said Stefania somewhat sarcastically. "I think we are compelled to accept your gracious invitation."

"Lest we end up corpses on the morrow," added Thomas.

"Phone this Harry person now," demanded Greschenko. "And put it on speaker, I want to hear the conversation."

"It's 0230 in London," explained Thomas.

Greschenko raised her brows and tipped her head.

"Now or never," she added with a smirk.

Thomas put his phone on the table and dialed Harry's burner.

"Thomas, by God, am I glad to hear your voice," said Harry. "I was starting to wonder."

"Sorry old chap, I trust I'm not too much a bother at this hour," said Thomas.

"It's no bother, I just got in from the pub," replied Harry. "Shh, love, I'll be right with you," Harry said to someone he was with.

"Listen Harry, there is a chap at MI6 named John Gabriel Tsang, find out what you can for me," asked Thomas. "Be as discrete as possible, as I'm concerned for your safety."

"Understood," said Harry. "Where are you?"

"That's not important," said Thomas. "Remember our last call?"

"Aye," replied Harry.

"I will reach out for you tomorrow at that time plus six," said Thomas.

"Right," replied Harry.

"And you take care," said Thomas.

"What time will you call him back tomorrow?" asked Greschenko.

"0700 our time," replied Thomas.

"That doesn't give him much time," said Greschenko.

"Harry will get the information by then," replied Thomas. "Believe me. What do you have on Tsang?"

"Other than what I've told you," replied Greschenko. "Not much. We have not been able to gather any personal history on him."

"John Gabriel Tsang," repeated Thomas. "Interesting name."

"How so?" asked Stefania.

"There was a Catholic saint," added Thomas. "John Gabriel Perboyre, a French missionary I believe, who was martyred in China."

"A mere coincidence," said Greschenko with a smirk.

Stefania stood and placed her hands on the table.

"I'm afraid Greschenko you've missed the fact throughout this ordeal, that there are no such things as coincidences."

Greschenko scoffed and rose from her seat.

"You will have your own rooms tonight," said Greschenko. "The orderlies will show you the way. We'll reconvene here tomorrow at 0700."

Greschenko stomped out of the room after barking orders in Russian to the woman attendant.

"You pissed her off," whimpered Anatoly with a frown. "Now no dessert. It was *sharlotka*, my all-time favorite, with black tea."

"I'm sorry Anatoly, that I cost you desert," responded Stefania with a soft frown.

The blonde servant stared in Anatoly's direction and winked at him.

"I think you are about to get lucky," said Stefania, who sat back down.

The staff brought in servings of a white cake powdered with confectioner's sugar, and black tea for Thomas, Anatoly and Stefania.

The waitress bent over, pressed her ruby red lips against Anatoly's ear and whispered something in Russian.

"What did the waitress say?" asked Stefania.

"Let's just say I don't think I'll be spending tonight by myself," replied Anatoly. "Oh and while they are wait staff, they are Russian Army."

Stefania finished eating the apple cake.

"This was delicious," she stated.

Anatoly nodded.

"I'd say a bit stodgy," muttered Thomas.

The blonde woman returned and whispered something again in Anatoly's ear.

"Have a nice evening," he said as he got up to follow the blonde leaving the room. "The other two staff will attend to your needs and show you to the living quarters. And I don't think I need to tell you this, but don't go snooping around. See you tomorrow."

Anatoly left Thomas and Stefania alone with the two male uniformed attendants.

"You were right," said Thomas with a laugh. "Anatoly got lucky, he got his cake, and he got to eat it too."

Stefania laughed.

"Seriously, as always I think they know more than their letting on," said Thomas.

"The question is, what is it?" asked Stefania. "We're still no closer to connecting the dots. We've got names, but no commonality of purpose."

"True," replied Thomas. "We've got the means and the opportunity, but no motive, or at least the real motive is obscured."

Standing up, Stefania gazed out the French doors into the wooded garden of the embassy grounds lit by the setting half moon.

"So let me get this right," said Stefania. "If the Princess dies without children, your friend Artie becomes heir to the throne."

"Correct. Where are you going?"

"Hear me out Thomas, please. What if Artie is a Catholic?"

"He's not."

"But what if he is?"

"Then under the Succession to the Crown Act of 2013, he's not the heir. Being a Catholic, he would be removed from the line of succession."

"Who's next in line after Artie?"

"His first born. His son."

"Assume his children are Catholic."

"Then it would be the Queen's first cousin, James."

"What's his religious affiliation?"

"Church of England, naturally."

"What's the story with James?" asked Stefania.

"He's in his late eighties, not in very good health."

"After James?"

"He's no children, so it's his younger sister, Princess Caroline. She's also in her eighties. Due to their advanced ages, James and Caroline have not been engaged in the business of the royal family for some time, which the Queen has not quibbled with."

"What about her children?" asked Stefania. "Are they well known or popular?"

"Not really. She's got two children. They've private lives. The daughter was a model, now retired, and the son is still an architect. She's a countess, and he a marquess. What are you getting at?"

"Nothing I suppose, just curious."

"That's a lot of questions over mere curiosity," said Thomas followed by a laugh.

"Sorry," replied Stefania. "I'm starting to worry we might not survive this time around. We got lucky two years ago."

"I fear, and regret to say, if it weren't for Greschenko's interventions, we'd have come to a sticky end."

"But why try to kill us?" she asked as she started pacing about the room.

"Let's assume that it's Tsang from MI6 and he's affiliated with Chen in some way," theorized Thomas.

"Yes, so what put it all in motion was your inquiry through Harry about Chen," stated Stefania.

"Right."

"And Tsang probably knows Chen's disappeared."

"Right. And with Tsang's MI6 connections he could probably monitor my movements, and perhaps even my communications."

Stefania put her hands on her hips. "So Thomas, for the sake of argument, if Chen was the focal point in connection with Wu's importation of weapons, including the RA-115, knowing that information would be pretty significant."

"Also correct Stefania. But we don't know why. It's a false flag operation with many layers."

"But Tsang doesn't know *what* we know."

"Whatever he assumes we know must be so damning that killing us is the only option."

"Yes, especially since your murder would be big news in the UK."

"And they didn't try to disguise the attempt as anything but murder, even in Richmond Park," added Thomas. "Extremely vexing."

"I think we can both agree that if we were killed in Mexico, the chances of the Mexican police catching the actual killer would be slim to none."

"Quite," replied Thomas rubbing his chin and leaning back in his chair.

"The only common thread is that Chen was Catholic, and that her father was the godfather of the Price of Wale's equerry, who was your friend Artie's mentor."

"And that Harrop was a disaffected Anglican seminarian associated with Bishop Hough, and Manhire was a disaffected Catholic seminarian," posited Thomas raising his index finger.

Stefania smiled. "Even in your world of 'there are no such thing as coincidences,' those are pretty thin connections. Plus, on Smith's list that leaves the Duke of Shropshire and Bishop Hough who don't fit any Catholic narrative," said Stefania.

"Greschenko seems to agree with that assessment. Or at least that's what she's letting on," noted Thomas.

"Unfortunately, as we've discussed, she holds all the cards at this point in time," said Stefania, her two hands leaning on the table.

"That she does," Thomas said in a monotone. "She most certainly does," he repeated.

"I'll guess we'll hear what Harry has to say in the AM," said Stefania.

"Shall we go through?" asked Thomas.

"Sir," said Stefania speaking to one of the two attendants. "Can you take us to our rooms?"

The young smartly uniformed attendant responded with a blank look. Stefania thought a moment. Thomas looked at her and shrugged.

"I dare say, I don't believe they understand English," observed Thomas. "That poses a dilemma."

"Sir," said Stefania in Spanish. "Can you take us to our rooms?"

"Yes," he responded in Spanish. "Please follow me. The rooms are on the second floor."

"Good show," said Thomas.

"I figured if they're stationed at the embassy in Mexico, they probably speak Spanish," said Stefania with a smile.

The two were led out the dining room into the wood paneled foyer where they followed the attendant up a large white marble staircase with a blue carpet runner, onto a landing and then up a side staircase to the right. The second attendant followed the group.

They walked by a male guard similarly uniformed, except he had a pistol, sitting at a small polished dark wooden desk at the entry to a short white walled cream carpeted hallway lit dimly with ornate crystal wall sconces. Half a dozen doors exited the hallway, three on each side. Some words in Russian were exchanged. The guard picked up the phone, said a few words in Russian and hung up. He nodded. The group filed down the hallway.

"This is your room miss," said the first attendant in Spanish, pointing to a white door on the right.

"And yours sir," pointing to a white door across the hall. "Should either of you require anything, inquire of the guard," he said in Spanish motioning toward the guard at the end of the hallway. "You are expected in the dining room at 0700. A guard will collect you just before 0700."

Stefania snuck a peak down the hallway. The other end consisted of a mere window.

"The only way out is going by the guard," observed Stefania.

"Sweet dreams," Thomas said to Stefania with a wink and a smile as he opened the door to his room.

"Yes, good night Thomas," she replied as she entered her room and closed the door, and turned the lock.

Slightly better in quality than an upscale hotel room, the door to the full marbled bathroom opened to the right of the entryway. A gray throw rug covered the cream ceramic tile floors, and a polished modern dark wood frame queen size bed awaited in the middle of the room. Opposite sat a small matching writing desk. A large framed photo of the president of Russia hung on the wall above the desk, his eyes lurking over the room. A matching chest of drawers sat next to the desk, with a flat screen television on top. Curtains drawn at the back of the room insinuated a window behind. Drawn to the window, Stefania opened the curtains to find a large sliding window. Below stretched the darkened Russian embassy compound, some gardens, and beyond the lights of Mexico City. She slid the window open a couple of inches, letting in the sounds of the chirping crickets and croaking frogs of the embassy gardens, and the street noise of bustling Mexico City beyond the embassy walls.

At least I'm safe, as an unwilling guest of the Russian Federation, she thought.

Exhausted from the day's events she brushed her teeth using a kit in the bathroom, kicked her flats off, peeled off her tight white jeans exposing her white lace bodysuit, leaving her pants crumpled on the throw rug. Deciding to sleep in the buff for lack of anything else to wear, she laid out her sweater and underwear on the desk chair. Turning off the lamp and plowing under the comforter, she pulled one of the two down pillows to cuddle next to. Her head nested deep into the other. Sleep overcame her and her mind descended into slumber, with the crickets and frogs serenading her to unconsciousness like a fine tuned orchestra.

Stefania's eyes opened, they gazed downward. She knelt on a bed of low heather. Terror once again gripped her. Slightly in front of her, to the right, knelt Thomas. Her breathing became labored. Panic set in. Death seemed near.

Oh Lord, please help me survive this. Oh, Madonna, through your intercession, please see fit to save me, she prayed.

Thomas looked back. He mouthed something to her.

Her eyelids jumped open. Her eyes darted around the room. Sitting up in the bed drenched in sweat from head to toe, all she could hear were the crickets and frogs from the window, safe and sound, it seemed, still in her room in the Embassy compound of the Russian Federation in Mexico City.

Settling back into bed, she lay on her back taking in the cavalcade of sounds from the window. She pulled the comforter up to her chin.

Was that another premonition? She asked herself. *But this time was it my death I foretold? Am I going to die with my feelings for Thomas unrequited?*

Morning, March 15, Mexico City

The four gathered in the same room where they had dinner the night before. Collected first by the guards, Stefania and Thomas were the first to arrive. Greschenko sauntered in wearing black skintight dress yoga pants, a see through white blouse barely concealing a black lace bra underneath, a waist length blue blazer with white piping around the lapels, and shiny black patent leather pumps. Anatoly slumped in, dark circles under his eyes, yawning in a somewhat disheveled in a gray suit, with white shirt and black tie, loosened, askew, and dangling somewhat from his neck. He sat down and immediately gulped down copious amounts of coffee. In a rare sign of disapproval, Greschenko stared at Anatoly, frowned, and shook her head.

The attractive blonde attendant served Greschenko, who sat across from Thomas, some black tea in a gold Russian tea holder. She didn't look as worse for the wear as Anatoly, and produced a nod of acknowledgment in Anatoly's direction followed by a slight smile. Stefania, sitting across from Anatoly nudged him under the table with her foot and smiled. He returned a slight smile and raised brow.

"There's breakfast on the buffet on the breakfront at the far end of the table," noted Greschenko. "Looks like we've got *kasha*, black bread, butter, *kolbasa* and cheese sandwiches, fried eggs, and *syrniki*."

Stefania stuck to the black bread, butter, and an egg.

Greschenko looked at her phone.

"It's almost 0700," she blurted. "Are we going to get this show on the road?"

"Impatient this morning, eh Greschenko," said Stefania with a wicked smile.

Greschenko scoffed and stared at Thomas.

"Well," she demanded.

"Right," said Thomas. He placed the phone in the middle of the table between them, and dialed Harry's burner number.

Greschenko stood and leaned in toward the phone, her hands on the table.

"Thomas," Harry answered.

"Good morning Harry," Thomas replied. "Sounds quiet where you are today."

"I'll explain that some other time," said Harry. "I did find out some news on Tsang."

"Anything useful?"

"Tsang is on an unauthorized absence from MI6," said Harry. "He's absent without orders."

"Interesting," replied Thomas.

"They're looking for him for misuse of internal and external assets," said Harry. "You know what that means."

"Quite," said Thomas, rubbing his chin.

"Last location they had for him was in Belize when he used one of his MI6 passports to get through customs into the country," said Thomas. "They think he may have fled from there to Venezuela or to a Caribbean Isle. They believe that Tsang and Chen were up to something, but they still haven't turned up Chen."

"That's a lot of activity in central America for someone at China desk," pondered Thomas.

"Thomas, Tsang is a field agent," said Harry.

"Crikey," blurted Thomas. "So we were really in harm's way," he murmured in the direction of Greschenko and Stefania.

"And one more thing I found out from my contacts, not directly related to Tsang, but I thought you'd be interested in just the same," said Harry softly.

"Go on," said Thomas.

"Are you aware of that small nuclear explosion in the States?" asked Harry.

"Naturally," said Thomas with a raised brow and a glance across the table to both Stefania and Greschenko.

"The Princess Mary and the Prince were at some musical fete nearby when it happened," explained Harry softly. "It's not public knowledge, and the royal household has held back this information. As soon as the bomb went off their team removed them from the area. Apparently no one knew they were there because everyone at the festival wears masks and costumes. They weren't immediately identifiable."

"Were they the targets?" asked Thomas still looking at Greschenko and Stefania.

"MI6 is working with the Americans," said Harry, still in a low voice. "But my contact wouldn't give me any more information than that. As you know the official American narrative is that it was an attempted terrorist attack on a nearby Army installation that went awry."

Thomas rubbed his chin and did not respond.

Stefania examined Greschenko's face for a reaction. Greschenko's face stayed expressionless.

She knew, Stefania thought.

"Given your close friendship with the Princess's brother," said Harry. "I thought you'd like to know."

"Thanks Harry," Thomas replied solemnly.

"One other thing," said Harry. "Bishop Hough apparently has gone on holiday, to parts unknown."

"Thank you Harry, please send me the usual remittance and take care."

Thomas pressed the end button on his phone and slouched back into this chair.

"How long have you known?" asked Stefania.

Greschenko sat back down and crossed her arms.

"*How long* have you known?" repeated Stefania in a louder tone.

"We haven't been able to confirm this information," replied Greschenko.

"MI6 believes it to be the case," exclaimed Stefania. "What, that's not good enough for you?"

"One of the hallmarks of a good intelligence operation is misdirection, white noise," added Greschenko. "It's possible that this is planted information, a ruse or subterfuge, to lead inquiring minds astray from the real story or objective."

"Or to make it sound like the Princess, who is widely unpopular, was close to being killed," said Thomas authoritatively. "Perhaps it's a ploy toward that end. A leak which then becomes a story to resurrect her sinking popularity."

"What if it's true?" demanded Stefania. "So no one would know who the real targets were," said Stefania. "It would appear a terrorist attack, and the Princess would be collateral damage."

"Yes," said Thomas. "As well as a significant number of rock stars, models, glitterati, celebrities, an anti-Russian Arizona Senator, your favorite Indie band, and others, of course."

"You yourself said that the Princess was the wild child," urged Stefania. "You said she's unconventional. Wouldn't it make sense for her to go to this counterculture festival? Wouldn't it be in her persona?"

"That," said Thomas, followed by a pause. "*Is* a logical deduction."

"I'm not going to argue the issue," blurted Greschenko. "Our sources have provided the same information. If they were at the festival, it could very well be happenstance."

Tears welled in Thomas' eyes.

"I'm proud then that I played a role in saving the life of the heir to the throne," said Thomas solemnly.

Stefania tilted her head back, looking at the ceiling.

"Are you two not connecting the dots?" demanded Stefania. "Who would benefit from the death of the Princess?"

Anatoly put down his coffee cup and stared across the table at Greschenko, still sitting with her arms crossed.

"The next in line to the throne!" exclaimed a now standing Stefania.

"That may be," responded Greschenko in a monotone. "But that's not my concern."

"It is if he used a purloined Russian nuclear weapon to achieve the result," added Stefania. "Isn't it?"

"I cannot believe or countenance the notion that Artie would undertake fratricide to become heir to the throne," said Thomas forcefully. "Not to mention the fact that it's technically treason under the Treason Act of 1702."

Anatoly again glanced in Greschenko's direction.

"It could still be a coincidence," said Greschenko in a monotone. "However, the Brazilian beauty here does make some sense," pointing at Stefania.

Stefania scoffed and sat back down.

Now looking at Thomas, Greschenko continued "Your friend Artie is connected to Smith somehow, Smith was connected to Chen, MI6 thinks Tsang and Chen are connected, and Chen's family was connected to Artie. Our fishing expedition got Tsang to take the bait. Tsang is small fry. Let's try to catch a big fish. Fortunately for me, and unfortunately for Tsang, he left the bait dangling on the hook."

"I'm not following," said Thomas.

"I think what Greschenko here is implying," said Stefania sarcastically. "Is that she intends to use us as bait again."

"I don't imply," responded Greschenko. "I intend to use you as bait again."

"If Chen and Tsang are connected," said Stefania. "Why don't we go back to Smith's flat. Maybe we overlooked something."

"Not an option," responded Greschenko forcefully. "Always lock the door behind you, and never ever return to the scene of a crime."

"What am I missing?" asked Thomas. "Who are you going fishing for this time?"

"If I had to bet," said Stefania. "I'd say Artie."

"Then you'd have gotten a fine return on your bet," responded Greschenko.

"What?" exclaimed Thomas. "You must be joking."

"The Assistant Director does not joke regarding such matters," said Anatoly after taking a sip of coffee.

Greschenko cut to Anatoly, frowning slightly.

"Well you don't," he followed with a shrug, wiping coffee off his lips with a fine white linen napkin.

"How are you going to bait Artie, and to what end?" asked Thomas.

"She figures," interrupted Stefania. "That if Artie is involved somehow, you'll get him either to spill the beans, or he'll have us killed. Either way, she'll know the motive for the operation and he's behind it. She'll then deal with Artie as necessary, blackmail perhaps?"

Greschenko slapped her hand on the table with a loud clap.

The attendants jumped slightly.

"If you survive this," said Greschenko. "I very well may ask you to join Russian intelligence."

"I'll pass on that, thanks," snapped Stefania.

"What if I won't cooperate to entrap Artie?" asked Thomas. "You'll be stuck."

"Do we really need to go through this again?" barked Greschenko snidely with a raised brow.

"You know she's right. It's either your hide or his," said Stefania. "And if he did try to kill his sister, together with thousands of innocent people, wouldn't you want to know? That prospect has to appeal to your sense of morality. He might try it again you know. Not to mention that someone tried to kill us at least twice that we know of. Who would have the motive?"

"Unfortunately I see your point," said Thomas solemnly.

"I thought you might," snapped Greschenko snarkily.

"What's your plan?" asked Stefania, her eyes cutting to Greschenko. "One that will actually *go to* plan this time."

"Thomas will phone Artie, spill some information, wet his appetite so to speak, ask for a sit-down," said Greschenko. "Hopefully the place and time are sufficiently convenient, and we can monitor the situation and protect you if necessary. But as

DiMaggio here mentioned, if he sets up a meeting with you and you disappear, I know who my culprit is."

"It doesn't sound like you came up with that idea on the spur of the moment," said Stefania sarcastically.

"Thomas will tell Artie that you are working on a story and you discovered a link between a group of international terrorists and Bishop Hough," added Greschenko. "Artie's name also surfaced in the course of Stefania's investigation. Thomas assured you that Artie's not involved, but he'd like to discuss it with Artie, in person, of course, before the article is published. That should be sufficient to pique his interest."

"I should imagine," said Thomas softly.

"Anatoly, get your laptop and hook it up to the flat screen," ordered Greschenko.

She pressed a button on the wall and curtains at the end of the room opposite the breakfront opened revealing a wall sized flat screen television which immediately powered on. Anatoly left the room and returned with a laptop, and pecked on the keyboard. His laptop screen materialized on the flat screen. In the meantime Greschenko fiddled with her phone.

"Here it is," declared Greschenko.

"Here is what?" asked Stefania.

"The Duke's phone number we found in Smith's apartment," responded Greschenko. "That's what."

She placed her phone on the table next to Thomas' phone.

"Call the number," she demanded. "Do it now. Try to get him to meet you on your territory, at Haverford Hall preferably, so we can make the most advantageous arrangements to monitor the situation and protect you both if need be."

Thomas's eyes cut to Stefania.

Stefania returned Thomas' glance and nodded.

Thomas let out a sigh and dialed the number on his phone and put it on speaker.

Greschenko stood and leaned in toward the phone.

"Hello," someone answered.

"Artie, this is Thomas."

"Thomas, good to hear from you. Last time I heard you were on holiday in Malta."

"Yes, since then we've gone to Mexico. Stefania wanted to visit the Guadalupe shrine."

"I see, well what do I owe the pleasure of your call?"

"As you know, ahh, Stef, Stefania is a journalist," answered Thomas with a slight stammer. "She's working on a story, and the story turned up some interesting twists."

"Yes," replied Artie. "What has it to do with me?"

"You see she, she seems to have uncovered a nefarious plot of some kind which is linked to Bishop Hough," responded Thomas still stammering. "Since you are very close to the Bishop, your name also came up and we thought it would make sense to discuss it with you before we approached the Bishop."

Artie did not reply.

"Artie," said Thomas. "Are you there?"

"Yes," he replied. "I'm here, I'm sorry but I was taken aback by your revelation. I can't imagine that Bishop Hough is involved in anything untoward. Certainly not I."

"Yes, yes," said Thomas. "I concur. I told Stefania the same. Nevertheless, we should like to meet with you in person to discuss Stefania's findings, naturally before we approach Bishop Hough, rather than discuss it by mobile of course."

"That would be best," said Artie.

"Can you meet us at Haverford Hall tomorrow?" asked Thomas.

"Well," Artie started, and then a pregnant pause permeated the room with silence.

After a few moments Artie continued, "I'm in Scotland hunting, and leaving wouldn't be practical. Why don't you meet me here tomorrow morning?"

"Byram?" asked Thomas.

"Yes."

"I think we can be there by 9 o'clock or so, after we collect the rental," said Thomas.

"Don't bother," replied Artie. "I'll have a car collect you two at the airport. Perhaps I'll ask the good Bishop to join us. Stefania *will* be accompanying you?"

"Yes, naturally, thanks Artie," said Thomas. "Look forward to seeing you tomorrow."

Thomas ended the call.

Greschenko sat back in her chair.

"As I suspected," said Greschenko. "He wants to meet you on his turf and he wants to be in control, even down to the transportation from the airport. Where's his place in Scotland?"

"It's Byram Castle," said Thomas. "His hunting lodge, near the village of Lairg. We'll have to fly into Inverness Airport."

"Anatoly, pull it up on the satellite and show it on the screen," ordered Greschenko.

The satellite view of the Scottish countryside popped up on the flat screen on the wall. A large manor house could be seen, with fields and forests as well.

"There it is," exclaimed Thomas pointing on the aerial.

Anatoly zoomed in on the castle.

"Quite grand," noted Greschenko. "Let's see. What is this wood here?" asked Greschenko pointing to the aerial.

"That's a forest of scots pine," responded Thomas. "It's probably about a quarter of a mile from the manor house."

"What's this here next to the wood?" demanded Greschenko again pointing to the satellite view.

"There's ruins of an old priory in the middle of a sort of small heath," answered Thomas pointing. "There's a formal walking path here from the house to the priory, through a small grove of other trees here, birches, alders and hawthorns mostly I think then over the moor to the priory."

"So the priory is not visible from the castle?" asked Greschenko.

"Correct," answered Thomas. "Not that I can recall."

"How many people in his entourage?" asked Greschenko.

"At Byram Castle there are servants, and Royalty Protection Group. If he's hunting, he may have a hunting party."

"What type of hunting weapons does he use?" asked Greschenko.

"Mostly rifles this time of year," said Thomas with shrug. "He's probably stalking deer, why?"

"Rifle calibers?" insisted Greschenko.

"He's got a small heard of fallow up there, so I believe he uses .308," answered Thomas.

"Won't he be holding all of the cards," snarked Stefania. "How can we possibly maneuver this to our advantage."

"I'm counting on him wanting to hear what you know," declared Greschenko now standing and leaning on the table. "I'm also counting on him not wanting anyone else to hear the conversation, including his bodyguards. If he wants to talk inside, you suggest a discussion outside for privacy. Thomas, you are going to try your damnest to get him to discuss the matter during a stroll along the walking path, through the copse of trees and to the field near the priory."

"Heath," said Thomas.

"What?" asked Greschenko.

Stefania smiled, and Anatoly held his hand over his mouth.

"Technically it's a heath," said Thomas. "A heath is different than a field."

"Whatever," snapped Greschenko.

"Artie likes to go for constitutionals down that path when discussing matters of significance, leaving his bodyguards in the castle," added Thomas. "Getting him there may not take much convincing."

"Excellent," declared Greschenko.

"How can this possibly help us Greschenko?" asked Stefania loudly. "Other than getting us killed without any witnesses."

"Anatoly and I will be hiding in the forest," she responded. "We'll hopefully be able to react to his actions. I just hope that we'll have enough time to hoof it from the road through the forest before you get there."

"And what if you don't?" demanded Stefania, now standing with her hands on her hips.

"Then," responded Greschenko calmly, "if you emerge from the castle alive, Artie is not the money behind the attack. If you don't, he is. As you've correctly surmised, I have my answer either way."

"Aces," snapped Stefania as she sat back down. "Why don't you let Thomas carry a pistol and hide a listening device on one of us?"

"Because it's possible he'll have his guards physically search you for weapons, or use a metal scanner," replied Greschenko. "It's probable that I can get a listening device by the guards, but in the unlikely event you're caught, you're screwed. If he's smart he'll employ a jammer inside anyway."

"He'll be on his guard, I'd wager," piped in Thomas.

"Given what you told him, for sure," said Stefania.

"How long does it take to get from the airport to the castle?" asked Greschenko.

"A little more than an hour," responded Thomas. "And there's really only one way to get there."

"It'll be close then," said Greschenko softly while sweeping her brunette mane back with her right hand.

"As to timing," piped in Thomas. "I'll try to get the driver to take us to Loch Shin on the way, to take in the view. That may add a good twenty to forty minutes or so to the sojourn."

"But if his driver is picking us up, how do we hide you two?" asked Stefania cutting to Greschenko and Anatoly. "If Artie does his homework, he'll make sure we're alone."

"That's quite simple," responded Greschenko with a broad smile as she sat down and turning to Thomas. "We will be traveling as Lana and Anthony Harris of Tucson, Arizona, your new found friends from the States."

"But you can't possibly come with us to see Artie," noted Thomas, his eyes cutting to Greschenko.

"Don't worry," responded Greschenko. "We have friends in Scotland who will be collecting us at the airport, we're just catching a flight from our friend here the Duke."

"What if someone makes you out?" demanded Stefania.

"That won't happen," bragged Greschenko. "In any event, that's a chance we'll have to take."

"It'll be fine," said Anatoly, then taking another sip of his coffee.

"Hearing you say that is somewhat reassuring," said Stefania. "Her, not so much."

"We had best get moving," announced Thomas. "We don't have much time, and we should leave by mid-afternoon if we are going to make it in time. I'll contact the pilots presently."

"Ugh," declared Stefania. "I've got nothing to wear. All my nice cold weather clothes are in the hotel room in London."

"To coin a phrase, very much to *my* chagrin," said Greschenko. "I feel compelled to loan you some of my things I have here. We are about the same size I think."

The thought of wearing her stuff gives me the shivers, thought Stefania. *Kind of like wearing the devil's cloak. Sounds like I have no choice, unless I want to freeze my ass off.*

"Well," blurted Greschenko.

"Thank you," responded Stefania reluctantly. "We don't have time to buy new things, and I must be presentable for Artie, and warm, especially if we are going to be outdoors."

"Yes," replied Greschenko. "And don't forget, this will be on loan."

"Believe me," responded Stefania. "I won't forget."

Early Morning, March 16, 42,000 Feet Over the Atlantic Ocean

Covered in a blanket, laying snuggly in the plush leather seat of Thomas' jet, Stefania's mind raced as she slept. As often happened in a light sleep thoughts darted about like lightning, and memories replayed over and over again, first Smith, his apartment, Wu, Chen, Espiranza, then the attack in Richmond Park and Tsang's attack in Malta. Like a photograph album, pages turned. Like a video stream, scenes rewound and reshowed again. The document from Smith's flat popped up, from top to bottom she examined it.

Was there a common thread, she thought deep in her subconscious.

Souchev in Ashgabat, the scene from Bolo's warehouse played out, and Harrop and Manhire haunted her. The tussle in the RV in Arizona. Her eyes darted back and forth beneath her closed lids.

Artie, what about Artie? She thought.

The memories of her conversations with Thomas arose, as if they took place presently. His explanations, and her research, cluttered her mind.

Then a jolt, and another. Her eyelids came unglued. She'd come to a revelation. A smidge of perspiration beaded beneath her nose and her upper lip. An ever so slight smile graced her face.

"What's wrong DiMaggio," snapped Greschenko sarcastically, sitting directly across from her. "Still can't take some turbulence."

"Thanks for your concern Greschenko," snapped back Stefania. "I'm fine, excellent in fact."

"Thomas," said Greschenko, turning to Thomas sitting across the aisle from her. "I'm curious, you indicated a distain for America. I find that quite surprising. Do you care to elaborate?"

"For the same reason I detest Russia," said Thomas. "As a gentleman, I despise bullies. Russia is an archetypical example of a bully frankly."

Greshenko disdainfully barked something in Russian and rolled her eyes.

"It's not so much a distaste for America, or Americans precisely, as its political system," replied Thomas. "It's my way or the highway system. The extremely polarized nature of American politics is incredibly toxic and counter-productive. There is no middle ground. There is no compromise. There is no discussion. Statues are torn down, historical figures are cancelled without debate. Both sides are bullies."

"You haven't much to worry," said Greschenko with a laugh and brief smile. "America is decadent. In five years there will be no America, not as we know it. Forty years ago it would have taken hundreds of billions of rubles to take down the United States. Now, we'll make a profit doing it."

"What do you mean?" chimed in Stefania.

"I compare America to the geography of Italy," theorized Greschenko. "On the surface it's beautiful, like an idyllic scene from a love story, but just underneath tectonic plates grind against one another, thrusting mountains and volcanoes into the sky, and like a ticking time bomb the Italians wait for the earth to move, the mountains to shake, the volcanoes to erupt, and their buildings which have stood for hundreds of years to collapse in a cloud of dust."

"I don't get it," interrupted Stefania.

"That doesn't surprise me," responded Greschenko sarcastically. "American society is a loose patchwork of cultures, languages, races, religions, political beliefs, all waiting for a precipitating event, a tremor, and then the whole house of cards will come tumbling down. That tremor can be caused by interior or external forces. Social media makes the instigation of such dividing forces an easy endeavor, and relatively cheap as well. We defeated America in Vietnam, not on the ground, but by propaganda. And outside forces import and sell drugs to an addicted populace and make millions in the process. There won't be much left in five years."

"Sounds like sour grapes to me, maybe due to events in Ukraine," snarked Thomas.

"Yeh, you Russians thought Ukraine would fall quickly, didn't go to plan, did it?" added Stefania. "Mostly due to aid from the USA."

Greschenko scoffed and turned to Stefania.

"DiMaggio, we are about an hour out from Inverness," announced Greschenko. "You'd best change. The high today is forecast to be about nine degrees, and the low close to one, overcast, with potential drizzle. I think the sweater, coat, and shoes will fit. You'll have to stick with your black leggings, as my legs are longer than yours. Everything is in the rear compartment closet."

Stefania went to the rear compartment of the jet and opened the closet. In it was a leopard print v-neck cashmere button-down sweater on a hanger.

This will work, especially since I have a black camisole which goes, she thought.

On the floor beneath sat black leather ankle high booties. Stefania picked one up.

Same size as me. Between the sweater and the shoes these cost more than I make in a month.

Next to the sweater hung a lambskin frock overcoat, with whipstitch piping and silver buttons, and a matching off-white cashmere scarf. On the hook behind the door hung a fur Russian winter hat, and on the shelf sat a matching fur muff hand warmer. She examined the overcoat's designer label.

Jesus, she thought as she shook her head. *This is worth more than another month's pay.*

She changed, brushed her long black tresses down a bit, pinned up her side locks, applied some makeup, and then strode down the aisle of the jet, with the outerwear in hand.

"Someone got a makeover," snarked Greschenko.

"You know damned well I could never afford this stuff," hissed Stefania. "I'm sure this is part of whatever diabolical scheme you've hatched."

"You look divine no matter what you are wearing," piped in Thomas with a smile.

"Thank you Thomas," replied Stefania, now smiling.

"What about you and Anatoly?" asked Stefania. "How will you get up to the castle?"

"My people will have transport waiting for us, hidden from your driver of course," she replied. "And they have a change of clothes waiting for us."

"Of course," hissed Stefania with a smirk.

"Just be careful with my Cossack hat, it's sable with fox fur trim," snapped Greschenko.

"Don't worry, I'd prefer not to wear it anyway as I'm not partial to fur," said Stefania. "Only if the weather demands."

"You westerners and your impractical sensibilities," shot back Greschenko.

Morning, March 16, Inverness, Scotland, UK

The jet pulled to a stop in the general aviation arrivals area of Inverness Airport. Stefania looked out the window. A pale overcast hung over the tarmac, and a spritz of mist covered the window. She buttoned up the lambskin coat, wrapped the cashmere scarf around her neck, and adjusted the Cossack fur hat.

Thomas got up from his seat in his beige hunting tweed breeks, with a gray heavy knit lambswool sweater, brown leather hunting boots, and a heavy tweed windowpane patterned field coat with baggy pockets and a brown collar. In his hand he held a green tweed cap.

Stefania examined him head to foot.

"I take it from your expression that you don't approve."

"I'm dressed like I'm going to a social party," said Stefania with a mischievous grin. "And you look like you're going on a hunting party."

"This is all I had packed on the plane left over from a hunting party just before we left on this adventure," replied Thomas. "Believe me, I *will* blend in the highlands."

"Oh, I believe you," replied Stefania. "Don't you worry. Remember I was at your castle on Seil. That was an experience."

"I reckon it was," replied Thomas with a smile. "The transport is here."

Stefania gazed again out onto the tarmac. There sat a hunter green Range Rover. The driver, a middle aged man wearing a tweed suit, with white shirt and green tie stood by waiting, leaning against the hood. The jet engines powered down and Greschenko and Anatoly stood aside as Thomas and Stefania made their way to the cabin door.

Anatoly took a second look at Stefania, and his eyes went from the bottom up.

249

"Oh my, Stefania you…," he said softly, catching himself.

Greschenko jabbed him hard in the ribs with her elbow. Anatoly grimaced, then opened the door and let down the stairs. Stefania stepped down first followed by Thomas. They walked over to the SUV.

"Good morning your grace and Ms. DiMaggio," said the driver in a slight Scottish brogue.

The driver opened the left rear door and Stefania entered and sat down. He repeated the exercise on the right side for Thomas.

"I'm Tony," the driver announced. "I'll be bringing you to his Royal Highness at Byram Castle. If there is anything you desire on the way, please advise me."

The Range Rover sped off the tarmac, and out the general aviation gate. Stefania turned back toward the jet. Greschenko and Anatoly stood in the doorway.

"What's that large body of water there?" asked Stefania.

"That's Moray Firth," replied Thomas. "We'll cross it, go through Iverness, and then be in the county almost all the rest of the way to Byram. A bit of forest and many moors."

"Are there any interesting sites along the way?" asked Stefania.

"As a matter of fact," replied Thomas. "Loch Shin has always been one of my favorites, and there is a magnificent view across the loch of the Ben More Assynt, the highest mountain in County Sutherland, from the A838."

"That would be nice to see," observed Stefania.

"Tony," said Thomas. "Would it be too much to ask to take a slight detour up A838 before Dalchork so Stefania can take in the prospect of the Ben More Assynt. It shouldn't take more than thirty or forty additional minutes round trip."

"Aye, your grace," responded Tony. "It'd be my pleasure, as I'm from Lairg I know the area."

"This reminds me of our journey two years ago from Glasgow to Seil," Stefania whispered in Italian.

"Yes," Thomas replied softly. "I don't think you have to whisper. I can't imagine he understands Italian."

"That was before I really got to know you," she replied softly. "I kind of thought you were a pretentious jerk at the time."

"I take issue with the 'jerk' part," Thomas said with a smile. "I can be pretentious. Can't argue with that."

"When we see Artie, please let me address the matter with him. It is my story after all."

"I suppose it is."

"Except this time at least I'm dressed for the conditions."

Thomas gave Stefania the once-over.

"Most certainly. I'd say you're prepared for a cool autumn day in Smolensk," continued Thomas in Italian.

Stefania laughed.

"I think Greschenko seriously wants you to look the part of a Russian."

Stefania laughed again.

"What if we don't come out of this Thomas?" asked Stefania.

"I'm convinced you're wrong about Artie, and nothing will come of it. So there's little to be concerned about. You'll see."

Thomas gently took her right hand out of her hand warmer, held it up to his mouth, and slowly planted a light kiss on her dorsal. He held it for a few moments and then carefully placed it back in the muff.

Goose bumps emerged on Stefania's cashmere covered arms.

"Your grace," said Tony. "Let me know where you'd like me to stop. There's a pull-over a mile or so ahead that offers a good view of the hills."

"That's fine Tony," replied Thomas. "I'll follow your lead."

The SUV flew down the barely one lane country road and came upon a turnout on the left. Tony pulled in and the SUV came to a stop. Thomas and Stefania got out and walked toward the loch.

A cool wind whipped across the white caps of Loch Shin. Grasses and reeds at the lakes edge rippled in the breeze. The waves bashed against the lake bank, the wind caught some spray, flinging it onto Stefania's face. The clouds, now interspersed with blue sky, cast a quilt of light and dark on the landscape which seemed to go on forever.

"Glad you took up Greschenko's offer for warm clothes?" teased Thomas.

"Yes, but I'll never admit it."

"There," Thomas pointed to a mountain in the distance. "That's Ben More Assynt."

"Magnificent," replied Stefania. "Truly magnificent. Is that snow on the peaks?"

"Perhaps, but the top is a lighter colored rock, quartzite I recall, giving the appearance of frost or snow. The summit is about thirty-two hundred feet. I climbed it once with Grandmamma, maybe when I was seventeen."

"Tony, would you mind taking a photo of us by the loch with the mountain the background," asked Stefania.

"My pleasure lass," Tony responded taking her phone and snapping a couple of photos of the couple.

"This reminds me of when you took me to Loch Ard," said Stefania.

"Yes, but this is a much more hostile clime, and that was in May. Shall we attend to the matter at hand?"

"I gather we must."

Sitting next to Thomas in the rear seat, Stefania admired the scenery as the SUV retraced the drive from Dalchork. Her eyes shifted slightly to observe Thomas. His boots laced ever so perfectly, his hair swept aside neatly, and his hunting cap sitting on his right thigh. His blue eyes caught hers. He smiled slightly, and offered a wink of the eye.

What if I'm right, and my dream was a premonition of death, she thought. *Shouldn't I tell Thomas how I feel. To let life slip away without knowing if we are on the same page.*

Stefania jumped as Tony's cell phone rang.

"Yes, your Royal Highness. His grace wanted to view Ben More Assynt from Loch Shin. We are turning up the drive now, strait away. Aye."

The SUV slowed and turned right up an unmarked gravel drive with leafless trees lining either side. After a few minutes it arrived at an iron gate, maybe fifteen feet in height, secured by two pillars of stone. Above the gate was a crest of arms. Tony pressed a button on the visor and the gates opened. The SUV continued through now onto a paved road continuing with leafless trees on either side, and the gate closed behind them. They came to a clearing where stood a large four story white washed manor home and slowed down to a slow roll. Two turrets populated the top floor above the double door entryway and then again at the end of the façade of the structure. Stefania counted twelve windows on each floor with gray surrounds dotting the front exterior matching the gray slate roof. Chimneys, more numerous to quickly count, with clay pots strutted above the gable rooftop, with dormers suggesting a fifth floor or attic. A large parking area occupied the front of the building with several SUVs and cars parked in front. After passing the house Tony accelerated slightly.

"Are we not going to the castle?" asked Thomas.

"No, your grace," responded Tony. "His Royal Highness has directed that I drop you just beyond, at the garden gate, where he'll collect you. He's just returning from stalking this morning."

"Stalking," whispered Stefania. "Sounds mischievous."

"It means he's hunting deer," whispered Thomas.

The SUV slowed and came to a stop. To the right stood a large stone and masonry archway surrounded by a six foot boxwood hedge which ran along the driveway. Tony got out and opened the door for Stefania and then did the same for Thomas and then motioned to go through the garden gate. Similar height boxwood hedges continued along the pea gravel path beyond the gate. The mottled clouds had now turned full overcast, although the wind had died down.

The dark day coupled with the high hedges gives this path a nefarious character, thought Stefania. Bothered by the turn in the weather, shivers ran and down her spine.

Thomas proceeded down the path, the fog of his breath wafting into the gloomy morning air. Stefania followed. They came to an intersection of four paths, all enclosed by tall boxwoods. At the intersection sat an old bronze sundial on a pedestal.

"That's useless in this climate," whispered Stefania. "Does the sun even come out?"

Which path to take? thought Stefania. *A microcosm of life, whichever path we take will decide our destiny.*

"Let's go straight," declared Thomas. "I believe this way will bring us to the forest path to the priory. Artie!" yelled Thomas.

"Here Thomas," said a voice. Artie emerged at the end of the path in front of them.

His tan seemed to have faded, and his close shaven brown beard seemed a little more than stubble now. Wearing a white shirt, with brown tie, gray tweed riding jacket, matching hunting cap, tan riding breeches and black leather mud stained riding boots, his dashing appearance did not disappoint. He held at his side a bolt action rifle, its barrel pointed toward the ground.

Stefania leaned in toward Thomas.

"What's the fascination with tweed?" she whispered.

"It keeps one warm here," he whispered back.

"I don't like the fact that he's got a rifle," she whispered again.

Thomas didn't respond.

The two approached Artie, as he seemed in no hurry to come to them.

"Thomas and Stefania," he started offering his hand to Thomas. "It's wonderful to see you and I apologize, I was out early this morning stalking, and didn't get back in time to change. There's a magnificent fallow stag in my herd I was eager to bag before he sheds his antlers. Also, given the delicacy of our conversation, I thought it best to speak beyond prying ears."

Shaking his hand, Thomas responded "It's wonderful to see you as well Artie, and thanks so much for this audience on such short notice."

Artie's eyes darted to Stefania as she slightly curtsied.

"My Stefania, you look delightful. I see the journalism business has been very good to you. Your hat is sable if I'm not mistaken, and is that fox trim?"

"Thank you Your Royal Highness, and you are correct about the hat, but business is not *that* good. Thomas is a top notch gift giver."

"Good show Thomas, and please Stefania, Artie to my friends."

"Thanks Artie," responded Stefania.

"Let's nip away down the path to the old priory," insisted Artie. "It's where I have my best thoughts and my mind is magically cleared of cobwebs and debris. I've left the security back at the castle so may have complete privacy."

"Where's the Bishop?" asked Stefania.

"Apparently on holiday," responded Artie.

How convenient, thought Stefania.

The trio strolled up the path.

"So you bagged the stag?" asked Thomas.

"Not quite," responded Artie. "Like Saint Hubertus, when I leveled my rifle he looked at me, like he knew me, like a friend. I saw Christ in him, so I let him live."

"These are incredible boxwood hedges," declared Stefania. "They must be a hundred years old."

Passing the last hedge of boxwoods, Artie picked a twig of boxwood and held it up to his nose.

"The early Christians associated boxwoods with the resurrection of Christ and that it symbolized eternal life," he noted. "The ancient Celts, and before them the Picts and the Gaels from this region, thought that the foliage and the wood offered protection from evil. The coats of arms of many of the Scottish clans contain the boxwood."

That sounds like something Thomas would say, thought Stefania.

Artie placed the boxwood twig in the buttonhole on his lapel as a sort of *boutonniere*.

Protection from evil, thought Stefania. *Works for me.*

She plucked a sprig of boxwood and stuck it in her lapel.

The pea gravel crackled underfoot as the trio proceeded through a leafless stand of trees into the glade beyond.

"On mid-summer's eve this heath will be alive with the pink and purple blooms of heather," remarked Artie somewhat dramatically. "You should come up then for a picnic here, truly enchanting."

"Yes, thanks for the invitation, but," replied Thomas.

"Now, fortunately, there are a few sprigs of Irish Heath blooming," added Artie.

"Yes, nice, but," interrupted Thomas.

They approached the ancient vine covered priory, now just a series of large crumbling gray rock walls, one with holes where presumably stained glass windows hung hundreds of years ago. The edifice seemed minimized in proportion, silhouetted against the forest of pine beyond. The wind, quiet until now, started to whip up. It whistled through the needles of the pines. Here and there little purple flowers showed through the dormant heather, the entire heath flowing like waves of a lake in the stiff breeze.

"But you want to get to the matter at hand," added Artie. "You said it had something to do with a project of Stefania's?"

"Yes, quite," replied Thomas.

"I see why you and Thomas are such good friends," interrupted Stefania. "You are very similar in many ways."

"Thanks for the compliment Stefania," replied Artie. "I admire Thomas you know. He's a man of conviction and morality. There's very few of those left."

"That he is," replied Stefania, turning to Thomas and then cutting to Artie.

Thomas smiled.

If only he knew Thomas is essentially being held hostage by the Russians under threat of blackmail, thought Stefania. *Of course, other than that, he's a man of great conviction.*

"So about your project," said Artie his brows now raised.

"Yes," said Stefania. "I was conducting an investigation into transfers of significant sums to one Stanley Wu involving an intermediary Charles Smith. I believe the purpose of the funds was to assassinate the Princess. Then I thought who would gain from dispatching the Princess? The best answer is the next in line for the throne, which would be you. Your private phone number was found in Smith's possession. You had contact with Charles Smith didn't you?"

"You can't believe I would have anything to do with any plot against my sister," replied Artie. "I don't want to be king. What would I gain, I have everything I could possibly want."

"Almost everything," replied Stefania. "The fact of the matter is you want to return the throne to the Catholic faith."

"You must be mad!" Artie exclaimed.

"Quite the opposite," said Stefania in a calm monotone. "Let me spell it out for you. Growing up, all attention was lavished on your sister, the heir apparent to the throne. Viscount Darby took you under his wing. Like the father you never had he influenced you in many ways, including in the Catholic faith, since he was a recent convert. You were jealous of your sister. You believed you were more suited to the throne than she, an awkward introvert who didn't take well to the public duties of the royal family. Then you met your wife a devout Catholic, through Thomas' grandmother, also a devout Catholic. Espiranza wanted you to convert, but you couldn't under the Succession Act and still be in line for the throne. But you did convert, but in secret, a fact known only by a few. Your children are secretly being raised Catholic. You didn't think it would matter because at the time you were third in line. Then your older brother unexpectedly died in Gstaad. Your plan was to have the Princess killed in a way that could not be attributed to an attack solely on her, and then become the heir. If suspicions fell on you, it would be treason under the Treason Act. It was an excellent plan, your sister would die in a nuclear conflagration with thousands of others, in a terrorist attack which would be difficult to trace back to anyone in particular, but given the Uyghur separatists' attack in New Jersey, suspicion would immediately fall on them, especially since some of the money came through China. Alternatively, investigators might reveal it was a false flag operation fingering the Chinese. Either way, your hands would be clean. Harrop and his friend Manhire were the stand-ins for the job if something happened to Smith."

"But that makes no sense," interrupted Thomas. "Even if that were the case, he couldn't become king if Catholic." Her eyes shot to Thomas.

"Artie is very popular," added Stefania continuing in her monotone, now speaking to Thomas. "He was counting on becoming king and waiting a few years and announcing his conversion, plunging the UK into a constitutional crisis. By then Bishop Hough would be the Archbishop of Canterbury. With his support, as well as the public's adoration, Artie was planning on undoing five-hundred years of the reformation in the UK, either through parliamentary enactment, or through force of will. And with individuals at MI6 on his side, he could count on them to tie up loose ends. The next in line are virtual unknowns and relatively unpopular. He would force a Hobson's choice on the country, a Catholic king, or the end of the monarchy as an institution. He placed his bet on the former. Isn't that right your Royal Highness?"

"Rubbish! What proof do you have to support this farcical account of yours?" demanded Artie. "I have no idea of what you're talking about!"

"It's the solution to a connect-the-dots puzzle," replied Stefania loudly.

"In God's name, how so?" quipped Artie.

"Bishop Hough is going to be the next Archbishop of Canterbury," snapped back Stefania. "He's high church and close to you. Harrop was his protégé. Lord Darby was your mentor, Lucia Chen's father was his godfather, and Lucia Chen was running the whole operation from the comfort of her cubicle at MI6. You were introduced to Chen and her father at some point through Viscount Darby, or through your wife. Chen had the means to clandestinely effectuate the Princess's assassination, and not have it traced back to you. Your wife is a religious Catholic. She had a scallop shell tattoo on her wrist, as did Chen, as did Harrop, and Tsang too. I'd wager they all hiked the camino together years ago. They're all about the same age. It'll be easy enough to confirm. They *can* be connected. I find it unfathomable to believe Espiranza would marry you without bringing up your kindred Catholic. And then there was something curious Espiranza said to me when we met, that the Anglican baptisms would suffice when the time came. That could only mean one thing, that your children would be confirmed into the Catholic faith. Lastly, there was the strange and untimely death last year of your brother Frederick in Gstaad. Only one person benefited by that tragedy, you. You had the means, the motive *and* the opportunity to pull this off. You suspected Thomas and I knew the facts and you had your inside man at MI6, Tsang, try to kill us."

Momentary silence enveloped the scene. A crow cawed in the distance.

"Artie, is this true?" asked Thomas.

"You and Stefania knew of my investment with Wu, which was orchestrated through Chen and Smith," said Artie calmly. "Frederick was a good soul and I loved him. I had nothing to do with his death, but it set in motion certain events. Frederick was the influential balance to my sister, the Princess and heir to the throne. After Frederick died that balance was gone, and once my sister became Queen she was going to cut me off. It was *she* who was jealous of *my* popularity. She felt threatened by me. I need money to support my lifestyle and the custom of living of my lovely wife. I was forced to make some questionable investments which promised guaranteed substantial returns. Did I look the other way? Yes. The investments through Wu resulted in an incredible return for me and my wife. If the investment of my money through Wu and those shady dealings ever came to light, my reputation would be gone, my sister, once she became Queen, would strip me of my titles, my military rank and honors. I'd be destroyed."

"I cannot countenance the death of the heir for such a purpose," replied Thomas in a contemptuous tone. "Your sister may well cut you off, but that does not justify murder, including the murder of other innocents. If your plan in the States had succeeded it would have killed thousands, and for what?"

"I have no idea what rubbish you're talking about Thomas," blurted Artie. "There was no murder plot in the States, only a scurrilous investment. But what I do know is that you and Stefania unfortunately know too much regarding my dealings with Wu and Smith. You are the most trusted upstanding member of the Lords, the most honorable man in the UK. You would not let this lie, would you?"

"I suppose not," replied Thomas.

Artie's head dropped, he stared at the ground.

"Unfortunately you've forced my hand. Any revelation of my investment will ruin me. Oh, and yes, being this is our last discussion Thomas, my children *are* being secretly raised Catholic," snapped Artie. "It shan't matter in the end. It's the twenty-first century Thomas. Other than perhaps you, no one cares what religion members of the royal family subscribe to, other than the heir to the throne of which I have no interest."

Out from behind one of the priory's walls stepped a man in a trench coat, gray slacks, holding a pistol with a silencer. He walked toward the group.

"Tsang," mumbled Stefania.

"Is Esperanza involved in your scheme?" inquired Thomas.

"No," responded Artie softly with a slight frown. "She knows nothing of it. She did, however, assist with the introductions to Chen and Mr. Tsang, with whom I understand you are acquainted. That assisted with the introduction to Wu, and my subsequent investment."

"What was Bishop Hough's role?" demanded Stefania.

"I have no idea what you are talking about," said Artie.

Sporting a black eye, facial bruises, and medical tape on the bridge of his nose, Tsang sidled up next to Artie facing the two, with Artie across from Thomas and Tsang in front of Stefania. His pistol leveled in Thomas and Stefania's direction.

"I now face a regrettable choice," grumbled Artie. "Not let you and Stefania live another day, or take it on the chin and go down in history as a disgrace to my family, my nation, go to prison for my investment, and let my sister destroy me financially and otherwise upon her ascension to the throne, which she will undoubtedly do."

"Get down on your knees, hands behind your backs," ordered Tsang, pointing his pistol at the two. "And stay where you are. Don't get too close DiMaggio."

Thomas and Stefania complied and knelt on the cold dormant heather, with Thomas slightly in front of Stefania to the right.

"You won't get away with this," said a solemn Thomas.

Thomas turned to Stefania and mouthed something to her. She couldn't make it out.

Again, my dream has come to pass, she thought. *I really must have a second sight. I'd hate for Greschenko to save my hide once again, but if there was ever a time it's now*, thought Stefania.

Her eyes closed, Stefania waited for the inevitable.

Oh Lord, please help me survive this. Oh, Madonna, through your intercession, please see fit to save me and Thomas, she prayed.

"Tsang," said Artie dejectedly, his eyes cutting to Tsang. "Don't shoot. I can't go through with this. I just can't. I'll take what comes my way."

Tsang lowered his pistol.

Then a strange sound, like someone smashing a pumpkin followed by a thud.

"Jesus Christ!" Artie yelled.

Her eyes jumped open. Face down on the heath lie Tsang. A gaping hole in his head oozed spongy bright red goop onto the heather. Hair covered skull fragments littered the ground in front of him. His pistol fell next to him, at Artie's feet.

"Very much the opposite," snapped Stefania as she got up and brushed herself off.

"Svetlana Greschenko more like," added Thomas, also righting himself. "Look," he said pointing to the forest on the far side of the priory.

Greschenko and Anatoly emerged from the forest in hunting attire. Anatoly held a rifle with a telescopic sight and silencer attached. Greschenko in a camouflaged outfit with a matching backpack, held a pistol with a sound suppressor pointed at Artie. They walked up to the trio, and Tsang's lifeless body.

"What took you so long?" yelped Stefania.

"You're welcome," snapped Greschenko, followed by an eye roll.

Artie stood there in shock, wiping some errant red fleshy gruel off his face with his hand.

Anatoly trained the rifle at Artie.

Greschenko turned to Artie, her pistol now at her side also pointed in his direction.

"I'm Svetlana Greschenko, Deputy Director of the Russian SVR," announced Greschenko.

"What?" Artie exclaimed.

"We have your entire conversation recorded," she continued. "Including the admission of your investment through Wu, which I can assure you involves illegal drug and arms smuggling, including an atomic weapon, among other disreputable activities. Whether you were aware of this or not is now inconsequential."

"Thomas," exclaimed Artie, turning to Thomas. "You bloody bastard."

Thomas continued brushing debris from his pants.

Stefania's mind raced through all the facts, like a computer on warp speed. Cataloguing the last week's events, statements and cross-referencing everything.

"You couldn't have recorded the conversation," confidently replied Artie. "From that distance, you're bluffing."

"She doesn't bluff," added Anatoly in a matter-of-fact monotone.

"He's got that right," interjected Stefania.

"Birders have extraordinary equipment used to seek out and record the calls of certain species," answered Greschenko. "Our parabolic equipment is similar, but much more sophisticated, and our recordings are very clear."

She took her phone out of her pocket with her left hand, fiddled with it, and replayed the portion of Artie's conversation with Thomas and Stefania. Artie's voice could be heard saying:

"Frederick was a good soul and I loved him. I had nothing to do with his death, but it set in motion certain events. Frederick was the influential balance to my sister, the Princess and heir. After Frederick died that balance was gone, and once my sister became Queen she was going to cut me off. It was *she* who was jealous of *my* popularity. She felt threatened by me. As the second in line, I needed money to support my lifestyle and the custom of living of my lovely wife. I was forced to make some questionable investments which promised guaranteed substantial returns. Did I look the other way? Yes. The investments through Wu resulted in an incredible return for me and my wife. If the investment of my money through Wu and those shady dealings ever came to light, my reputation would be gone, my sister, once she became Queen, would strip me of my titles, my military rank and honors. I'd be destroyed."

Greschenko stopped the recording.

"Crystal clear," snarked Greschenko. "And we've got corresponding video."

Artie's expression went from astonishment to dread.

"'Oh shit,'" that's what you're thinking," snapped Greschenko.

"Again," interrupted Stefania shaking her head. "You've really got to vary your expletives."

"So your Royal Highness," chimed in Greschenko. "You now are at the service of the Russian Federation. You will do what we want when we want it. Otherwise, this recording and other evidence we have becomes public. You'll be ruined, and probably prosecuted. We'll be in touch."

Seemingly content with herself, Greschenko smiled and raised her brow.

"Crikey," said Thomas. "This I didn't see coming."

"I don't know Thomas, it sounds awfully familiar to me," snarked Stefania sarcastically.

Stefania peered into Artie's blue eyes. Tears welled in them. A tiny drip flowed down the ridge between his nose and his cheek, catching on his upper lip before disappearing.

In less than a few minutes he's gone from being completely in control, to being a puppet on a string, thought Stefania. *He's finished and he knows it. The only question is how much pride does he have.*

His eyes darted from the direction of Greschenko to the ground at his feet. In an instant Artie dropped his rifle, crouched down, snatched Tsang's pistol, and held it to his right temple. Then, the tell tale sound of a muffled gunshot, followed by a thud, like a bag of potatoes hitting the ground. Artie lay face down nestled on a bed of heather with a bullet hole in his right temple. A trickle of blood slipped out and trailed down to the heath.

"Oh Madonna!" exclaimed Stefania, at the same time Thomas recoiled with a dramatic "Blimey!"

Greschenko bent down and with her gloved hand took the pistol from Artie's hand and placed it in Tsang's right hand, pointed it slightly toward where Artie had been standing and pulled off a single silent shot into the trees, then lay his arm on the ground, pistol in hand. She grabbed Tsang's feet and rotated his body, leaving the head in more or less the same position, picking up one of the bullet casings in the process. She handed the rifle to Anatoly, and checked Tsang's pockets, pulling out his wallet.

"Dammit Greschenko," yelped Thomas. "I've lost one of my closest friends. Again you vile creature, you've ruined another family."

"You say that now," Greschenko replied calmly. "But I suspect you'd have been singing a different tune if thousands of people were instantaneously incinerated in Arizona. I know you Thomas, you wouldn't have been able to live with yourself."

"I hate to say it," said Stefania softly. "But she's right."

"Such a shame," Greschenko calmly said, staring down at Artie's body.

"That's something I never thought I'd hear you say," uttered Stefania.

"Not that he's *dead*," hissed Greschenko. "Could care less about that, although I should have liked to have the future king as an inside source. It's just that all of his actions were for naught."

"What the hell are you talking about?" demanded Thomas.

"The Princess is barren," said Greschenko with a shrug. "Artie would have been king eventually anyway."

"Explain yourself Greschenko, for Christ's sake!" barked Thomas.

"The Princess has endometriosis, she had a laparoscopic treatment, which didn't work, and she's had several surgeries to remove cysts from her ovaries, all of which have rendered her unable to produce eggs, and so even IVF is not an option," replied Greschenko matter of factly. "Only a handful of people know. Apparently her own brother wasn't aware. End of story. Can't reproduce."

"Ah, so once the Princess died, Artie would have been king," said Stefania loudly rubbing her chin.

"Or his offspring, if he didn't survive the Princess," added Greschenko.

"So Artie was a secret heir. Now that Artie is deceased, his eldest son is essentially a secret heir," pondered Thomas. "Crikey."

"A secret Catholic heir," added Stefania.

"Quite," replied Thomas.

"Now what?" asked Stefania.

Greschenko cut to Anatoly. "The rifle," she ordered.

Greschenko took Artie's rifle.

"Take it," she said to Thomas.

Thomas demurred.

"Why would I do that?" he asked.

"How are you going to explain this?" barked Greschenko.

"How indeed," replied Thomas.

"Do I have to spell it out for you," snarked Greschenko. "You were talking with Artie and the rogue MI6 agent Tsang comes out of the forest and approaches Artie, pulls out his pistol and Tsang shoots Artie in the head. You snatched up Artie's hunting rifle, and shot Tsang in the head at short range. The bullet blows his skull apart. Afterward you checked his body for ID. A simple explanation, and pretty difficult to fuck up."

"How's that possibly believable?" asked Stefania.

"What's the alternative. That his Royal Highness had Tsang take you at gunpoint, but before he could do the deed he's shot by Russian agents, and then Artie commits suicide?" barked Greschenko followed by a laugh.

She tossed the wallet on the ground at Thomas' feet.

"His is the same caliber as my rifle, and I used a thin-jacketed .308 subsonic round commonly used in the UK," interrupted Anatoly. "Coincidentally, it's now the ammunition in his Royal Highness's rifle."

"A forensics team will never buy that a full metal jacketed round blew Tsang's head apart," snapped Thomas. "They'll figure out that the shot came from a different angle."

Greschenko scoffed.

"Just like they got the forensics of Kennedy's head-shot so accurate," she snarked. "They missed the mark by a mile on that one. The patsy took the blame and then in a strange twist of fate was shot dead himself. How regrettable."

A light went off in Stefania's head. The computer in her mind recalculated and stopped. Her eyebrows raised and her jaw dropped — a revelation.

Oswald! she thought.

"The round I used had the thinnest jacket available," replied Anatoly calmly. "It blew into a thousand of pieces upon impact with Tsang's head. The round will not be traceable to any particular .308 rifle. At close range it will cause a relatively large exit wound so that..."

"...so that the hunter has a blood trail to track his game," interrupted Stefania.

"Correct," replied a surprised Anatoly with raised brows.

"Like I said, my cousin owns a ranch in Brazil, and I've spent time there hunting with him and with my uncle."

"It'll be extremely difficult to tell the entry wound from the exit wound under the circumstances," added Anatoly.

"Let a forensics team analyze the scene," barked Greschenko. "Believe me, any theory other than what you tell them will be speculative and inconclusive."

Rain started to fall from the already sullen skies.

Stefania turned toward Thomas who stood silent, the condensation of his breath visible in the morning air, a look of dread pasted on his face.

"It might work," murmured Thomas.

"It'll have to work," stated Greschenko confidently. "The rain will also complicate forensics by the time they get a team up here."

"What if we just come clean, and tell the whole story Greschenko," argued Stefania. "What then?"

"Then Thomas will be destroyed," shot back Greschenko holding up her phone. "Not only was he working for the Russians under threat of blackmail, but we'll implicate him in Artie's death, his plot, the list goes on. That's not to mention that unpleasant information about the Vatican you uncovered two years' ago DiMaggio, and oh, I almost forgot, Thomas's grandmother's secret as well. The Radcliffe duchy will be tarnished beyond repair."

Greschenko placed her phone in her jacket pocket.

"Take it," said Greschenko, pushing Artie's rifle back at Thomas.

Thomas took it and raised the rifle, its butt tight against his right shoulder, his finger on the trigger.

"I should shoot you as you stand," he exclaimed.

"You'll be dead before you unlock the safety," announced Greschenko holding her pistol at the ready. Anatoly raised his rifle and pointed it in Thomas' direction. "And then DiMaggio here will come second. You think killing me would solve your problems? That's a joke. Explain the dead body of the Deputy Director of the SVR at his Highnesses' hunting lodge to the authorities. And what I know, the SVR knows. That, you can be rest assured of."

"Thomas, please," begged Stefania, as she reached over, putting her hand on the barrel lowering it toward the ground.

"Plus, Viviana Cantú is still out there, somewhere," added Greschenko. "Probably in Venezuela. You'd better hope she doesn't want to honor the contract even though Tsang's dead, although I'll find her eventually, she made it personal. Fire the rifle toward the forest," ordered Greschenko.

"Why on earth?" asked Thomas.

Greschenko rolled her eyes.

"Forensics, if they doubt your story, they'll check your hands and clothing for propellant residue," snapped Greschenko. "Although I doubt the local plods will be that sophisticated. Plus, in case anyone is listening, a rifle report must be heard."

Thomas fired the rifle, and then placed it on the ground.

"Your phones," demanded Greschenko with an open left palm.

Thomas and Stefania placed the Russian satellite phones in Greschenko's hand. She quickly stuffed them in her jacket pocket.

"You'll say nothing of the secret heir. It'll be between us, or else," Greschenko said sternly, her eyes cutting to Thomas.

"Of course," Thomas replied softly.

Her eyes shifted to Stefania.

Stefania rolled her eyes and nodded.

"By the way, the Duke wasn't involved in his brother Frederick's death, but it was *no* accident," added Greschenko.

"Greschenko, explain!" demanded Thomas.

"Oh, and congratulations DiMaggio," quipped Greschenko sarcastically with a slightly evil grin. "You solved this one just like the Vatican caper, at Thomas' expense, *again*. It seems to be a pattern."

"Greschenko," she snapped back with a devilish smirk.

"What DiMaggio?"

"You know what I think?" Stefania asked.

"Actually I've doubted you had the capacity," Greschenko growled.

"I was *so* hopelessly wrong," Stefania snapped. "I missed the mark by a mile."

"Hah, wouldn't be the first time," Greschenko replied sarcastically.

"The Catholic cabal angle was a ruse the whole time!" blurted Stefania. "And I followed it like a dumbass because you encouraged me."

"Dumbass, that's about right," responded Greschenko

"Artie had no idea that he was financing the importation of a nuclear weapon to the States or that it could be used to murder his sister, *did he*?" Stefania asked. "He had no clue whatsoever. He had no deal with Bishop Hough. Why deny those facts when he initially was going to have us killed? The only thing he was guilty of was making a shady investment."

"What's that?" asked Thomas.

Greschenko scoffed.

"You Russians wanted to rid yourselves of that pesky maverick anti-Russian Arizona Senator, perhaps the next president. Or, after the Ukraine debacle and sanctions, you wanted to get back in America's good graces by thwarting an atomic terrorist attack. Even more probable is that Russia was a silent investor, perhaps through Stasevich. With all the sanctions GRU needed an infusion of hard currency. Either way, it was the perfect ploy. Suspicion would fall on everyone, *except* Russia. Just like Lee Harvey Oswald. Who would believe a disenchanted defector with a Russian wife was a Soviet asset? No-one would because it was too God damned obvious. So vaporization of the Senator by a stolen Russian atomic warhead would cast suspicion on everyone because no-one knew who the real target was. Everyone—China, Uyghur separatists, the cartels, Artie, Bishop Hough, Manhire, Harrop, the Vatican even, would be suspects—except Russia, but you vaguely and conveniently tipped the American authorities off."

"Typically Russian, ruthless and diabolical, with little regard for human life," quipped Thomas rubbing his chin. "It's what Harry's spook friends would call 'fixing a phony', and it was *you* Greschenko who was leading us down the primrose path all along. You couldn't kill the Senator with a nerve agent or polonium, because the whole world knows Russian tactics. It's as clear as day."

"Exactly, and somehow Artie was roped into financing the project under false pretenses, and *presto*, a secondary purpose was to blackmail Artie who you knew would someday be king, but something changed. What changed?" demanded Stefania pointing her index finger at Greschenko. "What changed Greschenko that you had to retrieve the bomb, or was the plan all along to save the day?"

Anatoly grinned slightly and his eyes cut to Greschenko.

"The Princess!" yelped Stefania still pointing at Greschenko. "You didn't count on the Princess being at the festival. For whatever reason you didn't want *that* collateral damage. It's one thing to kill a Senator, but if it ever was discovered that Russia was responsible for the murder of the heir to the throne, there'd be hell to pay! Especially using a nuke to carry out the deed, there would *have* to be retaliation. Russia's president is a risk taker that's for sure. Perhaps he could count on America keeping it under wraps to avoid a nuclear war, but the UK, that was a risk Russia couldn't afford to take."

Greschenko's usually stoic lips flinched ever so slightly. Her left cheek rose a fraction of a millimeter.

"I'll also wager rogue elements within Russia, perhaps GRU, started the process, and after it was discovered you were ordered to stop it," said Thomas. "Which is why *you* were pursuing the RA-115 instead of GRU."

"Are you both finished?" Greschenko growled.

"And we were the insurance!" snapped back Stefania, slapping her leg then pointing her finger Greschenko's way. "You needed proof to show that Russia wasn't involved in the actual planting of the weapon. What better unwitting witnesses than a respected journalist and the sixteenth Duke of Radcliffe. That's why you killed Chen, Tsang, Manhire and who knows, even Wu, the two idiots in New Jersey, because they could've been aware of the Russian connection or they were just liabilities. You had no interest in questioning Devon or Giles, you wanted them dead. Cleaning up loose ends, just like last time. You wanted blame cast on others for the explosion, that Russia tried to stop it, and we could corroborate that to western intelligence. One big fat lie, covered by a snowjob, obscured by a smokescreen, and like magic, Russia is clear from blame, and in fact the hero! You just had to mop up the evidence. Boy *am* I good," exclaimed Stefania, followed by a clenched fist and a pump of the arm.

Greschenko's jaw visibly tightened and she raised her pistol ever so slightly from her side.

"...and you never told us what you found on Duce and Wanda's cell phones," added Stefania pointing at Greschenko. "You didn't follow them back from Buttermilk Falls; you knew *exactly* where they lived. I'll bet you took Wu's phone off his body before we got there. Plus you didn't question our story about Manhire. You never take my word for anything, ever. Hah! Yes!" Her arm pumped in jubilation a second time.

"Eminently reasonable actually," announced Thomas with a raised brow. "Frankly, I'd accept her theory as truth."

"What else did you find on Devon and Giles' cellphones you so conveniently confiscated? No answer? And I'll wager Smith was a Russian double agent, working for Russia and MI6. He had no connection with the Vatican. He wasn't a priest; that was just his cover. His London flat contained no religious items. Only a state actor could forge his Vatican passport. You went to the pantry in his flat before Chen got there – you knew precisely where the bank and contact information was. Wow! I'm awesome, feels exhilarating actually." Stefania hopped a couple of times in jubilation, followed by a *capoerira* swirl and kick.

Anatoly beamed at Stefania, as he turned to Greschenko. She leveled her pistol at Stefania.

"What was Bishop Hough's role?" demanded Stefania. "Another dupe who you intended to blackmail when he became Archbishop of Canterbury?"

"Too many bodies Greschenko," cautioned Thomas. "What will be your explanation? Moreover, killing Stefania or both of us will eliminate my intercession regarding the UK sanctions, which I might add Russia desperately needs me to do. So what's your play?"

"Are you going to take that fairy tale to the bank DiMaggio?" Greschenko asked in a brutal monotone. "Hmm?" she asked, her cheeks creasing as they tightened.

"Will they talk?" queried Anatoly.

Greschenko barked something back to Antoly in Russian.

"There is still Bishop Hough," blurted Stefania pointing at Greschenko.

"Unfortunately, he died of natural causes in his sleep last night while on holiday," responded Greschenko glaring at Stefania. After a pregnant pause, she blurted, "Well, *are* you going to take that fairy tale to the bank DiMaggio, are you?"

"I have no solid proof," meekly replied Stefania. "You took care of all that. We were played like a fiddle and I've got nothing. Although given Anatoly's statement, I take it I'm on the mark."

Greschenko huffed, the condensation of her breath seemed to linger in front of her for minutes. She lowered the pistol.

"Not a fiddle, played like a *balalaika*," said Anatoly with a mischievous grin.

“Indeed,” muttered Thomas.

“You can keep the clothes DiMaggio, your wardrobe needed a major upgrade, especially that knit hat of yours,” snarked Greschenko. “Compliments of Mother Russia. Thomas, you know what will befall you, your family, the Vatican, if any of this comes out. Not to mention DiMaggio. Well then, now that we’ve got that settled, *we* shall take *our* leave,” announced Greschenko.

“Right,” Thomas grunted with a frown.

“Hey Stefania,” said Anatoly. “When I’m in Rome or Rio, would you like to get together for an espresso or a cocktail sometime?”

“You’re not serious?” demanded Greschenko with a frown.

“Sure, Anatoly,” responded Stefania. “Do you want my number?”

“No need, I’ll know how to contact you. I’m a spy, remember,” he replied with a wink.

Anatoly and Greschenko turned and quickly jogged, guns in hand, behind one of the ivy covered priory walls, into the woods and out of sight.

“You can’t be serious,” asked Thomas.

“I’ll keep the clothes, no reason not to. I’m starting to reevaluate the ethics of wearing fur. It’s already a hat,” Stefania said with a shrug.

“Not that, I meant meeting up with Anatoly,” clarified Thomas.

“I wouldn’t mind,” replied Stefania. “I think Anatoly and I bonded a little during this ordeal, *and* it would irritate the daylights out of Greschenko, plus he’d be an interesting guy to have as a friend.”

“As a friend?”

“As a friend,” emphasized Stefania.

Stefania knelt down and examined Tsang’s right wrist.

“I bluffed and I was right. A scallop shell tattoo.”

“Incredible deduction on the Russia angle by the way,” remarked Thomas solemnly. “Rather elaborate, and it’s certainly consistent with devious Russian intelligence practices, but what sparked that analysis?”

“The mention of Oswald, and she took Tsang’s phone.”

“Say again.”

“There are theories that Oswald was in fact a Russian agent, even if just a patsy. Plus Greschenko took Tsang’s mobile out of his jacket pocket, I saw her,” commented Stefania. “So there must have been some connection between them.”

"Or she just wanted his phone," said Thomas with a shrug. "She's a spy after all."

"She didn't deny it, and I think Anatoly's response spoke volumes. Plus, we have one piece of information which she didn't count on us finding, the notes from Smith's flat with the phone and account numbers. I'll wager that's proof enough, and she knows it."

"Agreed, we should make our way back to the house and report what happened," announced a solemn Thomas. "It's a question of *oughtness* at this point."

"Oughtness?" questioned Stefania.

"I'm waxing philosophic," whispered Thomas.

"Now's not the time Thomas."

They both turned to make their way down the path back to the garden and the castle.

"Little thieves are hanged, but great ones escape," blurted Stefania. "Hah, isn't that the truth!"

Thomas sighed.

The combination of the rain and the near freezing temperature, chilled Stefania to the bone, although Greschenko's fur Cossack hat kept her head dry and warm. The pea gravel cracked under foot as a faint thunderclap could be heard in the distance. The heavy raindrops pelted the fallen leaves covering the ground in the small wood. Tree branches creaked as short bursts of wind serpentined through the copse of trees.

"Dearest," murmured Thomas.

"Yes Thomas," cooed Stefania.

"You understand our predicament?"

"Yes."

"It's possible that MI6 won't want to finger Tsang, and they'll place the blame on us instead."

"How likely is that?"

"I can't say," he responded. "If it wasn't me, who knows?"

Thomas stopped walking for a moment as they reached the grove of leafless trees as the rain came down in sheets, and turned toward Stefania. His blue eyes evinced stress, desperation and exhaustion. He clasped her right hand with his left and offered a slight smile. Muffled thunder reverberated across the heath into the woods. Like a waterfall the rainfall cascaded down onto the duo and streamed down their faces.

"You and I have been together through some of the most trying times of my life," said Thomas in a quiet tone, barely audible over the rain.

"True, but I feel as if both times it's been all of my fault," replied Stefania, likewise in a hushed tone.

"Don't be ridiculous. I knew what I was getting into. These matters were incredibly personal to me. You know today's narrative?" he quietly asked.

"Yes I do," she answered in a hushed tone.

"Let's hope it's convincing. Keep in mind, we may not be able to speak for some time after we're interviewed by the police."

"Thomas," she murmured.

"Yes, Stefania."

"When we were kneeling, waiting for Tsang to finish us off, you mouthed something to me," Stefania. "I didn't catch it."

"Dearest Stefania," Thomas began softly and paused as he took his hat off and swept his dirty blond hair back with his hand. "I thought we were goners and I couldn't imagine you not knowing."

Stefania's spine tingled and goosebumps popped up and down her arms.

"Not knowing what?" asked Stefania.

The cold winter chill that had permeated her body evaporated in favor of overwhelming warmth.

"Thomas!" a woman's voice screamed.

Esperanza, hair soaked down her face, ran up the pathway toward them in a rain drenched pink overcoat with black lapels she held closed with one arm, her other arm flailing about. Two security men followed in trench coats.

"Where's Artie?" she yelled as she approached. "Someone reported a shooting accident."

"Greschenko," muttered Stefania. "She leaves nothing to chance."

Thomas put his hat back on, walked up to Esperanza and took her hands in his.

"I'm sorry Esperanza," he said softly. "He's gone. He's up there," he said to the security men as he pointed up the path toward the priory. They took off in that direction.

Thomas pulled her close and hugged her. The wife who worshipped her husband fell to the ground on the side of the path, hunched over, wailing. Her tears melted into the rain, her eyes closed tight. Her right hand extended up, she grasped Thomas' hand. The fog of her breath hung in the air like the pale of death itself. Her soaked black locks clinging to her face, her knees let go. Sprawled on the forest floor the next to the path, wet leaves glued to her coat, mottling the pink fabric.

For the first time, after all the death she'd seen, and everything she'd been through, Stefania's gut stirred. Like a butterfly in her stomach, it crept upward. Her eyes closed slightly and a tear slid down her face, then another, and another. She crouched down, rested her face in her palms and sobbed uncontrollably. Thunder from miles away rolled across the landscape, and echoed through the glade, as raindrops pelted from above. The faint caw of a lone crow followed the last rumble of thunder. In that strange moment, her father came to mind. She wanted him back from the dead. As if the tempest read her thoughts, a ghostly voice blew through the trees saying, "I'm with you."

Five Months Later
August 15, Rio de Janeiro, Brazil

Running down a dark and foggy narrow street in one of Rio's *favelas*, Stefania tripped and fell into the wet putrid gutter. Her pursuer arrived, pistol in hand, ready to finish her off. Viviana Cantú looked down at her as she raised the pistol to Stefania's head now resting on the dank unpaved road. Cantú appeared just as she had in the photo Greschenko showed her at the embassy. Her black flowing tresses hanging down over her leather motorcycle vest, she pulled the trigger.

"Agh!" Stefania exclaimed and sat up in bed.

Thank God, a nightmare, she thought.

Sitting in a large bed as the morning light eked its way underneath the closed red draperies, she examined the room. The huge bed sat in the large dimly lit bedroom. Instinctively, she reached to her right and turned on the lamp on the nightstand. An ornate white marble fireplace faced the bed from the wall in front of the bed.

This looks like Haverford Hall, she thought.

On the nightstand stood a framed photograph of her in a wedding gown.

"What is it dearest?" asked a familiar voice. "Is something amiss?"

Thomas sat up next to her in the bed, caressing her shoulder.

Then bells, church bells, clanging loudly close by.

Her eyes flew open. The early morning winter sun crept through the venetian blinds covering her window overlooking the Atlantic Ocean to the east.

Assumption Day, she thought, now sitting up in bed, her thin pink cotton camisole draped over her nipples.

Our Lady of Peace's bells.

I'm at mama's in Ipanema, she realized. *My God, the dream.*

A smile slowly crept across her face from cheek to cheek. Happiness sizzled through her body for a moment.

Yes, the dream, she thought. *But which one, or both?*

Other books by C.J. Toca:

The Vacant Seat, the prequel to *The Secret Heir*.
The Lost Painting, sequel to *The Secret Heir*, coming soon.

Visit *www.cjtoca.com*